James Jackson

Bestselling author James Jackson has written several
acclaimed international novels includi... ...ic
historical thriller *Blood Roc*... ...he
specialised in future ... ...to the
Bar, and is a for... ...nant. He is based
...don.

PILGRIM

THE GREATEST CRUSADE

JAMES JACKSON

JOHN MURRAY

First published in Great Britain in 2008 by John Murray (Publishers)
An Hachette UK Company

First published in paperback in 2009

1

A CIP catalogue record for this title is available from the British Library

ISBN 978-0-7195-6934-0

Typeset in Monotype Bembo by Servis Filmsetting Ltd, Stockport, Cheshire

Printed and bound by Clays Ltd, St Ives plc

John Murray policy is to use papers that are natural, renewable and
recyclable products and made from wood grown in sustainable forests.
The logging and manufacturing processes are expected to conform to the
environmental regulations of the country of origin.

John Murray (Publishers)
338 Euston Road
London NW1 3BH

www.johnmurray.co.uk

For Harriet, Kate and Imo

In 1212, some seventy thousand children left Europe
in holy crusade for Jerusalem. They were to vanish
into history . . .

> When, lo, as they reached the mountain side,
> A wondrous portal opened wide,
> As if a cavern was suddenly hollowed;
> And the Piper advanced and the children
>   followed ...

From *The Pied Piper of Hamelin*
by Robert Browning

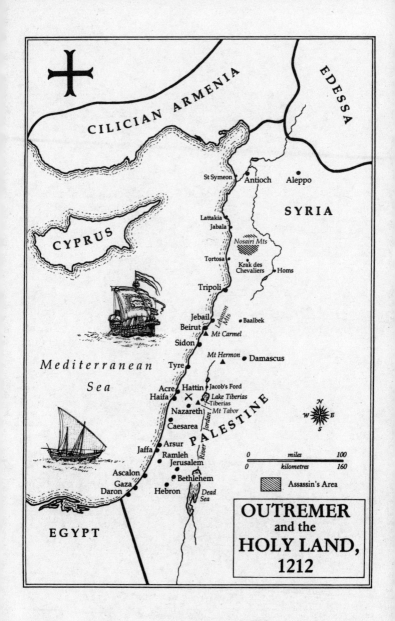

CILICIAN ARMENIA

EDESSA

St Symeon
Antioch
Aleppo

SYRIA

Lattakia
Jabala
Nosairi Mts

Tortosa
Krak des
Chevaliers
Homs

CYPRUS

Tripoli

Jebail
Baalbek
Beirut ▲ *Mt Carmel*
Sidon

*Mediterranean
Sea*

Tyre

Mt Hermon ▲ Damascus

Acre Hattin Jacob's Ford
Haifa ✕ *Lake Tiberias*
Tiberias
Nazareth ▲ *Mt Tabor*
Caesarea
PALESTINE

N
W E
S

Jaffa Arsur
Ramleh
Jerusalem

0 miles 100
0 kilometres 160

Ascalon
Gaza Bethlehem
Daron Hebron *Dead
Sea*

Assassin's Area

EGYPT

OUTREMER
and the
HOLY LAND,
1212

✝

Beginning

4 JULY 1187. THE HOLY LAND.

They should have known it would end this way, might have guessed when the old Arab crone had cursed them as they departed camp and the fire they set beneath her failed to catch. It seemed a long time ago, before weary miles of parched earth and dust-clogged throats, of constant skirmish and faltering advance, of gradual decline and encroaching death. This was the bloody conclusion. A final stand on a sloping and god-forsaken plain they called the Horns of Hattin. The end of Christendom, of Jerusalem, of everything for which they had fought.

'*To your fronts! They come again!*'

'Stand fast!'

'The Lord is with us . . .'

But they could not stand fast, could barely stand at all. And the Lord was far away. However hard they prayed, whatever sallies the Templars and Hospitaller knights made against the Moslem horde, the enemy pushed on, pressed in. The Turk horsemen wheeled their steeds, loosing their arrows on the move, the shard tips bringing down horses, puncturing chain-mail, winnowing the huddled and depleted mass of Christians.

Smoke billowed and drifted. It came from the bundles of kindling and brushwood placed by religious *muttawiyah* irregulars during the night, set ablaze to further torment the Latin army. A hellish place. The burning haze stung the eyes, scoured the lungs, joined the heat of the day to bear down on the crumbling defence. In the distance, the waters of Lake Tiberias glittered like a mirage, cool and unattainable. Most of the Christian infantry were streaming east towards it in a trampling panic of thirst and desperation. The Moslems were ready to block any exodus, to butcher any straggler. Their cavalry closed again, and the Latin foot soldiers disappeared in a broiling throng of swords and javelins.

Saladin, the great Salah ad-Din, unifier and commander of the Islamic world, had been clever, had drawn his opponents to this spot. He knew they would come. He had brought his forces across the river Jordan into Palestine, laid siege to the strategic town of Tiberias, planned to pick off the Christian enclaves one by one, fort by fort, and eventually retake Jerusalem itself. And so King Guy of the Latins had led out his knights and barons, the priest-warriors of the military Orders, the mercenaries paid for with the thirty thousand marks put aside for future crusade that would never be. It was a trap. Some forty-two thousand Moslems drawn up against twelve hundred cornered knights and their twenty-two thousand drought-crazed hirelings. No contest. Or at least none that would outlast the day. Now Saladin stood on a hilltop, a still figure attended by his emirs and Mamluk bodyguards, hemmed in by the armoured ranks of his *jandariyah* praetorians, gazing down upon grim and violent spectacle. Fluttering above them were the black and green banners of their cause, the yellow dynastic pennants of the Ayyubids, the horsehair standards of the Turcomans. A gathering of the elite watching the inevitable. He gave a nod.

Instantly the command was relayed by signallers waving flags, was received and sent on by the battle-field *jawush* and *munadi* criers stationed below. Their calls and whistles could be heard shrill through the clamour and clash of arms, redirecting and reorgan-izing, ordering tactical feint and rapid manoeuvre. A fresh assault was in train. In a travelling wave, the Kurdish archers and Arab spearmen drew back as the Moslem heavy cavalry thundered through, galloping on to the plateau in a stormburst of dust and war-yells, their couched lances crashing against Frankish shields, their swords rising and falling in the tumult.

'See, Count Raymond of Tripoli counter-attacks!'

Count Raymond of Tripoli had misjudged his moment. Valour or folly, it made no difference. It was the wife of this nobleman who was besieged in the citadel at Tiberias, this nobleman who even so had cautioned against rash move upon Saladin. He understood the strength of the Moslem foe, had cried out on the arid and inland march that all was lost and they were dead men. It did not prevent him from taking his knights and serjeants-at-arms in headlong rush against the enemy swarm. Perhaps he could break out, create escape for the rest of his brethren. The response was immediate. As the Count plunged through the scrub fires and rolling banks of smoke, the entire army of Saladin opened wide. The velocity of the charge carried the Christians on. They could not halt or turn, could not withdraw to their beleaguered comrades or their starting line. Then they were past, and the Moslem phalanxes closed once more. A simple trick, a different method of combat that had further disabled the crusaders.

Encirclement of the Christians tightened. Men fought or cowered, prayed and died. Killing time. There was little left to do. A knight lumbered haphazardly down the slope, his sword raised in challenge towards the crowding enemy. He took two crossbow quarrels in his shield. A third struck his throat, cutting short his mission, projecting a pink halo about his head before he fell. Nearby, a dismounted sergeant had retrieved a discarded Bedouin spear, was using it to jab wildly at the encroaching multitude. He did not see the approach of the Ghulam cavalryman behind, would not have felt the blow from the animal-shaped war-club that dashed out his brain. Nor would he have noticed the ragged band of five Hospitallers cut off on the flank by racing flames that burst around them, consuming their writhing shapes in an incendiary sea. Everywhere chaos, a thousand vignettes of pathos and pain and splintering defeat. Here a mercenary in chain-mail hauberk crumpling from heatstroke, there a soldier pinned by a lance that ruptured his chest and the English lion emblazoned on his surcoat. And always the furnace disc of the sun, sapping strength, evaporating the last impulse to resist. Yet the men would live long enough to regret responding to the *arrière ban*, the general call-up that had brought them to such plight. It was the Moslem year of 583. A terrible time to be an able-bodied Christian male in Outremer.

'*We cannot hold them!*'

'Commit yourselves to God, your lives to preserving the True Cross from the infidel!'

'Retreat to the royal tent and guard it to the last!'

That tent stood bright red and visible in the midst of their position, a totem of sovereign authority reduced to an isolated symbol of powerlessness and hubris. Fighting had erupted around it. On the adjacent plain, the northern horn of Hattin, the infantry were already dead or captured. This was merely the untidy finale. A few more forays by exhausted knights, clustered groups of ghostly forms standing back to back, whispering psalms, hurling rocks, presenting their shattered swords and dented battleaxes. All were swept aside. The hours had leached into the afternoon and it was done. Guy-ropes were cut, and the billowing structure of the royal tent sank.

'*Sanctum Sepulchrum adjuva . . . Sanctum Sepulchrum adjuva . . .*'

'Help us, Holy Sepulchre.' It was the prayer of the Crusaders, the words panting high and fast in the throat of the Bishop of Acre. He knelt and kept his eyes tight shut, a fat cleric sweating in fright and misery, far from the comfort of his sinecure. His head bent forward, pressed against the gold and gem-studded sleeve of the hallowed relic. It seemed to comfort him, to transport him to the moment when another man took the sins of the world upon his shoulders. He was at the feet of the crucified Christ. His arms held the gilded object close, for it was the holiest of holies, a gift to mankind, the very span of wood on which the Lamb of God had been nailed. The True Cross.

It could not save him. The arrows flew true, puncturing the instant, raking the corpulent form with multiple strikes. Wallowing confused in his own viscera, peering at the seven feathered flights protruding from his chest and belly, the Bishop pitched forward. His place was taken. The Bishop of Lidde had snatched up the Cross, was clambering across the rock scree, mewling and weeping in exertion, the precious burden weighing on his shoulder. If only he could gain height, could put distance between himself and the arrow-bolts, the blades, the spears, the howling onrush of the heathen. A lasso uncoiled and dropped around his neck. Quickly it tensed, wrenching him back, reeling him in. The sacred relic fell away and tumbled among the boulders. Possession had passed, and a torrent of colours, the *raj-jalah* regiments of Saladin, closed in. And at the centre of a charnel field the collapsed remnants of a royal tent covered the earth like a blood spill.

Saladin took his time. He surveyed his trembling captives with the cool aloofness of a leader whose most merciful God had delivered victory and would yet send the Latins crawling from these lands. They were a woeful sight, no longer the haughty princes of their Frankish realm, but subjugates with torn flesh and blackened faces. King Guy of Jerusalem and his brothers Prince Amalric and Geoffrey of Lusignan, Marquis William of Montferrat, Lord Reynald of Châtillon, Lord Humphrey of Toron, the Grand Masters of the Temple and the Hospital. All present, all uncertain of the fate he had chosen for them.

He breathed deep, let the perfumed interior of his tent filter to his brain. Frankincense could calm, the aroma of rose petals soothe. Yet they were overlaid with the scent of war, the sweat and sour despair of his prisoners, the cindered aftermath of conflict intruding from outside. Maybe it was how every meeting between Moslem and Christian should be accompanied.

Finally he spoke, his words translated by an aide. He knew the tongue, the mind, the tactics of the Unbeliever. But he would not stray from Arabic, would not honour these savages and barbarians.

'I see your Count Raymond of Tripoli departed the field in haste.'

'He performed his duty.'

'Or abandoned his post, as you would have been wise to do yours.' Saladin stared at the King, noted his quivering hands, his face contorting through fear and thirst. 'He is at present riding hard with his knights for Tyre. My men trail him, have followed him along the Wadi Hammam.'

'Then at least a few of my brethren make it home.'

The Saracen leader afforded him the slightest of

smiles. 'Home? You stripped your castles of every soldier, your coffers of every gold and silver piece, for a battle that you lose. There is no sanctuary, no crown, no army, no reinforcement from the west.'

'I remain a king.'

'Without a kingdom you are nothing. Soon I shall take Jerusalem, seize your remaining towns, restore each to the True Faith and the rule of my people.'

'Others will come, will avenge this day.'

'They will be too late, too weak.'

'With righteousness we may conquer all.'

'You have failed to conquer me.'

Saladin walked to a long table and poured iced rosewater from a jug into a pair of deep chalices. The Christians had not drunk for over twenty-four hours, had bypassed the springs at Tur'an, found the well at Lubiya dry. Small wonder their tongues were swollen, their lips cracked, their voices rasped with the desiccation of a desert. He felt the collective intensity of their gaze as the vessels filled.

'If it is of consolation, from when first you mustered and advanced upon us from your camp at the fort of Saffuriyah you had no chance.'

'There is ever chance.'

It was Gérard de Ridefort, Grand Master of the Knights Templar, who spoke. A zealot, a man who had broken every truce, abandoned all judgement, for the sake of perpetuating holy war. His bloodshot eyes radiated a venomous loathing.

'What is a man of religion if he possesses neither wisdom nor humility, Gérard de Ridefort?'

'Our fight is eternal.'

'Yet for the present I see it is over, your power is spent.'

'My authority is from a higher source. He will guide us to great and just victory. He will rain down fire and brimstone upon your head and the armies of darkness.'

'The same reasoning that brought you here, that impelled you to attack our reconnaissance force at the springs of Cresson. Each move has cost you dear.'

'I would glad sacrifice myself, ten thousand of my brothers, for the glory and sanctity of combat.'

Stupidity would ever find outlet in bluster, Saladin supposed. He should be grateful the Latins were so poorly led. Only two months before in Galilee, commanded by de Ridefort, one hundred and thirty knights and a few hundred lightly armed turcopoles had charged a travelling Moslem force some thousand strong. Three knights emerged alive, their foolish Grand Master among them. He had plainly not learned. But there were others worse, leaders whose base crimes and wickedness surpassed any outrage committed by a Templar.

'And you?'

His attention swung to Reynald of Châtillon, master of Oultrejordain. It was met with lifeless eyes and blank indifference. Saladin expected no less. The man was a breed apart, a monster whose domain had straddled the caravan routes, who raided with abandon, slaughtered without conscience. Reynald it was who mutilated women and children and murdered pilgrims on the hajj, who secretly built a fleet of pirate galleys

9

and launched them into the Gulf of Akabah. Wherever his ships had ventured, they brought terror and death, pillaging the coasts of the Red Sea, landing parties of cut-throats to forage for treasure and slaves. It was merely a foretaste. For the true purpose of the mission had lain hidden until soldiers disembarked at the port of ar-Raghib and marched inland for Mecca to seize the body of the Prophet Mohammed. They failed. But the profanity and insult were not forgotten. As Keeper of the Holy Places, as a devout Moslem, as a human, Saladin had prayed for this encounter.

He passed the goblets to servants who bore them first to King Guy and to Humphrey of Toron. Both gulped long and greedily, the younger noble sobbing with relief. It was more than water; it was the granting of life, for the Moslem code was that whomsoever received hospitality would come to no harm. The others watched, waited.

Saladin continued to study Reynald. 'You say nothing, Lord of Oultrejordain.'

'Of what is there to speak?'

'The reckless gamble of position. The loss of all you possess.'

'It was my intent to provoke, to bring you to battle.'

'And battle you have had.' Saladin peered closer. 'Some have obligation to God, but your sole master was avarice. It brought you wealth and influence, spurred your cruelty, and now brings you low.'

'I will not be taught by any Saracen.'

'But you will yet pay for your insolence and perfidy.'

King Guy had slaked his immediate thirst and passed the cup to Amalric. He too drank, before handing it to Reynald. The end of the line. Before he could put the rim to his lips, a Mamluk guard dashed it from his grasp. It clattered noisily, the declaration clear.

'We give you choice that you did not offer your victims, Reynald of Châtillon. Life or death. Renounce your Christ, choose our way, convert to the one True Faith, or you will suffer the consequence.'

Reynald laughed, and was still laughing as he was pushed forward, as Saladin drew his scimitar from its proffered scabbard and struck the head from its shoulders. Amid howls of disbelief, the freeze-tension of the moment, the arterial spray of blood, the shuddering torso of Reynald dropped. Wide-eyed, the prisoners cowered in the aftershock, some vomiting, others snivelling, lowing, frenziedly crossing themselves. Saladin had their attention.

Amalric of Lusignan could barely articulate a sound. 'What will you have done with us?'

'Whatever it is that Allah ordains, *Connétable*.'

They were dragged away to their new existence, a pleading and struggling rabble of dejected nobility. He would spare them, not through compassion, but for use. Princes and barons could earn good ransom. Grand Masters of military Orders could be co-opted to persuade fanatical followers into laying down arms. The rest would be less fortunate, condemned to slavery in the galleys and mines or to the blade of an executioner. War was capricious that way.

For a while he stood alone with his thoughts among

the body parts and abandoned water beakers. A waste of ice brought from the slopes of Mount Hebron, he reflected. At least he had rid the country of one miserable brigand. But there were many more to go before he cleansed the whole. He moved to the far end of the tent and ducked through its embroidered portal into the sarcophagus-dark interior of another. The scent of perfume was deeper here, the only light that of oil lamps shimmering weakly and barely picking out the lone figure standing in the centre.

'I commend you on historic success, Salah ad-Din.'

'God and the future will judge it.'

'You have dealt with Guy and his followers?'

'Only with Reynald of Châtillon. A king does not kill a king, passes no hasty sentence on the nobles he captures. Plenty others remain to be butchered before our departure.'

'It was my privilege to play a part in your achievement.'

'I cannot deny your role. Yet to me you are a jackal even jackals would despise.'

'You honour me, Salah ad-Din.'

The Lord of Arsur gave a low and ironic bow. He spoke Arabic well, but was no Arab. He had counted himself among the Franks, and yet betrayed his race without scruple. A difficult course had been navigated with consummate skill and ease, but the Sultan seemed grudging in his praise. That was his prerogative. Still, he could not ignore the facts, overlook the truth that subterfuge and sleight of hand had delivered up the enemy. It was the Lord of Arsur who had secretly persuaded the crusader ruler of Antioch to avoid committing to this war, the Lord of Arsur who had influenced King Guy to bring his army by this murderous route to Tiberias. And it was the Lord of Arsur who had slipped away with his retainers from the plateau on the Horns of Hattin to the Saracen camp the previous night. *A jackal even jackals would despise.* The jackal required feeding.

Saladin approached him. 'What is it you desire?'

'I ask solely for one thing.'

'The object that is called by your kind the True Cross you shall have. I will not break my word. But I sense in you a darker purpose, a further intent for power and control.'

'I seek merely to scavenge on the scraps of chaos.'

'Let it remain so, my lord. There is no room in our new kingdom for those who oppose, no toleration for any who would undermine.'

'I am aware of these conditions.'

'Then take your fill and leave by the morrow.'

Again the lightless form of the Lord of Arsur bowed. Such terms were acceptable. The Sultan was no fool, was right to feel unsettled, to have touched upon the possibility of hidden direction. A pact had been made with Satan, the aims and conclusion of which he would scarcely grasp. The Holy Land offered fine retreat for the unholy.

'May festivities commence, Salah ad-Din.'

A listless dusk of dancing shadows and undulating sound. By the light of fires and burning torches, Sufi mystics whirled, muftis chanted, and the forces of Islam celebrated victory. Among the clamour, high above the clash of tambourines and wail of flutes, came the screams of captured turcopoles impaled on stakes. They were renegades, Moslem apostates who had denied their faith and crossed to volunteer for military service with the Latins. For them there was no pity. So their cries welled, mingling with the rest. It would be a long night, a lingering death, for many.

Dawn broke, timid and grey on the horizon, threading illumination across the still-smoking battlefield. A haunting scene. Prayers were called and the faithful responded, offering thanks, promising obedience to the one God. There remained things to be done. In groups of ten, their wrists bound, their faces luminously pale in the gloom, two hundred and thirty Templar and Hospitaller knights were led out for execution. They were brought to a row of low boulders and forced to kneel. Around them the crowd jostled and jeered, ululating in frantic anticipation. This was sport, audience participation. The short sword-thrusts to the rectum, the necks of the victims rising in shock, the blades arcing downward, and the heads rolling to be hoisted on spears and paraded as trophies. A clean sweep.

Mounted on horses and leading a train of pack mules, the Lord of Arsur and his cowled officers made their way out of camp. Their task here was complete. They would leave the Moslems to their entertainment, let Saladin prepare for the next stage of conquest. The baron turned in his saddle for a parting glimpse of the show.

'*Traitor!*'

As his hood slipped, eye-contact and recognition came. The Templar stood at his stone block, his chin tilted in defiance, his expression fixed with accusation and hate. At the hour of his death, he knew. A handsome man, the Lord of Arsur thought, doubtless a great warrior. But there was a time for everything, an end to everyone.

'Judas. Betrayer of our cause.' The Templar called out again, his voice carrying, silencing those about him. 'I am happy to go to my Maker, glad to leave the earth on which you walk. A curse be upon you.'

Last laugh upon him. The Lord of Arsur shrugged and spurred his mount on. He would not allow the boldness of a condemned knight to penetrate, would not be troubled by valedictory sentiment. His party quickened its pace. Behind, they were cheering once more, and the rocks coursed red with blood.

In the weeks and months following, Saladin took many Christian towns and castles. Fifty-two of them fell. Surrounded, demoralized, their garrisons denuded of manpower for the army defeated on the Horns of Hattin, most offered only token resistance. Even those defended by the military Orders capitulated. For Saladin had sent envoys, the captured King Guy and Gérard de Ridefort, to parley and to order the laying down of weapons. The Templars had made solemn vow of obedience to their Grand Master. They could not refuse. The Latin kingdom of Outremer, land and forward outpost of the Franks – the Christian crusaders – seemed doomed.

Saladin eventually turned his attention to the main prize, Jerusalem. It was almost a formality. Swamped by refugees, unable to muster more than a handful of troops, commanded by a motley band of dispossessed nobles and two knights, the city tried to bargain. Saladin demanded payment, a hundred thousand dinars as ransom for the populace; the defenders responded, threatening to raze the Dome of the Rock. An empty gesture. On 2 October 1187, anniversary of the visit to heaven by the Prophet Mohammed from Temple Mount, the forces of Islam entered the gates. The cross adorning the Dome was torn down and ritually beaten through the streets, the al-Aqsa Mosque was purified with rosewater and prayer, the cheering of Moslems could be heard in every quarter. Ownership of Jerusalem had changed.

But the power of the Latins was not yet spent. Some clung on in their coastal redoubts, holding out, fighting back, depending for survival on resupply by sea. The cry went out to save Christendom. And it was answered. Knights and princes appeared from Europe, fired by conscience, inspired by faith to recovering Jerusalem and the lost relic of the True Cross. It prompted the next spasm of violence. In June 1191 the ships of King Richard I of England and a coterie of fellow sovereigns arrived off Tyre, and the Third Crusade began. Cœur de Lion did well, retook Acre, captured land, marched his army up and down. Yet he failed in his quest for Jerusalem. Others were to follow, their campaigns sputtering to ignominious conclusions, their efforts redirected to simpler ends. Few had the stomach or resources for war. Saladin, scourge of the Frankish empire, died on Wednesday 4 March 1193. He left unfinished business, a fractured dynasty, and an imperfect legacy to be fought over by lesser men.

Outremer had become the most beset of states, a narrow strip of territory and string of bastions running some one hundred and forty miles from Beirut to Jaffa along the Syrian–Palestinian coast and backing a mere ten miles inland. Within this compacted enclave barons squabbled and plotted; from here the military Orders mounted occasional raids. A strange and uneasy kind of peace. Around them, banditry and skirmishing swirled, intrigue and murder prevailed. To the north, another fractious Christian territory, that of Antioch and its satellite possession Tripoli. To the east and south, the Moslems. To the west, the sea. Christendom had its back to it. The days of glory, of triumph and dominion over the infidel, were gone.

A quarter of a century after the carnage at Hattin, Jerusalem remained a dream and the papal call to arms went unheeded. It was the turn of the children to try.

✝

Chapter 1

JUNE 1212. THE RHINELAND.

'We are called by God, my brothers and sisters, bidden by Him to right wrongs, to earn salvation, to count ourselves among the numbered ...'

He was only twelve or thirteen years of age, a boy preacher named Nikolas who stood on a cart and spoke with the fire of a demagogue, the fluency of a prophet. And the children listened. There were thousands of them, spellbound, their hands raised, muttering in tongues, crying out or laughing in ecstasy and joy. The Spirit of the Lord was come among them. It urged them on, forced them to sway and sing, to forget their troubles and discard their pasts, to dwell only on a future in which they would be saved. Behind the young orator, the great edifice of Cologne Cathedral loomed. It was a waypoint to crusade.

The boy stared from his platform at the upturned faces. They responded well to his address. He could see their rapt attention, sense the tidal surge of love and expectation and commitment. They sought, and he would provide. He lifted his arm, and the crowd stilled.

'Look upon yourselves, my brothers and sisters. You are the regiments of God, an army of innocence. And you have been betrayed.'

They waited for explanation, their features suddenly taut with concern at thought of duplicity, their eyes shining bright with conviction that all would be well. Their leader would offer solution.

'I say again, betrayed. By the princes and kings of Europe. By the haughty crusaders who lost our Holy Land to the Saracen. By the corrupt barons of Outremer, who even now revel in sloth and sin while Jerusalem and the True Cross lie abandoned. Must we let such wickedness and iniquity endure?'

'*No!*'

'Shall we remedy the impiety of our fathers, seize back what is rightfully ours?'

'*Yes!*' Mesmerized, German youth replied as one.

'As they used the sword against the infidels, so shall we use peace. The seas will part to aid our progress; the doubters will kneel in dread; the lamb will lie down with the lion. We are the pure at heart, and it is we who shall now conquer.'

Their cheers rose in tumultuous roar, washing over the square, lapping at the cathedral walls. Nikolas, the boy preacher, took comfort and certainty from it. He had prayed for guidance before the shrine of the Three Kings; he had toured the Rhineland with his message of truth and light. Children had flocked. As the Magi brought gifts to the Christ Child, so he would present his gift of a restored kingdom on earth. God had a plan, and the world would tremble and bend its knee.

A young priest bearing a hessian sack stepped up beside him on the beribboned and gaily painted cart. He reached inside the bag and withdrew the object nestled within.

'Behold, it is the head of St John the Baptist!'

It was indeed the severed head of a man, its embalmed Semitic features leathery and wizened with age. Sightless eye-hollows gaped at children who had fallen to their knees in reverence and awe. This was a sign, a symbol of what was at stake and what they would march for. Even the saints rallied to their cause.

Nikolas took the head and held it high above his own. 'The Baptist himself, my brothers and sisters. A saint who was sacrificed, who would have us voyage and be baptized in the holy waters of the river Jordan.'

'*Hallelujah . . . hallelujah . . . hallelujah.*'

'Do you search for paradise?' They did. 'Will you go on sacred mission?' They would. 'Will you come with me and take the Cross?'

'*We shall . . . we shall . . . we shall.*'

'Arise and make ready.'

Mass fervour was a beautiful thing. Their eyes glistened; their mouths opened and sang out to the Lord. They believed, for they wished to believe. They would follow Nikolas, for he offered vision and hope. Once lost, now they were found. Others would join them, dancing and tripping merrily in their wake as the colourful cart paraded through villages and towns on its southward journey. Children everywhere were bewitched and on the move, a simple cross of cloth sewn to their tunics signifying their aim. From Vendôme in France, thirty thousand had already departed for Marseilles in company with their shepherd-boy leader Stephen of Cloyes. But here there were more. With faith in their hearts, a pilgrim purse on their belts, a staff in their hands, they would begin their trek. There would be hardship ahead, travails aplenty. Yet they would endure. Because Christ bled for them, and the Holy Land called.

Kurt looked about him. He was bored with the sermonizing, with having to stand still and listen when he could be running, climbing, exploring, starting out on the expedition of his lifetime. Of course it would be an adventure. That was what he liked. What he hated were beatings from his father, enforced inactivity, finding nests whose eggs had already been taken. And Gunther. He detested him with all the passion a twelve-year-old could muster: despised his bullying nature, his greater height, his rotten teeth and mop of red hair. A year older than himself, this son of a woodsman was feared by the other village boys, who had often felt his fists. Mutual and lasting enmity was assured. So it made no sense that Gunther too came on peaceful crusade to Jerusalem. God most certainly worked in mysterious ways. Kurt would not drop his guard.

He caught sight of his friends among the throng. They were happy to be there, consumed like the rest in the bliss of the moment. There were the ten-year-old twins Zepp and Achim, the latter blind, the former guiding his brother for a miracle cure at the foot of the True Cross. Zepp smiled and waved, and Kurt returned the gesture. This was reported to Achim, who beamed and signalled his welcome. Close by were others: Hans the goatherd, Albert the crow-scarer, Egon the son of the blacksmith, little Lisa crying softly and being comforted by her cousin Roswitha. The village had been generous, was shorn of a generation. Kurt watched the salt tears stream, remembered how his mother had wept at their parting. He tried to put it from his mind.

His fall was sudden, the trip deliberate, and it caught him by surprise. Winded, his lip bleeding, he rolled on his back and peered up from the cobbles. Gunther gloated down.

'A pilgrim who cannot even stay upright to the edge of the square.' He planted his foot squarely on Kurt's heaving chest. 'Perhaps it is right you crawl to Jerusalem like a maggot.'

The youngster tried to rise, but was pinned. He tasted the blood in his mouth, was aware of the pressure and fury pulsing in his temples. A sense of justice and a hot temper were forever earning him punishment. He did not care. This was wrong, a crime perpetrated at the hands, the feet, of his mortal foe Gunther.

In vain he struggled. 'Let me up.'

'Is that a command, a whining plea? You belong where you are.'

'You tripped me, coward.'

'And I could crush you also.'

'In fair fight I would put you down.'

'What is fairness, Kurt? It is the strongest who rule, the weakest who submit. Do as others do, as I require.'

'Never.'

'I will hurt you, will get anyone I wish to hurt you.' The shadow of his angular frame blanketed his victim.

'Release him, Gunther.'

It was Isolda, her sweet face suffused with trembling ire, her gentle brown eyes glowing in indignation. At fourteen, two years older than Kurt, she was protective of her younger brother.

Laughing, Gunther slowly rounded on her. 'He needs a girl to guard him. It will not save either of you.'

'You would strike me?'

'Whatever it takes to teach a lesson.' He balled and raised a fist. 'Step aside, sister.'

'Samaritans do not walk away.'

She did not flinch. Her duty was to Kurt and the younger children, her promise to her mother to care for him and bring him safe home. She could not allow unchristian menace to daunt her.

Gunther grinned. He welcomed the challenge, the chance to stamp and punch authority so early in the mission. It was a mistake. His captive slipped free and scrambled to his feet, was upon him in a blazing instant. They were grappling, rolling blindly on the ground, Kurt flailing blows, Gunther desperate to shield himself.

'I meant nothing by it, Kurt.'

'I mean everything. You yield?'

'Please, we can talk.'

Kurt landed a hit. 'Surrender first.'

'Yes . . . yes . . . Stop, I beg you.'

Blood pumped from the nose of the woodsman's son and mingled with his mucous tears. The younger boy sat astride him, panting in his victory. He knew that it was not the end, but merely a marker, a prelude to future battles and increased hostility. Gunther was a dangerous adversary.

He became aware of the silence. Even the defeated Gunther had ceased his babbling. It was as though they were the focus of attention, at the centre of an arena in which a myriad eyes surveyed them. Self-conscious, Kurt twisted his head to see. His instincts had been right.

'How may we spread devotion, draw the infidels to Christ, when we fight among ourselves?'

Nikolas had descended from the platform to deliver his rebuke. In shame, Kurt hung his head and released his hold. He wanted to curl up in a tight ball of anonymity, wanted to crawl to oblivion through the dense forest of legs. But he was caught.

His voice glottal and wheedling, Gunther lay on his back and pinched the bridge of his nose. 'He attacked me without reason. Everyone knows he is a savage beast with no conscience or remorse.'

'That is a lie!' Kurt shouted in raw frustration.

'It is the truth, as I lie here wounded.'

'You shall be injured afresh for such falsehood.'

'See how he speaks and threatens me.' Gunther was garnering support, playing to his spectators. 'I am wronged, Brother Nikolas.'

'Then embrace him. Put resentment and child-ish things aside. Help and love each other. We have common cause, a single destination.'

They did as he commanded, and the children shouted in accord. *Hosanna! Hosanna! Hosanna!* All would be well. Kurt dredged a smile from his distaste and clutched at the bony shoulders of his foe. And Gunther whispered in his ear. *Depend on it, I will kill you.*

Isolda was fussing over him, tending his cuts, lightly chiding. He accepted her attention with sheepish good grace. After all, he had placed her in danger, exposed her to the perils of his personal feud. She had every reason to scold. But her exasperation would not last, was ever tempered by her kindness and sibling solidar-ity. They were inseparable: he the tousle-haired boy of energy and fire, she the thoughtful girl with brunette plaits and quiet ways. Together against the fates.

A different girl approached. She had emerged from the vibrating heart of the throng, a shy smile on her face, her limbs moving with the future promise of womanhood. Kurt stared. He had never before observed such things, was confused by her beauty and daunted in his response. He blinked. She remained in his sightline, drawing near.

'I saw the taller boy attack you. You were brave to fight, were not to blame.'

'They think me stupid.'

'You will not find me among them.'

Kurt flushed, comfortably awkward in her presence, stumbling over his words, near-falling over his feet. His heart raced. He wanted to say more, to tell and ask her everything. Yet he was rendered mute.

'I have something for your bruises.' She pressed into his hand a bag of poultice medicine.

Wordlessly, in wonderment, he took her gift. Then she was gone and he stood alone. The briefest of encounters, the quickest of farewells, and his inexplicable joy had turned to inexpressible loss. Around him, the excitable chatter and swelling murmur of anticipation were the same. But Kurt was in an altered state. He ignored the calls of his friends, the tugging at his sleeve, the companionable embraces of support and departure. A long march lay ahead. He vowed to himself he would meet the vanished girl again.

Exodus came, a triumphal scene of colour and fanfare, of singing and dancing children sweeping from the city. At the head of the procession was the decorated horse cart carrying Nikolas their general. He stood proud, his face to the front, a cross-bearer beside him, his progress flanked by an entourage of noble boys. At the rear of the tumbril, his legs dangling, a young flute-player piped a merry tune. And behind him came a tide of forty thousand, heading south for the Alps, for Italy, for Palestine, for Jerusalem.

People had travelled from afar to witness the sight. They whistled and applauded, called out their blessings, thanks and prayers. Never had there been such a happening. The children were embarking on glorious crusade and pilgrimage for them, for the sake of their souls and eternal salvation. God would smile upon them. They seemed so young – some only six or seven years of age, helped along by the rest, gamely keeping pace.

'God be with you, my children! Christ have mercy and preserve you!'

'The Lord speed and keep you!'

'Our Lady shall deliver you safe! You are in our prayers!'

If there was doubt or guilt or regret, it did not show. There were so many reasons to consign their young to the road. It would bring light to the darkness and faith to the heathen, would earn parents indulgence by proxy and entry to heaven free of sin. His Holiness the Pope had said as much. Besides, who knew with what kind of treasure their offspring might return? It was time they earned their keep. Intoxicated by zeal, delirious with religious fever, the good people of the Rhineland chanted and cast flower petals. They were sacrificing their children in the name of the Lord. No greater privilege or higher cause existed.

It took a day for the parade of minors to pass. When it was over, when the shadows lengthened and the dust subsided, the mad elation that had taken hold slowly settled to a grey and dull melancholy. Stray dogs whined and scratched fretfully at the scuffed earth, a church bell changed its peal from celebration to mourning, the funereal-scented petals lay scattered and abandoned in dried heaps. The streets had emptied and the children conjured from existence. But somewhere a voice cried out. It belonged to a small crippled boy left behind, a solitary figure backtracking and limping homeward to a life he had failed to escape. He vanished from sight. The bell ceased tolling and the land sank back towards nightfall and silence.

The four riders were to notice that silence when a week later they entered the town of Alzey. It was a pious place one hundred and twenty miles from Cologne, a favoured locale for wealthy merchants and wealthier monasteries. Hardly a setting for trouble. But it reeked of sadness, of a stagnant despondency that infected the streets and dwellings and grew from dreadful loss. Few bothered to observe the strangers. This suited them well, for they did not care to be spied upon. Those who did look would have seen travel-stained journeymen, a troupe of pilgrims, players or craftsmen making their way for money or faith to some other destination. Everyone had worries, their own private cares. There was nothing to arouse suspicion or fear.

They let their horses walk on. It was the oldest of tricks. Assume a purposeful air, adopt a manner suggesting work in hand or commands obeyed, and none would question. The quartet were masters of pretence. They could speak several languages, assume any role, had skin coloured light enough to place them anywhere in Europe. Direct them to shoe a horse, to summon music from lute or lyre, to fashion implements from wood and stone, and they were able. And they could kill. They had voyaged endless miles, were sent with single motive to eliminate a threat. Their target was close. The castle of Alzey.

'Peace be with you, strangers.'

'And with you, friend.' The leader of the group flipped a coin to the stablehand lounging at the inn hard by the castle walls.

It was accepted gratefully. 'You travel far, sirs?'

'Further than you may imagine. Our horses will be lame if they are not rested.'

'Allow me to tend them, sirs. I am not overburdened in my duties.'

'We expected busier times in Alzey.'

The ostler grimaced. 'Alas, you find a place of sorrowing and sighs. Rich or poor, many have lost their young in this holy venture to the East.'

'They will gain in heaven.'

'I pray it is so. Yet meantime not a hoop is chased nor ball kicked, not a laugh is heard.'

'There is ever a price for being instruments of God.'

The leader swung himself from his saddle, his companions taking their cue. They were amicable enough, the ostler thought. He squinted at them, tried to match their types, their faces, against his memory. Odd how he could not quite get a fix. There was something missing in their composition, something false in their bland engagement and deadpan smiles. He frowned and put it from his mind. One was not paid to refuse business.

'For how long would you wish your horses stabled, sirs?'

'Maintain and guard them at this post. We shall negotiate upon our return.' The principal pressed another coin into the appreciative palm. 'Our commerce in the castle will be brief.'

'What is its nature?'

'Stonemasonry.' It was not strictly true.

'A noble and worthy trade, sirs. But opportunity is scarce since the master rode out for Palestine. You would be wiser to approach the church. It is the bishops and abbots who have the riches and the inclination.'

'Our own inclination is for the castle. You say its master is away?'

'Almost ten years past. His son Otto, a mere stripling of sixteen, now travels in search of him.'

'Quite some quest.'

'He is brave and good like his father, and inspired by example of the children. I have no doubt he will succeed.'

The leader of the horsemen had equally no doubt the stablehand was wrong. 'How many days since his expedition set forth?'

'I would hazard five.'

'In company?'

'Alone, but for his black stallion and grey mare.'

His son Otto. The horsemen had not shown disappointment or surprise at news of their young quarry. Setback rarely deterred them. Challenges were to be expected, were part of such missions. They would track him soon enough. It had been six months since Otto of Alzey had sent message to the Grand Master of the Knights Hospitaller of St John in Outremer of his intent to trace his father. That quest could not be countenanced. There was no room for prying interference, no need for a callow squire of the Rhineland to investigate matters far beyond his experience. Word could spread outside the cloistered confines of the Hospitallers; curiosity could kill. So it was that the Lord of Arsur had dispatched his representatives to Europe with instruction to liquidate the sole progeny of a virtuous knight who had once devoted himself to the care and succour of sick pilgrims. The fledgling appeared prematurely to have flown. Too bad. Otto of Alzey would never reach Palestine.

They left the stablehand and made their way across to the main entrance of the castle. The burg was a low-built affair, modest in its scale, a squat structure of crenellations and arrow-slits designed more to protect than to menace. Yet it had its weaknesses. The guard responded well to the easy banter, the generous remuneration, of the visitors. They might have seemed a little eager, somewhat misguided in their hope of work. But all sorts came this way. He let them through.

Little disturbed the sedentary calm. They stood in the great hall, four artisans in a space dominated by a large hearth and a beamed ceiling. Tapestries hung on the walls, wood benches lined the circumference, flagstones scattered with straw reflected the dull glow of candlelight. The eyes of the newcomers noted the details. Three men played dice at a table, a spit-boy turned a haunch of venison. Beside him, a hunting-dog lazed in the heat. Occasionally a maidservant would enter with fresh candles or carry bread and beer to the engrossed participants in the game. They were ill-placed for action. The foursome marked time.

A steward appeared, a cheery fellow with rubicund features, a clutch of keys at his belt.

'We may offer food and drink, but at present have no use for your workmanship.'

'A pity, for we carry our tools.' The leader extracted a chisel from a leather pouch and unwrapped it from its cloth. 'Wherever we go, the gift we bring is through our hands.'

'Then I wish you well. Perhaps when next you pass I shall be able to provide the business you seek.'

'I doubt we shall return.'

'So stay awhile, share in our modest repast. There are but twelve of us remaining here to feed. And it was ever the rule of our young master and his father to offer welcome to whomsoever steps within these walls.'

'How fortunate for us. The townsfolk speak well of Otto.'

'They hold him dear and in highest regard. You will not hear a word said against him. He is the most caring of souls, most daring of spirits. Handsome too. Many a fair maid weeps bitter tears at his leaving.'

'Boyish youth may often act precipitously.'

'We are the poorer for it. But he would not listen,

would not tarry longer. If our children travel to the Holy Land, why not he?'

'Why not indeed?' The leader of the horsemen contemplated the gleaming chisel in his hand.

The steward continued to rhapsodize, unaware of the shifting positions, the change in tempo. 'I vouch that like his father he will make a fine and noble knight.'

'It is a treacherous road he travels.'

'At least he will find company. He follows the children out of Cologne, intends for blessing and news in Rome before onward passage to Outremer.'

'You should pray for him.' Instruments were being pulled from their covers.

Momentarily uncertain, the steward smiled, moving to usher his guests towards a trestle. 'From what part did you say that you hail?'

'We did not.'

A stone mallet swung and connected with the back of the steward's head. Bone and brain crumpled, eyes registered disbelief, the body sagged and sank shaking to the ground. The dog looked up. Already the killers had divided, three heading for the dice-players, one aiming for the spit-boy. It was merciless work. The youth had heard a sound, glanced round to see the incoming point of a steel gouge. He tried to fight, to dodge, to reach for a fire-iron. But he was too slow, too late, and the blow from the edge of a hand to the side of his neck knocked him prone across the roasting meat. He had enough air to scream before his face entered the flames, sufficient energy with which to thrash and kick before the spike pierced his lower back and cut the movement of his legs. Alight and helpless, he dangled, a boy immersed in his own cooking.

His assailant was loping fast to join his comrades in attack. There was nothing their victims could do. Instinctively, a hand rose to protect a face. It did not prevent a blade from plunging through the ear. Chairs fell, tankards scattered, and the dice-men fell to their final throes in a blizzard of blood and severed arteries. Their butchers stood over them, wiping weapons, readying to move on. Four down, more to go. Such deaths were unnecessary yet rewarding, an expression of art and faith, an outlet for skills, a matter of keeping in both eye and hand. It would have been a shame to come so far and depart without result. The leader of the horsemen gave a signal. Time to clear the rest of the fort.

Their entry to the remote chamber prompted no fear in the old man. He had a scholarly air, and regarded them with pale and steady eyes that lifted but slowly from their study of the Greek text. The intruders were objects of interest, as worthy of perusal as the illuminated tomes and apothecary jars around him. He gauged their intent.

'I do not seek explanation.'

'Nor shall you receive it. What can you tell us of Otto of Alzey.'

'Little, save that I am his tutor and mentor, that he will avenge this outrage.' He leaned back and placed his hand across the finely worked German cross pinned to his gown. 'I ask that you make it quick.'

They obliged, running him through, retrieving his brooch to add to their collection. The steward had not lied. He spoke of twelve residents, and the entire dozen were now dead. A task well done. Without pausing, the four riders left the room.

Later, as unremarkable as their arrival had been, the group slipped out from the castle gate. On the way, for good measure, they killed the guard and took back their coin; at the inn, they slit the throat of the ostler and emptied his purse. Then they mounted up and rode away. Their hunting expedition had only just begun.

In the great hall, the hound was lapping greedily at a puddle of coagulating blood.

What wondrous sight it made. One hundred miles from Cologne, along the road that unfurled beside the Rhine, spectators had gathered to watch the onward march of the children. Beneath the early-July sun, the youngsters tramped. They carried themselves well. Yet there was no denying their ranks were more ragged, their gait had lost its skittish vigour, their banners tilted with a wearied droop. Another day rolling into the next, another furlong reaching to an infinite distance. Feet were rubbed raw; eyes watered with the grime and dust; enthusiasm had frayed to grim determination. They would not let themselves down, could not betray God.

In a horse-drawn litter, a bishop from Mainz peered through muslin curtains and gnawed contentedly on a chicken leg. It was a perfect day for a picnic. He licked his fingers and tossed the bone outside, gazing with only mild interest as a dirt-encrusted waif darted forward to seize ownership. The poor half-starved mite. What a course these creatures had chosen, what courage they showed. He almost envied them their dedication.

A snatch of holy song reached his ears as he rummaged in his basket for a sweetmeat. Perhaps he could encourage the *Kinder* to sing for him, or would throw them a morsel to initiate a fight. He enjoyed a little diversion. With a satisfied grunt, he eased his hips forward and leaned back in the padded seat. The whore who knelt between his knees continued to perform fellatio on him, her head working expertly below his robe. He closed his eyes. It could make a man blaspheme, a prelate groan, distract him from divine pursuit.

He drew aside the curtain a fraction. 'They search for Jerusalem and the True Cross. I fear they will find doom.'

Hearing his voice, the prostitute emerged from her labours. He pushed her head back down. She obliged, a practitioner from one of the oldest professions taking instruction from another. Outside, the children trooped on.

'I wish to rest.'

Kurt called over his shoulder. 'Then do so, Gunther. We shall not prevent you.'

He would be happy to put distance between himself and his avowed enemy, would rather walk to

Outremer on bleeding stumps than concede position to the woodsman's boy. How his bones ached. At first he had welcomed the acclaim, had smiled gratefully at the adults who crowded to offer food and praise. They opened their hearts and inadequate larders to the young pilgrims. But they were not the ones who had to stride a thousand miles to Rome and thousands more beyond, whose role it was to cajole unwilling heathen into the ways of Christ. It was hard enough persuading his own friends to keep step. He tried to think of pleasant things, of the girl with flaxen hair and brimming smile who had entered his life in the square at Cologne a few days and an age since.

In front, Zepp was guiding Achim, describing the scene, picking and smelling wayside flowers, his sightless twin responding with laughter and tumbling questions. Hans the goatherd whistled a tune and whittled a length of hawthorn as he went; Albert threw clumps of sod at marauding crows scavenging the strip fields; Egon carried little Lisa on his back. The remainder kept their heads down, their feet moving. Ahead and behind, it appeared as though the youth of Germany had been disgorged in unending stream.

'I wager Nikolas is more comfortable on his cart.' Albert threw a well-chosen clod and the birds scattered.

'Why not?' Egon delivered a comradely slap to his shoulder. 'He is worthier preacher and prophet than you or I.'

'Prophet? He is a sorcerer who has placed a thousand blisters on my feet.'

'Each one of them a token of your faith.'

'A symbol of every mile I have dragged myself.'

The son of the blacksmith shook his head. 'Be strong, Albert. We cannot call ourselves pilgrims without expecting to endure, without bearing the burden that God assigns us.' He hitched Lisa higher on his back.

'You heard Nikolas in Cologne.' It was the turn of Isolda to speak, her words carrying soft. 'We are chosen and we are called.'

Hans spat in the dirt. 'No, we are sent. Your mother had a vision of the Virgin. Mine has dreams of gemstones the size of duck eggs. You, Albert?'

'I go to win my father and mother their place in heaven.'

'And you, Achim?'

The ten year-old was concentrating on the sound-path of a bee. He paused. 'God intends to grant to me my sight.'

They trekked on, buoyed by companionship and shared adventure. Kurt grinned at Lisa as she clung tight to the broad shoulders of her bearer. She reciprocated, her head lolling to the rhythmic tread. To the left, skylarks were rising, their song bubbling high; to the right, the Rhine flowed wide and steady. The children had never travelled so far. Kurt chewed on a sorrel leaf, let its sharpness ease the swelling hunger in his belly. There were too many to feed, too little provision for forty thousand swarming locusts. He sent another prayer heavenward. It was best not to ponder too hard or to dwell in the gloom, prudent not to glance back at the sullen and trailing presence of Gunther. He had not forgotten the threat.

Lisa piped up. 'How do you think Jerusalem will seem, Kurt?'

'A city of high walls and gleaming white towers.' He was focused on issues closer to his stomach.

Isolda caressed the youngster's head. 'It will shine brighter than the morning sun, Lisa. The people will run to greet us, will honour us as saviours, will bathe in the radiance of our truth.'

'If they do not?' A frown had creased the seraphic features of the seven-year-old girl. 'If they should send an army against us? If they deny the Word of God? If they should fight?'

Egon cocked his head. 'The son of the blacksmith here will protect you.'

'We all shall, Lisa.' Kurt jabbed at an imagined foe. 'No harm can befall you.'

'But they say that the infidels are more vicious than dragons, that they sup on the hearts of children.'

'Ignore these things. The Saracen has not the strength to challenge us.'

Isolda nodded. 'As Nikolas preached, we will carry all before us, shall bring every heathen from the path of wickedness.'

'I hope it is so.' Lisa still looked doubtful.

'Once the seas part and we walk for the Holy Land, there is no stopping us.'

Albert pulled an agonized face. 'I would rather the Lord gave us a boat.'

There were hoots of good-natured derision, the ribaldry of children attempting to shed their misgivings and overlook their discomforts. They were heading for rebirth, a better life. That was what mattered. But only a fraction of their journey was done and already the canvas and leather of their shoes were shredded. God would provide, they told themselves. God knew everything.

Lisa was asking more questions: on wolves and bears, on whether there would be mushrooms where they headed. It helped pass time. Cattle lowed, a further spur to discussion and onward report to Achim.

'Talk will save none of you . . .'

Ignored, Gunther had closed the distance, his words hissing close in their ears. He was unused to being disregarded, enraged at losing influence and the opportunity to coerce. Intimidation was difficult on the road. Yet he was not ready to quit, would continue to probe, to demoralize the weak and destabilize the strong. One needed sport.

'You consider yourselves prepared? You think you will survive the wild beasts, the brigands, the mountain passes, the heavy swell of the seas?' Lisa started to cry. 'Stay your tears for what will come. I doubt any of you shall reach the Holy Land.'

Kurt spun to face him. 'I doubt you shall reach another step without receiving a second blooding.'

His adversary hopped back, his smirk certain, his eyes aggressive and bright. The expression changed. Kurt did not waver. He expected a trick, anticipated a forward lunge as soon as he turned his head. But the

40

shout of alarm from Zepp, the fixed stare of Gunther, compelled him to look aside.

Isolda held his arm, was pointing to the meadows. 'Who are they, Kurt? What are they?' She was scared.

Bowed on all fours, cropping at grass with open mouths, scores of men and women grazed as oxen on the wild pasture. Dumbfounded, the children stood rigid and still. Occasionally, one of the strange and naked forms would bellow, would move slowly to browse on fresher ground. As zealots, they were performing their duty, an act of faith and penance. Man was unworthy to walk upright; man was a sinner, undeserving so much as to live and feed like cattle. Ultimate humility was the real path to godliness.

Troubled, in silence, the children renewed their journey.

✝
Chapter 2

They had seen him, communicated his approach with the mirror-flash of polished silver that rippled along the canyons and sparked from the tops of steep cliffs. The Lord of Arsur stared ahead. At the best of times, the Nosari mountains of Syria, crucible of hostility, nexus of the conflict between Islam and Christendom, were a dangerous place to be. These were not the best of times. He sensed the tension in his officers riding alongside, could smell their sweat. They had grounds for concern. Their hosts could kill for any reason or for none, for perceived slight or supposed lapse, for business or pleasure, for the gifts of gold and treasure carried in the packs of this small convoy. Murder was their way, and jewelled offerings and previous agreement provided no guarantee. The Lord of Arsur noted the buzzard floating high on a thermal and scanning below for carrion. He wondered if such birds had the power of premonition.

The horses forded the stream, splashing their way on to a track that entered another valley bounded by vertiginous walls of rock. More glints of light flickered news of their presence. The Lord of Arsur appreciated the effort. He relied on the abilities of these people, their lethal expertise, to carry forward his agenda, to play a part in conspiracy that would alter for ever the course of mankind. It was twenty-five years, almost to the day, since the bloody occurrence on the Horns of Hattin. Long enough. A fragile peace existed; Saphadin *al-Adil*, brother of the great Saladin, held tenuous sway in Damascus; John of Brienne governed as regent for the baby Queen Yolanda in Outremer. Few wanted war, none had the power to launch full military campaign. Except him. He had once told Saladin in a perfumed tent that he sought only to scavenge on the scraps of chaos. But contentment could pall, ambition grow. He had been waiting and planning for a lifetime. Saphadin and his Moslem cohorts, John of Brienne and the infant queen, the barons of Outremer, the Arab governors and emirs: all would succumb, would be consumed in the gathering darkness. Preparations were advanced, had brought him here to the land of the *hashshashin*, the hashish-eaters. The Assassins.

Al-Kahf was a structure that would not be ignored or forgotten. Jutting prominent on its sheer mountain crag, the fort was a man-made stalagmite, a soaring edifice constructed to impress, guaranteed to awe. Those who approached did so by invitation and temporary truce. The Old Man of the Mountains and his followers could be capricious. A delicate mission. The Lord of Arsur guided his mount on, led his troop in single file on to the winding uphill track. At any turn could be an ambush, behind every boulder and overhang killers might lurk. They would wipe a blade across his neck before he realized he was dead. But the only sounds were the plodding tread of hooves, the jangle of harness, the breathing of his men. The hashish-eaters had allowed them to live this far.

Ascent was achieved. It had taken an hour, a tortuous perambulation through blind gulleys and labyrinthine detours that brought them eventually on to a narrow ridge before the walls. There were no welcoming trumpets, no tell-tale whirr of a rampart catapult releasing its load. Not a sign of occupation existed. For a while, the Lord of Arsur sat in his saddle and viewed the prospect, taking in the unmanned castellations, the open gates. It would be foolish to interpret it as anything other than illusion.

He spoke calmly to his men. 'We advance two abreast. Unless attacked, you shall neither react to provocation nor reach for your swords. Be reserved; conduct yourselves with dignified purpose.' Responding to the press of his heels, his horse moved forward.

Revelation was dramatic. It came with smoke and flame, with a cacophony of cymbals and roll of drums. As the visitors attempted to steady their shying horses, ropes looped from the high windows of the keep to the courtyard below and figures in black swarmed down. Others jumped and tumbled into view, knives drawn and wielded in mock battle and choreographed display. Wood targets were held aloft and quickly pierced by flying blades. Silk screens were opened out and carved to ribbons in an instant. It was theatre and threat combined. The Assassins were the most skilled practitioners of their art. They were Nazari Ismailis, the *malahida*, Shi'a religious deviants bound by faith, blood and history to avenge themselves on the Sunni, to bring chaos and terror to the unrighteous, to martyr themselves for the cause of past injustice and future divine fulfilment. Death was a religious obligation, and they had grown rich and powerful on it. They were the perfect allies.

A circle was mapped on the ground with gypsum paste and, as the guests watched, two half-naked combatants entered the ring. There was no ceremony or emotion here. The rivals eyed each other, their bodies flexing, their daggers drawn and tracing air. Slowly, they orbited the circumference, feet shifting and finding balance, stares never wavering. They knew what was at stake. One dodged in and pulled back, the other lunging hard. Again the first man tried, feinting fast, switching hands, jabbing with his knife. His opponent leaped lightly back and accelerated to a different bearing. He slipped, rolled, and recovered. His challenger followed. Back and forth they went, trading moves, exchanging strikes, anxious to achieve a kill, determined to escape injury. There had to be conclusion. With three minutes gone, it arrived in a welter of glinting steel and flailing limbs. The men stepped apart. Blood could be seen, the smallest of scratches scored on a forearm. Without a word, the victim held it up for examination, his eyes widening as his hand clenched involuntarily, his teeth baring in a rictus grin of agony. He was dead shortly after hitting the ground, his face blackened and bloated almost beyond recognition, his body stilling after a few lacklustre flips. The bout had ended.

'*Poison serves to sharpen the response.*'

Unsmiling, his thin face dominated by agate-dark eyes and a grey-streaked and unkempt beard, the sheikh looked down from his balcony vantage. His followers were already dragging away the corpse.

The Lord of Arsur replied in Arabic, gestured to the deceased. 'I observe it well.'

'Remember it also.' Niceties were over. 'You bring tribute?'

'Sufficient reward to seal our understanding, enough gold to demonstrate the depth of my intent.' He raised his hand and the covers of the saddlebags were thrown aside to reveal the glittering contents within.

They seemed to find approval. 'Join me.'

Dismounting, the Lord of Arsur made his way to a stone staircase and climbed the worn steps to its summit. He emerged on to the roof of the keep, a panorama of hills, valleys and plains lying below him. It would provide any sect with a sense of impregnability. Attended by fifteen followers, the sheikh was standing to receive him.

'Here we are closer to God, and from here we may sortie to corrupt and destroy our enemies.'

'I depend on it.'

'As we in turn are glad of your trade.'

'A state of shared and happy convenience.' They walked a distance from the rest. 'I must thank you for assigning four of your *hashshashin* to my task in the Rhineland.'

'You pay well.'

'And it is merely the beginning. Soon we shall set tribe against tribe, faith against faith, the barons of Outremer against the rulers of the Moslem realm.'

'It will be pleasure to see them burn.'

'I have no doubt. You will be a spark to inflame the conflagration.'

The pair acknowledged common cause with a tepid exchange of looks. Instability was coming, followed close by war, and the Lord of Arsur would be beneficiary of both. He could depend on the sheikh to stay silent. It was the old code of *taqiyya*, secrecy, the Assassins' way to wreak havoc on all stability and orthodoxy. None would appreciate the scale of the project; no one would witness it unfold. That was its flawlessness.

He gazed across the mountain range towards the ochre dust of the flatlands. 'You have heard that John of Brienne, regent leader of the Latins, reaches fresh peace accord with Saphadin?'

'Peace is of benefit to neither of us.'

'Let us ensure it is temporary. One death will beget two, two will engender four, four will encourage mass reprisal. So it goes. Until there is clamour for parley, a meeting at time and place of our choosing and preparation. We must nurture every step, support every act.'

'You may rely on us.'

'I await to count the result.'

In reply, the sheikh turned and nodded once to his

entourage. A man stepped forward and, without pause or question, launched himself from the parapet. Again the sheikh dipped his head. Soundlessly, a second Assassin dropped into vertical descent. People died strangely in the Holy Land, the Lord of Arsur mused. Henry of Champagne had fallen from a window with his pet dwarf beside him; King Amalric of Jerusalem had expired from a surfeit of fish. Now these dedicated and glassy-eyed killers slew themselves as circus routine. Small wonder Saladin himself had feared them, had slept in a portable wooden tower to evade their homicidal clutches. Saphadin, his brother and successor, would not be as fortunate.

A seventh individual had plummeted to personal oblivion before the sheikh brought a close to his demonstration. He remained impassive.

'Death holds no fright for us. We embrace it, seek it out, yearn for paradise in which milk and honey flow, where virgin maidens walk among golden pavilions and laden trees of fruit. It is our destiny and desire, our strength, the very reason why men tremble at our name.'

'They shall quake the more when I am done.'

Out of anarchy and confusion would come new order, his order. *When I am done.* He was letting loose forces that would sunder accord and sow disaster, that would purify with violence. Each element would play its part, each stage would be mapped, each grouping would eventually be neutralized. He could not possibly allow the Assassins to outlive their usefulness. Such was the work of a master strategist. As of this moment, from a high fortress on a mountain crest, his object was to create hell on earth.

Children populated the fruit trees like feeding insects, revelling in the abundance, shaking free the cherries and plums to waiting hands below. It was a day of rest and forage, of rejoicing in sudden bounty. Feet could be bound or cooled in streams, limbs stretched beneath laden bowers, ravenous hunger sated for a while. They had changed much in the three hundred miles since Cologne. Weakness had gripped every step; hollow-eyed gauntness had set in. Yet they endured. Mannheim and Karlsruhe, Strasbourg and Freiburg, waypoints of pilgrimage, a shuffling trek bordered by the swollen waters of the Rhine and the brooding denseness of the Black Forest. They had reached the hills and meadows of the Basle *Land*. And so they clustered, pinch-faced and grateful to God, and devoured the produce of the orchards.

'Catch . . .'

Kurt captured the black plum thrown him by Zepp. The ten-year-old sat astride a branch, harvesting with the speed and fury of a born scavenger, Achim waiting beneath in blind faith and with an open pack. It was manna from heaven, the children said. Kurt was more concerned with eating. He bit into the fleshy ripeness, let the juice run on his chin, the sensation of food linger in his mouth and throat. What a moment, the briefest of respites. Around him, his companions gorged and lazed. Little Lisa played with a wood doll fashioned for her by Hans. Egon and Albert sat hunched over a game of five-knuckles, tossing a pebble and sweeping up a clutch of sheep vertebrae to the random applause of their audience. Occasionally, Isolda and Roswitha observed them from their forlorn assignment of patching clothes with bone needle and twine. Kurt smiled at his sister. Behind them he could see the sly and skulking form of Gunther. Even when relaxing, the son of the woodsman radiated malice. While others starved, Gunther would find himself provisions. Where others shared, he would hoard and boast of his fare. When others grubbed for roots and worms, he would return with full belly and knowing sneer. Kurt contrived to ignore him. The residue of the fruit tasted sour.

'Do not let him upset you, Kurt.'

He shrugged as Hans appeared at his side. 'I am more vexed by lack of food. Cherries are no answer to our appetites.'

'There is still the hare I trapped yesterday.'

'And the crow that Albert took with slingshot the day before. But we are growing weak.'

'Weak? I am becoming crazed.' The goatherd produced a lopsided grin on his roughly hewn face. 'Look at them. Innocents in the Garden of Eden, feeding on fruit that will cause the downfall of their stomachs.'

'I have already seen the serpent.'

'Gunther will keep. Avoid him as we do, and do not tread on his tail. Our little band will encounter greater terrors than he.'

Kurt glanced sideways. 'Do you ever doubt, Hans?'

'Always, at every step and for every minute. It is how the Lord tests us, how we test ourselves.'

'What if we should fail?'

'We should be cast into outer darkness or the fiery pit, shall for ever be damned. Isolda and Roswitha, Zepp and Achim, Egon and Albert: all will die. Yet I am sure the preacher Nikolas will remain comfortable and remote on his travelling cart.'

They shared the joke, their mood lightening with the sunshine and the merriment among the trees. Zepp had swung down to join his twin in bundling up their crop, Albert had won the game of knuckles, and Isolda was completing repairs to another set of threadbare garments.

'Your fingers bleed raw, Isolda.'

'They may hold a needle, do what is demanded of them.' She bit through a thread and laid the tunic aside before standing to join her brother and the goatherd. 'That should see us clothed for a few miles more. I am glad to have practised on Kurt these years past.'

'While I am glad to have a sister who cares for us so. It deserves reward of a banquet.'

'Such thoughts are for dreams, Kurt.'

'Not if I explore and find provision, if I should chance upon a wild pig or cat. One of us will discover something: a trove of roots, a fat river fish.'

'Be careful. You are as like to stumble on trouble as to unearth a morsel.'

She touched his cheek, and he dipped his head in rueful acceptance. She was right, always was, had learned from experience and the application of unctions to his many wounds that he and scrapes had common bond. He invariably chose the most challenging route and impossible of tasks. It made for excitement, caused Isolda alarm.

He squeezed her arm. 'I shall prove you wrong.'

'And I shall ever be the elder sister who worries.'

Their meeting had grown as youngsters wandered over to swap news and exchange supplies. They estimated the distance travelled and miles to go, traded rope belts and leather hoods, bartered pouches of calendula for handfuls of poppy seed. A boy carried a stick strung with field rodents and was instantly surrounded; a girl muttered prayers and gripped the injured foot of a comrade in pursuit of ecstatic healing. But there was further work to perform, the endless scouring of the upland and hunting through the low. To be still was to die.

Striding out along the rough uphill track, Kurt had soon left the chattering activity of the children behind. He was content to be alone, relished his role as provider to the younger of their troop. He would reveal his worth to a doubting sister, would one day stand full-grown and equal beside his proud shearsman father. It was that father who had ordered son and daughter to the Holy Land, for better or worse, for reasons of poverty and the sake of spiritual absolution. Kurt did not miss him.

Oak and birch gave way to the darker ranks of pine, the gradient steepening as he trudged. There would be plenty to find in the higher pastures if he were to look hard enough. His friends would welcome his return with cries of delight, would crowd to see what he had brought. Egon and Hans were fishing, Albert collected firewood, Zepp and Achim were stalking crickets and grasshoppers with a sack. He would achieve so much more.

A shadow flitted among the trees. He ignored it, then slowed, his attention drawn to a suggestion of movement.

'Gunther?' He shouted again. 'Is it you?'

Mind and sight could play games in the dappling light. He resumed his course, halted, stared back into the retreating shadow of the woods. Nothing lurked there save his imagination. He whistled a tune, remembered and tried to forget tales of trolls and dragons. A bear might be exploring, a mountain cat slinking low. Or it could be Gunther.

It began to rain, the heavy drops falling vertical and fat and accelerating into deluge. Water poured, running in rivulets from his body, coursing fast at his feet, drowning sound in torrential roar. Kurt stumbled blind and soaked through the sweeping grey. He had lost his bearings, was submerged in a gloaming that flickered in the shuddering storm. Thunder cracked. He shied. The path was now a stream, the forest an indistinct mass set against a wider darkness. He had to continue, had to find shelter, had to stay calm and succeed in his quest. It took effort to convince himself he was not frightened.

Lightning flared. Briefly, in its dazzling brilliance, he could make out the contours of a structure, the makeshift shape of wood beams laid as a haven for goats and cattle. He headed for it. Another flash, an immediate fade. He wiped the teeming water from his eyes, blundered on for the vanishing and emerging cover. Thank God for such mercies. His hand reached and found the rough-hewn timber, pulled him to it, hauled him into the damp interior. Panting with relief, Kurt leaned on his knees and let his clothes drain. Only slowly did he become aware of a warm presence, and only in the next bursting shard of radiance did he see the blood and the body from which it came.

The man was propped against a post, his expression unassuming, his chest pierced, a viscous stain saturating the front of his smock. It had been a recent kill. Kurt shuddered before it, wanting to run but held in check. One stared at the other, the dead inertness provoking inertia. Then Kurt fled. He was stumbling and crying, sliding to escape the horror and free himself of the clutching fear. So many questions invaded his mind. Yet they led to a single answer, to one solitary and unprovable fact. Gunther must have done this. The son of the woodsman had murdered as surely as he fed on the food of others and foraged on missions of his own.

It was a hard blow that struck the side of his head, his impulsive stoop that deflected its crushing impact to a glancing one. He dropped, stunned and semi-conscious, was being dragged through a dream of indistinct shapes and muffled noise to the edge of a slope. Vainly, he attempted to speak; powerless, he fought to stand. And far away he was moaning, beyond the sound of the thunder and the rushing closeness of a mountain stream. A pair of hands heaved him over, and he rolled down the bank.

Rain was also falling forty miles away, sweeping the road from Freiburg along which the children had travelled. In a cattle-shed nestling against a scattered coppice of trees, a handful of stragglers huddled from the storm. They had joined the crusade late, were anxious to find the tail-end. But for the moment they would keep dry, preserve whatever strength they had. The downpour would pass.

At first they thought they imagined the nearing rhythm and clop of hooves, then whispered uneasily and below their breath at the strange and foreign tongue they overheard. Rumour had it that bandits roamed in these parts. The children held each other close.

In a gust-spray of precipitation, the door swung wide on its eel-skin hinges and four riders stood framed in the opening.

'We seek one with the name Otto of Alzey.'

Vaguely he comprehended he was half dead, almost drowned. He had to be alive to be this cold, must have been immersed a long time. Ice seemed to pervade his thoughts and bones, occupy his very being. He remembered things. The hands that propelled him into the wide and turbulent stream, the expelled air and eructing water, the enfolding splinters of pain. He had clawed at the sides, at the rock and grass, had sought purchase against the foaming current. To no avail. He was carried on, sent through a mist of terror and submersion to a tranquil state of dark and comforting acceptance. That was where they found him.

He coughed again, and the water disgorged from his mouth. A hand was pummelling his back, its fingers wringing him out. So different to those that had gripped the implement used to club him, which had pushed him to a sodden oblivion. He would not tell his friends or Isolda of what he knew, of the dead stranger, of Gunther. Nor would he inform them of his dying thoughts and the image of the smiling and beautiful girl who had approached him in Cologne. She had come to him once more. They would think him mad.

'Kurt, you are with us safe. Do not move or fret. We will take you back.'

It was Egon, son of the blacksmith, who spoke. He was the strongest of them all, had the stolid nature and sturdy build of his male kinsmen. Happy fate that he and Hans had been catching fish downstream. Emptying on the ground, Kurt lay gasping, thankful and ashamed to be saved.

Hans prodded him with his foot. 'I have never landed an eel more difficult or large.'

'Ignore his words, Kurt. He rarely catches fish of any kind at all.'

'So speaks a blacksmith.' Hans tutted at the rescued boy. 'It seems you should sew and darn, and Isolda instead explore the mountain paths.'

'I would truly create disaster.'

'Your voice returns. A good sign.' Hans leaned and patted his head.

They hauled him upright and ferried him between

them, his arms dangling limp around their shoulders, his feet trailing on the earth. He was shivering. There would be no triumphal arrival in camp, no amusing anecdotes to relate. Just two older boys and their bedraggled and whimpering find. It hurt to have let them down, to have disappointed himself. He bit his lip and forced back the pricking tears.

'*Kurt, whatever has happened?*'

'You are drenched. Did you fall or slip? Did you miss your step?'

'Have you broken bones? Are you hurt?'

'We will find you dry clothing, a blanket, food. You are as frozen as ice.'

'Lie here. You must rest.'

He had been right of one thing. They did crowd round, asking questions, showing their concern. Little Lisa held his hand, Zepp and Achim clung to him as a prodigal brother returned, Isolda wept and kissed his cheeks. But a great tiredness had overtaken him. As his companions worried and busied around him, he sank down and slept.

When he awoke, the sun had gone and the light of a fire had taken its place. Green wood hissed and crackled, smoke billowed, and dampness evaporated in coiling wreaths of steam. Through this dusk-haze he could see the orange glow of faces, hear the murmur of voices. He was lucky to enjoy such companionship, a sister like Isolda. Ever watchful, she sat close and gently adjusted a rough horsehair cloak about him. He wondered if the girl from Cologne was thinking of him, and prayed she was safe.

'Are you awake, Kurt?'

'I am, Isolda. And I am sorry for the fear I caused, for the trouble and diversion I created.'

'You would not be my brother without occasional incident.' She found and held his hand. 'At least you live, though will not be exploring on your own for a while.'

'You have my word.'

She laughed. 'I know you too well to accept it. But I promised our mother that whatever befell us I would bring you to her unharmed.'

'What will befall us?'

'That is for God to know and for us to accept. I am sure He will be merciful if we persevere, if we are constant in our faith, if we continue in our endeavour.'

'I did not think I was on holy mission as I bobbed about in a mountain stream.'

'Yet it was the hand of Our Saviour that plucked you out.'

The hand of Gunther that pushed me in. As the firelight briefly dimmed, he could distinguish the stars shining cold and bright above him. At times, they could comfort, would wrap the heavens in a blanket of silver. Tonight they merely hung indifferent and cheerless, reminding him of his unimportance, of how alone and vulnerable he and his fellow pilgrims were. Best not to dwell on things.

'Take some food, Kurt. You must eat.'

Egon crouched beside him and pushed fragments of charred and indeterminate meat between his lips. He gagged, chewed and swallowed. It could be fox, might be pigeon. To follow, tree bark would suffice. There was little point in enquiring or refusing on this journey. He had, after all, failed in his search for a wild pig or cat. His blunder, his damn fault.

'Thank you for delivering me from the flood, Egon.'

'Where the waters do not kill you, these scraps will.' The son of the blacksmith fed him another piece. 'How did you come to be there?'

'I forget.' He lied.

'You have good balance, a fine eye, and sound fortune in spite of your escapades. And you arrive submerged at our feet.'

'Accident may catch any of us. It has taken a few in our village.'

'Until this moment not you, Kurt.'

The twelve-year-old winced as he sat upright. 'My tale is simple, the truth with it. I lost my way in the storm, must have tripped, received a blow to my head as I fell on the ground. When I came to, I was tumbling downstream, fighting to stay afloat and find handhold at the river edge.'

'Anyone who cheats death in such fashion, who survives immersion and cannot swim, is tougher than an anvil in my family forge.'

Hans had joined them. 'I know anvils that float better.'

'None that learn as fast as I.'

Kurt was happy to let them talk, to sit among them and absorb their joshing kindness and the warmth from the fire. Through the valley and into the hills, further lights speckled the blackness, other bands of children gathering round to ward off the spirits and their own night terrors. A wolf howled, its cry low and mournful and rising to an echoing scream. Its brethren replied ghostly in the forest vastness. Someone said they were demons on the loose, another that monsters prowled. Isolda hushed them and began to tell a story, a tale of kings and princes, of noble knights and fair maidens. It would help steady their nerves, revive their tired minds for the morrow and resumption of the march.

'And so it was that the evil baron marshalled his forces and set forth to conquer and rule the land of his neighbours . . .'

Sparks cascaded from the fire, showering illumination beyond the immediate circle. In its radiance, Kurt had noticed the eyes of Gunther glimmering empty and indecipherable.

Occasionally a camel would snort or groan, a desert fox yip and bark in the distance, but that was all. Out here in the Old Testament landscape, where acacia and thorn trees clung stubborn to the bone-dry surface, nothing would disturb the pre-dawn peace. That was how the commander liked it. His caravan was large, over three hundred camels tended by drivers, guarded by Mamluks, and loaded in Egypt with gold, iron ingots and weapons for Saphadin *al-Adil*, the Sultan of Damascus.

The patrol of Bedouin auxiliaries had not yet reported in. Its lateness would provoke neither comment nor concern. Any threat was unlikely. No group of bandits was strong enough to challenge the steady progress that they made; no marauding Christians would venture so far or find them in this wilderness. Stealth and size gave them advantage. It allowed them to sleep well, to avoid having to mass in the cramped confines of the caravanserai strongpoints. Walls had ears, towers eyes, local traders and herders mouths that could blab and spread a rumour. The caravan would stay from view and hide out in the night.

A guard dozed beside a group of hobbled camels. Behind him were the prone shapes of his travelling-party wrapped in their blankets against the desert chill, catching the last drifting moments of slumber before prayers and a new day recalled them to consciousness. Camel-dung fires would be lit, tea brewed, stew and bread eaten. They would set out again before the sun climbed too high, vanish ahead of any who might detect their presence. So the guard snored and broke wind and intermittently half opened an eye to reassure himself that things were as they seemed. Allah watched over them all. It was a wise course to trust in Him, to concentrate on idling time and chewing *qat*, on sinking into sweet narco-reverie once the amphetamine rush had palled. He yawned. A faint hint of movement had trespassed into his vision field, was agitating his unwakened state. He rubbed sleep from his face and strained to focus on the blurred figure approaching in the gloom.

'*Salaam 'alaykum . . .*'

'Peace be upon you,' the stranger murmured. The guard was stumbling to his feet, his mind too groggy to comprehend, his speech too slow to articulate response. He had not expected a visitor. There were instructions to kill those who posed a danger, to ward off those who came in close. But a lone wanderer offering felicitations was more surprise than risk. Besides, the guard had laid down his weapon, was attempting to find and retrieve it on the shadowed ground.

'You need no spear or sword to confront me, my friend.' The outsider spoke Arabic, his tone calm and reasonable.

'Do not come further.'

'Too late, my friend. I stand a mere five yards from you.'

'It is near enough. Step away. Return to your journey.'

'I cannot do that.'

'The alarm will be raised, soldiers called, your punishment swift. I have orders to kill.'

'We must all of us obey the authority of others. You and I, the soldiers and cameleers with whom you travel, the Bedouin sent out on patrol. Even the great Sultan of Damascus, Saphadin himself, answers to his family and tribe, to God, to the storms of circumstance.'

'You have no business in this place.'

'Yours has become our own, my friend.' The line was delivered in French, the tongue of the crusaders.

Aware that the situation had changed, was beyond his control, the guard shifted to meet the challenge. He was countered by a crossbow-bolt fired at short range. Its double head punched through his abdomen, exiting through his spine and carrying the stub quarrel and viscera behind.

Out in the desert, a single arrow soared skyward, its tip flaming, its trajectory curving in a graceful arc. The signal had been given. In a sweeping line abreast, and with a shuddering of hooves, mounted cavalry emerged in a headlong charge for the camp. Some had swords and clubs raised, others their lances couched, and all were intent on destruction. A man cried out and ran, through fear or to alert. His gesture was fruitless. The enemy were among them, hacking at the confused and rising Arabs, bludgeoning and pinning the inert or slow. Corpses lay blanket-clad, larva-like, the whinnying of horses and shouts of men eddying in the maelstrom. Dawn was breaking, but there would be no call to prayer. Instead, a process of elimination was under way, conducted with ruthless precision and total efficiency.

'Seize everything of value! Miss nothing and spare none!'

Climbing into the saddle of a charger that was brought to him, the killer of the guard negotiated his way through the murder zone. He gave orders as he went, directing, encouraging, bringing to a close. Before him, firebrands were being tossed into stores of oil and combustibles, the light flickering and catching the ongoing carnage. A squad of Mamluks tried to resist and were taken to pieces; a youth scrambled to escape, sprinting for the grey horizon, and was ridden down. Watching, the commander nodded in appreciation. He could report mission accomplished, the snatching of riches, the goading of the heathen, the gravest of blows inflicted on Saphadin. The Lord of Arsur had performed his opening move.

✝
Chapter 3

At an inn in the shadow of Basle Cathedral, cityfolk were drinking. Beggars and whores, young blades and tradesmen, the whole of humanity appeared to be represented in the riotous scene of colour and noise. A church spire could point to God. Here, energies were directed to earthier pursuits. In one corner, men and women crowded to watch a cockfight, cursing and yelling, trading money or insults as spurs struck and blood and feathers flew. Elsewhere, the inebriated slipped below tables, the insatiable fornicated against walls. Sodom and Gomorrah, a venue for loose morals and looser tongues, an excellent place in which to conduct a search.

The old Jew sat at a trestle, his ledger open before him, his assistant at his side. Naturally, the locals despised him, would mutter darkly of his hidden wealth and epic meanness. But he had the last laugh, if he cared to laugh at all. Anyone could be bought; everything had a price. Friends and security, influence and patronage, Church and state. Many came within his grasp; most were entered in his book or pocket. He was untouchable.

'You are?' He peered warily at the stranger who had slid into position opposite.

'A weary pilgrim who makes onward journey for the Holy Land.'

'Who is not a weary pilgrim? You are distinct only in your seniority over those who pass through of late. We have been infested with ravenous and needy children, are glad to be rid of them.'

'I am loath to consider myself distinct.'

'If it is charity or absolution you seek, find a priest. If it is a youngster, find a brothel of specific flavour. If it is money . . .'

He let the sentence hang, his eyes questioning and mildly hostile. The leader of the horsemen relaxed into the negotiation. His three companions waited outside, were available in case of hue and cry. He did not foresee trouble: the old Jew would not anticipate anything beyond the scope of his hook nose and basic greed. It made sense to convince him he discussed from a position of strength. People gave more of themselves when flattered or at ease.

'Citizens tell me you are a wise and informed man, that little occurs before or behind the walls of buildings without your certain knowledge.'

'Whether trade or wrongdoing, I discover all.' The ancient moneylender leaned forward. 'Do the citizens also tell you that they hate me, that they dream of cutting my gizzard from ear to ear?'

'I have not heard them speak so.'

'For they would not dare. Particulars are my shield and my sword, my security for long and contented life.

Between birth and death, everything is transaction, and every transaction requires funds. Without my kind, existence is impossible.'

'No idle boast, I am sure.'

A flagon of ale was brought. The horseman studied his potential victim through amicable eyes, observed how an air of suspicion clung to the man, could only hazard how he might attempt to cling to life. Even a stone could bleed if squeezed hard enough. What a pity this local font of knowledge had never heard of the sheikh and his followers at the Assassins' castle of al-Kahf.

Reaching for the jug, the old Jew paused. 'We talk in good faith?'

You have no concept of my faith. 'We do.'

'So state your aim and we shall agree a fee.'

'Information, news of a pious young man who travels on as I.'

'His name?'

'Otto of Alzey, a boy of noble birth whose family commends me to his side. They tell me he comes this way, that he rides a black mount with a grey mare beside.'

'An intriguing tale. And intrigue costs.'

'One gold mark for firm sighting and direction or I will depart for more favourable exchange.'

As though from air, he conjured the coin between his fingers. A flick, and it was gone, another and it reappeared. The features of the aged banker softened at its sight. He extended his palm, took the piece, and hunched over to examine it. When he looked up, his face was twisted with the semblance of a smile.

'Thus is friendship forged. You are a man of your word and your purse.'

'I await the words you may impart.'

'A youth Otto of such title and description indeed entered our city not four days past. He was eager to rest his horses, to purchase bread and varied fare for distribution to the starving children that he meets.'

'What worthy soul he is.'

'It was commented upon. His easy manner and generous spirit, his common touch and fine looks. Each drew its share of admiration or envy.'

'While you have earned my thanks.'

Libation was called for. The Jew decanted the contents of the jug into tankards, and the trio of new-found allies drank. One had become richer, another better informed. Toying with his cup, the horseman made his excuse to leave. There was arduous ride before him, the rigours of abstinence and the road to grow accustomed to. Tavern debauchery would hardly assist. The moneylender understood and bid farewell without remorse or a second glance. He should perhaps have taken more notice, for the long and contented life he had promised himself was now forfeit and rapidly approaching its end. Along with ale, he and his assistant had ingested sufficient digitalis, the poisonous extract of foxglove, to ensure massive and irreversible coronary. It would guarantee their silence, prevent casual remark or formal comment to the city authorities. Outside the inn, the horseman whistled and his steed was fetched. Ahead lay rendezvous and reckoning.

*

'We commend the spirit of our dear sister to God and give her body to the earth.'

It was at the beginning of the fifth week that little Lisa died. Like others, she had sickened and faded; like others, her mortal remains were laid to rest in one of hundreds of shallow graves that spotted the route along the northern shore of Lake Neuchâtel. Her fate and funeral were as commonplace as the rest. Just a small grouping of friends, bewildered or accepting, placing flowers, planting crosses, united in their grief. How many similar events they had passed in previous days. Their turn had come.

The youngsters rose from their prayers and tried to wipe the sorrow from their eyes. Little Lisa was gone, returned to God, buried with the wood doll carved for her by Hans. And that was that. Roswitha sobbed, Zepp and Achim clung silent together, Isolda and Egon held hands. Beneath the heaviness of their loss, the children still had each other, the holy imperative to struggle on. It provided their reason and remaining strength.

Kurt scuffed a stone with his foot and bit his lower lip. He did not care to cry, had no wish to display the weakness that he felt. Poor dead Lisa. He remembered her laugh, her curls, her devotion to them all. Consigned to moulder in the dust. There was no justice or purpose when she was merely seven years old, when more deserving candidates existed for the grave. At least she no longer suffered, was spared the toil facing them. At least his sister Isolda was alive, had discovered since Cologne a growing affection and regard for Egon.

He stared at them both, wondering for a moment if it were he as brother who should protect and comfort her. But she seemed satisfied with the brawny son of the blacksmith, happy to weep on his shoulder, to entwine her fingers in his and find tenderness in the misery. Kurt was pleased for her. His friend adored his sister, was good and honest and kind, had saved him from certain drowning. That already made them brothers of a sort.

'We have grieved enough.' Hans turned from the graveside. 'Brush away your tears. They will not feed or sustain us, will not take us to the Holy Land and the True Cross.'

Roswitha was bundling her meagre possessions, shaking her head. 'What do I care of that? My beautiful Lisa is ripped from me, my little cousin, my own blood. And you tell me to put away my sadness.'

'I tell you to look to the path in front.'

'It is a road of bones: our bones; the bones of every child who walks upon it. You are all too blind to see.'

Achim lifted his head. 'I am blind, but I see enough, Roswitha. The only way is to continue.'

'He is right, Roswitha.' Zepp chimed in in support of his twin.

'You are so sure. Yet it has brought us here, to throwing soil on a corpse.' She choked on her anguish. 'We were betrayed and lied to, by our parents, by the preacher-boy Nikolas, by our own heedless passions.'

Isolda stepped forward and held her trembling arms. 'What is life without suffering and sacrifice?'

'Where is salvation in this?'

'We are all together, all blessed in the sight of God, all embarked on our one true mission.'

'Little Lisa is not.'

'She finds a different way. Ours is not to question the workings of the Lord.'

Roswitha threw off her grasp and backed away. 'You believe it? You judge Him a forgiving God after what you have seen, after the hunger, the pain, the death, the burials you have witnessed?'

'How may any of us judge, my sweet sister?'

'I cannot go on. I cannot, I cannot, I cannot . . .'

Roswitha collapsed weeping to the ground, and Isolda was there for her as she had been for every child, caressing and soothing, rocking her in her arms. Kurt stood back, suddenly awkward at the emotion. The painful lump in his throat had grown, was forcing his distress and tears to the surface. He swallowed them down. At any moment he might break, could fall to his knees and pummel the earth. It would be inappropriate.

'Listen to me, Roswitha.' Egon had seated himself beside the two girls. 'I am schooled in nothing but the forge. Yet Nikolas commanded us endure, no matter what we face.'

'I have tried.' The response was muffled.

'We keep on trying, maintain our trust, as little Lisa did, as the apostles Paul and Peter did. It is our lot and our duty.'

'So do your duty.' Her face emerged raw and streaked with crying. 'It will be without me.'

'Are you to say that little Lisa died for naught, that you abandon us, turn your back on Christ?'

'I return to the Rhineland and our village.'

'*She is not alone.*'

Albert had ambled to the centre, a bird-scarer turned scarecrow, his feet bound in rags, his body grown skeletal and pitifully bent in the past weeks. Kurt was not surprised. It had become harder to inspire him, ever more difficult to push and pull him onwards. The death of Lisa, the decision of Roswitha, had brought him to his own conclusion.

'You also, brother?' Egon rose and placed a hand on his shoulder. 'We shall miss you both rather than condemn you.'

'I am tired, Egon. I grow more feeble and wasted with every furlong.'

'Then you must make your peace and go, and pray for us in our hour.'

'With all my heart.'

They embraced, and the other children joined as Albert and Roswitha prepared to take their leave. There was no clamour, simply the melancholy of further loss, the exchange of paltry gifts, the shouldering of forage bags.

'Take this willow basket, Roswitha.'

'And this handful of grain.'

'This shell is to be yours, Albert. Carry it and think of us.'

'Look after our dear sister.'

It was the turn of Kurt to say goodbye. He leaned and kissed Roswitha, whispered in her ear. 'Remember us to our families. Tell them of our love for them, that there may come a day when we shall meet again.'

'I will do that.' She pinched his cheek and sniffed through her tears. 'Return to us, Kurt. All of you must come back when this is ended and your mission complete.'

Gunther laughed, his tone jeering. 'A happy reunion, I am sure. You are unworthy, have no place in our midst.'

'Be silent, Gunther.' Hans was first to protest.

'What is one death or a thousand against the goal for which we strive? What is little Lisa, your fatigue, your swollen feet, your empty bellies, when measured against the prize of Jerusalem and the True Cross? Begone, strangers.'

Three down and they kept going. For the last time they had turned to wave, until the distant figures of Albert and Roswitha were sucked into invisibility. There was nothing else to do but continue, to put space between themselves and the earth mound and the memory that was little Lisa. For the whole day they walked. Kurt looked at the ground, tried to avoid conversation, attempted to ignore the despairing scenes unfolding at the wayside. Images merged. A young boy sitting alone and wide-eyed with the body of his brother; an arm projecting cold and bent from its makeshift scrape; children lying too enfeebled to move and too hungry to beg. The twelve-year-old shared what he could, distributing his reserve of carefully harvested water-lily seeds, giving away his precious flame-making flint and lump of iron pyrite. It would never be enough. And the son of the woodsman shadowed him, had sidled up and murmured his words of sham comfort. *Fear not, Kurt. I am still with you.*

Towards sundown he found her. The light was fire-bronze across the lake, geese flew in formation as if in salute, and weary children could pause to rest in the evening stillness. Her corpse was merely another waiting for interment. They would have muttered prayers and passed by, crossing themselves as they went. It was not a matter for them. Yet something drew Kurt. He had glimpsed her flaxen hair, seen eyes that were closed, lips that no longer parted in radiant smile for him. Her skin was so pale. Slowly, he moved towards her, sinking to his knees, reaching to touch her. And then he howled. It was a primal sound like no other, an expression of agony and of a boy whose greatest hopes were crushed and worst fears realized. His sister and friends tried to pull him away, but he resisted. Throughout the night, he kept vigil beside his girl from Cologne.

Heat shimmered off the Mediterranean and washed over the walls and fortress of Arsur. Perched on low cliffs, the town enjoyed a commanding view, benefited from its strategic location, its trading port, its role as conduit for goods and traffic from around the Christian and Moslem worlds. Close enough to Jaffa, the southernmost bastion of Outremer; far enough from royal circles in Acre to avoid prying eyes and the attention of the barons.

He rode out from his kingdom in late morning, attended by his captains, crossing the plain towards the forested hills of cedar and cypress. Twenty-one years before, Richard Cœur de Lion, King of England, had clashed with Saladin on this very ground as he led his army south. It had been a ferocious battle. The Moslems had attacked with Nubian infantry and Turcoman cavalry, the Christians responding with a mounted charge by the Templar and Hospitaller knights beneath a cloud of hostile arrows. Richard was at the forefront, cajoling, directing, inspiring by example and a brute force that eventually put the enemy to chaotic flight. Quite a scrap; quite some general. A high point in an otherwise disappointing campaign. What the Lord of Arsur planned would be a little more conclusive.

They followed the course of a dry river bed, slowing as they entered a narrow gully. The trees to either side were sparser here, stripped of branches and festooned instead with hanging and sun-dried human cadavers. They provided a striking if macabre processional route, gave stark warning that visitors were unwelcome on pain of death. Not that many would be induced to call or even to search for the location. The al-fresco morgue defined the boundary of a colony, a gathering-place for those with like minds and similar condition. In a valley beyond was the home of the leper Knights of St Lazarus.

A lone and hooded form astride an Arab pure-bred confronted them with his hand raised. The voice was a bronchial rasp:

'My lord deigns to venture from his marbled halls.'

'When there is business to attend, I would journey to Hades if required.'

'Welcome to nightmare of our own creation.'

The Lord of Arsur reined to a halt. 'You accomplished the objective with which I tasked you, seized gold and treasure beyond compare, arms destined for the infidels. I offer you my gratitude.'

'We proffer our allegiance.'

'It is as well. There are further targets awaiting your singular attention.'

'Should they come so easy as the last, should reward be as great, you may consider them already destroyed.'

'I vouch Saphadin will be displeased.'

'As I wager he will be none the wiser.'

Thus were plots born and wars begun, the Lord of Arsur reflected. He studied the green eight-pointed cross emblazoned on the mantle of the shrouded man. Like the Assassins, this band of rogue and leper knights were outcasts, reliant on his noblesse, dependable for he gave them food and water and motive. Without him they were sick and forgotten men. With them he had a catalyst, a fire-starter. One could not be fastidious when launching a bid for dominion.

An intensity shone in the reddened and unblinking eyes beneath the hood. 'Has the *barid* revealed more of its secrets?' The knight referred to the Moslem postal and carrier service interconnecting the centres of power.

'My agents are diligent in their endeavours. There is not a letter I do not read, a pigeon or courier whose path I cannot intercept.'

'It will prove useful.'

'Every step taken by Saphadin, I shall be ahead. Any move, alliance, employment of his forces, I shall learn of and counter.'

'Knowledge is your strength.'

'And lack of readiness is their flaw. They sign for peace with the Franks, believe that such concord will yet hold for five years hence. It seems we are to rouse each side from its tranquillity and slumber.'

'You will find us eager to play our part, glad at commencement of hostility.'

'I ask for nothing less.'

'From our Order will come chaos.' The leper knight wheeled his horse and beckoned to his visitors. 'Ride with me to camp and see for yourselves how we celebrate good fortune.'

Festivity could take many forms. The Lord of Arsur and his officers stared about them as they paraded through grim lines of severed heads placed in multitude on upright spikes. Simple pleasures for straightforward folk. Above them, in wooden watch-towers, sentries stood guard. Among the trophies, more hooded men, some bent and crippled, others grasping boar-spears or resting on swords, observed them pass. A reception had been arranged.

'You are industrious.'

'None may refuse us our basic delights.' The leper knight pointed.

Ahead, surrounded by stone dwellings, stables and sanatoria, a parade ground of impacted and sun-baked earth covered the expanse. At one end, mounted on chargers, a troop of cowled Knights of St Lazarus waited; at the other, tied to stakes two hundred yards distant, were their prey. Ten captives from the defeated caravan of Saphadin shook in their bindings. They mumbled prayers or gaped mute and bug-eyed at the building drama to which they would provide finale. There would be no pleading, no bargaining, no alternative outcome. A piteous sight, had the audience been inclined towards pity. Sport could begin.

In a stampede of dust, his long-hafted gisarme axe held high, the first of the knights accelerated for his target. The tethered Arab screamed throughout the run-in and went silent as his head split.

The Lord of Arsur squinted. 'A clean kill.'

'It helps to sharpen the edge of our brethren.'

'Alas, it denies an intact head for my tannery and onward shipment to Europe.'

He had done well in faking relics, in selling counterfeit heads of St John the Baptist to the rich and trusting fools of Christendom. They were merely part of the process, an element in wider actions that had amassed him a fortune. Where Reynald of Châtillon, Lord of Oultrejordain and victim of Saladin's wrath and blade at Hattin, had left off, he inherited, refined and continued. With one hand he traded with the Mohammedan and tendered his friendship, with the other he stole and snatched away. It was necessity. Vision and conquest, the raising of armies, cost dear.

The second of the knights completed his charge. A javelin flew, a body slumped. The next attacker was already formed up, raising his *masse torque* war-club in token salute before hurtling into the stretch. Face-off that led to face off: there was little left of the straining visage in his wake. Colleagues took their turn, galloping in, dashing out. An eleven-foot cavalry lance that pinioned, a steel-tipped lasso-flail that gar-rotted as it wrapped around. Then a sword, sweeping to sever torso and post in a single blow. All were tried and tested.

'My lord would honour us with participation.'

It would be ill-mannered to decline. The Lord of Arsur made his selection, picking a mace from among the weapons offered by his men. His choice was the morning-star, a spiked ball attached by steel chain to its shaft. It was capable of penetrating armour, liable to reduce a skull to pulp. Expertly, he lifted his arm at his side and let the killing-sphere dangle, spurred towards the impact point. The rush of air, the snorting of his horse, the looming and twisted grimace of a victim, the vibration of contact. Conclusion was swift.

He trotted back, restored the matted and bloodied instrument to its lender, and wiped a gauntlet on his surcoat. 'You will receive fresh orders in due course. Meanwhile, we take our tribute and return to Arsur.'

'As you wish.'

What he wished no man could hazard, neither Saladin nor Cœur de Lion could have foretold. He peered at the hooded creature.

'It is fortunate none suspect the Syrian Order

of St Lazarus might have spawned such demonic offspring.'

A clawed hand rose and pulled aside the covering. The Lord of Arsur's men shied in horror and disgust. Before them was a face replaced by a shapeless and atrophied mass, by the lesions and decay of lepromatous leprosy. The muscles twitched.

'Eventually all turns rotten in the Holy Land.'

Like a great serpent shedding its skin, the column moved into the Alpine foothills, discarding dead children, sliding onward with internal momentum of its own. Early August, and the harrowing sights and unbearable hardships had not diminished the pace. Thirty thousand had set out on this route, another ten thousand heading for the St Gotthard Pass and the eastern parts of Italy, and it was clear with each passing day that but a fraction would reach their destination. 'May their suffering be rewarded in heaven,' they prayed. And they buried more and spoke less.

'A bell, I hear it.'

'You imagine, Achim.'

'No, listen, Zepp. It comes this way.'

They paused, instantly wary at the possibility of trouble. News had come from the van that robbers and cut-throats were attacking pilgrims for their meagre rations and chance of hidden plunder, that farmers had killed to preserve their flocks and livelihood. How safe their villages had seemed.

The blind boy was right. A tinkling of a bell floated in the breeze, its sound presaging the appearance of a

snaking shadow heading their way. The image solidi-
fied. Nine grotesques, men or women it was impossible
to tell, shambled along in single file and, with aid of
a knotted rope, followed the lead of their guide. Ears
had been cropped, eyes gouged out, noses removed,
lips hacked away. Arbitrary justice, medieval style.
Only the leader had escaped total mutilation, had been
left with a single eye the better to steer, a tongue with
which to preach collective woe.

*'Let us serve as warning to others. Let us proclaim
before God our sins and heresies. Let man look upon
us and repent . . .'* The handbell rang.

Kurt nudged Hans and whispered, 'What devils are
these?'

'Cathars. They are Cathars.'

'They are unlike any beings I have encountered, the
most monstrous things I have ever seen.'

'It is punishment, Kurt. They were fool enough to
challenge the Church, to rail against the Pope. I have
heard a priest tell of their sacrilege and profanation, of
the crusade in north Italy and southern France against
them, and their resulting torment.'

With fascinated revulsion, the children watched
the Cathars pass. Kurt felt pity for them, a nagging
doubt that any deserved such harshness, should be
condemned to disfigurement and eternal wandering.
His was meant to be a forgiving God. Yet perhaps the
Church knew best.

'Stop, Zepp . . .' His sharpness forced the ten-year-
old to drop the stone. 'You think they are not already
persecuted?'

'They claim they are sinners and heretics. It is our duty to chastise them.'

'Not to find easy sport at expense of others.'

Disappointed, Zepp conceded the point and shrugged. There were plenty of other diversions. Kurt and Hans turned. They had heard the slightest of sounds, the quietest of cries from behind. Isolda had fainted. For uphill miles, she had struggled with a sprained ankle, Egon acting as her chaperone and support. Now he leaned over her, concern creasing his features, affection rendering him almost useless. His friends rushed over.

'Prop her against this stone, Egon. I have a rolled cloth for her head.'

'She is so grey. Quick, splash water on her face.'

'Isolda? Can you hear us?'

Advice was taken, random procedures followed. Slowly she revived, her colour returning, her eyelids flickering and glassy stare dissolving back to focus.

She gave a weak smile. 'By the hour, I seem to slow.'

'That is untrue, Isolda.' The son of the blacksmith knelt and gazed at her. 'Mountains are no barrier.'

'You encourage me in every step, sweet Egon. But I hold you back, have injury that may cause hardship to us all.'

'We share it as we do our food and faith, our hopes and pilgrimage.'

Kurt nodded vigorously. 'Without you we are lost, Isolda.'

'Yet at merest sight of those unfortunates I had cause to fall.'

'None would desert you for it.' Kurt leaned and kissed his sister, then stood. 'Egon will tend you, Achim and Zepp will amuse, and Hans and I will venture towards Annecy to discover provision.'

They climbed, eager to move, wondering what they searched for. Maybe they could find victuals, discarded boots, scraps of clothing or information. Revelations occurred in the harshest of times. Kurt was strangely elated. Twelve years old, he had the earth at his feet and glistening snowcaps around. This was freedom and responsibility and malehood, his very future. *Gunther* . . .

In a heartbeat, the rush of joy was gone. At the edge of the track, where it split to twist into a different valley, the son of the woodsman held a knife to the throat of a young boy. The victim was trembling, his friends on their knees pleading, piling their inadequate effects into an unfurled square of cloth.

'Things I might eat or trade, trinkets and baubles of any worth or none. Whatever you possess, I shall have.' He pressed the blade harder against the exposed neck. 'Make it quick. If you deny me, there will be blood.'

'Should you continue, it will be yours.'

Gunther reacted slowly to the shout from Hans, his attention swerving to record the knife in the hand of the goatherd, the wooden staff held by Kurt.

He was dismissive. 'Come closer and this little pig begins to squeal.'

'Release him, Gunther.'

'Or what, Hans? You charge towards me, attempt to wrestle me away?'

'It is not worth the pain and danger.'

'So continue on your way.'

'I took vow to protect my fellow pilgrims. As did you.'

'Conditions may change, needs arise.'

Kurt took a step forward. 'You remain under the oath and demands of the Cross.'

'I do?' Gunther narrowed his eyes. 'You among any should know of what I am capable, Kurt.'

Steel traced a line and the boy screamed. It was a flesh wound, a statement of intent, but blood flowed. Kurt retreated, the kneeling children continuing to empty the contents of their belt-purses.

Triumphant, Gunther ordered the kerchief folded and brought to him. He was simply collecting his dues. But he had not anticipated the flat tap of a sword-blade on his shoulder, the emergence of a stranger who had dismounted from a black charger and approached him silent from behind.

'It appears the contest is evened.' The newcomer grinned, his perfect teeth set in a faultless face. 'You care to joust the knife against the sword?'

His opponent seemed reluctant. The fight had not only been evened but was plainly over. Gunther had sloped away, his quarry released, and Kurt and Hans stood in awkward company with their ally and champion. There was no denying he had rescued them from a delicate situation, little doubt he was an important personage. He was a young and handsome noble some three or four years their senior, with piercing blue eyes and bobbed ash-blond hair. The tunic was green, the cloak blue, the upper body protected by a *cuirie* of hardened leather. Kurt and Hans had never before met such a deity, found themselves staring in deference and awe.

'We are grateful to you, sir.' Kurt bowed.

The boy laughed and slapped him on the shoulder. 'Arise. I am your friend, not your king.'

Then, friend, I am Kurt and this is Hans.'

'And I am Otto of Alzey.'

✝

Chapter 4

Neither the nightwatchmen nor the *ahdath* militia would catch the flitting shadows, pose a threat to the operation. At sunset the gates of Damascus had been closed and locked in a routine unchanged for centuries. But the danger was already within. The team of Assassins had entered the city several days before, had merged with the populace, moved among sympathizers, biding their time and laying their plans. These crowded alleyways, these hidden courtyards, these jumbled labyrinths of cellars and rooftops gave unmatched opportunity and incomparable cover. The ideal hunting-ground. Possibilities that would not be squandered.

There were myriad targets from which to choose. The mosques, the palace of the Sultan, the mausoleum of Salah ad-Din, the residence of the *Shinna*, the Chief of Police. All too easy. Besides, there would be plenty more occasion to visit, a thousand reasons to return and stoke the flames, spread the fear. For practitioners in the art of death and disarray, it was a question of balance, of pace. Terror at the unknown was the most valuable of tactics and tools. On this outing, and by order of their sheikh and the Lord of Arsur, they would keep it simple.

Commerce was the focus of their raid. Passing silently through the gloom, sliding sinuously over walls and obstacles, they made their way to the covered markets beside the Bab al-Faradis, the Gate of Paradise, and to the sprawling souk near the Amayyad Mosque. Guards were dealt with. Here there were vaults and storerooms piled high, recesses stocked with the heaped pungence of spices, the richness of silks and cloth, the oils and perfumes that made the streets famous and vulnerable to accidental blaze. The Assassins worked methodically, with practised fluency. Flax soaked in pitch and naphtha could act as accelerant, toppled amphorae could spread conflagration; flour dust sent airborne could serve as explosive. All was ready, and the spark was lit.

In living or recorded history, the residents of Damascus had experienced nothing like it. The fire raged for over two days, impervious to water and immune to any effort to smother it. Many fought to save their livelihoods, and failed. Many joined their friends and neighbours in ad-hoc groups to battle valiantly against the reaching calamity. The Assassins too were there. They were in the thick of it, concealed among the throng, directing and misdirecting, adding to confusion, seeing matters through. Left behind in the acrid aftermath, enveloped in a pall of smoke, were the glowing embers of what had been a thriving street life. None could quite comprehend the disaster. Yet in their shocked hearts they had an inkling that treachery and sabotage were to blame.

The Sultan came to visit. Stroking his beard, immersed in private thoughts of rage and retribution, he toured the scene with his advisers. He stopped to speak to the distressed and dispossessed, paid money from his purse, embraced and comforted the merchants and their kin. Saphadin, the great al-Adil, brother and confidant to the late Saladin, was a wise, merciful and benevolent man. But he was also a leader, a Moslem potentate whose grip on power forever suffered challenge and who had now lost face and revenue. Insult and threat would not go unpunished.

Yet the fire-starters were not alone in their aggressive acts that night. Elsewhere, in the mountains beyond Beirut, and in the region around Ajlun, bands of leper Knights of St Lazarus launched attack on the iron-ore mines of Saphadin. The campaign was as co-ordinated as it was sharp and decisive. Armed with battle-hammers and swords, the invaders fell upon the unsuspecting workers and engineers, cutting them down, burning their dwellings. Next they turned their attention to the mine-shafts. Within minutes, pit props were ablaze; after several hours, tunnel entrances were collapsing. By then, the knights had taken their leave, were heading for the hills behind Arsur, another task done. The body-count had been high, the destruction complete. News would soon filter back to a provoked Sultan.

During the week that followed, the Assassins departed Damascus and returned to their fortress at al-Kahf.

*

Some nineteen hundred miles to the north-west, in Switzerland, four other Assassins continued their pursuit. A lame horse and the need to replace it had delayed them in Biel; a false sighting of their target had distracted. But they rediscovered the scent. With renewed urgency they spurred on, following the trail, gaining on their kill. Assassins rarely accepted defeat. It would be the death of someone.

The leader raised his hand to slow them. For miles they had seen children, some living, others dead, some limping onward with the remnants of hope or dragging themselves back with the despair of surrender. Too bad. Christians and westerners had strange ways. He had noticed the two begging for alms at the side of the road, a tall boy and once-stout girl, peasant spawn languishing and needy in their plight. A nice spot to sit, overlooking a lake, hungrily watching the wildfowl and admiring the summer flowers. His agenda was different. Those who were still tended to observe, and those who observed always gave of their confidences.

He smiled and tossed a coin in the dust at their feet. They seemed grateful enough.

'You have names?'

The boy answered for them both, staring dully at the strangers through dark-ringed eyes.

Nodding empathetically, the Assassin remained open, pleasant. 'I can see you have endured much.'

'We have lost more: the young of our hamlet, the friends with whom we were raised, with whom we played and strove and came on pilgrimage. One day we march, the next we bury and wave goodbye.'

'Where now do you go?'

'Home to our village. We should never have left, should never have listened'.

'On occasion we learn through error and hardship.'

'Learn?' The boy hawked on the ground. 'Look about at our lesson. I discover only that death and stupidity are twinned.'

'It takes bravery to bow to fate, to recognize the inescapable. Those who doubt, who turn back, possess the courage to question.'

'I feel no courage.'

'Nor should you feel shame. At least you live to chase another destiny.'

Skilfully the horseman lulled and engaged, edged conversation round to issues more dear to him, higher on his agenda. Starved and careworn, the boy and girl would not suspect.

'You misplace comrades as do we. A young man of noble visage and bearing, adorned in green tunic and blue cloak, seated on a black horse with a grey mare attending.'

He saw the eyes of the girl spark and subside with the light of recognition. The boy again replied.

'He came this way these three days past.'

'His name is Otto of Alzey.'

'That too I remember. He dismounted to share bread and company with us, gave salve for our wounded feet.'

'A reputation that is one of kindness.'

'For the mercies alone he showed us, he merits reward on his journey and later in heaven.'

'Otto is of adventurous spirit. I am certain he will receive whatever recompense he deserves.'

'Be sure to thank him for his charity.'

'We shall endeavour in every way.'

As though weighing a decision, the horseman considered the children awhile. Finally, without word of farewell, he flicked the reins and urged his horse from trot into canter. His retinue followed. Left behind in the backwash of dust, Albert and Roswitha looked on and did not think of them again.

'You have made a friend of him, Kurt.'

The stallion snorted and flicked his ears in satisfaction as the twelve-year-old eased out the sweat and grime, rubbed down his coat with a cloth. At the rear, his back turned, Otto held a hoof between his knees and picked out debris with a metal tool. It was a moment of utter contentment for Kurt. In this gentle labour, in the well of a sweeping valley, he forged connection, shared time with his protector and new-found brother. Maximilian was the name of the stallion, Gerta the mare. He was happy to tend them, to talk and to laugh, to shed the deaths of little Lisa and the girl from Cologne, his parting with Roswitha and Albert, his discovery of the murdered man. And Gunther could not reach him now.

In the background, his companions fished in a stream and idled beneath the August sun. Isolda would not venture too close to where the horses stood. She blushed pink whenever she gazed at Otto or caught his easy glance. Even at a distance, her demure infatuation was plain, her confusion of emotions, her vulnerability to the lean muscularity and natural charm, writ bold. The traveller was an aristocrat, scion of a knightly line. Yet he was unaffected, had no arrogance in his manner, no haughty disregard for the unfortunate and the weak. Kurt was proud and grateful to have him near.

'Once we are done with Max, I shall make a bread poultice for the ankle of your sister.'

'She is obliged to you for walking her this far on horseback.'

'None are in my debt, young brother.' Otto lowered the leg and slapped the stallion on its haunch. 'As a Christian, as son of a Hospitaller knight, I am duty-bound to help.'

'It has slowed you.'

'What need for haste is there? We should rest, restore our strength and aching bones.'

'Our crusade demands we forever push forward.'

'Sense dictates we tarry awhile. There are many children whose lagging spirits we could revive, whose injuries we should dress. Jerusalem will remain a city, Outremer a kingdom.'

'In seeking comfort, do we not commit sin?'

The youth shrugged, checking over his saddle-pack. 'We shall each discover a path, whatever our pace and however it is ordained.'

'What is your path, Otto?'

'To be worthy of my name and true to the Lord; to find my father in the Holy Land.'

'He is lost?'

'Vanished these ten long years. Now I am of age enough to follow his trail and determine his fate.' He looked up. 'And you, Kurt. What is your preferred course?'

'Adventure and escape.'

'Not liberating Jerusalem from the Saracen? Not praying before the True Cross? Not lighting candles and worshipping in the Holy Sepulchre?'

Kurt silently reproached himself for his shallowness. 'You think me a fool.'

'I believe you honest. Adventure and escape is worthy reason. It is fervour and zeal that kills.'

They worked on, Otto combing out the tails of his mounts, Kurt arranging the saddle of Maximilian and the cargo of Gerta into semblance of piled order. Beside the stream, Zepp had caught a fish, was landing it with all the eagerness that starvation could bring. Four hundred and fifty miles from Cologne, and ribcages jutted more pronounced from wasted bodies, eyes had sunk deeper in their hollows. Thank God for respite and for Otto of Alzey, Kurt decided.

He unsheathed the sword, admiring and turning the blade, playing the light off its edges. What balance it had, what power it gave.

'Already the warrior, young brother?'

'I will never be a knight as you will be, but I may dream.' He slipped the weapon back to its scabbard and surrendered possession.

'Nobility is in the heart, Kurt. I have met lords with the blackest of manner, beggars who are courtly and chivalrous.'

'Then what is it to be a true knight?'

'A beret of quality will assist.' With a deft flick of his foot, the older boy propelled his discarded velvet cap from the ground towards Kurt.

The youngster caught it. 'I am serious, Otto.'

'It is to have courage and desire to serve; to acquire humility and a will of iron.' He held the sword in one hand, and leaned to retrieve his long *couteau d'arme* dagger with the other. 'These blades are mere symbol of more potent ideals.'

'Your father taught you well.'

'He left a memory of kindness. The rest I gained from my old tutor in Alzey. I would wish to disappoint neither of them.'

Memory of kindness. It would be nice to inherit that from a father, Kurt supposed. Older boy and disciple walked over to their friends. Another fish had been caught, was being divided and eaten raw.

His mouth bulging, littering scales and bones, Achim turned towards the footfall. 'Has Kurt told of our Cathars, Master Otto?'

'You are fortunate they suffered from debility.'

'They are dangerous?'

'It is rumoured so. They are heretics with two Gods, one good and in command of the spirit, the other evil and in control of the flesh. Their quest is to battle against the sinful God, to liberate the spirit by destroying the flesh. Children they hate. To them you are the continuation and product of man, of material and evil things. For a better world, you must die.'

'But we do nothing wrong.' The voice of Isolda was low with concern and confusion.

'When people are set in their minds and route, they are not always enlightened.'

'They would kill us for their divinity?'

'As others might for no reason.'

Kurt took a morsel of fish. 'Do not be afraid, Isolda. These devils live far distant, and Otto keeps sword and dagger with him.'

'I doubt I shall have use for either.' The sixteen-year-old broke off a piece of dry tack and offered it to her. 'Besides, we enjoy harmony and not enmity in our valley.'

'There is still Gunther.'

The children groaned and Otto chuckled. 'He will not again trouble us.'

Isolda received and chewed the biscuit as though it were holy sacrament. Her brother noticed how shyly her eyes dipped, how inexorably she was drawn away from her first love towards her perfect knight. Poor Egon. Against the wit and apparent worldliness of the older boy, the son of the blacksmith was dull and common fare. He seemed to accept his demotion with sad docility and stoic grace. Things happened; the seasons changed. There was little point in contesting.

Conversation and the sharing of food consumed the hours, reached into the late afternoon and the onset of evening. Shadows fell in the valley, and Kurt stood away from the group, listening to their talk, staring to the south. He had come too far to retreat as Albert and Roswitha had done, had cut himself loose from his past without knowing his future. The world was so wide and the mountains so high. He prayed fervently that what lay ahead was good.

Another mountain, a different place. Close to Tiberias in northern Palestine, rising from the wilderness, sat the hunched mass of Mount Tabor. It was the site of the Transfiguration of Christ, where the Messiah had taken three disciples to pray and appeared to them with his face and raiments shining as the sun, and the voice of God spoke from a cloud. That was then. In the year 1212 its contours hosted a forward encampment of the Moslem forces of the Sultan of Damascus.

It was early evening as the dust cloud travelled southward. Within it was a cavalry *tulb* of one hundred men, and at its head, accompanied by emirs and standard-bearers, was Saphadin. His back straight, his beard white and eyes piercing, he cut an imposing figure. As brother of Saladin, he had been the diplomat and trusted confidant, had negotiated with the Franks, duelled and battled with Cœur de Lion, King Richard of England, in an endless game of chance. Those days were gone. Or so it had seemed. For, in spite of peace treaty, the perfidious Christians of Outremer were again challenging his writ, manoeuvring for military advantage. Conciliation was far from the thoughts of Saphadin *al-Adil*, as he rode.

'Peace and blessings be upon you, my father.'

He dismounted and embraced al-Mu'azzam, his soldier son. The boy was youngest and most warlike of his progeny, commander of military formations in the region, leader of countless raids on the Christian lands. Occasionally the enemy required to be taught a lesson. Al-Mu'azzam was the man the Sultan entrusted to conduct it. They made their way to the collection of command tents behind the wood stockade.

'I expected your visit, my father.'

'When the infidels spit in our faces, betray the very truce we signed with them not a month past, my sole recourse is to turn to my son on this ancient mountainside.'

'I am for ever ready to do as you bid, my father.'

'At least there is one I may rely on. The rest snap and snarl as frightened dogs, are more concerned with themselves than with the honour and standing of our rule.'

'Does Damascus still smoulder?'

'The fires are out, but my anger rages.' Saphadin slapped the jewelled pommel of his sword. 'I ceded Jaffa and Ramleh to the infidels in the cause of peace, withdrew from Sidon and Beirut, abided by each agreement, nurtured trade with their coastal ports. Was it not I who placated them with return of their estates?'

'It was.'

'Have I not eased the passage of their pilgrims to Christian shrines in Nazareth and Jerusalem?'

'Indeed you have.'

'This is how they repay me. With scheming attack on my camel train from Egypt, with sly assault on my iron mines, with secret raid on souks in the heart of Damascus.'

'It is declaration of war.'

'Yet why now? I know of no reason why they should precipitate conflict. None would gain.'

'Though someone reckons benefit from such action.'

The Sultan frowned and continued to stride. 'True, we are in fragile and uneasy coexistence. True, each side will probe the other. And true, the infidel ruler John of Brienne last year allowed unleashing of force against our brothers in the Damietta mountains of Egypt. But this?'

'They condemn themselves by previous treachery.'

'There is no pattern or sense to it. I learn from spies that John of Brienne writes to his pope in Rome, demands crusade against us when our treaty lapses five years hence. Those five years are scarce begun.'

'He is sixty-four, his young queen dies recent in childbirth. Might a man not grow impatient as he ages, a king seek to reassert his power?'

'By a throw of the dice?'

'Perhaps he loses his mind, is maddened through grief. Perchance as fading regent he yearns for lasting triumph.'

'The course he chooses leads only to oblivion.'

They reached the central tent and passed inside. Al-Mu'azzam poured rosewater into glasses, and the two men sat. A sombre occasion.

Saphadin sipped brooding from his cup. 'This infidel outrage conjures memories of another, of the vile baron Reynald of Châtillon.'

'My uncle, your brother Salah ad-Din, removed his

head after Hattin with a single stroke. We shall do the like to all who confront us.'

'Sadly, we are blind to their identity. The regent himself? His barons? The military Orders of the Templars and Hospitallers?'

'Any could be culprit, my father. They require influence to buy secrecy and allegiance, resource to hire mercenaries and Assassins, stratagem to strip us of our arms and iron for our foundries. Each citizen of Outremer is guilty in association.'

'You suggest campaign?'

'Nothing else remains when honour is at stake. It is you who claims they spit in our faces.'

'And thus do we leave behind moderation, abandon negotiation in favour of battle. It may serve us poorly, drown us in blood.'

Al-Mu'azzam leaned forward and gripped the arm of his father. 'We must strike, al-Adil. The infidels are brazen, but they are weak. Their regent grows toothless, their lords are divided, their infant queen is but a few months old. No better time exists.'

'What of our own weakness and division?'

Saphadin rose and paced the confines of the tent. He was a man of energy trapped by circumstance, burdened with a thousand conflicting thoughts. Decisions had to be made, fury tempered and conditioned by reason and reflection. He could afford no rash move that would imperil the legacy of his late brother. Nor could he appear feeble, be mocked by his enemies, laughed at by his nephews and sons, by his own *iqta* vassals. There were always bolder and more impetuous pretenders waiting to usurp him. Action was required; *asabiyah*, family pride, was at stake. But he had no desire for wider conflict, no great standing army with which to fight it. Land needed to be tilled, grain harvested, industry and commerce maintained. Disruption to these could prove unpopular.

As though there had not already been disruption. The Sultan paused and stared glumly into inner space. Someone must know, yet none would tell. Even his contacts among the Christian hierarchs, his old connections with the Lord of Arsur, had borne no fruit. Silence was everywhere; hazard was all about. *No better time exists.* He looked at his son. The warrior hothead might be right, the moment for chatter past. Of one thing he could be certain. It would take months for the fools of Outremer to raise sufficient force, to garner support from the princes of Europe, to arrange reinforcement from Italy and France. And there was no guarantee the Franks would come. They were too indolent, too settled in their estates and ways, too occupied with easier and closer tasks against the Moslems in Spain, the Cathars in southern France, the resistance to their rule in Anatolia and Greece. Their pope had called for crusade before, and been rebuffed. Here was opening to exploit. Salah ad-Din had left unfinished business, an incomplete conquest of the Latin kingdom and restoration of Islamic rule. It was an affront to Allah the Merciful and Compassionate.

The Sultan stirred. 'Your views affect me. It is clear the infidels communicate with their swords, plain we have holy duty to respond in kind.'

'I am ready to act as your steel, al-Adil, to execute whatever is your resolve.'

'A pledge which heartens me. I trust that others within our nobility will be as loyal.'

'All shall rally to the cause.'

'Then it is set in motion. I will send officers to the central Syrian tribes, draw troops from Jerusalem, call in the *muqta* to provide the cavalry reserves we desire.'

'Have you role for me, my father?'

Saphadin spoke softly, as though in trance. 'Take two hundred and fifty of your horse across Galilee and descend on Acre. Kill everyone you meet, burn anything you encounter. They shall be in no doubt of our will.'

It was lost on neither man that the tented camp and its palisade overlooked the bleak and forbidding valley of *har megiddon*, Armageddon. Site of historic and spectacular slaughter throughout millennia, predicted scriptural location for the final battle between good and evil. Transfiguration and destruction. If one were to launch surprise attack upon the Christians, there could be few more appropriate springboards than the wooded slopes of Mount Tabor.

'More grandeur, Hans. More dignity and mannered airs.'

'You speak of dignity from where you sit?'

Otto laughed at the rebuke. Naked and reclining in a filled water-trough, he conducted his lesson in the arts of nobility and riding with the languid ease of a master. Class had commenced, and the goatherd was the most willing and comic of pupils. The children loved it. They whooped as Hans paraded by on the black charger Maximilian, yelled with glee as he acknowledged them with a dismissive nod or stately wave of his hand. The latter move almost unseated him. He was no horseman. But his mount was placid enough, tolerated the jester who had replaced his lord, who appropriated his beret and aped his ways. For the sake of sport, everyone joined in.

The noble boy submersed himself, let the cool water cover his face, the sounds of play ebb to dull vibration. It was restful in this broad valley beyond Chambéry. He was lucky to have found such fine companions, to have made such friends. Kurt and Isolda were already his little brother and sister. How journeying could change outlook. For too long he had lived carefree, revelled in the delights and wildness of youth, tested the patience and regulation of his beloved tutor Felix. That existence was ended. He had bid the old scholar farewell, kissed the local damsels goodbye, set out to find his father, to become man and future knight. Things would come to pass, he was sure of it.

He surfaced, his head streaming, to see Hans wobbling his way on a repeat circuit. There was no limit to the enjoyment his performance brought. The confidence of the goatherd grew. He punched the air in triumph. Even to clown as an uglier and simpler version of Otto was akin to being a demigod.

'Am I truly so absurd, Hans?'

'How may I answer, my pretty maid?' The goatherd doffed his cap to the noble boy. 'You will find I underplay your graces.'

'As you will find, with further instruction, I overplay my sword.'

'I shall abandon that lesson to others.'

Kurt threw a soaked and balled rag at him, prompting a barrage of laughter and missiles while Hans struggled to keep purchase on his steed. Throughout the entertainment, Isolda glanced longingly at Otto, Egon stared achingly at her. The young noble rolled out of the trough and started to dry himself.

'Kurt.' He whispered an aside to the twelve-year-old. 'If you wish to dislodge a man, more subtle resort is needed.'

'You have something in mind?'

As answer, Otto gave a low whistle that rose in pitch and volume. Its effect was immediate. Maximilian reared, kicking forward and back, bucking frenziedly until, with a cry, Hans pitched to the ground. Winded, he lay on his back, recovering with a look that passed from surprise through pain to dazed amusement. Slowly, he sat up, dusted down the beret, and replanted it on his head. Only then did he clamber shakily to his feet.

'Proof before all that manners and civility scarce exist among nobles, Master Otto.'

'I grant you, a cruel trick to be in league with a horse.'

'But a fine one.' The goatherd inspected himself for injury. 'What say you to a second bout?'

Otto had donned his hose leggings and now approached with his folded cloak. 'To be true noble, you require low cunning and dress to fit your new-found lustre. It will add colour and drama to any future plunge.'

'I will yet outwit you, you shall see.'

He fastened the cape about his shoulders and, with Otto holding the bridle, remounted to vociferous applause. Act two had begun. He was delighted with himself, had only ever ridden a village pony. To be on Maximilian, to have befriended a boy who lived in a burg and who wore fine clothes, was the stuff of dreams. He winked at Kurt, and the twelve-year-old shouted with mirth. The horse whinnied and stamped, Otto released his hold, and the demonstration resumed.

They had not counted on four horsemen. The strangers had appeared as though from nowhere, emerging from dead ground behind the hamlet and travelling along the track down which the children had walked. Hans had trotted ahead and turned, was cantering back on their bearing. He was the first to notice them. The chance to greet and preen before his fellows was too great. He was not about to pass up the moment, ignore present and future occasion to boast. It was a mistake.

The lead rider hailed him. 'Peace and good morrow, young sir.'

'And to you, brother. Safe travel, wherever you head.'

'A fine horse you have.'

'The better to travel the distance I cover. Is there assistance that I or my companions may offer?'

'I cannot tell. We come with message for one Otto of Alzey.'

'Fortune smiles upon you.' Hans delivered a lavish bow, hoping his friends watched. 'For I am he.'

In the fraction of a second that passed, a quizzical look might have shadowed the face of the horseman. Before him was not the boy described by others. He was no Adonis, exuded no natural and winning charm, no relaxed insouciance of one born to noble blood and gentle mother. So be it. People for ever embellished and overstated. It could not be helped. The boy could not be saved.

At the margins of earshot, but within their sight, the children witnessed the Assassins in the bloody act of execution. With a rush of dagger-blows, they closed to deliver sentence. Hans took a while to topple. He was flailing his arms, attempting to back his horse, to protect himself, to fight and evade. But he was surrounded, hemmed in, and steel turned crimson as butchery continued. There was little sound save for the grunts of the victim and the muttered exertions of his killers. He must have struck one of them with his shoulder or fist, for the man was unseated and fell. A small victory for so high a price. Hans slumped and disappeared.

In a haze of instinct and action, Otto and Egon responded, the son of the blacksmith running with a stirrup-iron to hand, the young noble snatching up his sword and leaping on to the grey mare to give chase and battle. The Assassins did not stay long. They were galloping fast, charging south with their blades raised in victory salute. Behind, Egon had caught their dismounted accomplice, was pinning him down, bludgeoning him to death in blind ferocity. Riding bareback, Otto was narrowing the distance on his quarry. While their horses were tired, Gerta was rested, eager to stretch her legs, to join pursuit, to obey the desperate urging of her master.

He overhauled them at two hundred yards. With a sideways slash of his sword, he removed the head of the nearest and went for the second. He would not go unopposed. The Assassin slewed his horse in a spray of dust and vectored round to meet him.

'*Allahu akhbar! Allahu akhbar! Allah! Allah! Allah!*'

Blades and horses clashed. But Gerta was a steady mare, her opposite an untested beast bought recently in market at Biel. Skittish with nerves, it jinxed and sidled, denied its rider clean angle of attack. And Otto had greater reach. He used it, sweeping his sword-arm in a generous arc, carving the heavy edge through air and bone. The trophy fell across him and he spun away in horror.

Along the strewn and spattered trail, the scene had evolved from its previous tranquillity. Egon was doubled-over, vomiting with shock. Otto slipped to the ground and knelt, his torso striped with blood, trembling and panting in his distress.

'Hans is dead . . . Hans is dead . . . I have killed . . . I have killed.'

In the distance, the surviving horseman did not pause in his flight. Closer by, the children were screaming.

✝

Chapter 5

On a day such as this, there was no need for the solitude of the loom or hours spent in contemplation and prayer. The warming ground was pulling in the sea breeze, the undulating terrain was sending it upward. Perfect conditions for falconry. Beyond the walls of the royal city of Acre, Lady Matilda looked about her and smiled. These were the moments she craved, when attended only by a single manservant she could ride out with her favourite saker or peregrine on her wrist, or gallop free and unrestrained for miles along the coastal sands. Aged seventeen, there was much to live for and everything to enjoy.

Behind her, the dune-coloured walls of the city rose as formidable as any fortress, as inviting as any prison. She was glad to escape the confines of court. While she loved and honoured her guardian, the regent John of Brienne, and his baby daughter Yolanda, there was still the clinging grief that came with the recent death of the young Queen Maria. His sorrow was immense. And encircling him, stifling her, was the boorish licentiousness of the barons and their secular knights, the cold-blooded zeal of the warrior brethren of the military Orders. The atmosphere in Outremer was an acquired taste. Yes, she was pleased to pass through St Anthony Gate and head for the wild.

A small Arab boy waved and shouted in greeting. She called back to him by name and in his native tongue.

'Peace be upon you, Hassem.'

'Upon you also, my lady. Where do you travel?'

'Anywhere that sport exists for my falcon and wind is present to carry it. Perhaps we shall go closer towards Tel el Fukhkhar.'

'Take care, my lady. There are bandits and robbers in every quarter of this land.'

'I shall heed your advice, Hassem. But I have friends enough to guard me.'

'I too am your friend, my lady.'

Wherever she went, Lady Matilda could turn heads and draw comment. She was a rare beauty, a vision of alabaster skin and dark coiled tresses, of green eyes and radiant smile. Peasant or noble, adult or child, Moslem or Christian, all responded to her warmth and compassion, were soothed by her empathetic charm. Talk was of whom she might wed. There were suitors and rumour aplenty, even idle and misplaced gossip that old John of Brienne himself might be tempted from mourning and widowhood by his ravishing ward. Little wonder they called her the Flower of Acre.

But this flower was not yet for the picking. With a flick of her leather quirt, she eased her horse into a trot and, riding side-saddle, travelled on past the orchards and citrus groves, the outlying and flat-roofed neighbourhoods, for open ground. It was easy to forget in this placid scene that the earth was steeped in blood. Both Saracen and Frankish armies had met here, had besieged those walls and in turn snatched ownership of the prize. Twenty-one years before, on 20 August 1191, as Saladin watched helpless from the hills, the army of King Richard I of England had led out the surrendered Moslem garrison and slaughtered them to a man. Salah ad-Din had failed to pay their ransom of twenty thousand gold dinars, had refused to cede possession of the one True Cross. Over two and a half thousand souls murdered: one event, a single stitch, in the hidden fabric of Palestine.

Beside a dusty plantation of olive trees, a mounted troop of Teutonic knights had filed from their compound at the St Nicholas Tower and were practising at the tilt. The business of war was never far from the minds or preparations of the warrior caste. To huzzahs and shouts, each lowered his lance and charged in for the imagined kill. There was something sinister in the faces hidden by enclosed steel helms, in the black German crosses emblazoned on white mantles. It was said a massed attack by Christian knights could rupture the very walls of Baghdad itself. Lady Matilda could well believe it.

She left the settlements and their rhythms of daily life, looked beyond the fields towards the barren land beyond. Hooded and held by jesses, the saker sat passive on her hawking-glove.

The servant shaded his eyes against the eastern sun. 'We should have brought beaters and dogs, my lady.'

'Where is isolation and sport in that?' Her horse crested a small rise and dipped into the shallow indentation of a valley. 'We shall stake our claim here and see what arises.'

Without exercise, the thrill of the stoop, her bird of prey would soon start to bait and agitate for release. She understood it well. They were old companions, the saker a link to the skills and accomplishments taught her by a beloved and long-dead father. How he had wished for a son and heir; how he had doted on her with the clumsy affection of a crusader lord. With him, she had toured Outremer, had learned to speak the Arab way, to respect the values and customs of local tribes. Once, she had even met Saphadin, had drunk sherbet as her father conversed with the Sultan and attended to diplomacy. Peaceful days. Her father had succumbed to illness, her mother shortly after. She would not betray their memory.

'The birds begin to fly, my lady.'

A flock of doves had scattered from cover, were wheeling directionless and low. Something had disturbed them. With a practised hand, Matilda drew off the hood and launched the bird into flight. It fluttered and spiralled upward, gaining height, searching for a cushion of air and the apex of a climb where it could hover and look down.

Instinct, or the short and breathless cry of her manservant, caused her to break concentration. Momentarily, her gaze dropped. It took time to focus, to redirect sight and mind from circling speck to a nearer mark. The ridge-line appeared to be alive.

Fascinated, she stared, unable to move, to speak, to fully comprehend. Facing her were horsemen, hundreds of them. Pennants fluttered from lances, light sparkled on helmets and bridles, a tension seemed to hold them in temporary pause before action. The Saracens. They were a magnificent and terrible thing to behold. Matilda continued to gape wide-eyed and open-mouthed. But her servant was screaming now, his words intruding on her torpor, and the stillness fractured.

'Away, away! We must hurry, my lady!'

She was already convinced. As the glittering mass curled forward, and the lances depressed to the horizontal, she spun her horse to flee. Gone was any pretence at decorum. She was astride her mount, driving it on, exhorting it, herself, her servant to greater effort and speed. There was much to lose and no reason to linger. The travelling wave came on, a tide surging and lapping with a roar at their heels. An arrow passed close, then another, and a third. Matilda ducked low, whispering a prayer, muttering encouragement in the ear of her beast. The animal obliged and forged ahead.

Only once did she turn to look. It happened when she heard the high and helpless shriek of her servant. He must have tried to cover her retreat, offering himself as sacrificial lure. It had worked. The feathered profile of arrow-flights protruded from his back. He wallowed atop his horse, his eyes beseeching, his mouth imploring, his hand gesturing weakly for Matilda to proceed alone. She imagined she could read his lips. *Do not concern yourself with me, my lady. Save yourself.* And he was gone.

Terrified, she galloped on, the noise gathering, the pounding of hooves, of blood, of war-chants, beating remorseless in her ears. She did not want to die, to fall to an arrow or the sharp end of a spear. It helped concentrate and direct her thoughts. Survival was all that mattered. She owed it to herself, to the sweet recollection of her parents.

They were almost upon her as she reached the outskirts of Acre. Like a storm-force of nature, the enemy crashed over and through the gardens and grounds, sweeping aside the running shapes that scampered to get away. Most were too slow, were caught and felled by the torrent. A drover herding geese towards the city gates sank beneath the weight of numbers; farmers picking fruit from trees were themselves picked off and hung limp in branches. Others were stampeded, corralled, cut down.

Counter-attack came, the line of Teutonic knights switching from rehearsal to reality in a valiant charge against the flank. It had no effect. The Saracen force absorbed the blow, surrounded and consumed the Germans in a crowding, piling melee of swords and maces. Men screamed and clutched at faces; men twitched dead and upright in their saddles; men were clubbed and disembowelled. Close-quarter battle was never pretty. The cavalry of al-Mu'azzam was getting into its stride.

Matilda crossed herself and frantically slapped the reins. Her horse was tiring, fading in its exertions.

She could hear the ceaseless drone behind, a metallic rattling at her tail. Her shoulders hunched. It was her body preparing for the fatal strike. O Lord, let it be swift. An Arab charger whinnied, its sound close and closing, transforming to a strange squeal of fighting ecstasy. The clatter belonged to a lance being aligned. A bell tolled, raising alarm from the city ramparts. Too late for her. She could see the narrowing gap of light as the great oak doors began to shut, the portcullis start its downward slide. Another trembling in the air, the hiss of passing shot, and a flaming arcuballista bolt flew low to remove Saracens, horses, the immediate threat. She was through.

High overhead, the saker hung on a thermal and called. Confused by the landscape, uninspired by sudden and turbulent change, it eventually soared to a new heading and disappeared. Hunting was more rewarding elsewhere.

'I thank merciful God you are safe, Matilda.'

John of Brienne embraced her, holding her arms and standing back to view the effects of her escape. His ageing and battle-worn face was creased with anxiety. As regent of Outremer, he had much to ponder, the political and military implications of the Moslem raid to consider. But the fate and well-being of Matilda were his particular concern.

'To bear the recent passing of my young wife Queen Maria was hardship enough. It would be torment beyond compare to lose you also to cruel fate.'

She leaned and kissed him fondly on the forehead.

'We both mourn her, sir. Yet this time, at least, I survive.'

'By dint of divine providence and your own horsemanship.'

'Through gallant and selfless sacrifice of my manservant and accurate shooting from your rampart guards.'

'Still, we lose much. My men take inventory, but the destruction is apparent all about. Loss of life, of property, of calm. A bleak day and prospect for our kingdom.'

'Our walls hold, sir.'

'For how long? I make peace with the treacherous vipers of Islam and this is how they repay me.' He stared in her eyes. 'You are a daughter to me, Matilda; your mother and father were my dearest of friends. It seems already I break my promise to them to guard you from any danger.'

'Not even a regent king may foretell every hazard, sir.'

'Here is one who has misread every sign, misjudged every aspect of our present circumstance. I believed Saphadin, Sultan of Damascus, wished for truce and accord, that prosperity and harmonious relations were in the interests of us all.'

'I know little of politics, sir. But I recognize we have benefited from the peace.'

'And, of this moment, that peace lies shattered at our feet.'

His eyes clouded, his shoulders hunched with the isolation and heaviness of his office. Matilda pitied him his responsibilities. He was a kind and righteous man, popular with the barons, respected by the Mohammedans, a force for stability and restraint. Wherever there was tension, he intervened; whenever there was argument, he mediated and brought solution. Often it was the runt of a litter, the smallest in a pride, which grew to outshine its siblings. So it had proved. There had been few rivals for the vacancy as king of Outremer, disquiet and perturbation at the arrival of an impecunious knight of Champagne to take the hand of Queen Maria. He was aged sixty-two at their wedding in 1210, she nineteen. It was rumoured he was exiled from the French court following a scandalous liaison with the Countess of Champagne, that Pope Innocent and King Philip of France had raised forty thousand silver pounds as bribe and dower to ease his progress to the Latin kingdom. Forecasts were poor. Yet he surprised them all: his love for the young queen infinite, his authority growing. Events changed once more.

He shook his head. 'I was a fool to believe this kingdom could ever rest in ease and tranquillity, a greater fool to accept position as its ruler.'

'Had you not landed in Outremer, you would never have wed and loved our dear queen, never have fathered your Yolanda.'

'Maria is dead and I am widowed. As for Yolanda, her inheritance will be nothing but a land beset by conflict and woe, rent by factions, invaded by infidels, clinging only to tenuous existence.'

'Existence alone is worth a psalm of exultation, sir.'

'Is it?' He flashed a look of melancholic resignation. 'I had hopes for more.'

'Surely one foray signifies merely that the Saracens are discontented, wish to communicate their message.'

'In Palestine, one attack begets another, one barbarous act promotes ten more, a thousand in reply.'

'Parley may follow.'

'Or war itself.'

He began to walk about the chamber, his head bowed in thought. Around him, richness prevailed: tapestries woven with gold and silver thread; candlesticks gilded and set with eastern gemstones. Trappings of office that shackled rather than consoled. There was rarely security of tenure in the Latin kingdom of the Franks.

'Hawks fly about us, Matilda.' The regent spoke as he restlessly moved. 'Pope Innocent condemns my treaty with Saphadin; his Templar fanatics agitate for the fray. Any excuse they seize upon to show me weak and my endeavours wrong. This single Mohammedan raid they will use to initiate escalation and foment tumult. And we are unready for it.'

'You will always have allies.'

'Of that I am certain and most grateful.' He sighed and smiled tenderly at her. 'I should not impose such worries on you, my sweet Matilda.'

'I am privileged you have reason to entrust me with them, sir.'

'As I am blessed to have you near. Would that you may one day find the happiness I once had with Maria, enjoy the fruits and bliss of wedlock.'

'I await my time.'

'It is said the Lord of Arsur searches for a new bride. He is rich, established, a true friend of this court, a presence of constancy and good in our land.'

'He is also chill and remote, has profited well from the deaths of two previous and noble wives.'

'Alas, he is stripped of love as I.'

'I fear I cannot replace it, nor add my estates about Mount Carmel to his own.'

'We shall talk again of it. Your father would surely wish it so.'

The regent turned as the doors were opened and a wet-nurse carried in the infant queen. Placid and sated with milk, Yolanda gurgled contentedly and stretched her limbs as her father billed and cooed above her.

'See how she is grown, Matilda. See how she responds to my words and smile.' He lifted and cradled the baby. 'I would give my realm to have my queen beside me now. But as God has taken her, he has in turn granted me the precious gift of this daughter.'

'She is like her mother, sir.'

'Each day she is clearer reminder of her beauty. The lips, the nose, the hair, these eyes that change from blue to brown. There is no kinder token of her life than this.'

Yolanda purred and burbled while her regent father held her and the nurse withdrew discreetly to the background. For a moment, it was possible to forget the outrage of that morning, to dwell instead in the innocence and pleasure of the baby girl. Her father passed her to Matilda, who caressed and bounced her gently in her arms. What simple delight, what incomparable means to banish the image of her manservant floundering on his horse, the sounds of pursuit, the fiery stench of the ballista bolt as it hissed past her head. Motherhood was a serene place. Matilda gazed down at the child. One day she would be lady-in-waiting to this queen, a mistress of the chamber and the wardrobe. And one day she would wed, not the dark and serpentine Lord of Arsur, but a boy prince or a true and perfect knight. She could dream and hope; she could fervently pray.

The wet-nurse looked on. She was one of two assigned to royal duties, a recent addition to the household. Quiet and conscientious, she had a plain face and ordinary manner, careful hands and full breasts with which to nurture the infant. Of greater import, she was deferential and colourless enough to go ignored. The Lord of Arsur expected it of her.

Otto led his grey mare slowly up the mountain path towards the village. The children had not blamed him for the death of Hans. That made it worse. It added to his remorse, to the heavy weight of guilt that sat solid on his shoulders. He had wanted to help his young friends, to assist pilgrims as his father did, to play-act a novice knight engaged in epic quest. Instead, he had seen an innocent slain. The killers had asked his name, had wanted a different victim from the guiltless goatherd found before them. Otto of Alzey they called for. The meaning was obscure, the succeeding horror all too real. He had to make amends, to atone for the desolation he had brought to the lives of his companions.

The walled village was like any other, a compact affair nestling among the alpine splendour. Travellers would scarce bother to look up. It was just another waypoint on the route to Italy, timber buildings clustered within the stone perimeter, protected from storm and hostile intent. Otto was hopeful. With a purse of silver, food and clothing could be coaxed from the most unpromising source.

'From where do you hail, my pretty youth?'

She was naked and large-breasted, a peasant girl astride a rock, swaying rhythmically, moving her pelvis as she spoke. A siren, a seductress. Otto stared.

'I come long distance, seek provision and apparel.'

'Fine boy, you will come many times ere we are through. As for apparel, there is no use for it here.'

He watched enthralled, hypnotized by her act, by her fingers pinching and kneading, by her hand sliding to work up a slick between her thighs. She moaned, her mouth open, her eyes bright. A finger rose to be licked.

'We are sinners, my handsome one, all abandoned in our fallen and natural state.'

Otto swallowed back his muteness, remembered to reply. 'Sinners should repent and seek forgiveness. It is why I must travel on, why I have duty to find food for my brethren.'

'One as you would be warm received in our midst.' Her legs parted in accommodating smile.

'I will pay for what I need.'

'Indeed you shall, and in kind.' She viewed him, her attention rapacious and lingering. 'I see you are cocksure, rise already to the occasion. You have much to offer in your hose.'

Strangeness bred its own ease and security. He was both repelled and drawn, confronted by her brazen sexuality and compelled by his own. There was noble and base motive in what he felt, a swelling ache, an urge, in both heart and loins. Carnality was not foreign to him. He had caroused and fornicated with the libidinous freedom that looks and position allowed. But this was something new. Perhaps she was a witch, had captured and enchanted her village. He would cast off such devilment, break free of her spell.

He backed Gerta away. 'I will find what I require in the next village, sister.'

'You are wrong. Two miles hence is Gluttony. Its citizens consume every morsel, will not share with you the merest scrap of bread. Beyond it is Sloth, its inhabitants too idle to farm or put aside provision. They come to us and beg for food. At the end of the valley is Anger. Visit it, and you will receive the quarrel and whipping of your life.'

'What kind of madness is this?'

'Not madness, but deadly sin. You have stumbled upon us here at Lust. Our method is gratification of the flesh, our purpose to consume misdeed, to use it up, to purify the earth so that God may again see fit to send his Son.'

'It is the blackest of trickery and magic.'

'In Lust we call it faith. Come hither, my lord, and

take your fill. By end of day, you shall have your packs and saddlebags swollen with supply.'

Rumours abounded of such sects, of heretics who employed wickedness as a means of finding God. Otto submitted meekly, unsure why he did so, unquestioning as he followed his temptress through the village gates. It was a sight and situation he had never before encountered. Strewn about the square, in doorways and windows, on steps and over tether-posts, men and women copulated in a reckless frenzy of orgiastic delight. Restraint was gone, minds fled with it. In their place were the grunts and throaty cries of coupling, the uninhibited display of congress in numerous forms and multiple formations, the building of sound and pressure towards ecstatic religious climax.

His guide was nuzzling his neck, nipping at his ear. 'Do you care to be lost as we, to partake in vice for the sake of our salvation?' She stifled his answer with a wet and deep and lengthy kiss.

He struggled for air, his mouth disengaging. 'I cannot.'

'You will.' She was rubbing her body against his, pulling him close, slipping her palm to engage his crotch. 'For such prize meat, we shall give fair trade.'

Another girl approached, wrapping herself sinuously around him. She too was naked, an auburn-haired beauty with arcing back and entwining limbs, her fingers probing and stroking, her mouth attending first to him and then to his escort. Nothing would hold them back. He sank into their combined embrace, giving himself over, losing himself to the moment, to the intoxication of mutual arousal and hot insanity. Someone proffered drink, unfurled straw bedding, removed his clothes. He was lifting a girl, planting himself deep, burying anguish and pain with thrusting hips and grinding abdomen. From a distance he observed her face contorting, sensed the vibration of her body, heard the joyous wail from her lungs. She clawed at him, fighting for breath and begging for more. The endless instant swallowed him.

Errand had turned to feat of endurance. Through drifting scenes of gratification he played his part, plunging in, oblivion alternating with total clarity. He was led around and offered up, welcomed and accepted into every fold. Release came. When it was through, when he stumbled drained and spent from the portals of Lust, his grey mare was burdened with cheese and hams, with gourds of wine, with leather and canvas footwear for his friends. Contract had been honoured. He was unsure if he had profited or lost.

Seven weeks after leaving Cologne, the children reached the top of the Mont Cenis Pass. It was a time to pause and reflect, to extract meaning from the desolation caused by the butchery of Hans, the loss of little Lisa, the departure of Roswitha and Albert. Their sacrifice had been worthwhile. Behind them was the massive bulk of the Grand Roc Noir, to its rear the slopes, the valleys, the lakes, the footsore miles they had traversed for God and glory and for the sake of their souls. And before them, beyond the mountain-fringed lake, was Italy.

'O Lord, we give thanks for Your great mercy and understanding, for Your protection and comfort in our days of woe. May You and the Blessed Virgin and St Christopher guard us and keep us safe in our onward journey.'

'Amen, Amen, Amen.'

Kurt ended his prayer, crossed himself, and fell to his knees to kiss the ground. He had not intended faith to intrude too obviously on his mission. But death and adversity had changed that. He needed to believe there was reason for burying his friends at the side of the road, for discovering the lifeless corpse of his love; he had to assume there was divine purpose in going on. Even Otto had proper motive for reaching Outremer. He would emulate the older boy, would apply more thought to his wanderings.

The young noble rested an arm across his shoulders as he clambered to his feet. 'Italy and the world lie to our fore. Are you not struck by wonder?'

'I am simply tired, Otto.'

'An improvement on your constant appetite.' They laughed and tussled good-naturedly. 'You are in fine and ancient company here, for Hannibal passed this way in his campaign against Rome.'

'Hannibal?'

'The greatest of generals. He outwitted his enemy, led his army through these very passes in dead of winter.'

'Then I shall never complain again of what we face.'

'You should be proud, Kurt. See what you achieve, the distance you have travelled.'

'We would not have reached so far without you beside us.'

'I would say the same of you, young brother.'

Side by side they stood and looked down towards the promised lands of Piedmont curving behind the far horizon. Around them were the jagged peaks they would soon leave, the Point de Ronce and Point Clairyo, Mont Lamet and Mont Malamot. Kurt had grown to hate them all.

Isolda joined them in their contemplation. 'I can scarce believe we are through the Alps.'

'There is still long way to go. The coast is arduous; the sea poses threat of its own.'

'The sea, Otto?' She frowned in bewilderment. 'Are not the waters meant to divide in the manner foretold by Moses, predicted by the preacher Nikolas?'

'I was not alive when Moses struck his staff, not present when Nikolas sermonized in Cologne. I expect to take boat for the Holy Land as any mortal would.'

'Should we pray more? Should we give ourselves to penitence?'

'Enough has been done, and it will not alter fate.'

Otto reached and took her arm, could not ignore how she shivered to his touch, how her eyes glowed soft with quiet passion. It would be different had she known of events in Lust, of his recent and sullied past. Egon was the better man.

He released his hand and gestured at the view. 'Hans would dear love to have stood where we now stand.'

'Little Lisa also.'

'For their sakes we shall keep strong and maintain our pace.' He called back to the blacksmith's boy. 'Egon, you prepare to resume the march?'

'As ever, Otto.'

'Zepp and Achim?'

'We too, Master Otto.' The young voices of the brothers piped up, their enthusiasm let down by fading energy.

'You wanted excitement and escapade, Kurt. It begins from here. No surrender to our fears; no diversion from our course.'

'I am with you, brother.'

The sixteen-year-old shouted loud to the rest. 'Are we together in this?'

They were as one. With focus in their eyes, renewed conviction in their step, they began the winding descent through the rolling banks of wild flowers. Otto walked the black stallion on, Kurt bringing the mare behind, Egon and Isolda shepherding the twins. The blind boy struck up a ditty, the others taking their prompt until their words rang out and cascaded joyous down the slopes. Just another dwindling band of children, one of hundreds en route for the unknown.

Yet not quite the average group. The surviving Assassin wiped sweat from his brow and examined the oncoming party from the cover of a line of spruce. These infidel young appeared in high spirits, in spite of their journey and cataclysmic encounter. A charming spectacle. It could not have been easy for them. Of course, it had not been straightforward for anyone. Mistakes were made, targets misidentified. As a result, it seemed Otto of Alzey was progressing freely and very much alive in company with his friends. Whether here or in Rome, resolution was needed. It was a matter of honour, of pride, of following instruction to the letter and the end. And it was a question of timing. This noble boy had been sentenced, would therefore be killed.

✝

Chapter 6

In the filtered light of dawn, a priest hanging dead from a rope and the branch of a tree presented an odd and forbidding silhouette. It might have been a bundle of rags, an effigy of sorts. But the bare feet gave it away. Unsettled, the children came to a halt and gathered close. They were on the broad river plain leading down to Turin and the river Po, the surrounding hills still unseen in the early-morning murk. The oak and its ripening fruit could mean many things: warning, suicide, the incidental handiwork of roving thieves. It was best not to linger. Yet, for all its horror, there was a grim fascination to the shadowy spectacle.

Kurt stepped forward. 'I will climb and cut him down.'

'No, Kurt.' Isolda gripped his arm. 'It might be cursed, a harbinger of evil things.'

'What is more evil than to leave a poor priest unburied and in a tree?'

'We do not know the reasons, do not know if he should be committed to holy soil.'

'He is Christian and we are pilgrims. It gives us

reason, Isolda. Can we pass and let him rot, ignore the plight of another?'

Egon sighed. 'He is beyond plight where we may aid him, Kurt. We should leave it to older and wiser heads.'

'Why?'

'There is no authority for us to act.'

'Yet we have the freedom. We have marched and suffered, thirsted and starved. And you think we cannot make decision?' The twelve-year-old turned to the young noble for encouragement. 'Tell them, Otto.'

'All be silent and on your guard.'

The boy had drawn his sword, as though intending to climb into the saddle and himself sever the rope. His words and the tilt of his head showed otherwise. He was concentrating on the dim and nearing distance, on points of light that had sprung to existence and were closing in semicircle about them. Debate ceased.

'What is it, Zepp? What happens?'

Achim clung tight to his brother. Perched behind him on the grey mare, and only partially awake, the blind boy had sensed the danger. His twin did not answer. He was trembling, staring with the rest at the flaming torches advancing towards them. The concave line stopped. There was silence, except for the sputter and hiss of firebrands, the inquisitive snorts of the horses and the shaking of their bridles. Ghostly forms had materialized into cowled figures clutching billhooks and scythes.

Otto shouted to them. 'Are you devils or men, friend or foe?'

'We are the Pure Ones.'

It was a deep and resonating voice that came from the leader garbed in black and stationed at the centre of the formation. A disquieting reply that made the children edge behind Otto. Unlike the young noble, they did not understand the Italian tongue, yet they could comprehend threat, discern the ritual in what they faced. Otto held his sword before him. He knew of these people, recognized that Pure Ones derived from the Greek word *katheroi*. He had his old tutor Felix to thank for that. They were Cathars.

The leader again spoke. 'He swings well, does he not? Are you approving of our sacred handiwork?'

'There is nothing sacred in foul murder. It is wickedness beyond compare, a crime offending the laws and custom of all reasonable men.'

'He was a prelate of Rome, a bloated suckling-pig feeding at the foul and poisoned teat of the papacy, of the whore seated on the back of the scarlet beast. For this he paid.'

'Who are you to make such decision?'

'A Perfect, chief of the Believers.' The man indicated his *credentes* with a sweep of his hands. 'And who are you to oppose us?'

'Otto of Alzey, son of Wilhelm. I travel for Palestine with my companions.'

'It seems your journey is ended.'

'A judgement I will keep for myself.' Otto tightened his grip on his sword, rocked gently on his feet to test his balance. He could see his opponents were preparing, was readying himself.

'Hand to us the children with you, Otto of Alzey. It is what we require.'

'So you may butcher them as you did the priest?'

'We shall liberate their souls as divine imperative and as act of purification. All matter is evil, its propagation through the rearing of young a deed in league with the Devil. Renounce sin, seek salvation, and surrender up your litter.'

'I would rather die.'

'A pity, Otto of Alzey. Even in this gloom you are as pretty as a damsel. You will doubtless fight and scream as such.'

'I shall give account of myself well enough.' He whispered behind him. 'Make ready to flee, my friends. At my word, Kurt and Isolda take Maximilian and ride as the wind. Zepp and Achim, you will follow on Gerta. Egon, you are to escape as you may.'

Kurt murmured back. 'How will you get away?'

'I will cover your retreat and put my faith in God These men are Cathars, see no reason in parley.'

'What is their intent?'

'To kill. I beg you do as I ask.'

Instead, the twelve-year-old placed himself beside him, his pilgrim staff held defensively across his chest. Isolda also moved up; Egon too. Astride Gerta, the twins were rummaging for their small knives. It was a united front, a statement of resolve and shared destiny. They might die, but it would be on their terms and at an hour of their choosing. Kurt peered at the flickering lights, at the reflection from the cutting-edges. He was in a place of evil, and it was right that he should stay.

They would not run, would not be cowed by Cathars or heretics of any hue or creed. He had preferred them without their lips, their noses, their ears, their eyes, he decided.

'Otto, we stand firm with you as you stood with us.'

'Choose a separate fate, young brother. There is little sense in us all falling to their savage blades.'

Egon stared ahead, his chin set firm. 'We shall not be found wanting for courage. If we are condemned, it will be together as grown men and women and not as frightened children scampering for our skins.'

'I thank you for such sacrifice, thank God I met you all.'

They waited, six youngsters counting time, holding their breath. Zepp and Achim had slipped to the ground to be with their comrades, to share in common fortune. Achim began to sing a hymn, his voice soft and sweet and valedictory.

The Perfect was unmoved. 'I see you face rebellion, Otto of Alzey. It will make no difference to the outcome.'

'You will taste my sword before you reach them.'

'As you will learn the error of your action, the sting of its result.'

With a motion of his hand, he gave the order. The line moved and the children huddled, their eyes big with anticipation of impending end. The words of Achim choked to a sob. He could hear the oncoming tread of feet, the rustle of clothing, the clatter and rasp of weapons. There was no doubt as to the conclusion.

Isolda placed a steadying arm about his shoulders and whispered in his ear. God would bring them smiling to His kingdom.

'Kurt, take my dagger and use it well.' Otto passed possession of the blade.

'You have my word.'

'All be strong in your hearts and in your faith.' The young noble advanced a pace and raised his sword. 'Bring cost to their triumph and do your duty by each other. Pray to Jesus and fight as demons.'

'Hallelujah! Hallelujah! Hallelujah!' Their chorus came in unison as the enemy closed.

'Is this dispute not a little uneven?'

Momentum paused. It had been a question delivered as a challenge, a challenge that issued as a roar. In its startled aftermath, attention swung to a solitary figure in the drab and shabby robe of a mendicant, a wandering and beggar friar. His years were great, his stature and presence imposing. And he stood alongside the children.

'What kind of justice is this? What religion may venerate the killing of innocents?'

The Cathar leader studied him. 'There are no innocents here.'

'Consider again.'

'You appear as though from air, grandfather.'

'It is to dust I shall consign you all should you dare advance further.'

'With what would you assail us?' The Perfect was entertained at the thought. 'Your trusty stave? Your bare feet? Your bellicose manner?'

'Mock while you may.'

'See how we treat others of the cloth, and continue your wandering. These spawn are nothing to you.'

'They are my lambs, and I will defend them.'

'Be on your way or hang beside your fellow priest.'

His instruction went ignored. The friar planted his feet more firmly, twisted the staff in his palms. He was not about to back away, had no interest in apology or climbdown. Matters would develop fast. He accepted the situation, intended to participate.

'I am Brother Luke, a penitent of Assisi, a humble pilgrim on passage for the Holy Land. I cannot deny God, will not scorn children in their hour and vale of darkness.'

'Old man, get you hence.' The warning was final, had lost its amused inflection.

Otto hissed at the friar. 'Heed him, Brother Luke. Preserve yourself and please begone.'

'And miss what is coming their way?' The Franciscan ran a thumb along the edge of his staff. 'I find myself already well preserved.'

'They will show no mercy.'

'Maybe so. But I will not cede ground to graceless Cathars. I will not allow harm to those engaged in holy mission.'

Stand-off was drawing to completion. His hand raised, his disciples poised, the Perfect addressed his new-found opponent.

'Time is done, beggar priest. You and your adopted brood are to be set free from your earthly and corrupted forms. Rejoice in it, and speak your final words.'

'*Firmitas et Fortitudo*.' Strength and Bravery.

Onslaught was as swift as it was pre-emptive. It was the friar who went forward, his speed astonishing, his agility taking all by surprise. The Cathars reacted. Three rushed to intercept, their blades jabbing and slashing the air, their rage vented in clamouring howls. They had not thought it through, had failed to judge their moment. Whirling to greet them, the old priest struck hard, his staff punching into ribs and clavicles, cracking heads, whipping down on joints and limbs.

He talked as he lightly laboured. 'I eschew violence, am one for brotherly love and peace.' A blow was dodged and countered with a side-sweep to the neck. 'Yet you test my vows and patience, persuade me from the sweet and gentle path of my brother Francis of Assisi.' Two further Cathars entered the fray, were dealt with in a single stroke. 'Do you not learn? Have you not suffered enough through crusade that His Reverend Lord the Pope sends against you?'

Plainly not, for another pair of Believers committed themselves, with ignominious result. They were felled like the rest, lifting and dropping in sudden impact, their weapons and lit brands scattered.

'A melancholy sight, and one for which I pray to the Lord for His forgiveness.'

Brother Luke rested his staff. Around him, the battlefield was strewn with the wounded and winded, with *credentes* clutching at their injuries or crawling for the sanctuary of their own. Theological debate was through. The Cathar leader waved his men back.

'From our hearts we thank you, Brother Luke.'

Otto extended a hand, felt it held in the firm grasp of his unexpected champion. 'Such feat of arms is more common of a soldier.'

'A skill I gain from long days on the road. Even a meek friar must learn to brawl.'

'We are fortunate for it.'

'As I am honoured to be in company of the brave. Let us seize the moment and retire. These sons of Satan may yet regroup and again attack.'

'You say you travel for the Holy Land.'

'That is my calling and intent. But on hearing of the children and their march, my brother Francis of Assisi bid me help and guide them in their quest. I will be at your side so long as you need.'

'Welcome, Brother Luke. My friends seek Jerusalem and the True Cross, and that is where I too head.'

'Then we go.'

They departed the hanging tree as the horizon lightened to grey, leading the horses, moving ever onward. Another incident lay behind them, a new travelling companion had been gained. Kurt cast a backward glance. The torches were extinguished; the Cathars stood passive and motionless as stone.

There was all the difference between abject retreat and tactical withdrawal. The Perfect stared after the tall friar and his adopted flock. He had pulled back his men for a reason; he did not intend to offer further battle, to squander energy and resource on such meagre pickings. A higher cause was his priority. Across Europe his brethren suffered, were being persecuted, hunted, butchered and enslaved. Their towns were burning, their bishops were hanged high by the neck as act of warning or vengeance. All on the orders of Rome. His Holiness the Pope had particular dislike for Cathars, viewed them as threat and disease, as a boil to be lanced. They would have no home that was not levelled. So it was they died or were forced to recant. Some went into hiding, some took the offensive, some stood to meet their bitter fate and make their final stands. Others had escaped to regions where they could nurse their grievance and pursue their aims. The Perfect was far from finished. He would never renounce his sacred vows, under no circumstance would bow before the papal throne. That was not what his God of truth and decency required. What He demanded of His faithful was that they endure, that they walk the path of enlightenment and harry the forces of darkness to the ends of the earth. An opportunity had arisen; the wronged would turn.

These children might believe they had shaken off pursuit, that they and their friar had outmanoeuvred a random and desperate band of heretics. If only life and death were that simple. Certainly, he would not give immediate chase. But he would follow and eventually overhaul, he would yet surprise with the plans he had laid. Brother Luke, Otto of Alzey and their spirited little grouping were not alone in dedicating themselves to crusade and pilgrimage for Palestine.

A pity these walls could not talk. Though on occasion they did: when he bricked up victims and left them to rot, when over days their shouts and pleas receded from muffled sound to echoing silence. Not today. The Lord of Arsur spat three times on to the inverted True Cross and muttered an incantation. Here in the crypt-chapel of his fortress he could nourish his soul and prepare, could add to his collection of sacred relics. A lock of hair from St Peter, a finger of St Paul, nails from the Crucifixion, the Crown of Thorns. Priceless artefacts stolen and plundered, gathered together as offerings to his demon deity, the one true Creator. Each to his own, everyone to his personal creed or heresy.

It was to Baphomet the sorcerer-being, the goat-headed god, to whom he owed allegiance and would dedicate his action. For some, the Word of God was all, while others spoke a different tongue. The great gilded idol looked down upon him, a flaming rush torch set between its horns, a pentagram etched upon its forehead. He abased himself before it. This beast divinity had brought him far; it would carry him to triumph. It demanded loyalty, merited the most precious of gifts, required the sacrifice of the regent, the barons, even the baby queen Yolanda. So it would come to pass.

He ran his fingers over the golden gem-soaked sleeve of the True Cross. It had not lost its lustre or allure, still glistened as it had that fateful morn when he rode from the camp of Saladin at the site of the battle on the Horns of Hattin. *Judas. Betrayer of our cause . . . A curse be upon you.* He could afford to smile at the memory of the bold Templar who had stood at the moment of his death and shouted after him. The condemned man had no idea of what was at stake, of what might one day be. Now he was dust, while the Lord of Arsur was poised at the doorway to supremacy. He caressed the piece. Such an object of veneration and love, such a powerful draw for the entire Christian world. It made its capture and defilement the more worthwhile. He knew its history well, its discovery in AD 326 by Helena, ailing mother of Emperor Constantine I, its confiscation in AD 614 by the Persian king Chrosroes II, its subsequent and circuitous return to Jerusalem when the Persians met defeat at the hands of Roman emperor Heraclius. Tens of thousands had perished for this relic, this item of shrouded flotsam. At the slightest mention of its name, armies would gather, states engage in war, men lose reason and drag themselves across land and sea to battle for its honour and possession. So it had proved before; thus would it be demonstrated again. He was counting on it. The True Cross would be put to the most imaginative of uses.

Noise intruded on his thoughts, pulled him from his reverie. There were shouts, the clamour and clatter of men descending stairways to his subterranean lair. In these opening days, he could not expect uninterrupted calm.

'My lord, I beg you come quick.'

His officer was panting, exertion and worry revealed in his sweat and the grimace of his mouth. Something was wrong. The Lord of Arsur observed him coolly, would not dignify the interruption with excitability of his own. He demanded discipline of his men.

'Make your report.'

'We have found a traitor in our midst, my lord.'

'Indeed.' The Lord of Arsur narrowed his eyes. 'If you have uncovered such a reptile, why the haste? Is he not bound hand and foot? Are you concerned he may yet escape?'

'All is possible, my lord. He had papers on him, careful observations of our strength and disposition.'

'Yet none know my intention.'

'It is his we have not divined, my lord. Whether it is for pay or some higher cause, whether he was sent by enemies unknown or merely took flight when opportunity arose.'

'I see we have mystery to resolve, a captive to unpeel. Take me to him.'

They made their way with studied haste along labyrinthine passageways and up spiral stairs towards the hidden light. Gloom prevailed everywhere, patterned with shadows cast by sputtering tallow. The men paced on, their own footfalls repeating and pursuing them on the blackened flagstones. It was a place where desolation and darkness presided.

Heat and dazzling sunlight grazed the eyes as they emerged on to a broad esplanade atop the castle rampart. All about below them was activity, the frenetic and purposeful motion of human termites engaged in a thousand tasks with a single aim. Within the walls of Arsur, an army was organizing. Mock combat was under way, soldiers hacking at straw-stuffed dummies and wooden posts or dwelling under the watchful instruction of their masters. On the other side of the square, pikemen were being drilled in the art of formation defence, raising and lowering, blocking and advancing, with their sharp-tipped ranks of lugged spears and ravensbills. Elsewhere, horses walked and trotted, barrels rolled, crossbow-bolts thudded into target butts. And above them all, the constant throb of industry, the beat of smithy hammers on helms and horseshoes, the tap and rattle of craftsmen applying piercing-tools to the production of mail hauberks and chausses.

The officer pointed. 'There, my lord. They bring him to you.'

A struggling man was being dragged between a pair of burly guards, accompanied by a posse of mercenaries brandishing clubs and wearing quilted jupon jackets. These were tough infantry who enjoyed beer and bloodshed. Their commander was loath to disappoint.

In a snivelling mass of terror, the victim was hauled upward over the sweeping steps and deposited at the feet of an impassive Lord of Arsur.

'Raise him.' The soldiers obeyed, and their leader reached to cup and squeeze the features of the captive in his hand. 'Did I not provide you sanctuary?'

'You did, my lord. Please, my lord . . .'

'Did I not feed and clothe you, provide your dying religion with new abode, allow you to steal by ship from Europe beneath the noses of your very persecutors?'

The shuddering prisoner nodded violently in

affirmation. He was aware it was hopeless. But breath and heartbeat could generate optimism, plight encourage a wishful grasping for alternative outcome. A finger stroked his cheek as the Lord of Arsur perused him from close distance.

'How many Cathars I have plucked from the stake and the noose in France and other kingdoms. How many more come hither to join us in Arsur, free from the inquisitive eye, the listening ear, of the Pope.'

'Your deeds will be blessed, my lord.'

'As yours shall be condemned. Ever since His Holiness and the King of France unleashed crusade against you these three years past, I have given your kind refuge from the branding-iron and sword.'

'This I know, my lord.'

'In return I have demanded only your loyalty and labour, your desire to serve.'

'I shall serve you again, my lord.'

'You betray me.'

His fingers tightened until the countenance of the prisoner was distorted and the eyes bulged. There was a curiosity to examine a life force shortly before its demise. Everything had come to this point, was reduced to an insignificant creature quaking before the fall. The Lord of Arsur smelt the sweat, the sour and primal breath of mortal dread. He felt good.

'To whom did you intend to deliver our secrets?'

'I was fearful, my lord, had no plan than to leave this site, to lay down arms and dwell in peace and quiet contemplation.'

'Instead you die in pain.'

'Mercy, my lord. I throw myself on your compassion.'

'Alas, it is found wanting.' He released his hold. 'You recorded our dispositions, noted and reconnoitred our capability and strength. That is the act rather of a spy than a thoughtful hermit.'

'I am innocent, my lord.'

'You are man made flesh, and flesh may be devoured.'

He nodded once and the victim left as he had arrived, his resisting legs kicking for purchase, his keening cries rising plaintive through the parting throng. Silence rippled outward across the open space. Men stopped their training; the steely clash of blades and hammers ceased. Anticipation hung, like the dust, heavy in the air.

The second in a row of three pits was the destination. Like its neighbours, it was twelve feet wide and excavated to a depth from which neither beast nor human could climb to liberty. Quickly, the man was strapped into a rope harness and sent over the rim, his terror escalating as his descent began. His screams reverberated from the hollow. Then a different and deeper sound, the enraged roar of a brown bear tormented by hunger and baited with whips. Its revenge, if not sweet, at least came with plentiful marrowbone and the muscled succulence of raw meat. The din mingled in a fur-ball frenzy before subsiding to the muted crack and splinter of feeding-time.

Fear was the key, the answer to cohesion. The Lord of Arsur looked on. There was no need for speech or explanation, no room for misconception. His troops well understood. Those he employed would toil and die without question; those who refused would simply die. He had hurled men from mangonels, had flayed them alive, had flogged and cut them so that insects could feed on their honey-covered wounds. Any cruelty the late and unlamented Reynald of Châtillon could devise he would exceed. Whether mercenary or Cathar, Assassin or leper knight, each played his part, would be an element in eventual success. The bear appeared to have had its fill of the traitorous Albigensian and was toying boisterously with the corpse.

A messenger approached and bowed, passing an encrypted note to the Lord of Arsur. It had come by carrier pigeon from the fortress of al-Kahf, and as he deciphered and read it it confirmed what he predicted. The Assassins had struck their next target; the schedule was maintained. He was pleased.

He glanced up at the officer beside him. 'Our Cathar danced well with his bear. Commit his two closest companions to the third pit.'

It was the one colonized by large and deadly fat-tailed scorpions.

'What sorcery is this?' Brother Luke conjured a fifth egg from the ear of Zepp and handed it to his assistant, Kurt. 'I declare your right ear more bountiful than your left.'

The ten-year-old yelled in gleeful amazement. 'Achim, my ear lays eggs! It provides us with eggs!'

In turn, absorbed by the mystery, the children

inspected the produce and the source from whence it came. Brother Luke observed them with warm benevolence. To his charges he was shield and talisman, a guardian as gnarled and weathered as an ancient olive tree. His own longevity inspired confidence; his very presence was proof that they too might survive. He smiled and talked, brought certainty and banished cares, and the youngsters listened with rapt concentration. None on their journey had displayed such kindness or shown such attention as this ragged friar with the lined face and pale compassionate eyes. He would have seen much, experienced the tempest and trials of many lands and threescore years. And he was an Englishman.

Otto caught an egg juggled and thrown by the friar and cracked it in a skillet. 'I had you marked as soldier, Brother Luke. Now it seems you are *jongleur* and magician.'

'Judge not a man by his manner or his words.' Another egg was flipped and expertly captured. 'I am the lowliest of beggars, yet read Latin and Greek and enjoy debate and scholarly learning. I speak seven tongues, including your own, but remain a son of Albion.'

'Tell us of England.' It was Kurt who asked.

'There is little to confide, for I left as a boy. It rains much, and I hear the wicked King John overtaxes his benighted people. My own thoughts are turned to a different kingdom.'

'Why is it you now make pilgrimage to the Holy Land?'

'To pray, to preach, and to die. I am old now, must prepare for the time when God calls me home and my carcass is rendered to the grave.'

Otto cocked his head. 'I have seen no hint of your decline.'

'The more reason to go while sight and strength remain. What worthier cause exists than to return to the sacred soil of Palestine, to retrace the steps where first I trod on passage to the Holy Sepulchre?'

'You have travelled there before?'

'Once. I was young, a novice monk at the great Cistercian abbey of Cîteaux. A group of brothers sailed for Outremer, and I, full of joy and wonder, accompanied them on their voyage. There were hard times, good times. Jerusalem was ruled by a crusader king; the Templars and Hospitallers swaggered with the inner fire of invincibility.' Wistfulness briefly misted his eyes. 'It was before Saladin and the years that led to the Horns of Hattin, before the Saracen prevailed over the chain-mail and lances of the Latin knights.'

The children had gathered round, eager to consume the wisdom and anecdotal scraps offered by this priest, this veteran, this most masterful of storytellers. They had told him of how Kurt had almost been lost to a river, how they had consigned the body of little Lisa to the earth, how they endured and toiled, had faced danger and Gunther and the four murderous horsemen who fell upon poor Hans. The face of Brother Luke had clouded when he heard. It was as though he knew of what they spoke, was troubled by memory of a rumour, by the ghost of distant legend. But the moment passed and new diversions arose. There were always tricks to perform, a hundred questions from his avid audience to answer.

Isolda, her chin perched in her hands, stared mesmerized at the old friar. 'How does Jerusalem appear, Brother Luke? Is is white and shining like the city of God?'

'Its towers are as tall as the sky, its holy places girdled by the strongest of walls. Yet happiness is scarce at a site where conflict is forever present.'

'Shall we bring peace?'

'I pray to God we do, for the land of Our Saviour cries out for it.' He gently patted her face. 'Love is what matters and conquers, dear daughter. And you and Kurt, Zepp and Achim, Egon and Otto will each and all bear witness and spread the message to the unbelievers.'

His voice muted with fatigue, the blind Achim whispered his doubts. 'Saracens lie ahead, Brother Luke. Infidels with swords and spears, with loathing in their hearts.'

'None could hate or harm you, for all are descendants of the tribes of Abraham. Besides, I am here, and who will match this humble friar in fair fight or foul?'

'There are still the Cathars behind.' Egon sat on watch at a small distance, was gazing back towards the route they had travelled.

Maybe he was anxious, or perhaps he smarted at the affection and regard in which Isolda held the noble

Otto, Kurt reflected. He felt awkward for his true and steady friend. Brother Luke rose and took the arm of the boy to bring him closer to the lapping campfire.

'No son of a blacksmith should be far from the flames. As for Cathars, dispel them from your thoughts. We have put miles between us, have crossed the river Po. Look forward instead. Genoa is close, and Rome beckons.'

Levity returned as they ate and sang, as a restful moon rose to hang above the warm late-August evening. There was trust and belief and friendship in the shared company and the simple act of breaking bread. The friar felt honoured to be among them as their guide. They had chosen him as he had chanced upon them, had welcomed him to their side. How young they were, how vulnerable they seemed to the ravages and vagaries of the world. He had left his tiny community on the plain of Porziuncola, bid farewell to his dear brother Francis of Assisi to protect the younglings and prepare them for their odyssey. Now they sat and ate among terraced vineyards not thirty miles from Genoa and the coast. The Lord help them, the Franciscan prayed, and the Lord advise them to turn back before they journeyed further.

Camped and clustered beneath the dark walls of Genoa were the remnants of the Children's Crusade. They had made it somehow, several thousand of them trickling in with shredded feet and harrowing tales, their faces grown old and their clothes dissolved to rags. From early June to late August they had marched, scavenging for provisions and burying their dead. This was the result. A desolate sense of loss and tragedy clung about them, glimmered dark in their shocked and recessed eyes. They could not quite believe they remained alive, could not conceive of what they had been through. Luck was a relative thing. As each frayed and diminished band slumped to a staggering halt, the scale of calamity became ever clearer. Most had not arrived. For those that did, one last affront and final betrayal greeted them. The seas had not parted to allow dry passage and onward trek to the Holy Land. It was hardly surprising the boy preacher Nikolas and his acolytes had vanished, apparently moving on towards Rome or into self-appointed exile.

Otto, Kurt and Brother Luke moved about the huddled groupings in the early-morning mist. Occasionally they would kneel to bind wounds or offer words of prayer and comfort, or distribute bread and biscuit from loaded sacks. The citizens of Genoa had been generous. But it would take time to banish the melancholy and repair the harm. Any who saw such a sight would have taken pity. So it was that litters were sent to carry in the ill and the lame, food and drink were brought to the exhausted young, and mothers came to plead with children who could be their own to stay and abandon their ongoing folly. Few of the arrivals had strength to argue. They were merely grateful to find rest, might one day be happy to be with the living.

Crouching to hold a goatskin water-pouch to the lips of a young girl, Kurt murmured encouragement and let her drink. She took his hand and squeezed it, wanting to hold on, wishing to cling to another human. Around them were the consumptive coughs of the road, the babbling of insanity and nightmares that refused to flee. Malnutrition and a driving pace had brought them to this. Kurt threaded on through the prone and huddled figures, his heart heavy and tread soft as he wandered in a landscape of scattered bundles and hooded forms. A wretched vista. He stooped again to proffer the gourd, but recoiled at the coldness of the touch. The boy was dead, his companions too tired or indifferent to weep or notice.

A head turned towards him, the tufted red hair, the mean face with its tight sardonic grin, familiar beneath the leather cowl. Kurt sensed his nerve-ends freeze before recognition dawned. Gunther, son of the woodsman, had been waiting for him.

'God smiles on us, Kurt. Be glad of our meeting.'

✝

Chapter 7

'*Pursue the ball! Put your foot to it!*'
A game of football was in full cry. Within the scrimmage of dust and feet, punches were thrown, teeth spat, curses traded, and the ball chased in bloody disorder from one end of the market square to the other. Genoa was used to tribalism. It often fought Pisa, its most sworn of city-state rivals, with drawn sword in deadly battle. Grievances were nursed, merchants vied and squabbled with merchants, ruling families indulged in violent feud between themselves. Sporting contest was never likely to remain immune to similar brutish aggression.

Kurt dodged again, pushing forward and ducking through the collision shockwave of two opposing players to regain possession of the ball. Moving fast, he swerved and kicked, watching the curving flight of the leatherclad pig-bladder and its impact on the wooden stool. Three strikes to one. The pilgrim boys were leading their hosts, and sportsmanship was suffering. Already Kurt had bruised shins, a cut lip and a blackened eye. But the sun shone, morale had climbed, and Isolda and Egon cheered him from the sidelines.

Otto too was there, stropping his sword and oiling it with linseed, shouting encouragement. Even the cityfolk stood and commented, impressed at the skill and boldness of these German young. Such children would make worthy sons of Genoa should they choose to stay.

'You do well, Kurt. Rest awhile and let others take the punishment.'

The twelve-year-old nodded and, gasping to catch breath, lowered himself to sit beside the young noble on a stone block. Before them, the match had become uglier. A stall of oranges was overturned, its contents spilling among the stampeding tumult, the complaints of the vendor drowned by hostilities and the mirth of onlookers.

'We lead them a merry chase, Otto.'

'Whether you gain friends or find enemies is unclear. But it is good to see.' The noble boy ran a cloth over the steel blade and squinted at his handiwork. 'They should have guessed that those who walk from Cologne are the hardiest of their breed.'

'Those who still stand are the most fortunate. I worry for Achim.'

'He is cared for by kindly people, attended by Zepp and Brother Luke, watched over by God. He will make recovery.'

'If he does not . . .'

Apprehension stole across the countenance of the youngster. His friend the blind ten-year-old with the voice of an angel and laugh of a cherub had sickened and faded, now lingered at the fringes of life. Zepp, his twin, talked to him and prayed, Brother Luke cooled his face and tried to spoon broth into his mouth. But Achim, who had achieved so much, who had brought light and levity in their darkest hours, was spent. They would have to leave him. It meant another departure that was one more death.

Otto put down the sword and gripped his shoulder. 'No weakness, Kurt. Face fortune as you play the ball, as you challenged the Cathars. Achim and Zepp expect you to be strong.'

'You are right, just as you spoke truly that there would be no parting of the waters, no travelling on foot across dry seas to Palestine.'

'It does not signal we shall not get there, young brother.'

'Must we reach Rome when there is boat set ready for sail from Genoa?'

'And miss fair adventure, the chance to see the greatest of cities, to receive proper blessing before we depart?'

'There are autumn storms approaching, Otto.' Kurt peered at his older friend. 'I have heard them talk at the harbourside in fear of the coming winds and waves.'

'Yet sailors prepare to put to sea.'

'Not for long. This ship is one of the last to head for Palestine before onset of winter. Should we walk for Rome, will there not be few in late September willing to risk destruction?'

'Merchants will ever seek trade, captains always try to earn a living. Caution and proud seamanship will carry us there.'

'I have never before viewed the oceans, never set foot aboard a vessel.'

'Nor I, Kurt. Though I have heard much from pilgrims and friends of my father, learned from what my tutor taught me.'

'Perhaps we will encounter sea monsters and discover mermaids.'

The sixteen-year-old smiled. 'I would vouch you had faced sufficient threat on land.'

'That land schools me well, informs me we may yet fall off the edge of the world.'

'Surprise and revelation will doubtless happen.'

'Gunther happens.' It was said with feeling.

'I recall he was no match the last time we met, that he near-fouled his hose and fled the scene.'

'He does not forget, Otto.'

'Then he will remember how it was to have my blade pressed close to his throat. It should temper his actions.'

'He will wait and watch.'

'As shall we. So put him and other demons from your mind.'

Kurt would try. Yet he glanced about to be certain, to gauge if the son of the woodsman was near. Old habits, familiar routines, were hard to abandon. Isolda left her seat and approached to apply unction to his wounds. She enjoyed her role as older sibling, welcomed the excuse to edge closer to Otto. Her brother submitted to her care with his usual resignation. Only when the cuts smarted and he winced at their sting did the pang of remembrance enter his heart and the image of the girl in Cologne with the flaxen hair flicker into view. So many days since, and so many dead.

Otto had noticed the shadow of anguish. 'Noble or pauper, we all of us die, Kurt. It is how we live that matters. Resume your game and show Genoa of what you are made.'

He obeyed and, with Egon at his side, charged back to the fray.

Money was changing hands. Among the squat stone houses and dusty recesses of the medieval port, Gunther conducted business with a local street tough. It was a simple transaction, one that would lead to the infliction of pain, the maiming or death of his enemies. Targets of opportunity had arisen. He would be foolish to ignore them, less than a man to pass up the chance to exact retribution on those who despised and rejected him. Like flies, the surviving children of his village had tramped their filthy way back into his reach. They seemed alarmed at such touching and sudden reunion. With them came others: the handsome peacock from Alzey so quick with his sword and chivalry, a nomadic holy man with his bare feet and tattered habit. Punishment was called for.

Gunther pressed stolen coins into the open palm of his hireling. 'Now is the time. Take your friends into the game and aim for the boy named Kurt.'

'What harm do you intend?'

'As much as you are able. Strike when there is confusion, treat his head as the ball.'

'We take a risk.'

'I pay you for it. There will be more if he is carried off; further if he dies.'

'You dislike him much.'

'Each one of them I hate, but he is worst. He questions me, defies me. That way lies hurt.'

'Be sure we shall execute it well. None fight harder than my crew. The Rhineland scrap will be damaged beyond repair.'

'He deserves it all.'

They shook on it. How fortuitous it was that local boys possessed commercial sense, knew a smattering of German and the foreign tongues of every merchant dealing at their quayside. Enmity could be so worthwhile. Kurt was enjoying his game, was heading unaware for rendezvous with a nailed boot. Rarely did football end without a casualty.

A shadow enveloped them, a pair of hands gripping the two conspirators by their necks.

'What manner of plot is this? A Genoese oaf confers with a Rhineland carrot?'

'Put me down.' Gunther struggled against the calm intensity and unyielding hold of Brother Luke.

'A peevish carrot.'

'You will regret this! You shall pay for your offence.'

'I tremble at such frightening prospect.' The friar lifted the writhing miscreants further from the ground. 'There is nothing so undignified as to whine and bandy threats when dangling in the sky.'

'I have friends who will do you harm.'

'While I have righteousness and the power of God to do as I see just.'

'Unhand me, friar.' The snarling voice of Gunther rose to a screech.

'Is it not the truth that reason comes when two heads are brought together?'

'You are mad, beggar priest.'

'Yet I still see you plan injury to blameless innocents. I still have might enough to divert you from your wrong.'

'We shall give you wrong.'

'And I shall teach you lesson.'

As though playing cymbals, the friar clashed the boys together, stunning them to limp submission. The son of the woodsman groaned.

'Let me confide in you a secret.' Brother Luke murmured conversationally to them both. 'I do not like knaves or rogues or bullies or braggarts. They are an affront to the sight of God, and they disturb me from my purpose and from preaching to the birds of the air.' He received no argument, so went on. 'I urge you to repent. I ask you to strive to be better men. Are we agreed?'

'We are.' It was an answer shaken from the local boy.

'You, carrot?'

The flame-haired German was less coherent, but managed to nod.

'Then I am filled with gladness at our compact, happy to find unity and accord where prospect was bleak. Give your hearts and thanks to the Lord. Offer up your purses.'

He released his hold and deftly, without invitation,

ripped the money-pouches from his captive and bewildered audience. Their protest was clumsy as it was unfocused. Brother Luke ignored them, tipping the contents into his hand, inspecting each piece with expert eye.

'Give me the money.' The knife wavered in the nervous grasp of the city lout.

'I cannot.'

'You will, or your heart shall be clean pierced.'

Unruffled, the friar continued his examination. 'These proceeds are ill-gained, stolen I vouch from the defenceless and weak.'

'We keep what is ours.'

'That is no way to enter the gates of paradise. Surely you would wish me to disburse such riches to the poor and the sick?'

'*Stick him with your blade, friend.*' Gunther was circling, encouraging attack.

Negotiation seemed void. Resignedly, almost with regret, the Franciscan replaced the coins and launched his foot direct into the groin of the young thug. The boy doubled over, Gunther shrank back, and Brother Luke, whistling a merry tune, proceeded on his way to distribute their generous contribution.

John of Brienne, regent of Outremer, stared out a long while from the high ramparts of Acre. Across the land, down towards the gentle course of the river Belus, the sun was dipping and casting its fire-glow. Perhaps it set on his own rule, on the tenuous hold the Frankish Christians maintained in this fragment of the Holy

Land. He had once enjoyed standing here, breathing the citrus-scented air, listening to the drifting sounds of raucous laughter, the snatches of troubadour song that climbed from the great hall below. Pleasure was now gone. In its place were unease and foreboding, reports of Moslem raids, news of Templars leading counter-strikes from Tortosa and Hospitallers riding out from their mighty castles of Krak des Chevaliers and Marqab. Strong walls surrounded him, yet he had never felt more vulnerable or beset.

He toyed with the gilt chain of office at his throat, let his fingers pick fretfully at its metalwork and gemstones. If only Saphadin would talk, respond to the messengers that were sent him in haste as courtesy and need. But the Sultan of Damascus stayed silent. Much could be read into this. He was clearly intent on provocation, evidently waging undeclared war in preparation for a wider conflict. Outremer required time and manpower. Neither was available.

A harp played and words of knightly love reached faint to his ears. He laughed sourly to himself. Anything could happen, collapse might be nigh, and somewhere a court singer from Aquitaine would be crooning of romance and gallant deeds. How remote it seemed. His concerns were closer: the well-being of his baby daughter Yolanda; the longevity of his kingdom.

'I spoil your reflections, sir?'

He turned at the voice of Lady Matilda. 'Interruption is welcome. It is best I do not dwell too long alone with my pondering.'

'Would that I could ease your burden, sir.'

'Nothing will relieve the weight of office save knowledge that I am not destined to be last ruler of Outremer.'

'There is not a man in this realm who would think it so.'

'They do not see as I see, cannot hear what I hear. I am surrounded by drunks and roisterers, counselled by warmongers who know little of war.'

'All will stand by you, sir.'

'Or they may share in our destruction. A sharp wind snaps at us, my lady, threatens to scatter and blow us to the sea.'

'God in his wisdom will preserve us.' She stepped up beside him at the castellation. 'My father would bring me up here as a child, point out to me every feature and mountain, each tower and gate.'

'He loved Outremer as the kingdom loved him. I would value his presence now.'

'My company is poor substitute. But I will honour him and serve as well I may, shall bear whatever burden is placed upon me.'

The ageing ruler gazed intently at her. 'Swear to me that should troubles multiply you will take ship to safety in France.'

'How could I flee at such critical hour, sir? How could I abandon those who most need me, lands and possessions my family have owned since the Second Crusade?'

'To outpace a unit of Saracen cavalry is not to outlive a general conflagration.'

'I shall face whatever fortune has ordained.'

'For one of such youth and rare beauty you have the heart of a lion.'

'Where you and your infant daughter dwell, I shall be found. You are my regent king, she my queen and akin to baby sister, this my home. No Mohammedan or promised battle will force me from my duty.'

'I cherish your loyalty and affection to us.'

'As I prize your blessing and your kindness.' She linked her arm through his. 'None would dare defy or bring us down, sir.'

He chuckled. 'Maybe, after all, we are not destined for oblivion.'

They watched together as the light bled to a deeper hue, as the dusk stole closer on the rooftops. Seventeen-year-old noblewoman and sixty-four year-old king, each immersed in thought, thankful for the presence of the other. Matilda wondered if these quiet moments were borrowed, if they were hurtling to extinction.

Below them, the nurse to baby Yolanda scurried from the palace en route for assignation. She was a large and cheerful woman, repository for several appetites and eager sexual voraciousness. This night she would indulge. Naturally, life possessed challenge and was not always sweet. She detested the sour and silent ways of her new associate, the wet-nurse so recently imposed as her shadow and her second. But hers was not to reason or protest. At least it offered chance of respite from the beloved infant queen, opportunity to carouse with menfolk as desire and time allowed. My, how she serviced them. Of late she had chanced upon the stuff of lust-soaked dreams, a god in the guise of a sergeant employed with the royal guard. The man was dark and strong, had stamina and ardour, the rough-and-ready manner of a soldier who liked to love and loved to revel. She was flattered and mounted, and that was all that mattered.

She proceeded into the maze of buildings and tight alleyways as fast and light on her feet as she could manage. Her anticipation climbed. Occasionally a guard hailed her, a familiar face called out in quest of conversation. She murmured her replies, tugged her muslin wrap closer about her hat and face, and bustled on. Soon she was through a gate and across the narrow stone footway north into the quarter of Montmusard. There would be fewer questions here at the periphery of the city, fewer prying eyes to scan her hurrying progress. Within minutes she was at the foot of a flight of steps leading to the upper floor of the two-storey dwelling. It could be any place, belong to anyone. She paused to catch her breath, to straighten her smock, and ascended.

'You are late.'

'I am as prompt as my duty to the regent and the baby queen permits.'

'Ah, duty.' The sergeant hawked into the corner of the room. 'How fares the mewling babe?'

'She is as pretty as any I have seen, as placid as any I have cared for.'

'While her nurse is far from docile.'

'I have my wants, and you provision well.'

He indicated a basket filled with jars, dainties

and rolls of cloth. 'See what I bring you. Fruits and perfumes, frankincense and silks.'

'All, I wager, filched from the court of the regent. You are a bad man.'

'Appreciate it so.'

The soldier approached and kissed her forcefully, making her squeal with hurt and pleasure. How strong his hands were, how muscled his arms and chest. She gasped for air, felt the hardening of his groin, the obvious give of her response. It was not her fault he made her act this way. His tongue searched her mouth, his teeth nipped at her ear and neck, his fingers undressed and travelled. She wanted to blaspheme, to scream and curse, to bawl every gutter obscenity that Satan could invent. God, this was good. For a time they stood, swaying and sucking, discarding their clothes, fumbling their way towards greater passion. She slid downward. His groan reflected her effort, her head pumping, her lips engaged, her cheeks full. Anything to keep her man.

They staggered to the piled horsehair blankets and fell greedily upon each other.

'We are fortunate to meet.'

She giggled as his fingers clawed between her thighs. 'A hound will always find its truffle.'

'As a soldier will ever leave his mark.'

'You may stain me however you choose.'

'A lady would put up sound fight.'

'I am no lady.' She pulled him closer, ran her nails hard across his back. 'Yet I will brawl on this bed until you cry out.'

He kneaded her flesh, forced wide her plump and unresisting knees. 'Such pity you leave yourself open to attack.'

Orders were strict and were expected to be followed. So he straddled her, made the right moves and noise as she bucked and bellowed like a heffer. What a performance. To think she believed he coupled with her through honest choice. She was too engrossed to understand or care, shaking and shuddering, rocking her porcine carcass to and fro. There was something pathetic in her vulgar enthusiasm and base vulnerability. He would see to it, when the moment came and his master the Lord of Arsur directed, that this fat nurse would be dispatched without bother or delay. She was keeper of the royal nursery, protector of Queen Yolanda, and for that she must die. Her replacement was already deputized and in position, ready to assume the senior role as vacancy occurred.

'Grind me, you soldier dog. Pound me to the floor . . .'

Dutifully, and without much pleasure, he obliged. Intrigue and strategy demanded it of him. She was not to know their chance meeting had involved no chance, that she had been selected, cultivated, groomed. Handover of the infant was assured.

'It is you, Kurt. You come to bid me goodbye.'

Achim turned his sightless eyes towards the footfall of his friend. He lay propped on a straw pallet in the hovel room, his skin damp and grey with sickness, his enfeebled body as thin and brittle as kindling.

Beside him, Zepp crouched silent in his anguish, too despairing to stay, too loyal to leave. Kurt understood. For the ten years of their twinned lives they had been inseparable, Zepp guiding Achim, Achim supporting Zepp. They had never before thought it possible to be separate, to lose their own shadow. Now death was close, and that prospect drew near.

The blind boy smiled, even in his weakness lighting up the space. 'Forgive me the trouble I cause.'

'Always.' Kurt dropped to his knee and clasped him tight, wanting to hold on, to convey a thousand fractured feelings.

'We tried, Kurt, at times did well.'

'Such a journey they will set down in history, Achim. How we found passage through the Alps, challenged the Cathars, lived for weeks through drought or storm.'

'I would not change it, brother.'

'What a band we have proved. You lifted our spirits, made us sing, encouraged us on.'

'In truth, I was never so skilled at forage.'

Mirth vibrated through the emaciated frame, and Kurt found his laughter dissolving into tears. The stoicism of the younger boy seemed to rob him of his own. Otto had been wrong, for Achim had not pulled through. It stripped their group of two more, left despair and incomprehension in their place.

The ten-year-old gently pushed him back. 'No mourning, Kurt. We celebrate, for you carry me onward in your head and heart.'

'I would rather bear you each step on my back.'

'Instead you must travel without us, reach the Holy Land and kiss the True Cross for Zepp and me.'

'That I will surely do, Achim.'

'You have Isolda and Egon beside you, our new comrades Otto and Brother Luke.'

'They are as pained to leave you as I.'

'Who knows what may happen?' Achim reached out with both hands and began to map his face. 'Until we meet again, this is for remembrance.'

'I could not have asked for finer brothers and companions.'

Fingertips brushed across his mouth. 'Smile for me, Kurt.'

He tried, fixing a grin so that Achim might recollect more than simply the dampness on his cheeks. The youngster was satisfied, had made his peace, accepted his destiny as readily as he embraced his blindness.

'Brother Luke?' The blank gaze swivelled for the doorway in which the Franciscan was silently framed.

'I have come to fetch Kurt. It is time.'

'You also bring food.'

'It would be thoughtless of me to tend your soul while ignoring your belly.' The friar carried over a wooden bowl of gruel.

Achim waved it away. 'I ask only for your blessing and your benediction.'

Kurt blinked into the sunlight and gulped back his grief. It was as though he stepped from a mausoleum, had left Brother Luke to perform final unction. Isolda and Egon were waiting for him, their bundles packed and pilgrim staffs ready in their hands. The next stage of the journey was soon to begin. In Rome they would find blessing from the Pope. It would be worth the extra miles.

'Where is Otto?'

'He fetches his horses, prepares their shoes and fodder.'

Her eyes crimson-ringed with emotion, Isolda stared at the ground. Each of the children had taken turn to say farewell to Zepp and Achim, had trooped out changed by the event. For Isolda it was especial burden. She had mothered them this far, had told them stories, had kissed them goodnight as they went to sleep in lie-ups and ditches. And as Achim waned, she too appeared to falter, to lose the passion that had carried her across mountains. Kurt bit his lower lip, aware that her dark wretchedness reflected his own.

'We can do no more for him, Isolda.'

'I know it, and I know too that he will be at peace, that our destiny calls us to Rome with Otto and Brother Luke. But in parting we betray him; in leaving Genoa I lose my brothers and my heart.'

'Look at us. We have each other and still stand.'

'For how long?' Her eyes lifted, her look tortured and beseeching. 'Little Lisa, Roswitha, Albert, Hans, Zepp and Achim. Every step we have abandoned a friend, cut loose another brother or sister from our village.'

'Isolda, they understand.'

'They are wiser than I.'

Quietly, he went to comfort her, found strength in being of use, in clinging on. As a rule, he hated weeping, despised it in himself. But his sister cried only arid tears, had been wrung dry by her experience. Egon stayed mute and reserved in his sorrowing.

Isolda murmured to her brother. 'Death stalks us, Kurt. It sits outside these walls, trails us, catches us.'

'It has not defeated us.'

'We have given so much, hungered, suffered, cast aside and buried our comrades in the name of Christ. And He covers His face, turns our pilgrimage, our crusade, to dust.'

'I steal eggs and fall in rivers. I cannot answer such things.'

'What if the preacher-boy Nikolas was wrong? What if he lied?'

'In time we will discover.'

She gripped his arm tight. 'I am not scared for myself. But I could not bear to live if you should die.'

'You will not shake me from your side.' He pressed her head against his own. 'We will be all right, my sister.'

Saying it with conviction helped to console her, persuade himself. They would honour the dead and Zepp and Achim by going on. Meaning would have to come later.

Brother Luke emerged from the interior, his task discharged. 'I leave them joyous with prayer and resigned in the sight and instance of Our Blessed Lord. Amen to my sweet and precious lambs. Are we ready to part from Genoa and follow our holy way?'

'We are, Brother Luke.'

'Then let us walk.'

Egon interrupted. 'I remain and take ship from this harbour.'

His face flushed with determination, yet his gaze confused, he seemed as surprised by disclosure as his friends. There was hollow stillness in the after-seconds, consternation that might have passed for calm reflection. Kurt and Isolda hunted vainly for reply.

It was the Franciscan who spoke for them. 'If this is your resolve.'

'It is.'

'Unshakeable it would appear. I am sure you have your reason, certain you will not be otherwise persuaded.'

'My decision is made.'

'So long as it is not dictated for you, that you search your soul and ask guidance from God.'

'All these things I have done and more.' The son of the blacksmith hung his head in solemnity and shame. 'I did not ever wish to deceive or abandon you.'

'Please, Egon.' Kurt stepped forward, his voice low and imploring.

'I am not worth the concern.'

'You are to me and to Isolda, to Brother Luke and Otto.'

'We divide as friends, and will meet again that way in Palestine.'

Isolda was trembling. 'Why, Egon? Why this?'

'Because you do not love me.' He ran.

Kurt started after him, but the friar held him until resistance ebbed and impulse waned. He talked softly.

'Let it be, Kurt. You cannot bind him hand and foot, cannot drag him where he has no wish to move.'

'He is my friend.'

'Value and treat him as such. For us, other necessities arise.'

A slow handclap drew them to the vision of Gunther revealed at a distance upon a low stone wall. He was triumphant, his face split in spiteful sneer, his blackened teeth bared in challenge.

'Journey safe, beggar priest.'

'My intention is ever to do so.'

'You are low in mood and number. Would you care to have me with you?'

'At present I see no grounds.'

'In future you may have no choice.' The boy folded his arms. 'Like Egon I secure berth aboard ship, depart from Genoa direct for the Holy Land. I will reach it before you ever shall.'

'We are well rid of you.'

'I am not finished, friar.'

'No?' Brother Luke raised an eyebrow.

'Your progress falters; your small and timid group reduces. Darkness surrounds you.'

'It may yet be banished.'

With a sudden flick of his wrist, the Franciscan sent a stone spinning to strike the wall between Gunther's feet. The son of the woodsman yelped and disappeared.

Brother Luke grasped the hands of the two children. 'Light returns, my lambs. Gird yourselves and fill your hearts with hope. Say it with me. *Firmitas et Fortitudo.*'

Strength and Bravery. They chanted it with him, repeated his mantra as they gathered their simple possessions and headed for the city gates.

Brother Luke striding in front, then Otto leading the black charger, and Kurt, Isolda and the grey mare following, the modest caravan set out for the coast road and Rome. Behind them, pigs were being slaughtered for the day. Their frantic screams swelled and chased out other noise, pursued the pilgrims far along the track. Even the horses seemed unnerved. Long afterwards, Kurt imagined he could hear the sounds, smell the panic stench of beasts assembled for throat-slitting. Experience had taught him to ignore the past. He gripped his staff more tightly and continued to walk.

The Cathar scout tailed them for a while. They appeared to have discarded three of their number since the last encounter. A positive sign. And they still had no idea of what they faced. With a song in his heart, and holy gratitude on his lips to the god who hated mortal flesh and procreation, he turned back to make report to the Perfect and his Believers.

✝

Chapter 8

A late hour, and the regent of Outremer remained in closeted discussion with the Lord of Arsur. He was grateful his baron had braved the journey from his southern domain, appreciative of his presence. In this vaulted and cavernous palace chamber lit by tallow lamps and draped in tapestries of silver thread, they could confide free of interruption and the intrigues of court. Eyes and enemies were everywhere. John of Brienne needed his friends.

'I am fortunate for your support, to have one as you so loyal and trustworthy beside me.'

'You will ever have me to watch over you, sir.'

'There are few I would prefer in such duty. Propelled by events, I fear we head fast for the abyss.'

'Outcome may yet alter, crisis be contained.'

'We would wish it so. But there is little at present to raise our spirits.'

'You have worthy companions to protect you, knights and lords devoted in their service to your realm.'

'Who among them may I rely upon? Who among them may I depend on for wise counsel and calm reflection when their estates burn and coffers dwindle?' Brienne stood grim-faced before a tapestry panel depicting his royal city. 'Where once the Saracens inhabited Acre, they could occupy again.'

'We shall repel them, sir.'

'I admire your certainty. And meantime Saphadin gathers forces to his side, dispatches raiding parties, harasses our interests and our lands.'

Indeed he did, mused the Lord of Arsur. It was perfect in planning and execution. Of no small consequence was that messengers sent from each side had been intercepted, letters offering negotiation and urging settlement had been lost. None were in mood for compromise. It showed in the farms laid waste, the corpses nailed by their tongues to barn doors, the livestock slaughtered or driven away. He had passed through blighted scenes and smouldering landscapes on his passage north from Arsur. Quite some achievement. His Knights of St Lazarus were doing well. He allowed a glimmer of satisfaction to enter his chill heart.

The regent stared at him. 'Do you believe my treaty with Saphadin and his infidel emirs is now void?'

'Some have wished it annulled since first you put your seal to it. Not I, sir. We can ill afford full confrontation.'

'Such reasoning little moves the barking dogs of the military Orders. They bay for war, for the red meat of Saracen dead.'

'Templars and Hospitallers cannot be sole arbiters of our response and fate.'

'When crisis beckons, they carry others with them. If I urge caution and restraint, attempt to still their fiery blood, I seem weak, am deemed a coward.'

'You are no faint-heart, sir.'

'Action not wisdom is demanded. I am grown isolated at Council, am buffeted by argument in favour of battle.'

'Better to be live ox than dead lion.'

'Not if I wish to placate the feverish warriors in our midst.'

'That way lies Hattin, the defeat of our army, the conquest of our lands by Saracens who outnumber and outfight us.' The Lord of Arsur peered earnestly at his regent, managed to volunteer a shudder. 'I was lucky to escape the field when so many did not, remember each incident and every knight who fell. I smelt the burning flesh of my Christian brothers, saw with my own eyes the royal tent sink, heard the terrible clamour, the clash of steel, the strike of the Mohammedan arrows. Peace is discarded easily by those who do not know war.'

A pretty enough speech, and he believed not a word. John of Brienne, however, appeared to draw comfort from it. He would be less than content had he known he was in the presence of his nemesis and that downfall was near. The royal guard was infiltrated, the royal infant nursed by an impostor, the royal palace threatened by forces unseen and within. There would be no stopping the realization of prophecy and vision, no counter to the dark might of the lord god Baphomet. Matters were in hand. The Lord of Arsur would smile and offer counsel, a shoulder on which to weep. Whatever it took, wherever it led. A plot matured over twenty-five years was bound to be ambitious in scope. The death agonies of a kingdom were more rewarding in close proximity.

In gesture of solidarity he reached and gripped the arm of the ageing ruler. 'I am here with you, my regent lord.'

'I can think of no greater reassurance.'

'Then be heartened, sir. Allies and like minds as ours are all about. I see the standards of the Lord of Jebail and his vassal Sir William de Picton too are presently in this city.'

'They come as you to pledge fealty and assistance.'

'Thus already are we a power to be reckoned.'

'Perhaps so.' John of Brienne massaged the fatigue from his eyes. 'Valiant souls, each one of you. Yet what are we against Saphadin? What course is there against an infidel sultan who, once so calm and cautious, turns rogue?'

'There will come a day of reckoning.'

'I hope it will be when we are equipped and manned and may hold our position.'

The Lord of Arsur stifled a yawn. John of Brienne could bellyache and whine, but he would not be saved. Saphadin too would be vexed, for events were accelerating beyond his control. In the meantime, inconsequential chat would suffice.

'How does the infant queen, your daughter, sir?'

'She prospers, is my joy and light in this desolation, the hope for Outremer.'

'Long may she reign. She is dear to us.'

'Mercifully, she is too young to gauge the turbulence in her kingdom. Thankfully, she is well protected from the ravages of politics and those who might wish her ill.'

'I pray it remains so.'

What he prayed for, planned for, was significantly darker. It was good to keep faith. As in every coastal city in the Latin realm, from Beirut to Jaffa, the gates of Acre were closed for the night and the portcullises brought down. As if evil could be so easily shut out. The Lord of Arsur listened and spoke, assumed the guise of confidant and friend who had at heart the interests of this noble king and his subjects. They were of value solely as dupes. He studied the face, wondering at the shape it might make when forming a scream.

'Lady Matilda.' The Lord of Arsur proffered a courteous nod.

'What brings you here, my lord?'

Things to do, people to kill. 'I come to provide buttress to my sovereign, to stand with him against gathering storm.'

'He is in need of your solace, my lord.'

'Alas, I cannot bring good news. There is too much distress in our land to speak otherwise. But I may at least provide amity and resolve to the court.'

'You honour us.'

'As you enchant Outremer with your beauty and grace, my lady.' For once he strayed from type and did not lie. 'Your father would well approve of how his daughter beguiles, of how she has grown in rank and reputation.'

'I try to serve his memory and to continue his work.'

'You could emulate none more revered.'

Her father had been a sanctimonious fool with a weakness for meddling involvement and for prying into matters beyond his concern. It had been unwise of him to follow the strands of conspiracy, to pursue phantom tales of treachery and double-dealing, of the location of the True Cross. A diligent man, now a dead knight. He had never quite liked or trusted the Lord of Arsur, and with the hindsight of the grave that judgement was astute. As it was, he had succumbed to surprise illness and bloody flux, had writhed his last in a soiled bed attended by a loving and grieving daughter. Case closed.

The Lord of Arsur contrived affectionate concern. 'News travels, even to Arsur, my lady. We have heard of your escape from the clutches of the Saracen horde.'

'Many innocents were caught.'

'Such is the nature of these raids, the bloodlust of the infidel.'

'Yet it was Saphadin who signed treaty of peace.'

'My memory is longer, my lady. But you will not hear me call for war. Like your father, and like John of Brienne, I will for ever champion the cause of harmony.'

'Some might find fault.'

'Let them. I am accustomed to the jibes of rash young men who know nothing of life but the inside of a wine flagon.'

She laughed lightly, tilting back her head, allowing him to appraise her exquisite features, her dancing green eyes, her long neck shrouded in its cloth *barbette*, her forehead ringed by gold-embroidered circlet. Such a very vulnerable throat. The gown was low-cut and scarlet: the colour of martyrdom. He took it as a positive sign.

'Your estates avoid the worst excess of the Saracens, my lady?'

'For the while. Yet I learn terrible things befall those in neighbouring land.'

'The enemy strikes at will. None are safe.'

'All who at present seek refuge in our city tell so in their eyes. My father would be stricken by this turmoil and their plight.'

'We must be glad he is with Our Lord and the saints.'

'Since Queen Maria died, it is as though we are cursed.'

Empathy exuded. 'Who may know?'

He did, of course. But revelation was for another time. With the same crafted politeness, he excused himself from her company and went on his way. Behind, Matilda watched, confused by courtship that involved no warmth, a presence defined by its absence. Without determining cause, the young noblewoman was troubled and discomforted. She stood for a long while.

*

Others were less concerned. In the palace stables two men conferred over the relative merits of their horses. One, the knight William de Picton, was large and bluff with the swagger of a true crusader, the worldly bearing of a veteran who had served with Richard Cœur de Lion. Equine flesh was his passion. But he was no fool, had seen enough death to value life and to cherish harmonious relations with the Moslem. Beside him was his liege baron the Lord of Jebail. Here was something more exotic, a perfumed creature robed in silks, a nobleman turned native, an ally of the regent who craved tranquillity, song and dance, who liked the Arabs and was rumoured to be partial to their boys. They were an unlikely but successful pairing of friends, and Outremer had benefited from their sway.

'Regard the neck, Sir William. It arches high, has elegance enough to see it stabled in the finest courts of Araby.'

'Keep your beast, my lord. My Norman would trample it as straw in battle.'

Jebail sighed in mild reproach. 'I trust it will not come to that.'

'In present clime, trust and hope may roll either way as dice.'

'Banish your gloom, Sir William. Even as Armageddon approaches and we live in the end of days, we should make merry and drink well.'

'Yet I still believe my steed has more pace and strength than yours.'

'Persist in your delusion. I have bred horses the Viceroy of Egypt himself covets.'

'Perhaps we shall ask him when his army arrives with that of Saphadin before the gates of Acre.'

'Again your melancholy.' The Lord of Jebail walked over to fraternize with a horse whose head extended in inquisitive greeting above its stall door. 'Is this not the animal that bore Lady Matilda away from the horrors of the Mohammedan attack?'

'It is.'

'A clever mount. We too should run for cover when all about is chaos.'

They shared the joke, pausing at the appearance of the Lord of Arsur in the dim light of the lantern. Mutual respect rather than warm camaraderie was their common bond, but they enjoyed the patronage and regard of the regent and gave him loyalty in return, promoted his commitment to trade and conciliation with the Saracen. Or so the Lord of Arsur made it seem. He smiled at his companions, would keep them guessing to the last.

'What say you, Arsur? Could my horse best that of Sir William?'

'In running or mating, my lord?'

'Excellent answer.' The nobleman turned to the knight. 'Shall we see how they fare when put to another?'

'Male or female, my lord?'

'In truth, I find it hard to choose.' The Lord of Jebail tittered and waggled his head.

The Lord of Arsur stared past him towards the silent stalls. 'How far we are here from the commotion of court and the fears of the realm.'

'I agree, my lord.' De Picton was happy to remain with the subject of horses. 'Grant me the odour of any stable, the stench of dung and hay, over the smell of crisis.'

'And crisis there is, Sir William. It is why I visit John of Brienne.'

'Why we too gather in Acre.'

Jebail waved his hand distractedly. 'I see none of it in my fief, for Jebail is left untouched by discord or raid.'

'You are fortunate, my brother lord.'

'Fruit is picked, goats are herded, fish are caught. Only a village simpleton would wish for war.'

'They may yet take over the village.'

'Not while I and Sir William live.' The Lord of Jebail peered enquiringly at his fellow noble, his gaze more astute than his plumage suggested. 'I know the Arab, the Turcoman and the Kurd, am intimate with his wiles and ways.'

You are closer than most to their rears, the Lord of Arsur silently conceded. 'We each of us have had our dealings with the Saracen.'

'There is not an emir or sheikh who would embrace the prospect of needless conflagration. Misunderstanding abounds. I shall take it upon myself to pay visit to the Sultan in Damascus, to cool the rising heat and break this wheel of hatred and anger.'

'Praiseworthy hopes, my lord. You are indeed a dove of peace.'

Flattered, Jebail smoothed his garments with well-kept fingers. 'I am a strutting peacock who still finds time to serve my king and Outremer.'

'You offer more than you will ever know. Journey of a different kind is called for.'

De Picton snorted. 'Riddles are not for me, Arsur.'

'So I shall make it plain.'

He sauntered across the flagstones and took up position at a distance. The scene was set, the stage cleared, and the pair of actors seemed confused. They looked about them, attempting to glimpse what sixth sense informed. A shiver of movement, a shadow, a falling away of certainty. Something jarred; something presaged danger. Doors swung and fears gained solid form. The Assassins had come to call.

'How is this, Arsur?' De Picton reached instinctively for his sword and found it was not there.

'Is this a trap?' The voice of Jebail followed, high-pitched and tremulous. 'Is it a trick? A jest of some kind?'

'Explain yourself, Arsur. Desist from this folly.'

Jebail shrank behind the protective bulk of his vassal knight. 'Defend me, Sir William. It is perfidy, treachery. What shall we do?'

'We will fight.'

A decision of no consequence, reflected the Lord of Arsur as the trio of killers closed. People died in different ways. The Lord of Jebail chose to shriek, attempted to dodge and plead and claw his way to imagined shelter that did not exist and would be hard to achieve with multiple blade-thrusts to his back. William de Picton performed as he had pledged, grappling and wrestling his opponents aside, until he staggered bellowing to his knees and pitched forward in a pool of his own blood. The Lord of Arsur observed dispassionately, a still figure in a dark cloak and with a face that did not move.

There was a muscle-twitch in the knight, residual energy that flipped him on his back. He should never have left his castle in Wales, thought the Lord of Arsur as he accepted a sword from an officer emerging through the murk and teased it through the ribs. Spasms ceased. Yet there remained unfinished business, the simple matter of three Assassins standing mute in docile surrender. They had done as demanded. The Lord of Arsur gave his direction and they were instantly cut down. As he watched, he pondered idly on their compatriots sent to Europe for the purpose of dispatching Otto of Alzey. Every conceivable aspect was covered, one successful outcome planned.

He knelt and began to apply blood to his face and clothing. 'What dread catastrophe has befallen our dear and gallant brothers, what sadness we stumble in, too late to prevent such hideous crime. Inform the regent. Call out the guard. Tell all we at least gave this unholy trinity of vile murderers a taste of our vengeful blades.'

It would not take long before palace and city erupted in alarm. Until then, he would sit quietly in contemplation while future hopes for the realm leaked away in a thickening and crimson slick around him. The doughty knight and effete baron were so much more useful in death. They were victims, icons, rallying points for an avenging Outremer. Conversely, he would be a live hero, a man on whom the weakened regent king would have no choice but to rely. Dependence bred control, would in turn facilitate conquest. Not bad for a brief encounter in a stable.

Nearby, spooked by the strangeness and proximity of events, horses were stamping and neighing fretfully in their boxes. The late Sir William de Picton would have appreciated that.

Stupefied by what he had seen, mesmerized by his own terror, the stablehand inched further back into the lightless reaches of the passageway. He should have resisted sleep, should have found the straw-lined berth less inviting. Now he was for it. He might be a simple lad, a worthless speck in the firmament populated by lords and ladies, but he knew treachery and unlawful slaying when it was laid before him like a butcher-shop. This noble Lord of Arsur was nothing more than a foul fiend, a cold-hearted slaughterman without morals or remorse. Whether to report or ignore it, that was the inconvenient question. Best to slip away, to clear the head, to weigh the rewards and drawbacks of bearing witness.

The decision was made for him. An arm circled from behind and pressed a blade against his throat, sour breath and a harsh whisper scraping at his ear.

'What prize have we here?'

'I saw nothing, I swear it to you.'

'Yet you quake as though you did.'

The stablehand trembled in dumb confusion. 'I was sleeping, unaware of things. I beg you, spare me.'

'Verdict is already reached.'

'No harm is done, you have my word. On my life, I will stay silent.'

'We believe such promise.' The officer of the Lord of Arsur planted a Judas kiss lightly on his cheek.

News spread and men came running. They had heard of murder and of heroism, of the Lord of Arsur confronting and slaying a host of heathen Assassins. It was not idle rumour. What they found was a scene of contained carnage and a noble lord bloodied and victorious in his duties. The Lord of Arsur could do no wrong.

'Again, young Otto.'

The sixteen year-old pranced forward, whirling a quarterstaff in concerted effort to break the defences of the friar. He had been taught by the best, had learned the art of fighting with sword or stave, the tricks and acrobatics that would allow him to fell a bullock let alone a ragged Franciscan of well-advanced years. But so far Brother Luke remained impervious to attack.

'I thought the Church more welcoming, friar.'

'It may yet upend the rich and unrepentant sinner.' The priest lazily rolled the haft between his palms. 'You must work with your hands to know how to use them. Pretend you are a mean vagabond of the road and not a delicate princeling from a castle.'

'You will have delicacy served down your throat, Brother Luke.'

'Oh?' The Franciscan smiled and lowered his weapon.

'Put up your guard. I am more practised than a Perfect and his slovenly band of Cathars.'

'Though clumsier than a blind mule with a missing leg.'

'You slight me.'

'I goad you for a purpose.'

'And what purpose is that, Brother Luke?' Otto spun the staff adroitly in his hands. 'To make your sputtering apology the sweeter to my ears?'

'To jangle your nerves; to test you; to rouse you to fury and misjudgement.'

'I am as cool as any snowcap on a mountain.'

'As likely to melt away.'

The friar lifted his heavy stick. Tips met and eyes engaged. Mock combat could be an intense and hard-fought game.

'Prepare to be vanquished, Brother Luke.'

'Instead I shall prepare your landing.'

Riposte provoked charge. The young noble moved on his opponent, working his staff in a clattering rally of strike and counter-thrust. They battled on, trading blows, the friar conceding not an inch of ground, appearing to expend not a scrap of effort. Otto pummelled in vain. The staff went airborne, spinning from his grasp.

'Less haste and more thought, Otto of Alzey.' Brother Luke hoisted his winning stave across his shoulders. 'Should you lose your balance, you are dead. Should you lose your arms, you are dead.'

'I will remember it.' Otto leaned on his knees, gasping breathless from exertion.

'Impetuousness is the finish of many young men. To dance well you must learn the steps.'

'I cannot match you in mastery of the staff.'

'Yet you may improve.'

'That is my intent, Brother Luke.'

'Speed, cunning . . .' The friar sidestepped as Otto flew at his midriff, tripping him into a tumbling sprawl. 'And judgement. These are concerns for the eager pupil.'

Lying winded on his back, Otto managed a croaking laugh. 'I concede.' The end of a staff tapped on his chest.

'We shall never foretell fate, so prepare for all instance.'

Brother and sister sat beside each other and watched the display. Here on the coastal plain before Livorno they could rest awhile beneath a tree, could bind their feet and gaze at an autumn-marbled sky stooping towards a darkening sea. More miles had been covered, another calendar month entered. Behind them, the rugged seaward tail of the Apennines, the generosity of Sarzana, the brooding wariness of Pisa. Ahead, the trudging pace towards Venturino, Grosseto, Civitavecchia and Rome. New words and places to encounter, fresh incident and danger to greet.

Kurt rested his head against his hands and closed his eyes. There was no escaping the absence of his friends, no ignoring the dull pain that reminded him of their loss. At times he thought he saw them, could sense them at his shoulder. But like ghosts they would vanish when he turned. Of ten who had set out from their village, only he and Isolda remained. Perhaps they were touched by God, or maybe they were cursed. He missed the tomfoolery of Hans, the steadfast-ness of Egon, the knowingness of Albert. He grieved for the tinkling voice of little Lisa and the optimism and chattering mirth of Zepp and Achim. Goatherd, blacksmith, bird-scarer, a generation gone.

'Why do they rehearse combat when we go on peaceful pilgrimage, Kurt?'

The youngster shrugged. 'You heard Brother Luke. We prepare for all events.'

'But Nikolas in Cologne told us there would be no fighting, that we would reach Palestine with words of love.'

'He told us also that the seas would part.'

'It is not the same.'

'Hospitallers nurse the sick and carry swords. Templars pray as monks and wear chain-mail.' He turned on his side to look at her. 'Would you prefer we were captured by Cathars or submitted to the blades of the killers who slew Hans?'

'I do not know.'

'Whether it is Gunther or a band of heretics we face, I am glad for the friar and Otto beside us, happy they sharpen their skills.'

'We would for certain be in worse circumstance without them.'

Her look softened, her breath grew more shallow, as she traced the movements of the young noble. She could never criticize Otto for long.

'He is a lord and we peasants, Isolda. I cannot see him taking you as his bride.'

'I may dream, Kurt. I will let you visit when I dwell in a castle and sit in the great hall on a throne.'

'Will you throw me in a dungeon for claiming you a fool?'

She smiled, her attention still resting on the older boy. 'I would forgive you if my lord and husband demanded it.'

'Search elsewhere, Isolda.'

'He is so fine a boy.'

'Egon too was fine, was loyal and devoted, humble and kind. You wronged him, Isolda.'

She glanced at him, contrition reddening her cheeks, hurt and shame flickering in her eyes. 'Would that I could ask his forgiveness.' Her hand reached out for his, pressing his fingers between her own. 'When did my little brother turn so wise?'

He had no answer. Yet he was aware that he had changed, that he was not the happy-go-lucky child who had stood in the square before the great cathedral of Cologne. Too much had been lost, and too much learned. What he had once dismissed as mere escapade, as chance to discover and strike out from his village, had evolved into more. It was a feat of endurance and faith invested with the cries of others and the lives of his companions. He owed it to them to continue, to see what they no longer could, to carry back what they had sought. One hundred and eighty miles from Rome. A pilgrimage and crusade with meaning, after all. Whatever he faced, he would reach the Holy Land and bring home the True Cross.

Trumpets called, cymbals clashed, and a thousand infantry marched in step across the square. Their commander-in-chief Saphadin, Sultan of Damascus, reviewed them from his balcony dais. Flanked by senior emirs, resplendent in his robes of state, he knew the meaning of presentation, the importance of majesty and spectacle. A ruler could last beyond usefulness and life-expectancy if his nerve held and his image impressed. Perception could quell unrest, awe put down a coup. Armed troops drawn from Mosul and the Jezireh also helped.

'What splendid sight, al-Adil.'

The elderly leader stared down his aquiline nose at the scene. 'It will soon be the turn of the horsemen, and then you shall see something to inspire.'

'Already the infidels cannot match us in standing force. They will tremble, cower at our advantage in men and arms.'

'I have yet to witness it. But should it cause them to abandon their folly, to pause in their blind action, I will be glad enough.'

'Abandon? Pause?' The officer scoffed. 'Al-Adil, they send the Assassins against us, wage war on our caravans and trade, unleash their Templar and Hospitaller madmen against our defenceless villages and towns.'

'I am aware of the tally.'

A Turcoman replied. 'You are aware also, al-Adil,

of the silence of these Frankish dogs. They will not speak, do not intend to parley.'

'And what is our message and intent? We already pull men from the fields and farms, strip cities of their garrisons, frighten our Moslem rivals in Aleppo with our gathering of strength.'

'It is good to scare them, al-Adil.'

'We scare ourselves, convince ourselves there is no alternative to armed engagement. Effects may be unforeseen, results beyond our control.'

Another general spoke. 'For thirty years I have served your family in peace and combat, al-Adil. I know the devils of Outremer as well as any, have stared in their eyes, walked on their corpses, planted banners on their ramparts, charged their ranks at Hattin. The sword is the only message they understand.'

'They comprehend too the subtlety of power, the weighing of risk, the exercise of caution. Why else did they entreat and sign for peace?'

'To purchase time we can ill afford.' The old military campaigner fixed his leader with accusatory glare. 'We know crusade will come. Let us strike now, rip the landing-stages from beneath their feet.'

'You may pay on the battlefield with your life the consequence of error. Mistake on my part, and I forfeit the kingdom and the sacred lands of Islam.'

'Your brother Salah ad-Din would not have hesitated to right wrongs and avenge slights.'

'My brother Salah ad-Din was advised by me.'

Saphadin raised a hand and his coterie fell silent. He welcomed debate, the guidance of his closest. But he would not permit them to stray into outright dissent, would not accept the heedless ways and untrammelled aggression of his cavalry son al-Mu'azzam. Bellicosity had to be tempered by judgement; the unleashing of punishment raids on Acre and Haifa and the outlying estates of the Christian nobility should ever be twinned with negotiation. He was sixty-nine years old, John of Brienne sixty-four. Old men could talk; aged rulers could compromise. Nothing was too late.

For a moment he appeared hypnotized by the rhythmic pace below, by the crash of armour-scaled feet on compacted earth.

The trance broke. He turned, his eyes seeking out and finding a portly *hajib*, a chamberlain, loitering silent and diplomatic in the background.

'Take cavalry escort and proceed under flag of truce to the infidel regent John of Brienne. Demand explanation, unearth the truth. If we are to go to war, it shall not be until we exhaust the trail of possibility and accord.'

Bowing low, the chamberlain retreated to his task.

In Acre, the broken body of a stablehand was discovered lying at the base of a high fortification known as the Accursed Tower.

✝
Chapter 9

From beneath the cover of a wide-brimmed hat, a wayside beggar observed their arrival in the city of Rome. They seemed weary, justifiably so for young and old who had journeyed far and suffered the privations of the road. Even the two horses plodded with the somnolent tread of sleepwalkers. Tired travellers were unwary, and that was to the good. They would not be anticipating threat. There was Otto of Alzey, young noble, principal target. Still a thing of rare and fine looks, his face begrimed yet gracious and cheerful in its aspect. A pair of children accompanied him, a boy and girl, sole survivors of their party. And with them was a weathered and tattered friar of no consequence. Hardly a group to impress, insignificant but for the fact that Otto of Alzey should not be alive, that Otto of Alzey was destined to perish here in the streets of this city. He and his companions were heading south-east, and the lone Assassin began to follow.

'Mind your step, you cur!'

He dodged a barrel and found himself facing the choleric eyes and wrathful tongue of a cooper. The man was being unreasonable, took the submissive dip of his head as excuse for unleashing further oaths. The Assassin backed away. He wanted no argument or attention; he was bent on more important venture. But the barrel-maker did not accept the generous offer of continued existence, seemed to think whipping a vagrant fine sport. He raised his fists and filled the ground this miserable stranger and beggar had conceded. That beggar now viewed him through narrowing eyes.

Shouting and belligerence were so uncouth. In a second, he could break the arms and collarbone of the man; in two, could drive his nose through his head; in three, could hook out the eyes; in four, could castrate. A clean down-stamp and the windpipe, the spine or the chest would be crushed. All in the line of duty and professionalism.

Deftly, in spirit of supplication, he grabbed the wrist of the craftsman, all the while pleading and sobbing for mercy. Pressure intensified. The man gasped, whimpering and falling to his knees as bone and cartilage compressed, as severed nerves fired pain direct to a disbelieving brain. The Assassin walked on, leaving behind a crippled mass that had lost its livelihood with use of a hand.

The Rhineland youth and his friends were making steady progress, the heads of his grey mare and black stallion nodding above the street throng. There could only be one destination, the Lateran Palace, home to Innocent III, the Sun Pontiff, Bishop of Rome, Vicar of Christ, greatest and most crusading of all the popes in history. Audience and blessing were what every pilgrim craved. Each to his own calling. The killing he himself intended was not merely for religion or his sheikh, nor solely to please the Lord of Arsur. Since the slaying of his fellow agents on the road beyond Chambéry, it had become more pressing and personal. He would inflict vengeance with a long knife, would stick it to young Otto when the time arose. Ignored in the multitude, the beggar maintained his shuffling pace.

Had he waited at his station on the verge of the city, he would have seen later that day the arrival of a different and larger group of dust-shrouded pilgrims. Like the Assassin, they too were disguised. The Perfect was bringing his Believers to a place they hated with all their might. But when in Rome . . .

'Rise, my children.'

Cupping their chins in his hands, Pope Innocent III smiled and gently encouraged Kurt and Isolda to their feet. Trembling and wordless they complied, their eyes bright and wide in trance-like amazement, their tongues tied in trepidation. Before them was the most powerful figure on earth, a priest prince in papal tiara and raiments of white. He could launch wars and absolve sin, excommunicate kings and converse with God. None could challenge his authority without facing eternal damnation. So brother and sister remained silent and stared at the ground.

Innocent surveyed them, his voice soft and German fluent. 'I am higher than man and yet lower than God.

It is He alone you must fear.' He bent towards Isolda. 'What is your age, daughter?'

'I believe fourteen years, Reverend Lord.'

'And you, my son?'

'Twelve summers, Reverend Lord,' Kurt managed to mutter.

'Too young for such long journey, for the perils and rigours you have doubtless faced.'

'We find Rome, Reverend Lord, intend with our souls and strength to reach Jerusalem.'

'Ah, Jerusalem.' Innocent nodded. 'A name to fill our hearts with both bitterness and joy. Jerusalem is lost. Jerusalem has resisted capture by the Christian princes of Europe, by Cœur de Lion himself.'

Isolda spoke. 'We are not knights or princes and have no army, Reverend Lord. But we are the young and humble, the ones who carry love for Our Saviour to the lands of the Saracen. They will see the truth of what we speak.'

'I have seen many lost who hold the same conviction.'

'Bless us, I beseech you, Reverend Lord.'

'My daughter, I will not order you back to whence you came, nor deny you the sanction for which you ask. Each of us has a quest, attempts to walk closer with God. But pilgrimage is for the grizzled and old such as Brother Luke, for those who stumble towards their end, rather than virtuous youth so early in their life.'

Summoning his courage, still gazing downward, Kurt spoke up. 'Reverend Lord, Holy Father, we are the two left from our village. Our friends all are gone. There is nothing left to return for. We must continue, must travel to the Holy Land.'

'I commend your valour and admire your odyssey, my son.'

'Preachers told us that only the pure at heart will conquer the infidel, will reunite the True Cross to Christendom.'

'They must have been persuasive.'

'We still march, Reverend Lord.'

'Although it is my decree and indulgence that send so many thousand forth, I weep for their piteous torment.'

'There is Otto and Brother Luke to guard us, Reverend Lord.'

'Is that so?' The pontiff raised his eyes to the friar and the noble boy before patting the shoulder of the youngster. 'Then I shall hold them to their duty and will blame them should they fail it.'

Kurt blinked, imagined he was tricking himself, inventing the scene. He had never before met a pope, never entered a palace or seen such things, never witnessed the richness and display. There were the treasures and tapestries, the painted frescoes and reliquaries. There were the berobed prelates and richly dressed ambassadors, the white habits and emblazoned blood-red crosses of the Templars, the black mantles and eight-pointed crosses of the Hospitallers. This was the centre of the world, of the known universe. And he and Isolda, Otto and Brother Luke, stood at its inner core.

'What of you, Otto of Alzey, son of Wilhelm? Do you also make pilgrimage?'

'Of a kind, Reverend Lord. I seek my father, a Hospitaller knight from whom I have not heard these ten years past.'

'I am told you bear a sword and don *cuirie* of leather. While this boy and girl undertake mission of peace, it seems you are inclined to more warlike persuasion.'

'I aim not for battle, Reverend Lord. But where there is threat I must prepare.'

Innocent inclined his head. 'At least there is one I may trust to carry blade against the heathen Saracen. I find the royal courts of Europe less eager in this task.'

He made the sign of the cross and in Latin committed his visitors to the care and mercy of God. A precious moment. Interview was closed, and the children were ushered from the chamber by a severe and elderly cardinal less welcoming than the Pope. Kurt glanced at him, noted the curl of his lip, the disapproval cloaked in simple piety. The man appeared more desiccated than the rest, perhaps dried out by decades spent in prayer and study. Kurt felt the urge to converse.

'Was that truly gold on the handles of the door?'

'It was.'

'And the incense-burners. Were they set with precious stones?'

'You saw correct.'

'I wish we could tell our friends of what we

experience, of how our Reverend Lord has blessed and sanctified our journey.'

'The Holy Father is charitable and generous with his time.'

'He honours us.'

'No, he bears and suffers you, bids you go on your way.'

Cardinal Cencio Savelli did not much like the young.

The Franciscan had remained behind. In the background, a bell tolled distant and muffled from the basilica of St John Lateran, cathedral seat of the papacy. It was a comforting sound, the heartbeat of a religion, the pulse of a body politic whose influence spread far with fire and word. Yet here was a more basic scene. A humble friar and an all-powerful pontiff, two priests separated by rank and age and speaking only feet apart.

'It is four years since last we met, Brother Luke, when you came to Rome with the poor man of Assisi.'

'I remember it well, Reverend Lord.'

'As do the cardinals of the Sacred College. There were few in favour of the audience I granted.'

'Brother Francis and our fellow penitents are beholden, Reverend Lord.'

'I have no regret. The world is fairer and more sweet for the ecclesiastical tonsures I allowed you, for your preachings of repentance and love.'

'We are unworthy of such praise.'

'I speak nothing but the truth.' Innocent stepped to a carved wood table and decanted water to a pair of chalices. 'Where now is Brother Francis?'

'He sets sail from Dalmatia for the Holy Land, bids me follow and shepherd children he hears are destined for that place.'

Innocent paused and put down the silver jug. 'For seven hundred years, since the reign of Emperor Constantine, a pope has reigned in this palace. I fancy none ever saw a thing so piteous as these innocents and striplings struggling towards Palestine.'

'Your plenary indulgence, your offer of absolution to those who send proxies on crusade, encourage such event.'

'You criticize, Brother Luke?'

'I comment.'

And he noticed much. Experience had taught him how to read his fellow man, how to penetrate the mask of office. He would never underestimate Pope Innocent III. The pontiff had the mind of a canon lawyer, the groomed charisma of a prince, the ambition of an emperor. It was a powerful and dangerous combination. Son of the Count of Segni, nephew to Pope Clement III, scion of the noble Roman house of Scotti, he had been a cardinal by twenty-nine, was in 1198 at the age of thirty-seven elected supreme head of the Church. Success and magnificence abounded. The Franciscan would not forget that this was the pope who had sanctioned the brutal sack of Constantinople, the extinction of the Byzantine Church. Capable of shedding a tear, certainly. Able to inspire and lead, to manipulate and control, without a doubt. He wanted something, otherwise he would not have invited discourse.

Innocent approached and proffered the goblet. 'My apology it is not wine.'

'Such comforts are not for me, Reverend Lord.'

'Indeed not. So drink instead the produce of a lowly spring.' They both sipped. 'Strange is it not, Brother Luke? Christian knights answer my call to arms with victorious crusade against the Moorish infidels in Spain, triumph at Las Navas de Tolosa in this July past. They strive too with holy war against the heretic Cathars in France and other places. Yet they dare not strike against the Saracens in the east.'

'Travel is arduous and the risks high, Reverend Lord.'

'I thought God demanded of us such sacrifice.'

'Man is frail and weak.'

'The leaders of Christendom weaker.' Innocent lowered his cup. 'Even the Templars, my angels of death, lose their impulse to kill for our faith. Even John of Brienne and his idle lords seek easy life with the Sultan of Damascus.'

'They have their reason.'

'Sloth and cowardice are no reason. Thus do mere children take their place, stride with cheerful purpose for the sacred shrines we claim to venerate.'

Thus do you prepare to reveal your aims, the friar thought. He waited. The restless energy of the pontiff alighted on him and did not shift.

'Reports come to me, Brother Luke. They tell of

unrest and disturbance in Outremer, of strife where there has been calm, murder where there is typically none.'

'I know nothing of it, Reverend Lord.'

'But you shall. You will work diligently to find cause and fact, will pry and probe, will search from highest tower to lowest cave. Then you will make expeditious dispatch to me.'

'I am to be your spy?'

'My observer. What better concealment than the filthy rags of a mendicant, the aged and dusty bones of a roving friar?'

'There is my obligation to the children.'

'They will add lustre and detail to your story, divert suspicion from yourself.'

The Franciscan gazed back unwavering. 'Reverend Lord, I am a man of simple outlook, a beggar and preacher of eternal love.'

'Yet we live in state of eternal war. Your loyalty is to me, Brother Luke.'

'It is to God.'

'I am leader of His Church on earth.' The pontiff leaned close, his eyes searching. 'Do not disappoint. There is narrow margin between those who wear sackcloth and preach in open fields and heretics who hate Rome and must be consigned to the fire.'

'Torture and death hold no fear for me, Reverend Lord.'

'Though you may fear for Brother Francis and your brethren of Assisi.'

'You would threaten us?'

'I shall do what is needed to protect and preserve the concerns of the Lateran. Go forth and discover. Be my eyes, my ears, my diviner of intentions.'

'To what end?'

'Power, Brother Luke. It is ever about power.'

Follow the road inland from Ascalon and the coast, continue past Blanchegarde and the dusty town of Latrun, climb into the Judaean hills, and with three days march behind him the average general would have brought his forces to Beit-Nuba. Arab country; waypoints in crusader history. Perched on its mound, the squat fort dominated the land about, acting as lookout and defence, guarding since Roman times the western approach to the city of Jerusalem that lay twelve miles beyond. Twice in 1192 King Richard I of England had reached this spot. He had been hampered by weather, by the desertion of the French, by impending starvation, by threat of encirclement from an avenging Moslem army tramping up from Egypt. And so he had retreated, taking his Englishmen back to the enclaves of Outremer, losing for ever the chance to capture the holy city he coveted.

A wasted opportunity, the Lord of Arsur reflected. He was walking the battlements with the fort commander, an unlikely ally given his status as Moslem and Turcoman, as dependable officer in the service of Sultan Saphadin. Trust could be so misplaced. When an emir was passed over for promotion, he could grow bitter; when a functionary had costs and needs, he could be bought. The commander's grievances had

not been difficult to exploit. They made him suscep-
tible to bribery, in turn opened him up to blackmail.
Of such things were the most fruitful collaborations
born.

'You have our last consignment of weapons?'

'Yes, my lord. Stored as you command and ready for
use when called upon.'

'I count on your similar readiness.'

'Rely on it, my lord.'

'It is important that I may. And should you falter in
any way, you shall meet ten thousand agonies before
you enter paradise.'

The man understood, swallowed hard in his
response. It was part of his working relationship with
this brooding Frank from Arsur. He could live with it,
would do his utmost not to die for it.

'May I ask why such quantity of items is required,
my lord?'

'You may not.' The Lord of Arsur stared him down.
'Nor may you enquire of the seven of my chosen men
left here with you at my departure.'

'Seven, my lord? I already have a garrison.'

'Consider it enlarged. They are to be lodged in
the gate towers, will not fraternize with any but their
own.'

'My soldiers will ask questions.'

'To which you shall avoid reply.'

'It will take money to quarter and feed extra mouths,
to purchase the silence and loyalty of my troops.'

'I am glad it is no matter of conscience.'

The Lord of Arsur continued his tour, pacing to

a flight of spiral steps and descending into the cooling gloom of the interior. Richard Cœur de Lion was not the sole leader who could use Beit-Nuba as start line and forward base for grand strategy and all-conquering design. He, Lord of Arsur, would improve on the record of the English king. For months, covered wagons had arrived full-laden at this site and soon after trundled home lighter on their wheels. Pre-positioning was under way, a build-up that paralleled his steady dismantling of Mohammedan and Christian kingdoms, his staggered destruction of John of Brienne and Saphadin. As their worlds burned, he would seize the day and take Jerusalem; as their eyes were diverted, he would strike them down and assume their crowns. No easy undertaking. Yet he was confident of victory, certain his enemies were unprepared for the looming apocalypse. This bleating Saracen officer would be grateful for having chosen the winning side.

They emerged into the castle grounds, a lower ward protected by walls and girded by workshops and stables. It reeked of abandonment, reinforced the image of a forgotten outpost of previous conflict. The very illusion he desired. For twenty years the fort had gone ignored, its manpower dwindling, its importance dismissed in a land now under Moslem control. The threat to Jerusalem had evaporated as quickly as the fortunes and army of King Richard. So it seemed.

At the barked order of a sergeant, men came running. In front of the baron and his Moslem turncoat, the cultivated scene of dereliction fell away, its layers of camouflage pulled aside to reveal the hidden reality within. False walls dropped, earth-encrusted frames and trapdoors lifted or slid back across the ground. Exposed were the engines of war. There were the fork-beams of catapults, the counterweights of mangonels, the wheeled platforms of ballista machines. Everything that either besieged or besieger might require, of which a campaigning emperor might dream.

'We have not been idle, my lord.'

'And you convince me how appearance may deceive.' The Lord of Arsur did not show a flicker of satisfaction. 'I expect you to keep up your guard, to present a usual aspect to the world outside. Nothing must draw attention to Beit-Nuba.'

'You have my word.'

'As I also have your soul. While the rulers of Damascus and Outremer choose in their maddened dotage to tear each other assunder, you shall sit tranquil in this crumbling fortress.'

'Until what time, my lord?'

His master was advancing to inspect the lowered structure of a giant battle-sling. 'At the hour of my choosing, you will learn.' He patted the timber, ran his fingers along the coiled rope. 'We have more active purpose for our hands than to wring them as the rest do in these benighted days.'

'It is privilege to serve in your employ, my lord, an honour to offer what aid we may.' Obsequious Mohammedans could say the kindest things.

'Are the dungeons prepared?'

'Arranged as you desire and primed for their occupancy, my lord.'

'Then we are set fair for the venture that unfolds.'

He looked upward, shading his eyes to gauge the position of the sun. A glorious day. By his reckoning, and through intelligence gleaned from Damascus, the next phase of collapse was about to begin.

This infernal heat. It seemed worse in the gully, the rocks reflecting glare, the high cliff walls stilling the air to the heavy consistency of a swamp. The *hajib* cursed and swatted away a fly. He preferred indolence and the sybaritic pleasures of court, was trained as chamberlain to manage the palace household, to assess slaves, to choose the dancing-girls and delicate platters that would grace the daily routines of his sultan. True, Saphadin was a little more austere than was quite necessary. But he could be generous, was always fair, right up to the moment when he chose his senior chamberlain to act as dove of peace to the Christians of Outremer. It was unjust and absurd. A sorbet flavoured with almonds would be welcome; a mounted servant able to angle the parasol more effectively would be a miracle. He cleared his throat of dust and spat it to the side.

'Where are the scouts?'

A captain replied. 'Well ahead, your honour. They will soon appear if encounter is made.'

'Ensure the pennant-bearers carry high our flags of truce. I do not wish to be misjudged as commander of a raid.'

He backhanded the sweat from his brow, rocked uncomfortably in his saddle. It was no way to treat a fat man. There were others more suited to the role of ambassador: those who were born to the saddle or the diplomatic joust. They could keep their vocation. He was an urbanite, a traveller only between cushions and across silk carpets. Perhaps it was why the Sultan had plucked him from among his coterie. The infidel Latins would listen to one so close to Saphadin, would recognize that a chamberlain spoke from the heart and home of his Moslem overlord. War would be to the detriment of all.

The captain offered his water-flask, and the chamberlain drank. 'What attraction is there to this life of soldiery?'

'Had you charged the infidels on horseback, you would not ask, your honour.'

'I have not, so I do.' He gulped again and returned the bottle. 'The flies, the burning sun, the ache of the body. If Allah had wished me to suffer such conditions, He would have made me a lizard to dwell beneath a rock.'

'There is no disgrace in leaving behind the harems and perfumed baths, the fountains and shaded courtyards.'

'And precious little point.'

'Our calling is more harsh, our reward different.'

'I see no reward in lowly *jamakiyah* payment, no reward in blistered skin and a lungful of dust.'

'One day you may need to fight, your honour. One day you may feel the joy of lifting a sword in anger, of pitting yourself against a brutish Frank and cutting him through in the name of Allah the Most Merciful.'

The courtier managed a weak laugh. 'It shall be an age yet.'

He was wrong. Ahead, a figure had appeared on a pale horse, emerging from the cover of a *tal*, an artificial mound of debris favoured by bandits and ambushers in these parts. Yet there was nothing to cause alarm. He was alone, a curiosity dressed in the plain mantle of an unidentified knight, his face obscured by a hood. A peculiar sight in a strange place. The chamberlain craned to see, turning to look at the captain and back to the apparition. Heat and light could create mirage, chance encounter stretch the bounds of courtly protocol. The visitor raised his hand.

Speaking in French, the *hajib* called out. 'We greet you also, friend. We come in peace and under flag of truce for parley with John of Brienne, regent of Outremer.'

Not a word was uttered in reply. On the advice of his officer, the chamberlain attempted Italian and English before resorting to his native tongue. The fool did not answer, but sat immobile and staring, his arm elevated in challenge or welcome. Frustrated, unable to summon explanation, the courtier shouted louder.

'Move aside. We will proceed.' Horse and rider failed to obey.

On command, twenty Mamluk cavalrymen lowered their spears. Whatever the mission of this soft and scented chamberlain, they were not about to cede ground or honour to an infidel who blocked their path. Silence was disrespectful, as good as a declaration of threat. They should have checked to their flanks.

The hand dropped. In a shattering instant the scene was blood-drenched, jerked from the recognizable to the unbelievable in a matter of seconds. Crossbow-bolts, double-headed and travelling straight, punctured the air, striking men and horses, tearing from them sounds that were seldom heard. Had he time to think, the chamberlain might have appreciated the trap. But he was otherwise occupied, penetrated by a brace of steel-tipped quarrels that quite took his breath and spine away. Around him, the tableau was folding in on itself, reduced to a last stand where no one moved and no one stood.

At the head of the extinct column, his sword drawn, the captain urged his horse in final and vengeful charge for the knight. The ploy had been anticipated. Caltrops flew, the small and spiked devices scattering in a metal snowstorm on the ground, piercing hooves, throwing the rider. Rage and instinct must have driven the man on. Climbing to his feet, he succeeded in a few tottering and ungainly steps before slumping in the dirt, a host of the deadly burrs embedded in his back. Far behind, one of his troops was making poor his escape, galloping in headlong dash for the rear of the canyon. A hawser uncoiled and went taut across his path, its grapple-iron catching on an opposing rock. Rope and neck connected, and the body spun.

In the quiet aftermath, the leader of the leper knights limped among the dead. God bless St Lazarus and all his works. Carefully, painfully, he picked at the flap of the document-pouch carried within the saddlebag of the chamberlain and extracted the letter. It would be from Saphadin to John of Brienne, a personal plea for negotiation and understanding. Henceforth, and by order of the Lord of Arsur, it was surplus to requirement.

His face provoked a memory, distant or recent she could not say. Isolda scanned the crowd. It had been the briefest of glimpses, a beggar man with a wide hat, just another adult in a press of humans that thronged and swamped the senses. Yet that single glance disturbed her. The eyes were too intense to mean well, the mouth too tight to ever want to smile. Surely there was explanation. But Kurt was busy conversing with Otto, Brother Luke was carving passage through the Roman streets. She would put it down to fatigue. Besides, her young brother would only laugh and tell her not to worry.

'We are arrived.'

The friar motioned them to his side as he stood before the strong oaken door of a preceptory set behind an iron grille. It was a modest affair, a dormitory building with narrow windows and few stylistic features of any note. Its occupants preferred such anonymity.

Kurt squinted at it, puzzled. 'What kind of house is this, Brother Luke?'

'The kind that is closed to the outside, which wields clandestine power and holds all manner of privilege.'

'Does a family live here?'

'Of a sort.'

Otto joined in. 'Why do we visit?'

'A question I should ask myself.' Brother Luke reached for a bell-rope and tugged. 'Observe.'

It took several minutes and a number of peals before activity stirred within. Eventually, a hatch swung aside and a pair of suspicious eyes surveyed them through the opening. A male voice followed, its tone as unwelcoming as the glower.

'We have no alms to give.'

'I seek neither food nor sanctuary, brother.'

'Then if it is confession and absolution you demand, go instead and find a church.'

'Is this the way to treat one you have known through previous visit, one with whom you have in the past broken bread?'

'I know you not.'

'Come, Brother Mario. I am old, but my memory does not fail.'

Slowly, with a pace that suggested both reluctance and calculation, the bolts were thrown and the door pulled wide. Confronting the Franciscan and the three youngsters was the stark red cross of the Temple.

'Peace be upon you, Brother Mario.'

'And on you also, Brother Luke.' The Templar made no effort to unlock the metal gate. 'What brings you to our door?'

'The spirit of friendship and chance journey through these parts.'

'You bring attendants.'

'They are the waifs and lambs I take with me to Palestine. What better way to imbue them with the fervour of pilgrimage and sacrifice than to acquaint them with your Order of Poor Fellow Soldiers of Christ?'

It provoked a sneer from the Templar. 'I do not recall we have ever served as example to you, Brother Luke. The Knights Templar embrace holy war, the purity of violence, while you eschew it. The Knights Templar ride out to do battle with Lucifer and his heathen Saracens, and you roam with bare feet and preach repentance and kind acts.'

'We are all of us Christian.'

'Not all of us garbed in the sackcloth of a vagabond.'

The friar smiled. 'Did you not as I make sacred *charism* of poverty? Did you not as I undertake to comfort the weak and helpless?'

'Each interprets that as he must.' Distrust was solidifying to hostility. 'Your sermon is done. You should depart.'

'And miss occasion to greet old friends? What of Knight Brother Julius? Sergeant Brother James?'

'Away on holy retreat.'

He lied. It was in the nuance, the tilt of the eyes, the unscripted language of the body. Everyone had their secrets, Brother Luke decided. After all, he would not be telling the children of his conversation with the Pope, would not be confiding in Innocent tales of his travels and of how he had made discovery in other places and far-flung parts. Templar commanderies had been emptied, Templar estates denuded of their workforce. Hidden exodus and concealed reason were in play. *You will work diligently to find cause and fact.*

He always did, with or without the authority of the pontiff. Arrogance was the fault-line of the Templars. It was time to utilize and follow it, to pick out further strands of his investigation. The Franciscan was sure they would lead to Outremer, that he walked in a true direction.

'You dream, Isolda. We must keep pace.'

She turned at his call, seeing the excitement in his face, the cheer this city brought to the soul of any boy. If only she shared the confidence of her brother.

'I thought I remembered something, a man behind us, Kurt.'

'Among this horde? You imagine.'

'I have seen him before, I know it.'

'Every merchant is the same; every drover and storeman wears similar dress.'

'It was the face, Kurt.'

'Do not fuss. We have our nobleman and friar near.' The twelve-year-old wrapped an arm across her shoulders and skipped her on.

She was right: Kurt had laughed and told her not to worry.

✝

✝

Chapter 10

Candle smoke and incense fumes filled the interior of the basilica of St John Lateran, and the prayers of Brother Luke rolled strong and reassuring in the dimness. Kurt squeezed shut his eyes and repeated the incantations. Alongside, Isolda and Otto knelt in veneration before the cross, their heads bowed and lips moving. After so long on the road, there was something comforting in the ancient solidity of these walls, something disquieting in making preparation to leave.

The friar faced them. 'Our prayers are done, my lambs. If we are to catch ship, now we must away.'

'Can we not stay in Rome a while longer?' It was Isolda who asked.

'We may wait, yet neither weather nor any mariner shall. The sea grows fierce, the risk of shipwreck with it. So let us gird ourselves and march before we come to founder.'

Kurt clambered to his feet. 'Will you teach us new conjury and song, Brother Luke?'

'It will be my delight.'

They proceeded outside, Otto buckling on his sword, the Franciscan pointing to the cityscape and telling tales of previous emperors and popes. Each account encouraged a stream of questions.

'Did Caligula truly make his horse a senator?'

'How could Nero wish to burn this city?'

'And you say Commodus struck off the heads of senators who refused to laugh at a prank?'

Brother Luke nodded. 'History is laden with such incident. All point to the corruption of man, the need for vigilance against evil, the harm done by rulers who know neither compassion nor humility.'

'It is as well we live in better times.' Otto fixed the beret on his head.

They walked across the square towards the horse-posts where Gerta and Max were tethered. The animals had been well cared for, fed and groomed by a band of industrious and scurrying hands who provided to the passing traffic. In Rome, pilgrims were a treasured commodity. Kurt was busy recounting to his sister a story of gladiators pitted against wild beasts in the great Colosseum. She listened dutifully, her gaze wandering ahead to Otto.

The face once more. It could not be coincidence, another chance encounter. She stopped. Oddly, the man was no longer dressed as a rootless vagrant, but wore the smart clothing of a private servant. All the better to blend in. Perhaps he waited for his master. Yet his eyes were turned elsewhere, bore in upon the friar and young noble.

'Isolda?'

She did not hear the query of her brother. Her attention was on the stranger, tracking him through the fluid scene of colour and movement. He did not belong. It was as though he tensed for a fight, coiled himself to pounce, a loner surrounded by people and horses but operating to a different beat. Briefly, his face was framed then obscured by a rearing steed. And in that moment she remembered, was borne to the track where Hans had died, where four horsemen had converged to hack her friend to pieces.

Horror and realization dawned with a scream. She was yelling her warning as the man moved, as his dagger rose and plunged straight for Otto. It seemed the only action in a world that had stilled. She watched, her sound cut short by dread, her brother reflexively twisting to see. He was already springing forward in futile gesture of defence. But it was too late. The point of the knife travelled fast, was accompanied by the high-pitched cries that had once propelled the young goatherd to his grave. The beggar was revealed as the fourth man, the Mohammedan who had fled the last clash to try again. He could not fail. *Allah! Allah! Allah! Allah!* Isolda covered her ears and clenched tight her eyes. She would not be witness to the inevitable.

But others saw. In a steel curve of light, a sword emerged from its scabbard into Otto's hand, descending in bisecting line as he pivoted to greet the threat. It did more than intercept. The Assassin stumbled, his effort cut short, a heavier blade than his own implanted deep between his eyes. Those eyes registered nothing. Then he fell away, and Otto stood alive and bloodied at the epicentre of shocked silence.

Brother Luke was the first to move, enveloping Kurt and Isolda to his side. 'Take comfort, my lambs. Young Otto proved the most quick and sure between them.'

'It is my fault.' Isolda sobbed and buried her face against his sleeve. 'I wished to warn you, wanted to tell you I recalled this evil stranger from past meeting.'

'I already had noted him.'

'You had?'

'Why yes. He was garbed as a beggar when first we entered Rome, followed us like an obedient ass.'

Kurt sounded reproachful. 'Otto might have died, Brother Luke.'

'He was never in danger. We had to draw this knave from the shadows, lull him with confidence to bring matters to conclusion.'

'How could you know his purpose? How could you suspect him from any beggar in the street?'

'When you wander as much as I, every soul reveals itself, every man walks with a step as particular as a noble and his signet seal.'

Isolda clung to the friar. 'Are we not Christians, Brother Luke? Could you not counter this villain with your staff, parry him as you did the Cathars?'

'In Rome I am become again a mild and reflective priest.'

'We might have captured him, placed him before proper court of judgement.'

'A cornered beast is more frenzied than a roaming one. And, until this moment, we had no proof of his treacherous intent.' The friar stooped and kissed her head. 'May God forgive me. I am sorry you have beheld more woe and slaughter than was ever meant for a child.'

Before them, Otto crouched beside the corpse; around them, spectators gathered to observe and comment. The sixteen-year-old had opened the belt-purse of the dead Asssassin and was examining its contents. He held up a piece between his thumb and finger, a silver German cross inlaid with garnets.

'What is it, Otto? What is its meaning?' Brother Luke had stepped forward.

'Meaning?' The boy gazed up at the friar, his voice hoarse with emotion. 'These murderous hounds who trail me have paid earlier visit to Alzey, have invaded my home, put those I love to the sword, butchered my old tutor Felix to whom I gave this token.'

He did not weep. It was too great a blow for mere tears. But his face was ashen pale, his grimace set with total anguish. In silence, he pulled further objects from the canvas bag, each of which he laid on the ground, some of which drew a sigh, a nod, a clenched fist. They were confirmation of his fears.

The Franciscan lowered himself to his haunches. 'Your deceased prize here is Assassin, a *hashshash*. They come from the mountains of Syria, are hired and sent by those unhappy to see you venture east.'

'Why, Brother Luke?'

'That is uncertain. Yet we may suppose it will be for neither kind nor generous reason, and you are viewed as danger to persons in the Holy Land.'

'I menace none.'

'Others have more jaundiced eye. Of course you seek your father. But you will ask questions, peer through doorways, offend interests.'

'My name and honour compel me to find truth.'

'However unsightly?'

'Wherever it leads and whatever the cost.'

The friar nodded. He had expected such answer. 'You have chance to turn back for the Rhineland, Otto.'

'There will be little but corpses left for me in Alzey. Someone wishes me dead, commits these killers to ensure it. You have my word I will discover the secret.'

'Forgiveness and love are more noble than vengeance, Otto.'

'Only in the robes and bare feet of a Franciscan.'

New commotion entered the surrounding hubbub. The crowd parted and Cardinal Savelli appeared in company with a squad of Lateran guards. Men bowed; women curtsied. He ignored them, his demeanour as unchangingly severe as it was when first he met the children.

'I should have foreseen the most recent visitors to our see would also prove the most troublesome.'

Brother Luke faced him. 'Such trouble is not of our making, your eminence.'

'Yet blood flows and a corpse lies prone.'

'Not the blood of an innocent; not the corpse of a guiltless traveller.'

'Who is ever guiltless, friar?' Savelli let his withering gaze move to the bloodied youth. 'You are quick with your sword, Otto of Alzey.'

'It is why I am alive to address you, your eminence.'

'Then you are fortunate that witnesses speak of heathen curses uttered by this wretch.'

'He came at me without warning, had deadly intent in his eye.'

'Our duty is to kill the Saracen, and you perform it well. No stain will mark your soul, no condemnation affix to your family name.'

'I am not to face tribunal, your eminence?'

'There is no crime committed here. You have blessing from Innocent, our Reverend Lord. Be glad and be wise, and be gone from Rome within this hour.'

'We head anyway for Nettuno.'

'That is to the good, for I hear two ships remain in harbour preparing to set sail.'

'They will be the last this side of winter.'

'Still greater reason for your urgency and speed.' The cardinal spread his hands and the pike-bearers fanned out to bar the press of citizenry. 'Incident is done and we need no more. Now leave us.'

Life had regained its daily rhythm; signs of death were being sluiced away. How readily a populace could shrug off act of violence, for there was always the next to take its place. Cencio Savelli stood on the cobbles and observed the work of his underlings. It would soon be time to retrace his path to the Lateran, to ascend its marbled stairs to the Sancta Sanctorum, the private chapel of the pontiff, and there report on happenings in the square. Yet he could afford to linger awhile and think.

He had pondered much of late: on the nature of power and abuse of influence; on the bending of will to a higher design. Maybe he was old, but ambition still burned. Undoubtedly he was cardinal, but one day he would climb higher. It was why he had agreed to serve not God but the shadow master the Lord of Arsur. There could be no withdrawal from their compact. Too much was at stake, too much already done. A month past, five thousand French children, wretched survivors of their original movement, had reached Marseilles for embarkation and crusade. They had been overjoyed to find boats, overwhelmed by the warmth with which they were received. Only now would they recognize their terrible folly and desperate fate, as they stood caged and captive in the slave-markets of Alexandria, as they were sold into deeper bondage in Egypt. Whether catamite or handmaiden, fair skins carried rich premium. Their tragedy was his gain.

Five thousand drops in an ocean, Savelli mused. There would be more: the Rhinelanders who had not died and were stupid enough to proceed. They too would suffer, would earn money for the secret coffers intended to fund the ships and pay the soldiers for the real crusade. It would come. When the Lord of Arsur raised his standard above the citadel in

Jerusalem, when he revealed his discovery of the True Cross, every king and prince, lord and knight, would scramble to attend. The heathen Mohammedans might try resistance, but it was likely to be token. Saphadin and his emirs would be dead, the Viceroy of Egypt constrained in sending relief by false rumour spread from Venice that Christian armies headed for the Nile. Shock and fear would keep them in their place. And so the Lord of Arsur would rule over all, a natural leader and sole successor. John of Brienne deceased, the barons extinguished, the infant queen Yolanda terminally deposed. A happy coincidence that the new overlord of Jerusalem and Palestine, sovereign of Outremer, would enjoy the support of Cencio Savelli, future-appointed pope. It was right to back a victor.

As though the strength and reach of the Lord of Arsur needed to be proved. The final bloodstains were sprinkled with sawdust and ash, the ground spotted with holy oil to rid it of polluting Saracen trace. One could never be too careful. Assassins might return with modified agenda and a different target, could lurk disguised as prelate or pauper. Even this failed attempt carried message that none was immune, anyone could be struck. Cardinal Savelli would ensure he remained among the vigilant and the living.

A priest hurried over. 'Such occurrence is a terrible thing, your eminence.'

'I agree.' He would be sending word to the Lord of Arsur that Otto of Alzey had survived.

*

'Oh, fair princess sitting in your tower . . .'

The nurse bounced the baby queen in her arms and crooned a little ditty. She returned the smile of the infant, but it was done with calculation instead of love, performed with the lukewarm ritual of one who knew already how the story would end. A long and fruitful life was not part of the intended narrative for this child. Below, the cultivated land stretched away from the walls of Acre. It was wrong to have taken Yolanda from her nursery, forbidden to bring her to the tower roof. But it was a fine day and no harm was done. Not yet.

She swung the infant and sang to her another stanza. What privilege to have such access to the future sovereign, to be entrusted with her care. The poor mite had no mother, no one to comfort and put her to the breast save a hard-working stranger in the employ of the royal house. It was a thought that brought a malevolent smirk to the face of the nurse. She was being paid well to deliver up the booty, the precious bundle, when commanded. Until that moment, she would be diligent and unobtrusive, would keep them guessing. John of Brienne, regent of Outremer, was destined to lose his kingdom, his daughter, his everything.

'What is this?'

Sharp admonition carried in the tone of Lady Matilda. She stared at the nurse, a questioning frown on her brow, cold displeasure in her green eyes.

Excuses tumbled. 'My lady, I mean no harm. I thought the air would benefit her young majesty, believed she might enjoy excursion to new parts.'

'In spite of rules forbidding it.'

'On occasion I forget myself, my lady.'

'You are paid to remember, engaged to guard and cosset the person of our queen.'

'I beg you not to report me, my lady. Such offence will never be repeated.'

'Should the matter again arise, should I catch you in illicit place, you will be beaten and discarded.'

'It shall not happen, my lady. You have my promise.'

Matilda let her scurry away. She could not pretend to like the strange and shadowy woman, could not dismiss her hint of defiance even as she cowered. There was knowledge and hidden purpose in the blandness. But she had no time to dwell on such considerations, to reflect on her greater regard for the senior and more cheerful of the nurses. A mistake had occurred and now was dealt with. In future she would attempt to curb her annoyance, control her sharpness with deficient staff.

Easier said than accomplished in these trying days. For a while she paced fretfully on the battlement walkways, her thoughts distracted and her worries bearing down. Children were her concern, thousands of them rumoured to be sailing for the Holy Land with optimism in their hearts and yet without hope of triumphant landing. Arab traders in their dhows, Maghribs and Levantines in their fishing caiques, had already reported on the sorrowful sights in Alexandria of sick and malnourished waifs herded to auction by whip-carrying slave-masters. It was almost too harrowing to contemplate, was too vexing to ignore. She had to act, needed to ensure that those who made it to the shores of Outremer were gathered up and protected, were taken to her care. This she could do. If the regent and his barons were engaged in higher matters and affairs of state, she would dwell in the affairs of the forgotten. They had no one else.

She had known where to find him. In a welter of thrashing limbs, and pursued by affray, he landed violently through the open doorway at her feet. Somewhere in the minor dust squall a tooth was spat out, a drunken oath emanated as a groan. Matilda stood back. As a young lady of noble birth, she rarely mixed with the lowly denizens of the Acre taverns and guardrooms. They were unspeakable types, thieves and murderers marooned in the darker recesses of Christendom, soldier ruffians more likely to desert their posts than ever defend the masters who paid them. Vice was their virtue, whoring, gaming, fighting and drinking their pleasure and pursuit. Worst among sinners was this man.

Rocking feverishly on his back, he began to sing a bawdy shanty of a fisherwoman and her friendship with an eel. At least he was alive, Matilda thought. The song reached for a climax and abruptly stopped. He had noticed her, was struggling to sit upright and focus through bloodshot eyes.

'Am I in heaven, my lady?' He belched and delivered a conspiratorial wink.

'I know of no paradise that would take you, Sergeant Hugh.'

'Then I am condemned to drift and wander as a spirit.'

'What happened to the warrior and bodyguard who protected Richard Cœur de Lion, the bowman who saved his beloved king from Saracen ambush near Jaffa and Blanchegarde?'

'Richard is gone, and I with him.'

'Twenty years have passed since he departed these shores. Yet you choose to linger, prefer to drink and carouse than pursue the noble art of soldiery.'

The Englishman sighed. 'The weather is conducive to me.'

'Do all your countrymen sink to such low and sorry state when left in foreign climes?'

'It is our disease, my lady.'

'I intend to provide its cure.'

He hiccuped and fell back, an act which triggered delivery of another rambling song. Matilda was uncertain if he mocked her or had merely forgotten her presence. She let the ballad run its course.

His head lolled. 'Hugh of York at your service, my lady.'

'You are in no position or mind to be of use to any.'

'Such cruelty from one so young and pretty.'

'I perceive you with my eyes.'

'What green eyes they are.' He stared up insolently at her. 'And what sharp tongue that cuts me to my soul.'

The man was impossible. She flushed at his oblique flattery, the suggestive manner with which he caressed his words. Sergeant Hugh was playing with her. He was a rogue and chancer, a mischief-maker who cut deals and created trouble, who lived off the fat of others and the sweat of his associates. Whatever glory there had been was vanished; however brave he once was he was now its spent and indolent shadow. But he still had the rugged and stocky build of a fighter, still possessed the shoulders and eye of the finest archer in the Latin world. She would find employment for him.

'You helped my father, Sergeant Hugh.'

'Like King Richard, it is history. Like all good men, he is dead.'

'If you revere and cherish his memory, you will listen to me.'

'I listen.'

'There are children, countless number of them, that head this way to Palestine, driven by fervour to liberate Jerusalem and uncover our lost relic of the True Cross.'

'They are fools.'

'They are innocents doomed to fall prey to Saracens and slavers, liable to suffer the most terrible of fates.'

'So, I weep.' His concern seemed less than profound.

'Are they not worthy of our aid and comfort?'

'Who is worthy and who is not?' The Englishman gazed at the sky and began to whistle a little tune. 'The Lord of Jebail and Sir William de Picton were deemed worthy, yet they were cut down here in Acre itself. It happens.'

'We may change events, do what is right and merciful in the sight of God.'

'I am out of practice, my lady.'

'Are you out of conscience also?'

'Leave it to the regent. Leave it to the nobles. Leave it to any but myself.'

'I turn to you, Hugh of York.'

He rolled his eyes. 'Why so? Even my horse Zephyr creates more wind in his belly than beneath his feet. Yes, I was renowned as archer without compare. True, I was with Cœur de Lion when he rode in the hills above Emmaus, when he caught distant glimpse of Jerusalem and raised his shield to prevent further sight of the city he would never reach. All is in the past, and my privilege too is to avert my face.'

With theatrical sigh he clamped his hands across his eyes and lapsed into contrived silence. From this position he could pretend she had departed and he was once more alone. The ruse did not appear to work. His fingers spread, his pupils contemplating her with dull resentment.

'You intrude, my lady.'

'I will pay you well for your endeavour.' She was loosening the purse at her girdle, emptying silver pieces into her palm. 'Should charity have price, it will reward you more than any other of your schemes.'

'What role is this to hunt children?'

'One of the highest calling. Saddle your horse, patrol until the new year the coastal length of Outremer and

Antioch, wrest the young from danger and carry them to the safety of my friends at the great Cistercian abbey in the hills above Tripoli.'

The soldier slowly raised himself again. 'From there?'

'We will bring them to Acre, restore them to their liberty.'

'While I see my own trampled in the dust.' He held out his hand to receive the coins.

She smiled and repeated his words. 'It happens.'

Horses stamped and whinnied, men haggled, and the sounds of argument and trade rose in solid confusion above the market square of Nettuno. Otto was selling his mare and stallion. A merchant with pinched face and mean eyes circled them, lifting their hooves, prodding their flanks, as the beasts stood patient and understanding. They had carried their master well, had escorted him these long miles. To the young noble they were most loyal of companions; to Kurt and Isolda they were totems and friends. There was pain in losing Maximilian and Gerta.

'Regard their necks, the carriage of their heads. Your animals are sick and broken.'

'They are tired as are we all.' Otto ran his hand along the black coat of the stallion. 'You will not find better mounts.'

'Perchance before you started your journey. But now they are done, ruined by the travel and the harshness of the road.'

'I see no ruin, only strength to be restored by fodder and rest.'

The man gave a sour laugh. 'Rest? They would be of more use if put beneath the blade of a butcher. I will give a silver mark for the pair.'

'It is quarter of what I ask.'

'They are less than what you promise.'

Kurt abandoned them to their debate, wandered through the teeming and evolving scenes. There were stalls and side-streets to explore, goods to examine, and spectacle to observe. Everyone was arriving or departing, going somewhere. Above the stench of animal dung and human waste, he could smell the sea, the harbour where his ship waited, the horizon for which he aimed. So many times had he bid farewell to people and places, moved on to the next. But never before had he left a shoreline, leaped so decisively to the distant unknown.

A noise drew him. It was the clamour of excitement, the baying of a mob. He pushed through, worming his way between shifting walls of humanity to reach open space and a better vantage. From here he could see, could catch glimpse of the target of jeers and catcalls, of venomous abuse. The crowd heaved and parted and a woman burst through.

'*Make way for the whore!*'

'See how she ensnares a bird as she catches the pox!'

'Watch how she makes a feather bed in which to pleasure us all!'

She stumbled and the mirth grew, her bare form

white and dirt-flecked as she scrambled to seize a fluttering chicken. The fowl dodged and the young woman slipped and fell. More laughter, more oath-laden shouts. It seemed she had cheated on her husband, was suffering the consequence of her infidelity. Kurt saw her tears, the beseeching panic in her eyes, the quivering shame in her nakedness. He turned away, angry at his powerlessness and her plight.

Edging to the periphery, he ducked through an alleyway and emerged into a courtyard ignored by the general flow of populace. He would sit and catch his breath, expunge the brutal picture from his mind. The poor, haunted woman. At least she was not being branded for her crimes or burnt as a witch.

A shadow fell across him, the light displaced by the presence of a tall man. His face was obscured by a canvas cowl, his shape distorted by a capacious smock. But there was no doubting who he was, no need to guess the identity of the three men beside him. They were Cathars, and they had already made acquaintance. Kurt gazed dumbly at the spectres, consumed by desire to flee, paralysed by sudden nightmare that transported him to the foot of an oak in whose branches a dead priest hung.

'It is not finished, child.'

The twelve-year-old shrank against the rough-hewn stones, tried to make himself small, to make himself scarce.

He stammered a response. 'I have no business with you.'

'Yet our paths cross, and it is fate which brings us to this confluence.'

'You follow us.'

'No difficult task.'

'Keep away from me, stay distant from my friends. Otto has a sword, Brother Luke a staff that will beat you roundly as when first we met.'

'They are not with you.'

'I have my fists, my feet, my teeth. Step back or I will show you how I fight.'

'Such spleen and intemperate spirit for a pilgrim.' The deep voice, speaking this time in German tongue, was mocking, dangerous. 'You will not shake us in our sacred quest, will not divert us from cleansing the earth of its impurities and sin.'

'You are mad.'

'We are chosen, elected to show the way and to harvest the corrupt flesh of man.'

'What if I should call out that heretics are loose among us?'

'Would they believe a boy? A dead boy?'

The Perfect reached and tousled his hair, an act of gentle familiarity designed to menace. Kurt shied. Yet the fingers tightened on his scalp, the grip of the Cathar leader pulling him close.

'Take care, child. We shall meet again.'

Kurt pivoted free and ran.

It was Brother Luke who confronted him as he scampered into the marketplace. 'A hare, and a frightened one. What fearful thing propels you so quick, my lamb?'

'Spirits, shadows, imaginings that mean nothing.'

'Stay close and I will banish every one.' The friar took his hand and clenched it between his own. 'We shall prevail over all.'

And Kurt believed, absorbed the confidence the Franciscan emitted. The old man had seen the world, encountered threat and lived this long. He had earned the right of self-assurance. The twelve-year-old would not trouble him with tales of his encounter.

Otto appeared and hailed them, Isolda at his side. 'Max and Gerta are gone, delivered up to new possession.'

'A travelling merchant? A local knight?'

'Isolda persuaded me to do other. I gave them both to a poor family whose need was greatest and whose regard and care for them will be unequalled.'

Brother Luke nodded. 'Then we are set fair. Onward, my lambs. A distant shore beckons.'

Their walking was over. Before them in the harbour were two vessels, three-masted merchantmen low in the water and laden with the barrels and bundles of trade. Otto and the friar had negotiated passage, the young noble offering security to the master with Hospitaller documents proving payment would be made. It would reduce the chance of a crew resorting to murder, avert the risk of an avaricious captain selling passengers on to Barbary pirates. Brother Luke kissed the ground and blessed the youngsters.

'We are some thirty miles beyond Rome, at the

very limit of our landward crossing. Come aboard, my lambs. Our voyage is begun.'

He strode up the gangplank, Otto behind, and jumped as effortlessly as any matelot to the deck. But Kurt and Isolda hesitated. They stood trembling on the wharfside, studying the hull, the masts, the folded sails. The waters were so deep, the blue Tyrrhenian Sea so vast and wide. It was a leap of faith to a gaping chasm.

The friar peered at them. 'Winds wait for none. There is no turning now.'

'We cannot.' Isolda wrung her hands, desperation clinging in her throat.

'You may have lost your army of children to conquer the Holy Land, yet you may still find glory and carry home the True Cross.'

'How may we find glory when we lack courage?'

'*Firmitas et Fortitudo*, my lambs.' The Franciscan spread his arms. '*Firmitas et Fortitudo*.'

Sister and brother looked at each other and raced to climb aboard, their friends helping them over. The four pilgrims embraced. 'Strength and Bravery,' Kurt whispered to himself. 'Strength and Bravery.'

As their ship cleared the breakwater for the open sea, the Perfect was leading his Believers on to the second of the two vessels.

In the Holy Land, south of the city of Jerusalem, lay a bleak and wind-blown valley named Gehenna. It was in this desolate place that Semitic and Assyrian tribes once made burnt offerings, sacrificed children to Moloch and Baal, the supreme deities and ancient gods of fertility and youth. Later generations set fire to refuse here, the smoke and flames blackening the sky, wreathing the land in dismal haze that conjured furnace-images of its past. Children would visit again. Gehenna, site of eternal torment. *Gehenna*, the Hebrew word for hell.

✝

Chapter 11

December 1212, and winter storms had raged along the coastal length of Outremer. Winds beat against the ships and galleys tethered fast to their moorings, rain lashed the walls and fortifications of the Christian enclaves. And the Franks waited for spring, wondered if it would bring the full wrath of the Saracens, speculated whether dark skies and roaring thunder were portent of their own annihilation. Nowhere was the mood bleaker, relations more turbulent and divided, than in the great hall at Acre. Voices were raised, insults hurled, threats exchanged. The very walls and flagstones gave off dankness and despair. It seemed the tempest had reached into the very heart of the Latin kingdom. The Council was in session.

Around the long table were the secular and religious rulers of the land. At the head sat the regent king John of Brienne, arrayed to either side his allies and his critics. An uncomfortable mix. There were the lords of Beirut, Caesarea and Sidon, the lords of Jaffa, Haifa and Tyre. With them were other barons and senior clerics: the Patriarch of Jerusalem, the bishops of Acre and of Tyre. Alongside too were the Grand Masters of the military Orders: Guerin de Montagu of the Hospitallers, Hermann Bardt of the Teutons, Philippe Du Plezier of the Templars. All present and angrily opinionated. Watching, keeping his counsel, resting back in his chair, was the Lord of Arsur.

'Your brothers are murdered, your lands pillaged, the Lord of Jebail and Sir William de Picton cut down. And you cower as whipped hounds.' The fist of the Grand Master of the Hospital slammed on the table, and a flagon of wine spilled.

A grey-bearded noble responded. 'What would you have us do, Grand Master? Ride out with paltry force to our deaths? Invade the Bekaa? Lay siege to Damascus?'

'You may fight as the military Orders fight, resist as we resist.'

'To what avail?' The baron made no attempt to hide his antipathy. You holy warriors are quick with your swords, zealous in your pursuit of Saracen blood. Yet I see no lessening in the pace and fury of the infidel raids.'

The Hospitaller leaned forward and jabbed a finger. 'Your honour is at stake, Aymar of Caesarea.'

'There is no honour in foolhardiness, no credit in rash adventure.'

'Beware your tongue, noble lord. It is the knights of the Hospital, the Temple, the Teutons, who guard your threatened kingdom.'

'Guard? You provoke.' It was the Lord of Haifa who spoke out.

'You have never liked us, never approved of our sacred purpose.'

'At last, a Knight Hospitaller who observes the truth.'

There was laughter, and the Grand Master of the Hospital glowered and reddened. Particularly fine sport, the Lord of Arsur mused. Better than any bear-bait, more savage than fighting-dogs placed together in a sack. The scarred and sardonic veteran from Haifa was well matched to the bull-headed aggressiveness of the Hospitaller chief. Play on.

The Grand Master stared venomously at the baron. 'The Pope himself commands us in our holy task to wage eternal war against the infidel.'

'And where is the Pope? Passing edicts in Rome. Idling in the sumptuousness of the Lateran while we suffer and toil to preserve our weakening hold on this corner of Palestine.'

'Our hold is weak since you are weak.'

'I have slain with these hands more Saracen than a troop of Hospitallers or Templars.'

'Yet now I see they tremble too much to hold secure a goblet of wine.'

The Lord of Haifa rose slowly from his seat. 'You insult me.'

'I inform you.' The Grand Master had touched a nerve, sat back to appreciate his handiwork.

His pleasure was short-lived, the moment punctured by interruption from John of Brienne.

'My lords of Caesarea and Haifa are right in what they say, Grand Master de Montagu.' The regent gestured to the Lord of Haifa to be seated. 'The Pope will not save us, nor the princes of Europe. They are unhappy with the peace I struck with Saphadin, yet remain unwilling to send armies for a war. Instead, fate plays cruel trick on us, washes bands of ragged children up along our shores.'

'At least those children have more daring than these lords about your table.'

Uproar ensued, the hammering of fists on seasoned oak, the cries of men offended and shouting for retraction. The Lord of Arsur sat it out, waiting for the squall to abate. There would always be the next twist of events.

'Silence!'

John of Brienne held up his hand and the noise stilled. He studied the unrepentant face of the Hospitaller, his patience spent, his voice edged with the harsh defensiveness of authority undermined.

'Your violence leads to nothing but desolation and despair; your assaults on the Mohammedans bring greater woe upon ourselves.'

'It is your timidity that reaps the whirlwind, sir.'

'Remember to whom you owe your allegiance.'

'To the pontiff and to God.' De Montagu gazed unblinking at the regent. 'And you should consider well on whom your authority rests.'

'I was elected king and regent by the barons here. Such state of things remains unchanged.'

Philippe Du Plezier, Templar Grand Master, smiled without humour. 'Age may weary a man and render him feeble.'

'Not me, Grand Master.'

'Then some might discern your reluctance to raise arms against the infidel as treason to our sacred cause.'

'How do you perceive it, Grand Master Du Plezier?'

'My eyes are turned to more spiritual concerns.'

Sour and ill-disguised mirth erupted in snorts among the gathered nobles. The man was a butcher, an earthy Templar who delighted in leading out his knights to harry and kill the Saracen. Soldier or villager, the nature of the target little troubled him. All that mattered was the victims were Mohammedan, their liquidation a religious duty. He and the regent rarely shared common cause.

'I am realist rather than traitor, Grand Master.'

'Reality is a war you choose not to see.'

'What I see are warehouses filled with goods and trade; our vaults and coffers groan with gold and silver earned through commerce with Damascus and Aleppo. You would squander this for squalid dispute and confrontation with the enemy?'

'We would not exist were there no heathen threat, were there no reason for our skills. It is fortunate for you our joy and calling is to fight.'

'It encumbers any chance for peace.'

'Peace is illusory, is worthless when based on conciliation or concession.' The expression on the face was unyielding above the white Templar surcoat and red Latin cross. 'Saphadin is sixty-nine, wishes to draw events to conclusion, to complete the vision of his brother Saladin and drown us beneath the waves.'

The Lord of Arsur received a nod from John of Brienne and climbed unhurried to his feet. It was important that the regent and his lords witnessed the coming quarrel, necessary for them to believe the drama they beheld. He would make it easy for them.

'I have heard more sense spoken by my pet dwarf, Grand Master.'

Response was immediate, as he had expected and rehearsed. Inflamed by rage, the Templar leader jumped up and made to lunge towards him. Fellow Grand Masters struggled to restrain him, to mollify and calm, to no avail. Du Plezier shook them off, his hate-filled shouts and wild punches aimed at an unrepentant adversary.

Protected by the table width, the Lord of Arsur stood his ground. 'Quite some display, Grand Master. I can only surmise how the Saracen trembles at your approach.'

'Cowards!' Arrogant disdain had evaporated into rabid fury. Du Plezier was trembling with ire, his face mottled red, his eyes bulging from an unseen pressure. 'You hide beneath your rocks and stones, recoil as Jerusalem suffers under the demonic yoke of Islam. You lie, you appease, you bow timorous before the Antichrist Saphadin.'

He did temper well. The Lord of Arsur regarded him, his fingertips resting on the table edge. 'I was at Hattin, saw how the infidels outnumbered us, the consequence of recklessness, the result of stupidity and belligerence by your former Grand Master Gérard de Ridefort.'

'He was a loyal servant of God.'

'De Ridefort was a dolt.'

'You dare affront our Order, besmirch our reputation?'

'I would challenge any I deem to threaten the security and integrity of the realm.'

'The Knights Templar are blessed by the Lord, sanctioned by His Holiness in Rome.'

'And they are led by bellicose simpletons.'

Rage had few boundaries when pride was assailed. Had swords been close, there might have been deaths. Guards were called, the tussling interests physically parted, and John of Brienne pounded the table to reclaim control. Even the Bishop of Acre was involved, had the Lord of Haifa by the throat.

'Is this not what our enemies seek? Division, confusion, schism that will deliver up our broken kingdom into heathen bondage? I beseech you . . . No, I *command* you to your places.'

It was the weary irascibility of a ruler who maintained his throne but had lost position. He owed his presence, his authority, to his late wife Queen Maria, to their infant daughter Yolanda. Neither could help him. There was scant quarter given to the wounded in Outremer.

In the wavering silence the moment passed and the flame of discord between the barons sputtered to mute and uneasy truce. Only the voice of the Lord of Arsur could be heard, his words low and measured.

'Your regent majesty, my brother nobles. We are seized in the grip of madness, a choleric fury that consumes us. Like the blind, we totter towards a war we cannot win, fritter a peace we cannot afford to lose.'

'The Saracen attacks us and that is enough!' Hermann Bardt of the Teutons bellowed in disagreement.

'It is never enough, never sufficient to let chance slip through our maladroit fingers. To this end I make proposal and vow. I will take horse to Damascus and seek audience with Sultan Saphadin himself.'

That had their attention. Dreamer or fixer, he would be viewed as peacemaker, hailed as a symbol of virtue and conviction willing to travel the distance and see concord prevail. He might fail, could die. But at least the inhabitants of Outremer would for ever regard him as the man who offered a last push for reason. All to the good, all for a hidden intention that was supremely bad. He would indeed deliver the final heave. It would topple the Holy Land over the edge.

As he spoke, his leper Knights of St Lazarus were preparing to attack Moslem pilgrims gathered to make the annual hajj to Mecca.

Over one hundred miles north along the coast, south of the town of Tripoli, the weather was breaking. The seas were still rough, the caps of the restless waves white with spume, but the gales had eased, the winds gusted less, and passage could be forced to the foaming shallows. A small boat pitched towards the shore

It dipped and rose, first perched on a crest, then sinking into steep descent, its soaked passengers braced and huddled, its lone oarsman battling valiantly in the surf. The bow struck sand, and four figures abandoned the craft to leap and stumble to the safety of dry land.

'Where was Moses when we cried out to him?'

Brother Luke plucked Isolda from the draining sea and set her down upon the beach. Beside her, Kurt was scrambling waterlogged to observe his surroundings, Otto dragged his pack to higher ground. The faces of each carried expressions of wonderment and relief.

The Franciscan looked at them. 'Near three months, and we are here, my lambs, arrived on this sacred soil I visited and left so many years past. Our Lord has been merciful.'

God had certainly given them cause to be thankful. Their ordeal had been long, their journey full of hazard and incident. The sea claimed their first ship, for it had foundered near Messina. Their second vessel was boarded by Greek cut-throats who themselves had their throats cut; their fourth and fifth were no more than fishing-craft that had inched them east across the Mediterranean map. Finally they had reached the island of Cyprus, had sojourned in Limassol for a fortnight while the friar made preparation for the onward step. And at every stage they had heard news of the children from France who had gone before them. Grim tales of shipwreck and piracy; stories of how thousands had perished on the rocks off Sardinia, how thousands more had been traded to the Arabs.

Survival was sweet. Kurt breathed deep and watched the cloud dissolve above the distant mountains, a flock of gulls wheel and fight over a morsel of food. The land of the Bible, and his feet were upon it. This was what Hans and little Lisa had died for, what Egon, Zepp and Achim had tried to reach. He and Isolda alone were left standing. The voyage had changed him. He felt older, stronger, wiser, perhaps appeared so to the others. But Isolda still mothered him, and his friend Otto, now seventeen and with a light stubble and hair grown long, still treated him as a younger brother to be indulged and protected. It was comforting in its way.

The noble boy whooped. 'Who could imagine our exploits, Kurt? Who would conceive we might come so far?'

'Many times I thought we would not.'

'Put it behind you, my brother. Everything we seek is here. Honour, glory, feats of every kind. You will discover the True Cross, and I shall find my father.'

'Where to begin, Otto?'

'Revelation will come. People talk, clues unfold. We are in a place to which thousand upon thousand of good Christians have travelled before.'

Kurt shrugged. 'I have met enough unlikeable ones on the way.'

'The four of us will confront any who wish us ill. We have triumphed over previous threat, will do so again.'

'Why do we land at such a place?' Isolda was wringing salt water from her sodden tabard dress. 'Why did we not sail on to proper port?'

Otto laughed. 'Because the old friar wishes to teach us humility; because he feels a drenching will remind us of the power of the Divine.'

'And because our ship heads for Tripoli while our goal is southward for Beirut and Acre.'

The Franciscan had dropped to his knees, had bent and kissed the sand with reverence and joy. His charges were safe; his mission of pilgrimage and wandering piety could resume. There were many who required a healing and helping hand, a multitude of sinners and unbelievers ready to receive the Word of the Saviour.

He clambered upright, his pilgrim staff held tight in his hand. 'How better to arrive than as newborns on a deserted beach with nothing here but nature and the elements?'

Reply came from an unexpected quarter, with a wailing shriek from an arrow that pierced the air with the high-pitched noise of its flight. The youngsters threw themselves flat. Yet Brother Luke faced the danger unperturbed at the whistling approach, motionless even as the steel head struck and shattered his wooden staff.

A figure had materialized, a sturdy European in motley Arab and Frankish garb, with a yew longbow clenched in one hand and a broad grin creasing his bearded features.

'It scares them every time. Yet not you, holy brother.'

'I do not frighten with ease.' Brother Luke met him with a level gaze.

The man tilted his head and studied him. 'I have

seen the bravest of Saracen warriors run at the sound of my flying she-devils. You act as though versed in these dark arts and trickeries of war.'

'I am more versed in acceptance of fate.' Brother Luke switched from French to English tongue. 'You use a longbow, play pranks and speak words as though born and raised an Englishman.'

'A Yorkshireman. They call me Sergeant Hugh.'

'While I am known as Brother Luke, bred in the English county of Somerset. And with me Otto, Kurt and Isolda.'

'To be without weapons in these parts is rash. To venture here with mere children is unmatched folly.'

'We take our chance.'

'You have no chance. The land is in turmoil, the risks abound. Everywhere there are enemy patrolling. Mamluks, Bedouin, the cavalry of Saphadin, the brigand troops from Lattakia, Arab foragers or Italian errants ready to profit well from the easy capture of the meek and inexperienced.'

'From whom do you profit, Sergeant Hugh?'

'I cannot deny I am paid, rewarded for every head I find and deliver up safe and attached alive to its body. But it is in good cause, at behest of young Lady Matilda of Acre, the most kind and fair of all noblewomen in Outremer.'

'She has evidently bewitched you.'

'I know of no man resistant to her excellence and charm. She commands me protect the children, and I obey.'

'Thus now do you wander lovestruck and loyal.'

The Franciscan snapped the arrow from his staff. 'I am grateful to her, thankful your aim is both straight and true.'

'Silver pennies improve the eye and steady the hand, outweigh my lack of practice.'

'You must have been peerless in your day.'

'The best, the personal guard to Richard Cœur de Lion.'

'Well, Hugh my brother, it seems we are become acquainted.' The friar proffered his hand.

As afternoon light shaded into evening, the small party made camp within a cluster of Greek temple ruins. Sergeant Hugh had led in his horse and laid out blankets, Brother Luke built a fire from kindling and dung-bricks brought by the soldier, and the young explored. The Yorkshireman, a long-poled battleaxe resting at his side, stretched out against a crumbled pillar, unstopped a gourd of wine, and casually observed the activities around him. To the amusement of Kurt and Isolda, Otto was poised atop a fallen block of marble and was struggling gamely to draw the longbow.

'A heroic picture.' The sergeant gulped a mouthful of wine and wiped his mouth with the back of his hand. 'As sculpted as a statue, as fair as any maid. And still you are no archer.'

Crestfallen, the youth lowered the bow. 'I thought I had strength enough for the task.'

'A yew bow defeats all but the most sturdy. It has taken me a lifetime to bend her to my will.'

'She?'

'The most capricious of mistresses. Yet I have tamed her, have learned to put three arrows in flight at any time, to pitch a man from his horse at over four hundred paces.'

Kurt was examining the quiver of arrows and plucked one at random. 'What is this, Sergeant Hugh?'

'Three feet of finest ash, with flight of goose-feathers and steel bodkin-head as sharp as a pin. It will punch through oak doors, pierce the mail or plated armour of an infidel.'

'And this?' The boy held up a black-painted arrow for inspection.

'I call her my night terror. Unseen in darkness, she puts the fear of a thousand heathen gods into the hearts of men when she arrives silent among them.' He nodded as Kurt extracted another. 'That you have encountered: the she-devil with a whistle I have hollowed beneath. Beside her, the barb, a fish-hook no man may pull from his gut. Next, the blunt-head or hammer.'

He described each, lovingly providing explanation, illustrating with tales of his past. The soldier seemed wistful, more at ease with vivid recollection than in the disappointment of the present. He was a fighting-man left stranded, a survivor who had cheated death and now made a living by cheating almost anyone. While the flames of the fire climbed, the children and friar drew nearer to catch its warmth.

Brother Luke eyed him. 'Your German is good, Hugh.'

'When one has dealt with the Teutons, lived so long in Outremer, one acquires the ear for several tongues.'

'I would not cast you for ambassador.'

'Tact and manners are not my bent.' The sergeant started on a second flask of wine. 'It was I in drunken moment who removed and flung down the banner of Duke Leopold of Austria from the conquered towers of Acre and ignited his lifelong feud with my master King Richard.'

'Did he not repay such insult by taking captive the Lionheart two years later on way home from crusade?'

'I hear ransom was given and the King released.'

'It cost England dear.'

'Further reason why I stay remote and afar in the east. Yet life has been dull since Cœur de Lion left.'

Seated cross-legged, his face eager, Kurt chewed on a piece of salted fish. 'Was King Richard the greatest of all warriors?'

'None equalled him. He was impulsive, reckless, brave, strong, fought like no other man I ever saw. If he committed to battle, it would turn in an instant. If he charged the Saracen, they would melt to his strike.'

'They say he killed many men.'

'Scores by his own hand. On the route down to Ascalon, I was at his side when he led the Hospitallers and Templars and put the infidel to flight. He must have slain twelve with his lance and two dozen more by his sword.'

'And you?'

'Sufficient to merit my post as his chief protector.'

'You must be proud of such exploits.'

Sergeant Hugh paused to reflect and take a pull of his drink. 'Satisfied at a role performed, ashamed of excesses committed.'

'You did wrong?' Kurt had stopped eating.

'There is such a thing as too much slaughter. At Acre I partook in the bloody and joyous killing of near three thousand unarmed souls surrendered to our charge. At Daron the following year I was with Richard when we threw the captured garrison to their deaths over the ramparts.'

The Franciscan reached and held his arm. 'All sinners may repent, Hugh.'

'Not this one, Brother Luke.' The Englishman held up a hand, his thumb and fingers splayed. 'See, the fingernails are vanished. They were lost to the disease we call *arnaldia* as our troops besieged Acre. Twenty years on and these are my keepsakes, reminder that I am but a common brute, am unchanged and beyond repair.'

'In the eyes of God we are equal.'

'The conclusions of men are not so generous.' He emptied the contents of the bottle into his throat.

'Yet you help us, and that itself is step towards salvation and the light.'

Sergeant Hugh yawned. 'My charity is bought; my endeavour lasts until I deliver you to safe keeping at the monastery of Belmont in the hills above Tripoli.'

'How many else have you saved in this manner?'

'Too few to earn my fortune, a handful of half-drowned young. The rest?' He poked a stick into the fire. 'Who may tell what has befallen them?'

Discussion concluded, the soldier settled himself down to sleep. It was only later, when darkness fell and the quiet conversation of the children had lapsed to slumber, that the Englishman stirred again. While Brother Luke prayed on his knees in the blackness, the sergeant prowled by dying firelight among his weapons, tightening the horn nocks of his bow, oiling with linseed the blade of his axe, applying a clove of garlic to the tips of his arrowheads.

The low and gentle voice of the friar intruded. 'Habit is difficult to break, my brother Hugh.'

'We each of us make our preparation for death.'

'Garlic?'

Sergeant Hugh rubbed the clove along a steel barb. 'It spreads the poison, ensures a wound will never cleanse.'

'I prefer to spread the Word of God.'

'My creed is simpler: is one of wenching, carousing and killing. Does it make me a bad man, Brother Luke?'

'A lost one.'

The sergeant chuckled. 'A fellow countryman is with me, and a holy one at that. I consider myself found.'

Morning came obscure and grey across the mountains. Brother Luke was at prayer, Otto and Sergeant Hugh rebuilt the fire, and Kurt and Isolda had wandered to inspect the remains of a collapsed necropolis some two hundred yards distant. Alexander the Great had once marched this way, the route of his army littered with signs of civilizations destroyed and imposed. Phoenicians, Greeks, Romans, Semites and Franks, all had left their mark and buried their dead, all had conquered and in turn been vanquished. New arrivals had disembarked, a Franciscan and three children. Their footprints were unlikely to be noticed in the sand-buried tracts of history.

'*Razzia!*'

A single word from Brother Luke, a warning in Arabic that a raiding-party approached. Sergeant Hugh rolled to the ground, motioned for Otto to do the same, and crawled up beside the friar to peer to the east. He was about to speak, prepared to dismiss the alert as nothing more than the hallucination of an aged mind, the illusion thrown up by weakening eyes. But he blinked and the shadows had gained size and formed into recognizable shape. Horsemen, perhaps twenty, maybe thirty, and they were hostile.

The soldier whispered back to the youth. 'Stay low, young Otto. Don your *cuirie* and keep your sword close.'

'I must rescue Kurt and Isolda.'

'You will keep where you are.' Brother Luke reversed sinuously into cover. 'To show yourself is to invite the onslaught. Signal my lambs to remain mute and unmoving. They are wiser to go to ground.'

As though called, Kurt appeared in the chamber

entrance to a tomb. He smiled and waved, took the gestures of the noble boy as encouragement to shout. His words carried faint, his movements suggested elation at a great find. He was not the only one to make a discovery.

'They perceive us.' Sergeant Hugh scowled at the evolving formation.

The friar added his own observation. 'Now the cavalry spread.'

'The easier to overwhelm us.' The archer selected an arrow and stood to fit it to his bow. 'What pity they fail to conceive the artistry of my craft.'

'Will they not parley?'

'Saracens on horseback have no time for settlement, no use for talk.'

'Then may God be with us all.'

'Amen to that, friar.'

Sister and brother had started to walk back towards their companions. They were ignorant of events, unaware of the developing pace. The Saracens were readying for the charge. A command was given, the horses moving from trot into canter and pounding to a gallop, the mouths of their riders opening in full battle-cry. Earth vibrated. Kurt and Isolda halted. Across the divide, Otto was gesticulating violently, pointing, his face contorting to give voice to a call that had acquired the accompaniment of distant and more disturbing sound. The children turned. Before them, bearing down, was something they had never met, a vision they had not expected. Hand in hand, they ran for a hiding-place and for their lives.

Sergeant Hugh discharged the arrow, a prized she-devil that accelerated with unnatural scream towards its closing target. Impact was abrupt and catastrophic. The horse reared at the onrush of noise, the steel arrowhead piercing its neck, driving through to pinion the rider in the chest. The cavalryman dropped his curved Turkish scimitar, rode the dying and bucking beast groundward as he himself died.

'Welcome to the Holy Land, my friends.'

Collected and fluent, the longbowman released another flight. His indolence was departed, replaced by the confident ease, the focus, the trained actions of one who might have been vying in Sunday contest at the butts. This was his element and his very being. Otto cheered. The second shard had made contact and penetrated mail, the hit quarry flung aside in bloody confusion. Sergeant Hugh worked on, methodical and rhythmic, aiming at the leadership, taking out front-runners. He had moved forward for better view, stood alone at the periphery.

'My second quiver. Fetch it to me, Otto.'

'You must get back, Sergeant Hugh.'

'When moment is right.' He shied a little as a volley of Saracen darts bracketed his position in puff-bursts of powdered stone. 'If I put them from their horses, I diminish their advantage.'

'They still outnumber and engulf us.'

'By whose estimation?' The Englishman aimed and shot, his muscles bunched and straining to the effort.

Behind him, the friar and young noble made

preparation for the fray. At any moment the travelling force of the attack would reach them, the Mohammedan horsemen arrive in their midst. The cries of the foe became louder, the wet and heavy impact of arrows on flesh closer on the ear. Otto crouched and waited. Brother Luke seized a burning brand from the fire and toyed with it in his hand.

In a cascade of loose chippings, Sergeant Hugh vaulted a fallen slab, his inelegant retreat chased by mounted Mamluks. A javelin flew straight and missed his vanishing back. He laughed, spun low, and drew his sword.

'Calm yourself, Zephyr. We shall prevail.'

Tethered to a pillar, his decrepit mount champed and whinnied anxiously at the spiralling scene. His master had often led him into rash and desperate venture, and this was such occasion. In demonstration, a large Turcoman in fur-edged helmet and brandishing a sword filled the space vacated by the soldier. The man twisted to shout to his comrades, encouraging them on, urging them forward to erase the cowering band of infidels. He had the advantage, the higher ground. The pelt and scalp of the fleet-footed longbowman were his for the peeling.

His grunted exhalation was one of surprise. He faltered, poised in the interlude between bafflement and realization, a warrior whose advance had been strangely checked. The Turcoman looked down. Protruding from his abdomen was the unwelcome head of a battleaxe, its blade buried deep, the hands of a young and handsome Unbeliever wrapped around its haft. Surely the boy was too untried to have inflicted so grievous a blow. With a hiss, the Moslem teetered and dropped.

'They are among us, Otto. Withdraw to the centre.'

'There is no centre.'

'So make your quarrel with them.'

Sergeant Hugh ducked, a blade striking the column above his head and sending sparks and fragments showering down. He slashed with his sword, cut through to the bone. Another assailant dispatched. It was a fighting retreat that was disorderly brawl. Otto darted among the ruins, parrying, thrusting, attempting to hold the ever-diminishing line. He emerged from behind a block, but tripped and fell, rolling ungainly to escape a downward stab. A Mamluk held his sword high, prepared for the finish. Something caught his eye, a rock hurtling fast and connecting hard. As he clutched his shattered face, Otto completed the assignment.

'May God forgive me, my lamb.' It was the familiar voice of Brother Luke.

The Rhineland boy called back. 'That is for Him, but I am grateful.'

More were closing in, pushing the three Christians to a point of no breakout or return. Archers had dismounted to join the fray, and the terminal phase would not take long. Trapped, the Franciscan fended off approach with his firebrand, harrying and baiting with the aplomb of an acrobat. Yet he would not kill. That was for ardent and noble youths who wore *cuirie* breastplates and had learned to joust from the cradle. That was for soldiers who had rediscovered their form. He would go to his Maker with clear conscience and clean hands.

✝

✝
Chapter 12

Through the drifting haze and pounding commotion, a trumpet-blast echoed. The sound of salvation, of ambushers being ambushed. Within seconds, tempo had changed, direction altered, and the Saracens were pulling back in blind haste. Inward rush had become outward torrent, men stumbling to flee, fumbling for bridles and reins, mounting up, spurring on. They did not get far. A detachment of Frankish cavalry, its lances couched and horizontal with deadly intent, struck them at a gallop.

The screams were of a different timbre. Fear displaced the joyful ululation of pursuit; cries of anguished panic filled the air once loud with expectation of quick victory. Defeat could be equally rapid. Token resistance was bludgeoned aside, stragglers soon dealt with. In the wavering aftershock, only the wild and terrified dash of a riderless horse, the wasted pleas of wounded Mohammedans, encroached on the silence.

A Templar knight rested on his bloodied sword and surveyed the unusual trio of survivors emerging from the debris-field of stones and corpses. The knight did not speak. He was exemplar of his kind, a Christian warrior clad in mail, his hauberk and chausses draped in the white mantle of his Order, his padded shoulder espaliers worn and rusted through patrol and skirmish. God's work was never restful. Behind him, mounted on warhorses, men of his squadron trotted by, armoured and clattering behemoths hidden by triangular shields and the steel helms encasing their heads. Even their chargers seemed of unearthly form, their powerful chests double-strapped, their immensity swathed in hanging caparisons. It was a picture at once disturbing and reassuring.

Sergeant Hugh crouched to frisk a cadaver. 'I cannot fault your intervention or its timing, knight.'

'As I cannot claim surprise to find you at the midst of this escapade.'

'You honour me.'

'It is not intended as praise.' The Templar nodded cursorily at Otto and Brother Luke. 'And these?'

'Otto of Alzey and Brother Luke of Assisi, voyaging pilgrims to our holy shores.'

'They could not choose more bleak or brutal incident for their arrival.'

The Franciscan offered a calm and pious look. 'We embrace such happening as we find.'

'You will need to, should you live.'

'If it be the will of God, I shall carry His message of light and love throughout these desolate parts.'

'We too strive to spread it, through the point of a lance.'

At his feet, the English soldier had expertly stripped one body of its valuables, was tugging free a silver ring from the finger of another. The knight made no attempt to disguise his scorn.

'You scavenge like a jackal, Hugh of York.'

'And you preach like a bishop, knight.' The souvenir-hunter relieved the carcass of a trinket and began to unbuckle an ornate belt. 'Observe the *hiyasa*. Its plates are gilded, its patterns intricate and finely worked. These are no militia, no random group of foragers. They are the best the Saracens may send against us.'

'We have noticed it of late. They strive to test our mettle.'

'At least we are not found wanting.' Sergeant Hugh bundled his trophies into a linen bag and stood to scan for further plunder.

'Where now do you go, archer?'

'Wherever my fancy or my new-acquainted friends direct me, knight. Perchance I will rest awhile on the shore, or take my spoils of war to sell, or pick over fresh cadavers that I find.'

'You trifle with me, Hugh of York.'

'I do not take orders from you.'

The eyes of the Templar narrowed. 'Take care with your impudence. You are far from Acre and protection of your kind, beyond the bounds of your customary refuge.'

Sergeant Hugh shouldered his quiver. 'I am fortunate to have ability and arrows that may outmatch the thickest of mail jerkins.'

'Is that so?' The point of the sword ground harder in the earth.

Coolly, the soldier drew a small knife and held it at his side. 'Proof will lie in the heads and shafts I liberate from my kills.'

There was intensity in the passing seconds that might have escalated to violence or petered to nothing. With Templars it was hard to calculate. Their justice was often summary and extreme, their hand forced or guided by the spirit of the Lord. God was plainly a mercurial creature.

'Brother Luke, Sergeant Hugh, come quick!'

At wordless instruction of the friar, Otto had slipped away to determine the fate and well-being of Kurt and Isolda. Now he reappeared, hurdling obstacles in his haste, his face pallid-white with shock, his voice cracked by discovery. The Franciscan seized and held his shoulders, gazed with forceful understanding in his eyes. Dread answer was already given. The two children had vanished.

'What is to become of us, Kurt?'

He did not know, had never considered in his bleakest imaginings their voyage would finish this way. Otto dead, Brother Luke dead, Hugh the rough and vulgar bowman dead. And he and his sister snatched from their hiding-hole and carried off by rampaging heathen. The Franciscan had encouraged him to be strong, to be brave. Simple words and easy to heed when horsemen were not yipping and wheeling in threatening display, when despair did not envelop, when Isolda was not beside him weeping soft and silent tears.

The rope tugged and they jolted forward again, their hands bound, their pace determined by the plodding tread of the horse to which they were tied. Details were muddied, actions distorted in the chaos of the battle. There had been the noble boy calling, the dark insect-cloud of mounted enemy, the glint of swords and the dream-like wrench from sanctuary. He hoped his friends had not suffered greatly in their dying moments. But tales of Saracen cruelty abounded, were fed with breast-milk to every infant in the Christian world. A new reality, and he could scarcely pretend he was not terrified.

'I am with you, Isolda. That is to the good.'

'You have no choice.'

He twisted his hand to touch her fingers, attempted to show solidarity, to transmit support. Confidence that was nothing more than a confidence trick.

'While we live there is hope, Isolda.'

'I see none. I see evil men on horseback who carry us towards hell, infidel warriors who do not speak our tongue or share our God.'

'But we still breathe, sweet sister. They have no wish or cause to harm us.'

'I would rather they did, prefer it should they put us from our misery.'

'Hush, Isolda.' His whisper was harsher than he intended, was directed as much to his own aching fears. 'We must keep faith.'

'Why do they seize us? Why do they drag us onward for their sport?'

'It is their way.'

She staggered and recovered, held upright by Kurt, pulled forward by the straining tether. Her brother murmured encouragement, willed her on. If she fell, they might beat her; should she faint, they might dispatch her with a blade. He let her lean on his shoulder.

With frenzied whoops, a Saracen horseman circled in from the flank and decelerated beside the children in virtuoso performance of balance and control. Silently he observed the captives, a remote figure with dark eyes and long moustache. Then a single cry, and he spurred away in a flourish of martial showmanship.

'His stare, Kurt. It held such hate for us.'

'He was curious.'

She turned her head to glance at him, seeking reassurance. He bit his lip and concentrated on the path in front, on the flicking tail of the horse, on bringing circulation back into his wrists. Surely these infidel would not have made the effort of their capture only to kill them at the wayside. Yet nor would they be rejoicing at the manner in which Hugh of York had peppered them with his arrows. Decision on survival could be a finely balanced thing.

'Otto, Brother Luke, Sergeant Hugh. They gave their lives for us, Kurt.'

'That I recognize. It is for their sake we must endure.'

'I try, Kurt.'

'How may we fail them, disgrace their memory, by our weakness? Do you remember how Otto saw off Gunther, drew his sword against the Cathars? Do you recall how Brother Luke levelled those hooded murderers with his staff?'

'Of course.' She managed a sad and quiet laugh.

'They blessed us with example. Then there was Sergeant Hugh, a stranger to us, a wandering rogue, yet a master with the longbow.'

'Such sacrifice they made for us.'

'And never did they waver.' He slowed his pace as the horse negotiated an incline. 'We are children, low-borns from the Rhineland. Not nobles, not friars, not bowmen. But whatever we face, we will act as though their knowledge and resolve were our own.'

He blinked the dust from his eyes and cast a look heavenward, hoping for a sign, wishing he had been more prayerful in the past. God would have a plan. Somehow He would glimpse through disorder, take pity on a twelve-year-old boy and his fourteen-year-old sister, deliver them from slavery and exile and the terrors before them. *Save us, O Lord*. Kurt saw the snow-brushed slopes of the mountains ahead, the valley entrances gape wide like portals. And he understood that he and Isolda were alone, that they would soon be swallowed up and their world close behind.

Victors behaved as victors did, beheading corpses to ensure their spirits did not attain desired Mohammedan paradise, tying feet to drag away human battle-trophies in debasing and bloody trail. Tortosa was their destination, the great Templar stronghold further up the coast. Their job was done. It had been the smallest of victories, nothing more than rehearsal and training for what was to come. Lances pricked the sky, horses pranced excitably with the fight still in their nostrils, and orders were hollered and passed down. The cavalcade moved out.

Otto and the English bowman had followed a different path. It was the initiative of the youth, an impulse that had made him snatch at the bridle of a riderless Saracen mount and swing himself up into its saddle. He would not let his friends disappear without a chase, would not admit defeat until he and every prospect were exhausted. It made no sense. Yet loyalty, comradeship and honour required neither logic nor explanation. Brother Luke also had volunteered. But he was too old, too peace-loving, too earth-bound, to be of use. Disappointed, he had accepted the verdict of others. So it was that Hugh of York became second member of the pursuit. He had not stopped complaining since.

'You think we shall achieve a thing with such lunacy?' The Englishman looked sullen from beneath the brim of his purloined Turcoman hat. 'A boy your age should be sticking his dick in a wench, drowning himself in bowls of ale and malmsey.'

'I thank God my tutors have been more wise than you.'

'How you squander their instruction.'

'They taught me duty, Sergeant Hugh. They schooled me in the noble objects of gallantry and fidelity.'

A derisive grunt emanated from the soldier. 'Here

you need blacker arts, boy. Low cunning, the mind of an Arab, the agility of a barbary ape.'

'And plainly a steed able to carry the plunder of a thief.'

It drew a reflexive and quickly suppressed smile. Astride his burdened horse, the archer appeared as nothing more than a raggedy tinker festooned with amulets and charms and ferrying his worldly possessions at his side. Trade or fight, there were items aplenty from which to choose, and all were close to hand.

'What do you find in these children, Otto of Alzey?'

'Friends I will not abandon.'

'To me, they are nuisance, burden to my purse, beyond the scope of my employment.'

Otto halted and scanned the horizon. 'My soul sheds tears for you, Sergeant Hugh.'

'Your vainglory and romantic notion will see you killed, boy.'

'Your complaints shall do likewise for you, bowman.'

'A boy of such wit. It will be lost when the Saracen boils you alive.' The Englishman drew alongside. 'What are we against an entire *razzia* group, Alzey?'

'An undefeated force with sword, longbow and poleaxe.'

'You forget participation of the Templars to our benefit, overlook how near-overrun we were among the ruins.'

'Perhaps fresh miracle may yet save us.'

'I doubt it. Our foe is from Homs or the great hilltop castle at Saône, is not comprised of mere goat-stealers from Holy Valley.'

'We shall challenge them as they are.'

Otto began to walk his horse on, adjusted to the arcing course now set by the crop-haired Englishman. The soldier had picked up the track and was slowly assuming the lead. It had not taken long for nature and instinct to return. But his truculence stayed.

Irreverently, the seventeen-year-old called after him. 'You are in ill humour with me, Sergeant Hugh.'

'Is it so plain?'

'As daylight and the mountain crests.'

'I know these lands, know too we should not be in them.' The soldier peered about, tasting the air, testing the wind. 'If you wish to survive, you will do as I command. I am your senior, boy child.'

'While I outrank you.'

'What is title in a wilderness, noble blood when it possesses no sense?'

'I fought beside you, parried deadly blows in thick of battle.'

'Bravo. Yet it was I who rescued your fragile neck.'

'Not so.'

The longbowman flashed a baiting grin, happy to prick the skin of the Rhineland youth. There were few he could not irritate or outjoust. It merited a drink. He extracted the flask-seal with his teeth and tipped the neck to his lips.

Refreshed, he tried again. 'Your aged friar taught you prayerfulness, Alzey. I will educate you in life.'

'Existence at the bottom of a wine vessel is no life, Hugh of York.'

'*Be still.*'

In a jangle of wares and pilfered booty, Zephyr was reined back. Sergeant Hugh dismounted, sliding to kneel and inspect horse-droppings half-covered on the route. The raiders had slowed. They were taking some care in disguising their route, were accompanied by individuals on foot. And the dung was fresh.

'We close on them, German boy.' The soldier studied the ground, tracing the direction of scuffmarks and prints. 'Curse our fortune, we close.'

Always start with the Templars. Brother Luke sat low on the piled nets and cordage of a fishing-dhow, scanning the waves, watching the small island grow in his vision-field. He would keep busy while Otto and Sergeant Hugh were elsewhere engaged and Kurt and Isolda were held captive. There was nothing else to do. He was simply a mendicant, a wandering friar who had chanced upon the Templar fortifications on Cyprus, who had espied the comings and goings at their stronghold in Limassol, who for two weeks had reconnoitred their estates and garrisons at Gastria, Khirokitia and Yermasoyia. They masked their intentions and capabilities well.

The Knights Templar, Order of the Poor Fellow Soldiers of Jesus Christ, at the heart of the Christian and crusading worlds, at the centre of everything. Poor they might once have been. But no more. They were far removed from the grouping of priestly knights founded a century before by the humble Hugues de Payns and Godeffroi de St Omer to guard the pilgrim trail. Their wealth was vast, their influence great, and even kings and princes paid rich tribute to this warrior caste. They had pledged themselves to fighting eternal holy war against the Saracen, were committed to retaking Jerusalem and their sacred site on Temple Mount. If conspiracy were afoot, the Templars would be drawn in. How fortuitous to be in their company.

Brother Luke felt the breeze stiffen, the dhow heave as its lateen sail filled. Behind him, the Templar fortress of Tortosa, its great *donjon* keep intimidating and heavy-massed above the waterfront. He had strolled unchecked among its bastions and winding alleyways, visited its Cathedral of Our Lady of Tortosa to pray. That the church was built with arrow-slits and thick defensive walls spoke much of Christendom in this land. Ahead, less than two miles offshore and to the south-west, the brooding and fortified isle did not present a welcoming countenance. It was why he had come.

Arwad, the hidden redoubt of the Templars. None landed who were not invited; none were invited who were not brought under escort. Measuring only nine hundred by six hundred yards, and protected by a high wall, the territory contained a tight concentration of storehouses, watchtowers and strongpoints. Atop its highest elevation was a fort; at the side of its harbour entrance was another. It would be hard to take by seaborne assault. The perfect fallback, an unrivalled position in which to regroup should the Saracens push them to the brink, should existence on the mainland opposite become untenable. Or it could act as venue for plot.

Fishermen rarely asked questions. If the friar wished for a closer look, they would oblige, be eager to help a holy man whatever his belief. He might bring them luck, would surely bless them in their labours. They adjusted the canvas, bringing the dhow near to the north of the island. Like the southern side, it possessed a boatyard, its foreshore scattered with the skeletal ribs of vessels under construction or repair. Nothing to draw attention. But the old man in his dun-hued rags appeared engrossed.

'Ease the sail, I beg you, my brothers.'

They did as he commanded. With an exhortation that they recover him on a later pass, the Franciscan swung himself sinuously on to the gunwales and slipped overboard. The fishermen shrugged. There was no fool like an ancient wanting baptism in the chill December sea. Yet they marvelled at his willpower, his strength.

Part swimming, half wading, Brother Luke reached the shoreline and clambered low up the sand shingle. He had not been seen. That was to the good, for he had observed ships in the harbour, detected the reflective glimmer of steel-tipped pikes, the *chapel de fer* helmets of sentries on patrol. The Templars were protecting their hive. Seamless, unhurried, avoiding clumsy movement that might catch the eye, the friar crawled forward. There were sheds to inspect, large borms and excavations to investigate.

He wiped salt from his eye and stared again. It could not be, was not suggested by the rush-woven screens that circled the site. Everything was artfully arranged and the camouflage carefully set. Beneath it, behind it, were the wooden hulls of galleys. They were pulled up in rows and sunk in their hollows, each long and graceful in form, each with masts lowered and oars removed. An invisible fleet of ships. One hundred and fifty slaves were required to man the oars of a single galley, and here alone there were six of the type. Elsewhere there would be more, vessels dug into crevices, part dismantled and biding snug until call to arms and the moment of war. On this grim island of Arwad, over a thousand imprisoned souls were likely to be sweating and suffering, kept ready for some future act. It was time for the friar to leave.

A few hundred yards distant, closeted in a chamber of the main fort, a visitor sat in conversation with the Grand Master of the Knights Templar. Their meeting might have surprised others, would certainly have dismayed those present at the Grand Council in Acre. The two men were not friends. Yet for the while they shared common purpose and a single cause, a desire for conquest, a hunger for power that would be sated only through bloodshed and force. There were no onlookers to their conference, no others privy to its secrets. The Lord of Arsur had stepped ashore on Arwad.

'It was fine theatre we conjured at Council, Grand Master.'

'The longer the regent and his barons believe we are enemies the better.' The Templar toyed with a richly inlaid rosary. 'None must recognize what we are about or suspect us of ill deed.'

'They will not.'

'Yet risks increase as the hour approaches.'

'Set aside such concerns. Every precaution has been taken, every provision made for concealment of our capability and intent.'

The Grand Master gave a thin smile. 'Perchance they do indeed swallow the truth that we feed them.'

'Truth we bait with poisoned barb. And all the while our troops muster on Cyprus for transport to Arsur, our ships lie out of sight in their berths.'

'You unleash a storm that shall not be easily contained.'

'How else to blow away the old and decayed, the dying embers of Outremer?' The stagnant eyes barely hinted at the fathomless deceit. 'Why, I am regarded as saviour and peacemaker, as loyal friend to John of Brienne.'

'He will soon have neither friends nor kingdom.'

'Within days will be shorn of daughter and heir.'

Thus were overthrow and regicide arranged. The Lord of Arsur regarded his accomplice in crime. He had done much for the man and his Templar knights, had cultivated alliance, assiduously courted goodwill. Moreover, had it not been for his involvement eight years before in the sack of Constantinople and disbursement of its seized lands, the Order would never have acquired new estates in Thrace and the Peloponnese.

Even for religious zealots, greed could provide ample motive.

He gazed towards the light of the Norman window, pondered fondly on the dying hours of that city-jewel of Byzantium. Insanely brutal and magnificently rewarding times. He and his men had raped noblewomen and slit the throats of Varangian guards on the silver throne of the patriarch in the cathedral of Santa Sofia, had tortured priests to discover the location of relics and treasures at their church of Christ the Pantocrator. Satisfying work that filled a need. All to this end.

The Grand Master let the rosary dangle in his fingers. 'My Order provokes the resentment of many. The Church envies our privilege and tithes; the people begrudge our power; the Pope castigates our perceived inaction and inability to destroy the hated Saracen.'

'I give you your crusade.'

'For it, I am thankful. It will be good to march once more upon the Holy City, to prove ourselves supreme among the military orders, to win again the regard and affection of all Europe.'

'Once we have Jerusalem, none will question your ascendancy. Every king and prince will bend his knee, every noble offer tribute, every bishop crawl at your feet.'

'And you?'

'I will begin my reign.'

It was said with quietness and certainty, with the focus of a leader-in-waiting whose planning neared fruition, whose destiny would be realized.

Du Plezier caressed the rosary with hands as

comfortable with a sword. 'Much relies on how Saphadin will receive you in his camp.'

'He was born to negotiate, will not pass up chance to parley at such critical hour, such moment of truth.'

'What is truth?'

'However we describe it to our credulous spectators. As John of Brienne deems me his friend, so Saphadin *al-Adil* will welcome me as bringer of truce, of salve for his woes. He has no choice but to listen, no other course than to agree to meeting with our regent.'

'I trust you have selected well the place for their gathering.'

'It shall be one fecund with surprise and complete with Assassins.'

Sallow lord garbed in black faced Grand Master dressed in white. Opposite and complementary sides of the same scheme. They understood what needed to be done, the scale of butchery to be unleashed. Saphadin dead; John of Brienne dead; Moslem emirs and Christian nobles dead. Then the march on Jerusalem would commence, a steel-clad force of Templars and hired mercenaries leading an army of Cathars and arrow-fodder inspired by its own heretical desires. Disparate formations melded into one. Ironic, the Lord of Arsur reflected, that he employed Templars whose brother forebears he had betrayed at Hattin. He kept much to himself.

Words entered his head, whispering soft and resonant from the past. *Judas. Betrayer of our cause.* He tried to scrape their bitter residue from his mind, but it clung. More words came, floating with the image of the condemned Templar standing before his execution stone. *A curse be upon you.* The eyes of the knight stared vengeful at him. He turned his head, averted his face from the red Latin cross.

The Grand Master had not noticed. 'Solitary and disquieting matter remains. It appears the youth Otto of Alzey is alive and landed on our shore.'

'Matter that is no concern. Have you never wandered near the sea and crushed its shell-creatures underfoot?'

'We kill him?'

'At our leisure and determination.' The Lord of Arsur waved a dismissive hand. 'Not even the son of Wilhem of Alzey will change event, challenge the outcome we have set.'

'My Templars will delight in slaying the worthless offspring of a Hospitaller.'

'Dwell on more vital things, on rehearsal for the fray.'

Du Plezier had worked through to the small crucifix at the end of his rosary. 'By the Lord our God, we shall have the Holy Land.'

And by mine. 'I shall leave you to your company and away to rendezvous with the Sultan.'

'All hail to the next king of Jerusalem.'

Raised from baron to ruler, promoted from obscure fief in Arsur to pre-eminence over all. The title sat well with him. And yet it was merely the start: of a new kingdom on earth, of a dark majesty that would devour the weak and control mankind. His inheritance.

Baphomet, sorcerer-god, would be watching. Let chaos proceed.

'You see them, Sergeant Hugh?'

'I do not.' The soldier lay prone and still on the wintry ground and let his breath-vapour filter through the wool cloth about his face. 'Yet I can report I favour being beside a large fire with wine goblet in one hand and cut of venison in the other.'

'Brother Luke did not complain so.'

'The friar is a man of god. I am a bowman who delights in fine roistering and devilish maids.'

'Who is the better man?'

'Who is the man lying frozen in hostile land on wild chase dreamed by a German boy of short acquaintance?'

Otto pulled himself up beside the Englishman and raised his eyes slowly above the frosted earth ridge. Whispered argument kept his mind from the cold. But he trusted the soldier, had seen the light of expectation in his eye and promise of skirmish and affray persuade him onward. His skills might be needed.

The enemy had established camp at the forested mouth of a valley. They were in no hurry, were on terrain controlled and patrolled by their own. Occasionally the Templars and Hospitallers might ride out in force to make a point, to raise the tempo and tension of exisiting conflict. Yet Moslem spies near the great forts would forewarn of their approach. It was part of the game, an element in the escalation that presaged full-scale war.

'They raise shelter, Sergeant Hugh.'

'Then they have more sense than ourselves.' The bowman adjusted his position and squinted across the divide. 'Like any Arab, they shun the routine of patrol, will not place guards to much effect.'

'It is to our benefit. The foe will scarce suppose we trail them.'

'I scarce believe it for myself.'

Sergeant Hugh grimaced and cupped his hands about his eyes. Before him, the raiding-party was at rest, its horses tethered, its riders gathered and crouched beneath canvas cover to eat and discuss. There were casualties to mourn and the surprise attack by Templars to debate. They could lie-up here, might again sortie out intent on vengeance and improved pickings. Rhinelander and Englishman studied them from their vantage.

'I could creep near and release their mounts, Sergeant Hugh.'

'You could further receive a Saracen dagger in your back.' The soldier reached and jammed the Turcoman helmet lower on the youth's head. 'Think, German boy. First, horses are their occupation, possessions they defend and hold most dear. Second, your diversion will fail. Third, even should our disguise hold and we walk boldly into camp, chance is slight we may set free your companions.'

'Create a plan of your own.'

'Let me in silence and I shall try.'

Quiet it was, broken only by the occasional whinny of a horse, the floating conversation of Mohammedans easing down from chase and battle. The noble boy and archer were perched above it. They had left their steeds at secure distance, had made the approach by foot. There would be no rapid escape.

'Something moves, Sergeant Hugh.'

'My bowel and your imagination, if I am not in error.' The Englishman blew on his hands.

'Beyond the camp, approaching from the east.'

'Mere result of wind on trees.'

'I have yet to see trees journey in caravan. They are horses, camels, men on foot.'

He was right. Merchants and traders had arrived, long-distance travellers making slow and steady progress for the wharves of Lattakia. In their packs and saddlebags were carried the produce of Araby and Persia, precious merchandise of fine silks and pungent incense, rare spices and dyed skins. They had room for more, were happy to collect.

It was starting to snow. Within the camp, Kurt and Isolda huddled shivering beneath a blanket and clung tight to each other for warmth.

✝
Chapter 13

Even the jester had been dismissed. The noble men and women of the royal court at Acre were in no mood for festivity, were not inclined to talk and laugh as they once did. Low and murmured conversation was of crisis, of the latest rumour and most recent outrage. The Pope was raising an army; the Pope had left them to their fate. The Saracens were preparing for mass attack from Mount Tabor; the Saracens were dug in east of the Jordan. Lies based upon gossip and founded in despair. There was a yearning for better times, and reminiscence of the past. Advent in the Latin kingdom, and countdown was towards not the birth-anniversary of the Christ Child but the end of epoch in Outremer.

John of Brienne nodded graciously to the wife of a knight, noted the anxiety-tic and the gleam of pity in her eye. They were all concerned, all ready to abandon him without knowing really where to go. Yet some remained true. To his right, Lady Matilda chatted lightly and attempted to lift the despondent mood. A difficult task.

The regent cut a piece of mutton and threw it to his

nearest hunting-dog. Showing no interest, the beast turned its nose away.

'Now too my hounds lose their appetite. It is a poor sign.'

Matilda smiled at him. 'Be of cheer, sir. They will find it again when sporting passion is regained.'

'That will not be for a while, for at present my knights engage in chase of deadlier kind.'

'I hear daily the hammer-ring of the smithies, the clatter of our cavalry as it ventures on patrol.'

'It is the sound of preparation and of war, Matilda. Look about this table, at the empty spaces where men of rank desert us, persons who once placed their hands between my own and pledged to me their solemn fealty.'

'I see them, my lord.'

'When trouble rears, hearts grow faint and the strongest may scamper for their lives.'

'Many stay.'

'Too few of them whom I trust. Templars, Hospitallers, Teutons: military Orders whose swords imprison me as much as they guard against the Saracen.'

'We have none else to rely upon.'

'The pity for it.' He reached with his knife and stabbed a hunk of bread. 'On matters irksome, how fares your knavish Sergeant Hugh?'

Matilda lowered her eyes, ashamed. 'I crave your pardon, sir. It was wrong of me to assign him to casual mission of my choosing.'

'Think nothing of it. He is least nuisance when

sent on errand far from here. I vouch he will fail.'

'I can merely pray he will not. There are child pilgrims who may be aided by his bowmanship.'

'Let us hope. My own child, our infant queen, would benefit from a miracle.' The grizzled leader chewed contemplatively on the bread. 'Like your father, I believed we could live in peace with the heathen, at least until we mustered and were ready for crusade.'

'Is that not fleeting truce instead of peace?'

'However it is termed, it seems ended. I would rather Saphadin, Sultan of Damascus, called off his Mamluks and Turcomans, recoiled from the furnace-pit of impending confrontation.'

'Where there is chance, it may be realized.'

His silence might have shown he concurred, could have signified disagreement. The face was grown too worn to read. But there remained unspoken empathy, the affection between a girl and guardian, a daughter and her proxy father. Matilda listened to the desultory exchanges of the lords and ladies. They were poor at masking their fear.

A Templar was momentarily silhouetted in an archway, his presence backlit by the fire-glow of the kitchen ovens beyond. It was a sight not lost on the regent.

He growled beneath his breath. 'Observe how these dark apparitions prowl, Matilda. They haunt my every step.'

'I confess I am made uneasy by them, sir.'

'Do not lose such instinct. Their knights are devils

cloaked in white surplices, never to be relied upon. Why, it is said Cœur de Lion on his deathbed claimed in jest he bequeathed to their Order his vice of pride and arrogance. It seems they have sufficient.'

'Banish your vexed thoughts, sweet sir. Dwell on the lighter things, on friendship and laughter.'

'There is precious little laughter. But friendship I recognize and will drink to.' He gulped from his chalice. 'It is on the shoulders of a friend that perhaps the entire fate of our realm now rests.'

'The Lord of Arsur you shall tell me.'

'You frown, Matilda.'

'Disregard it, sir. I am seventeen years of age, a maiden unschooled to give advice.'

John of Brienne laughed gently, his eyes brightening with fondness. 'Yet since your earliest years you have never baulked at proffering counsel. This time, however, I take my own. In our perilous state we turn to the baron who serves us well, the ally who risks his life to negotiate with the Mohammedan foe.'

'I bow to your wisdom, sir.'

'We must hope the Lord of Arsur succeeds in all his labour.'

Another part of that labour was now in train. In the nursery chamber of the palace, the plump and hearty wet-nurse stood as her replacement entered the room. She was eager to get away, keen to cede the night watch to her characterless junior who was ever prepared to assume the more tedious of her duties. There were better ways to while away the evening hours. Already she found herself growing slightly breathless at the thought. Her lover in the royal guard would pummel her hard tonight, would make her sweat and squeal with the ecstatic agony of his ways. His rough touch and muscled torso were worth every sighing second of the wait.

She bustled happily through the passageways and alleys towards her assignation. Some might once have laughed at her, tittered meanly at her graceless ways and shapeless form. But she had a man who loved her. That was what counted. He gave her things, mounted her like a caged demon, whispered secret and sweet affection in her ear. A clandestine coupling. He had made her swear on her life and soul to tell no one, had cajoled and bribed her to maintain their liaison in the darkest of shadows. Because she wanted him, yearned herself to be wanted, she complied. Her undershift was becoming damp with perspiration and the wetness of expectancy.

Without pausing, she climbed the stair. He was waiting for her, stripped to the waist, a casual and lopsided smile beckoning her close. She took a step forward. Even vulgarity had its ritual, its little mating-dance routines. She jigged with pleasure, puckering her lips in a fat version of winsomeness. His expression changed. Had she noticed, she might have backed away; had she detected the thin-bladed knife clenched in his fist, she would have propelled herself to instant retreat. She was too slow and unwary. Escape had been forfeited, her fate long since decided. As the dagger emerged from behind his back and plunged for her belly, she was still reminding herself of her wondrous luck, still preparing for the blissful act of penetration.

In the royal quarters of baby Yolanda, the recent appointee slowly rocked the cradle. Back and forth it went, rhythmic and hypnotic. The infant slept on. She had grown used to the presence of the thin and unsmiling woman, accustomed to her smell, her breasts, her milk. That was to advantage, for adult and young queen would spend much time together. The nurse leaned over and watched the gently breathing form. What privilege it was to serve this function; how vulnerable the tiny girl seemed. So helpless and alone. She was born to become ruler of Outremer, but would have her life sacrificed to something far greater. The nurse reached in and carefully lifted the bundle.

Later, when the frantic alarm was raised and a search ordered, no sign could be found of the baby queen or either of her two nurses. They had simply vanished. There was talk of the Devil and of dark magic, speculation that grew of involvement by the Saracens. But conjecture would not restore Yolanda to her inconsolable father. Frenzied with despair, John of Brienne rode for miles into the countryside, took men with lanterns into the deepest recesses of his city, calling for his daughter. He was not to be rewarded.

Transaction had been made, the deal struck with silver pieces and Koranic verse, and the traders moved on with their new acquisitions. The pair of children would fetch good price at market, for the boy was strong and the girl shy and graceful in spite of her rags. Young and fresh things they were. They would clean up well, had already washed ashore into the clutches of the raiding-party. The soldiers had been happy to offload them. Back at their fortress base, their garrison commander would claim their hard-won cargo, would sell it on and profit for himself. His men had pre-empted such occasion, and both they and the travelling merchants were the richer for it.

'We head again for the coast, Isolda.' The twelve-year-old looked back over his shoulder at the receding mountains. 'It will be warmer, closer to where we left Otto and Brother Luke and the English bowman.'

'Our friends are dead, Kurt.'

'Though we are not.'

She raised her tied hands. 'But we are still captive and bound fast, still surrounded by men with menace and with spears in their grasp.'

'Each step we keep our hope will be closer to rescue.' He indicated the camel train walking at their side. 'Who else in our village would ever glimpse these creatures?'

'What are they?'

'Perhaps horses of some kind, or the camels of which Brother Luke spoke, beasts as mean and poor-tempered as the men who drive them.'

'It is a strange world, Kurt.'

'One I intend to see for as long as I am able.'

Her features brightened to a smile. 'You were ever hopeful, always my young brother who raised the spirits and banished the gloomiest of clouds.'

'Without my sister I am nothing.'

'Do you recall when as a small boy you climbed the highest tree and refused to come down?'

'I was beaten for it.'

'For many things, Kurt. Every jape and misdeed, you were its champion and I your defender. You and Egon lost for a day and night in those caves. You persuading Albert to lower you by rope deep inside that well.'

'Exploration has often brought me to trouble.' He shook his head in rueful memory. 'Did Hans and I not find a cart abandoned and ride it down a hill?'

'Direct into a trotting line of proud knights and squires.'

They allowed themselves the comfort of the moment, the distraction of the past, before awareness crept back. Albert the bird-scarer was left behind, Egon the blacksmith's son had deserted them, Hans the goatherd was butchered with knives on a remote track in northern Italy. Kurt felt the grief burn once more in his throat. Everyone whose life he touched was gone.

His sister spoke softly to him. 'You did good and true things too, Kurt. Few of the young did not depend on you to protect them from Gunther.'

'It is a name I have not thought of for a while.'

'A name with no cause again to be mentioned. And I alone know it was you who warned Edda the village scold that our bishop planned to burn her as a witch.'

'She paid me twenty hen-eggs for her escape.'

'What is the value to be placed on our skins, Kurt?'

Brother and sister tramped on. Their pace, set by the plodding walk of the animals, was gentler than it had been with the soldiers. At least they were not tethered to a horse, were roped only to each other. The merchants left them alone, intervening on occasion merely to prod and direct with the tip of a long whip. Assessment and examination were already made. The mouths of the youngsters had been forced open, their teeth checked, their limbs squeezed by expert hands. Mute and obedient, the children had accepted this. There was more reason to be livestock than roadside carrion.

A sharp cry from Isolda, and she sagged in sudden pain as her ankle buckled beneath her. In an instant, the two children were surrounded, jabbering Arabs pointing their whips and goading them forward. Isolda tried to stand. But the injury from Europe had returned and her sprained leg would not hold her weight.

She sat, her eyes wide with trepidation. 'I cannot. Please, Kurt, tell them. It is impossible.'

He began to remonstrate, attempted to push back the angry and crowding group of men. A finger jabbed his chest, a whip cracked threatening and close to his ear. He struggled harder. They did not understand his protestations, were too loud with their own shouts to care about his. Furious, he swung a punch clumsily and double-fisted at the nearest face.

It was a grievous error. For all his bravery, he was outnumbered and a boy. They would teach him a lesson, would break him until he grasped the meaning of his folly and the power-balance of slavedom. Until he bled.

The attack dissolved before the first blow. High above, a banshee shriek caused them to stop, drew their eyes upward to follow the arcing noise-curve of an arrow in flight. Kurt recognized the howl. It was a she-devil, the sky-signature of Sergeant Hugh, and it meant the soldier was alive and salvation close at hand. Isolda too was staring.

Somewhere ahead, a voice called in Arabic. 'Greetings, my friends. Better an arrow screams so than a trader when punctured by its steel head.'

Those traders now shuffled exposed and uncomfortable into looser formation. Facing them was a drawn longbow and a muscular archer, and beside him a young warrior in leather *cuirie* and holding a flaming torch. There was little to do but play for time and devise a stratagem.

Sergeant Hugh stopped them. 'My arm grows tired and I seek excuse to unleash this shot. No sudden movement, no hostile design, or you die.'

'We outnumber you, infidel.' It was a senior merchant who spoke.

'Then step forward any who would enter paradise.'

'What is it you wish for?'

'The boy and girl. Release them to our charge or suffer consequence of my wrath.'

'They cost us dear.'

'Will cost you more should you disregard me.' The bowman gestured to Otto, who moved forward and threw a canvas bag at their feet. 'Within are treasures, baubles and precious trinkets that may compensate and enrich. In return I ask for the children and a single horse.'

'You seem persuasive, infidel.'

The stance and gaze of the bowman remained fixed. 'Try me.'

One did. With a yelping scream and cry to Allah, a camel-hand rushed from the periphery brandishing a long and lowered spear. Almost careless, Sergeant Hugh responded. He swivelled to pass the arrowhead through the firebrand of the young noble, rocking back to loose the shaft. It sped fast, spewing flame, impacting deep in the chest of the assailant in incendiary eruption of hog-fat and pitch. In seconds, the Arab had transmuted from human to firework, his robes catching, his body falling, the funeral pyre engulfing and consuming. Point made, and fully taken.

A further arrow was already fitted to the bow. 'Consider our talking complete.'

Delight and relief were too great to contain. Kurt and Isolda hugged their rescuers, laughing, tripping over their words in haste to ask and tell. They wanted to know everything, wished to speak of their own experience. There was the raid and skirmish to discuss, the survival of them all to celebrate, the details of capture and release to debate. Otto cuffed Kurt in backhanded welcome; Isolda kissed Sergeant Hugh.

The Englishman rolled his eyes. 'Enough gaiety. We are still in Syria. We remain on dangerous soil.'

'But we are reunited.' Kurt slapped him enthusiastically on the shoulder.

'I am unconvinced of the merits of this.'

Otto jeered. 'Do not listen to him, friends. He is as pleased to see you as I.'

'My purse is considerably lighter.'

'Proof of his affection and regard and his readiness to buy you both from your imprisonment.'

'It was my mother, God rest her soul, who warned I was a halfwit.'

Isolda looked enquiringly at him. 'Yet where is Brother Luke?'

'Your blessed friar is alive, you may be sure. He is too frail for a venture such as ours. He went with the Templars to their command at Tortosa.'

'Will he join us?'

'At his own pace and once he has preached to every man, stone and lizard on these shores. Then he will come to Acre to meet us and preach some more.'

Kurt voiced their disappointment. 'That could be weeks or months, Sergeant Hugh.'

'I am merely bearer of the tidings. Blame it on the vagaries of an old man, on his holy mission, on the curious twists of fate.' The soldier strode to Zephyr, his horse, and mounted up. 'Now, I have as good as bought you, you are my chattels and those come with me. Noble boy, you will bring them. We head once more for the Cistercian monastery above Tripoli.'

Confident in his command, that the youngsters would follow, he flicked the reins and allowed his mount to travel on. It had been an eventful morning, and would be more so if they did not avoid further patrols or the caravan he had waylaid and whose possessions he had lifted. He pulled the wood stopper from a goatskin flask and put it to his lips, grimacing and spitting its contents on discovering only water. The gods were perplexing. He turned in his saddle.

'You dolts, fools, ingrates!' He wheeled his horse, roaring in livid disbelief, riding to catch the children setting out on different bearing. 'Why is it you disobey me? Where is it you think you journey?'

Otto answered. 'The Hospitaller fortress of Krak des Chevaliers.'

'Madness.'

'At least it is my madness, Sergeant Hugh.'

'We had agreement, a plan.'

'Your agreement and your plan.' The youth grinned winningly at the thunderous face. 'My father is Hospitaller knight, and my task to find him.'

Astride another horse with his sister, and led on a rope by the noble boy, Kurt chimed in. 'Our own duty is to go where Otto goes.'

'And where do you believe your mighty castle is? How do you intend to reach it?'

'I shall enquire, will seek direction from others.' Otto was calm at the edge of the storm.

'Others? Others who wish you ill, who do not speak your tongue.' The exasperation of the bowman had translated into shouts and wild gesticulation. 'You have no allies or support, no knowledge of these parts.'

'We learn as we journey, Sergeant Hugh.'

'Then you will cruelly find your well-bred notions and appealing ways no match for Saracen malice. I have risked myself for your infant pelts. I have saved you more times than I may count.'

A plaintive note had entered his voice. It had no effect, for the three youngsters continued on their way. With a prayer and an oath, the soldier nudged Zephyr forward. Irritation, professional pride, would not let him stay behind. He called after his stubborn charges.

'Defiance is an ugly thing, Otto of Alzey. Mark my words, your Brother Luke would not approve.'

Their Brother Luke was busy. He had talked and perambulated his way about Tortosa, always willing to stop and offer a blessing or kind word, ever eager to tend the poor and sick of the town. Visibility rendered him unseen. Yet he noticed. He spoke the language of the Arab, could ask questions, pry where others could not, carry his investigation into the darkest and most threatening of reaches. How many boats had come to the harbour, how many forays had the knights made, how many men patrolled the castle walls. All needed answers.

Rumour and observation travelled fast at the bottom of the dungheap. Tortosa was a key bastion guarding the crusader sea routes from Europe. News and trade, supplies and manpower converged on this point. The Franciscan too was newly arrived, just an aged friar in a habit as stained and shabby as the surrounding streets.

He crossed the central courtyard of the fortress and passed below an archway to a worn flight of steps. Most of the brother knights would be at prayer. It was an opportune moment to burrow further beneath the Templar skin, to push the bounds of their Christian hospitality. Begging for alms was not part of his itinerary this day. He descended the stone stairs past an open doorway, keeping to the shadow, flitting beyond the radius of a murmured conversation. Here a drapier hurried to discuss matters concerning holy vestments; there a turcopole snored off the rigours of a previous night on duty. Brother Luke went deeper.

No guards were present. The Templars could play their own games of dissemblance and masquerade. They belonged to a secretive Order, felt no compunction to throw wide their cellars and chambers to the world outside. But an air of concealment could breed inquisitiveness. Perhaps they were confident that none would make discovery; perhaps they believed that overt security would fan speculation.

The friar paused and listened. In the cool subterranean gloom, only silence pervaded. He sniffed the air and pushed on. Ghostly light dappled the flagstones through narrow openings set high in the walls, seeming to cast more darkness than illumination. At intervals, oil lamps had been set, and the friar took one as he progressed on. Vaulted passageways divided, the underworld labyrinth winding through a series of crypt-like halls. More steps, additional corridors.

That smell. It was the faintest of traces, carrying the suggestion of naphtha and nitre, of sulphur and pitch. He went forward and raised the lamp. Before him, laid out on racks and trestles, were clay pots with thin necks, vessels designed not for drinking but instead moulded small and spherical for a human hand to throw. Beside them were stacked short lengths of tow, hemp and flax cut to order and able to be flung. Brother Luke swung the lantern and searched into the black. Against the walls he could make out the taller shapes of amphorae, possibly filled, probably sealed. He could not leave them ignored.

As he stooped to put his nose to earthenware, a voice broke harsh into the stillness. 'You are an unusual wanderer, Brother Luke.'

'Forgive an old man and his curiosity.' Chuckling disarmingly, the Franciscan straightened and turned. 'A weakness for wine takes me to all manner of place.'

'Today it brings you here.'

Three Templars blocked his escape, sergeants whose faces glowed hostile in the restrained light thrown by their lanterns. Rush torches were too flammable for these cellars. Brother Luke noted it, had already discerned much. He backed innocently and imperceptibly against the large jars close to the wall.

'Why, if it is not my old acquaintance from Rome. Can it be you, Sergeant Brother James?' He leaned forward, blinking at the leader of the group.

'I am promoted *turcopolier*.'

'Indeed? A battlefield commander of other sergeants, a position of responsibility deserving of respect.'

'Your own position creates only doubt.'

'You know me, Brother James.'

'I recognize you as a man whose age belies his actions, whose rags disguise a scout who came ashore by fishing-boat to spy upon our isle of Arwad.'

'Such reasoning is misguided.'

'Interrogation may tell us otherwise.'

They advanced upon him, threat implicit in their bearing, intention evidenced by the heavy cudgels in their hands. Brother Luke viewed them with calm and passive interest. Three brutes who betrayed a great deal in what they did.

'Kneel.'

The friar replied without a tremor. 'I bend only to the will of God.'

'We shall see.'

A blow struck his chest, a second his abdomen. He swayed slightly and recovered, a tree buffeted but unfelled. They tried again, pummelling with bone-jarring ferocity, driving their clubs hard into ribs and back and head. He breathed harder and stayed upright.

'Yield, friar.'

'Did Christ do so before Pilate?'

'You blaspheme.' The wooden baton impacted on his nose and the blood gushed free. 'You wish to be flayed alive, to be burned as a heretic?'

'What I wish is of little consequence to your conduct. I sought you out in Rome as a friend, Sergeant Brother James.'

'You discover me as your enemy.' The club rose and fell.

A pink loop of saliva hanging from his mouth, the friar stood serene for the next violent contact. The Templars had something to hide and protect, a clandestine matter that had brought them in number from Europe, that had made them lay-up boats and put down traps. His instincts had been correct.

He offered conversation while they gathered their energy and breath. 'Are we not both of us Christians, Sergeant Brother James?'

'You believe in peace as I put trust in war.' A mailed fist slammed into the cheek of the Franciscan. 'And, as I have advised, my rank is become *turcopolier*.' The balled and steel-clad hand pulled back and punched forward, this time to the temple.

Collapse came, Brother Luke toppling across jars that split and spilled their contents. In the wreckage, the friar was motionless. He was aware that the three Templars continued to beat him, conscious too that what he detected were the component substances for one of the deadliest weapons of war. Liquid seeped around him. He tasted vinegar, the drink with which Christ was taunted on the Cross, the one material able to contain and douse the blaze created by these demonic armaments. The Knights Templar were making wildfire. It would permit them to take and hold a city, to defend its seized ramparts by raining fiery death on any who besieged them. As he drifted towards grey oblivion, the old friar congratulated himself on his find. It was worth the suffering. There could be only one city, a single target. The Templars intended to conquer Jerusalem.

There would be pandemonium in the royal city of Acre, much wailing and gnashing of teeth at the sudden disappearance of the baby queen. Grief-stricken, howling conspiracy and blaming the Saracens, her father the regent would be ordering a general search. All to no use. It was simply another stage in the disintegration of Outremer, a further prop ripped from beneath the power-base of John of Brienne. Sad and worrying times. Such were the thoughts passing through the mind of the Lord of Arsur as he headed for the cold and wooded slopes of Mount Tabor.

He spotted the cavalry of al-Mu'azzam riding out to greet him, a silent display of strength that fanned out and fell in to either side. The Mohammedans were taking no chances. He guided his horse on, refusing to acknowledge their presence, secure that the Sultan of Damascus intended first to talk rather than kill. His moves, like those of John of Brienne, were so predictable, so easily manipulated and countered. Each leader was absorbed in his own concerns. Neither would foresee the coming strike.

Attended by two bodyguards, Saphadin received him in his tent with studied graciousness and appraising eyes. They had not met since the days of the great Salah ad-Din, when each had acted as negotiator and go-between, when the Lord of Arsur had delivered up the Christian army for annihilation at Hattin. Matters for discussion and reminiscence were plentiful.

'I am sixty-nine years of age, older than when last we met.'

'The years sit well with you, al-Adil.'

'Not so with the land we inhabit.' The Sultan looked gravely at his visitor. 'How has this come to pass? How has truce between our nations slipped to the brink of an abyss?'

'Hot temper and ill judgement may for ever carry men towards conflict, al-Adil.'

'I thought I could trust your regent king John of Brienne. I believed we had treaty, supposed that even while he planned long-term crusade he wished peace and reason for the present to remain.'

The Lord of Arsur held and returned the steady gaze. 'It is not he who agitates for war, al-Adil. As in your own court, there dwell in Outremer rash and emboldened nobles, zealots and provocateurs who rouse the furies and stir the blood.'

'Which are you, Lord of Arsur?'

'A friend to amity and accord, a bearer of the seal and confidence of John of Brienne, a supporter of the very compact you made with our Latin kingdom.'

'Yet you are the viper in the bosom of that kingdom, the creature who betrayed the Christian forces for profit and for gain.'

'The more reason you should embrace my intervention and good office, al-Adil.' He produced a sincere and reassuring smile.

Sultan and envoy sipped mint tea in silence, each man perusing the other, reflecting upon motive and intended move. The Lord of Arsur was content to wait, satisfied with the dialogue he had already created. Saphadin was intrigued; Saphadin would fall all too easily in his trap.

The Moslem ruler was cautious. 'What advantage is yours in coming now to me?'

'Peace brings reward to us all. I own land and wealth, have earned much from prior association with Salah ad-Din your brother.'

'Why should I see truth in your counsel?'

'For that we both are witness to the destructive destiny of battle. For that I am no Templar or Hospitaller knight chafing to slaughter every Mohammedan. For that I am the sole chance you possess to draw back from looming fray and devastation.'

'Perhaps devastation is required.'

'And what then, al-Adil? The Pope and the European princes will raise armies, send fleets, engage you in fresh cycle of bloodshed and brutality.'

'I shall crush them all.'

'At supreme cost to yourself and instability to your realm.'

There was recognition in the face of the old man, awareness behind the white beard that for every strength there was opposing weakness. He might be able to summon troops, could raze every Frankish town and bastion the length of Outremer. But the conflagration might yet consume him.

The nobleman was patient and persuasive. 'Conciliation is ever a more certain and placid creature than war, al-Adil. It is twenty-five years since Hattin, less since Richard Cœur de Lion stormed ashore with vengeance in his heart. Reasonable men have no wish to repeat in haste such history.'

'You have suggestion?'

'Negotiation, al-Adil.'

'I have sent to Acre messengers of peace, ambassadors for mediation, my own senior chamberlain. None return to me alive.'

'Killed no doubt by those desiring confrontation. Let us confound them. Let us seize the moment and sue for harmony.' The Lord of Arsur stepped closer to the Sultan. 'Confer with John of Brienne in private discourse; bring your emirs to meet the barons. Only then will order be restored from present chaos.'

'We shall choose the site of assembly.'

'As you demand, al-Adil. Pick also your hostages to pass to our safe care for duration of the gathering. In good faith I will tender myself as captive to your charge.'

'A brave decision.' Saphadin waved an imperious hand. 'You have place in mind for the keeping of my pledge-made-flesh?'

'Your chosen emirs will be imprisoned at the small fort of Sephorie close by Tyre.'

The irony was not lost on Saphadin, for it was the stronghold from which the Christian army had set forth that July morn in 1187 for eventual destruction on the Horns of Hattin.

His dark eyes narrowed. 'As my honoured guest and future hostage, as baron who has worked for our sultanate and cause, where is it you would desire to be lodged?'

'At the castle of Beit-Nuba.'

The Lord of Arsur was no stranger to the place.

*

Twilight dropped across Mount Tabor, broadened over the hills of Galilee and the valley of Armageddon. A still and peaceful night. The eve of Christmas in the Holy Land.

✝

Chapter 14

'Identify yourselves.'

'Otto of Alzey, son of Wilhelm the Knight Hospitaller, and three companions.'

They were dwarfed by the soaring edifice. Unassailable on its rock bluff, a monumental bulwark of concentric defences and thirteen outer towers, it was the mightiest of all crusader castles. The stone essence of Frankish power. Never taken by siege, it sat above the valley pass and astride the route to the Syrian interior, a constant presence, a visible reminder to the Saracens and their sultan in Damascus that the Christians were unlikely ever to leave. A bastion set within a stronghold wrapped inside a fortress. Breach the walls and an attacker would find himself confronted by an interior moat. Cross the moat, survive the catapult-shot, and the same attacker would face a steep glacis, would be channelled into killing-zones overlooked by angled ramparts and hidden galleries, by murder-holes and defensive passageways. Krak des Chevaliers in all its harsh glory.

Kurt glanced uncertainly at Otto. 'You said they were Hospitallers, Otto.'

'They are.' The noble boy kept his gaze on the gate tower. 'Yet they are also Knights of St John of Jerusalem, men who both tend the sick and wage war against the heathen.'

Sergeant Hugh nodded. 'I know it well, for I have ridden into battle with them when King Richard marched towards Jerusalem. It was they who charged first at the enemy, who compete only with the Templars in fervour and ferocity, who are the sworn enemies of Islam. A Hospitaller is as gentle in the infirmary as he is barbarian in the field.'

'This castle is proof of it.' The twelve-year-old let his stare traverse the daunting heights.

Isolda too was looking. 'I cannot believe a father of yours to be barbarian, Otto.'

'He was the most temperate and beloved of men and kindest of fathers, was never known to raise voice or hand in anger. His mission east was to nurse pilgrims and care for the weak.'

The English soldier heaved a sigh. 'Ah well, it is how many of us start.'

In groaning succession the portcullises lifted, and the small band of riders passed through to ascend the ramp. Kurt gaped open-mouthed, noted only dimly the cocked crossbows, the silhouettes of the giant slings, the distant figures of patrolling sentries. The scale was as monstrous as it had once been beyond his imagination. Seated behind him, Isolda clung tight.

'We welcome you, Otto of Alzey.' A burly sergeant had appeared from the guardhouse. 'I see you are accompanied by Hugh of York.'

'He acts as our guide.'

'Then it will not be for spiritual concerns.'

Sergeant Hugh pulled a wounded face and dismounted in a jangle of accumulated chattels. 'That is no greeting for an old friend to your Order.'

'We have friends enough in the infidels we fight.'

'Such meagre salutation in this time of Christmas cheer.' The Englishman handed the reins to a stable-hand and looked about. 'A good fire, a belly of roast pig, a flagon of wine are all a poor and humble traveller requests.'

'Poverty and humility are not reputations which precede you.'

'At least I am recognized.'

He helped the children down, patted their Arab mount, and gathered up his longbow and quiver. There was something in the piety of the military Orders that made them the butt of his jokes, something in him that drew wearied acceptance and resignation from the religious knights. To survive was to earn respect. The Hospitaller watched.

'You brave weather and enemy to come here, Sergeant Hugh.'

'My very reasons to keep away. But Otto is on quest to find his father, and I fool enough to assist.'

'A wasted journey. Brother Wilhelm left our Order many years ago, a famed and goodly knight, before my service.'

Otto had lowered himself from his horse. 'He did not return to Europe.'

'Who knows what befalls a man in these parts?'

The sergeant brother was phlegmatic. 'He may lose his mind or his life faster than an insect on a piece of dung.'

'You do not reassure the boy.' Sergeant Hugh placed a protective hand on the shoulder of the youth.

'It is not my duty. You would strive better to visit our coastal fortress of Marqab, to speak there with the Grand Master and his senior brethren.'

'For the while we will avail ourselves of his lower ranks here.'

Without invitation, Sergeant Hugh began to cross the bridge spanning the deep divide hewn from the rock. None was about to challenge him.

He was a strange and unnerving sight. Surrounded by runes and cabbalistic symbols scored in the walls, his attention focused on a small fire, the ancient sat as though in trance. In the guttering glow of the lamps, the youngsters listened to the drip of water and waited for the old Hospitaller to speak. Perhaps he would not, thought Kurt. Maybe he was dead, preserved for ever in the dank gloom of this chamber and kept upright by a stalagmite growing inside. The boy shuddered. It had been the idea of Sergeant Hugh to visit. He had ushered his protesting companions down a series of dog-leg stairways, had brought them to the hidden watercourse and bathing-rooms carved out beside the moat. There was someone he wished them to meet.

The head turned, revealing features shrunken and leather-skinned with age. Hair was vanished from the scalp, sight almost gone from the eyes, and the face dipped at the end of a spine twisted by the pressing weight of years. He was nothing more than the composite of a black habit thrown over a collected heap of bones. Brother Luke would have seemed young by comparison.

A small tongue flicked dry and lizard-like between the colour-drained lips. 'You gather children to me, Hugh of York.'

'It is important they meet with you.'

'Imperative I should speak with them.' His voice was faint and breathless. 'Draw close, my brood. I shall not eat you.'

They took some convincing. The three glanced at Sergeant Hugh, who encouraged them forward with a nod. Hesitant, they shuffled nearer.

Otto glimpsed back at the bowman. 'He is known to you, Sergeant Hugh?'

'Hugh of York is known to most.' The rheumy eyes of the Hospitaller were still and staring. 'It may not seem so, but we were companions-in-arms, fellow soldiers who fought in the army of Cœur de Lion, I as Hospitaller, he as protector to the King himself.'

'We have often heard his tales.'

'Each, no doubt, growing more vivid with the telling.' If there was humour, it was lost in the thin tones and wizened countenance. 'Yet trust him, rely on his craft, for he is your sole surety in these troubled realms.'

His speech drifted to silence, the moment extending while the children and archer stood and the old knight sat. There was a sense that long time could pass in reverie, that days were akin to seconds, and seconds could stretch to days. None interrupted.

The mouth moved. 'You may wonder why I choose to dwell in darkness, why I should inhabit the deepest chambers of this fortress. Take yourselves to the roof of our great keep and you shall see, will perceive the distant bastion of Castel Blanc, will observe how we are nothing more than remote islands of Christendom placed upon a sea of troubles and buffeted by infidel storm. I have already witnessed and foretold the end, given warning of our final days.'

'So you hide?' Kurt blurted a question before Isolda could restrain him.

'I choose to keep from the sins of the world and the agonies of man. We build castles that are no defence, offer prayers that will not save our souls. The Beast walks on the earth, and will soon devour us.'

Kurt would not be hushed. 'You are a soothsayer, a prophet?'

'I am a seer of things.'

'What manner of things?'

'Our past and future, the nature of being, the fears and shadows in all our hearts.'

Otto crouched to peer level at the face. 'I search for my father, Wilhelm of Alzey.'

'A courageous and onerous task.' The Hospitaller cast a pinch of powder to the fire and watched the flame turn to purple. 'He was fine exemplar to the religion, the best among our brotherhood.'

'Yet he bade you all farewell.'

'That was his chosen destiny. He went like many

knights on holy errand, in pursuit of discovery and the True Cross.'

Isolda took a pace forward. 'It is why we too travel to these lands.'

'Then you may be swallowed up as he has been.'

The young noble was insistent. 'Tell me, I beg of you. Where now is he? What do you find? Does my father live or die?'

'He lives in death.'

'Such oracles deceive and have no meaning. Be clearer with your words.'

'There is no clarity where he is gone. He has moved to the lightless side, to the service of the black and murk.'

Otto rose dismissively to his feet. 'We are done, for it makes no sense.'

'Did it make sense that four apocalyptic horse-men and Assassins should pursue you on your path? Or that heretic Cathars should surround you at the hanging-tree?' Different powder was thrown, another flame blossomed. 'And you, sweet brother and sister? Did it make sense when you buried a young girl at the wayside, or when unseen hands thrust you in the mountain torrent?'

They were stripped of response, dumbstruck at the understated revelation. Mood had changed, and yet the elderly Hospitaller had not.

'How?' Otto swallowed his dismay. 'What secret magic is used to know this, which enchantments applied to your thoughts?'

'No magic or charms, but the gift of vision. As

everything is linked in nature, so everything beyond it also. The True Cross, your father Wilhelm, the murderous riders, the crusade on which you travel, the darkening skies that threaten brimstone and fire. Even the stalwart friar in his dun rags is shackled like you to the single flow of providence.'

Sergeant Hugh groaned. 'I suppose I too am touched and tainted by event.'

'You are deeper immersed than you may think.'

'I feared as much.' The Englishman scratched his head. 'And your talk is of the Beast.'

'One man who comes among us, who seeks dominion over all. A false lord, a friend and dissembler, a dark and fallen angel made flesh. He sets people against people, drives kingdoms from peace towards war. He collects power to himself, will usurp and overthrow established order, intends to seize the throne.'

'Saphadin?'

'It is not he, nor any of the infidel.'

'I can think of no Frankish lord with such malice or authority.'

'Yet you will recall Reynald of Châtillon, the baron whose head was struck off by Saladin in his tent at Hattin. His spirit walks, and monstrous deeds are done. Legions of Belial assemble, and innocents die.'

Kurt was rooted to the spot. 'All this you see in coloured flame?'

'Message carries in the wind, in the song of birds, in the fall of mountain rain.'

'And what are we to do?'

The question drew no immediate answer. The aged

311

Hospitaller was again focused on the flickering light, had sunk further into reverie and himself. Kurt and Isolda craned to see, anxious to detect in the blaze a sign or a truth. They stood a long while before Sergeant Hugh shepherded them away.

'Search others for wickedness and yourselves for strength.' The voice trailed after them, yet the figure was still. 'Answer is ever within.'

Firmitas et Fortitudo. It seemed pertinent to his circumstance. Brother Luke watched the flagstones pass beneath him, felt the pressure of hands beneath his shoulders as the guards dragged him onward. For days he had languished in the dungeon cell, had dwelt in the company of rats, roaches and faeces. A solitary precursor to what was to come. There was method in the Templar malice. It was their special way and Christmas rite, a technique crafted to soften the victim and nourish him with diet of his own anticipation and terror. The friar was content to allow them their confidence. Such welcome change to be on the move.

They reached a large chamber, its light painful to the eyes in the aftermath of gloom, and he was flung hard to the ground. The scattered straw did little to break his fall. He raised his head and peered about, could not be optimistic in what he saw. Philippe Du Plezier, Grand Master of the Temple, sat enthroned in a wooden chair. Both men viewed each other, one a jailer with vicious intent and predator instinct, the other a prone and elderly friar who seemed uncowed by the occasion.

'You enjoy your sojourn with us, Brother Luke?'

'I have scant complaint.'

'There will be time for it, and for regret.' The Grand Master bent to study his captive. 'I have heard of Franciscans, yet until this moment have been denied occasion to meet one.'

'More of my brethren head this way on pilgrimage, Brother Francis of Assisi our founder among them.'

'Alas, they will not discover the fate or position of their brother Luke.'

'That is a pity.'

'Is it not? But my hand is forced, my patience tried by your trespass upon our generosity, your meanderings about our possessions.'

'I meant no offence, Grand Master.'

'Though we are quick to take it.' Du Plezier had already betrayed his decision with his eyes. 'What meaning and purpose lie behind your presence, friar?'

'My trade is to preach and to nourish the wasted spirit of man.'

'Your appetite is to meddle in the affairs of the Order of the Knights Templar.'

'By accident and fortune, Grand Master.'

'Through treacherous design. You are found within our cellars, seen in a boat traversing our domain, land south of Tripoli in company with the young noble Otto of Alzey.'

'I do not choose my path or the companions with whom I journey.'

'Nor will you choose your fate.'

The friar listened to the distant tolling of a chapel bell. It reminded him of the sound from the belfry of St John the Lateran in Rome, returned him to his audience three months earlier with the Pope. Innocent III had engaged him as a spy, and here was the drab and logical conclusion. Templars were not famed for acts of clemency.

'Such crude and brute power, so sinewed and muscled in form for an old and pious creature, Brother Luke.'

'Travel renders a man strong.'

'We shall test that strength.' Du Plezier nodded to his men. 'Scourge him.'

Quickly, they cut away the sackcloth habit and forced him naked to his knees. The Grand Master surveyed the scene. He had expected trouble, a struggle of sorts, but the beggar spy was as pliant and meek as a sheep stitched within the pelt of a bear. Holiness, acceptance, might be only a flayed skin deep, however.

The Templar leader raised his hand. 'Wait.'

He stepped from his seat and walked slowly to inspect the striped scarring to the back and shoulders of his prisoner. The marks were not livid or fresh, but were historic remnants, the rough and ossified layers of a previous life and of savage beatings.

'Again you surprise me, friar.' Du Plezier deliberated. 'Are you flagellant? A criminal? A former slave?'

'It is record of my years, of the many towns and villages from whence I have been driven.'

'At least you discover shelter here.'

A joke of sorts, followed by a gesture to begin. Rawhide was used, and with each strike there was a shuddering crack of sound, the grunts of energy expended and the groans of air expelled. Truth would out, even if entrails came with it.

Brother Luke had not flinched. He lay quiet, his skin torn, his face in the straw as Du Plezier stood over him. The Grand Master casually emptied a pail of salt water on the welts and lacerations and watched the body spasm.

'Is it wasted effort to apply the lash to you, friar?'

'You must do as you consider just.'

'Justice is not my endeavour.' The Templar had yet to finish with his project. 'Put his feet to the fire.'

It was the oldest of tortures and slowest of ends. The feet would be coated in pig-fat and placed before the hearth, the flesh roasting, the bones detaching, the victim screaming his tormented way to a superheated demise. He might take days to die, would do so with the stench of his own cooked and cauterized meat in his nostrils. Few who suffered thus ever rose to walk or talk again.

He was bound and his propped and shackled legs stretched out, the greased soles of his feet set towards the flames. Perhaps it was better this way, preferable to strapping, the monstrous art of tying wrists behind back and winching them upward until arms and shoulders dislocated and the writhing unfortunate expired. In the event, hard to make comparison. Sweat coursed on the torso of the friar, and Du Plezier stoked the blaze with workmanlike vigour.

'Have you nothing to confide, Brother Luke?'

'Only that I am wronged, that I am a simple mendicant with no cares save to help my fellow man.'

'Or to help yourself to rumour and information we wish undivulged.' Another jab of the cast-metal poker. 'Already your skin blisters.'

'My spirit soars. It is beyond the reach of any furnace, or the hand of any evil-doer.'

'I am guided by God, Brother Luke.'

'As I am protected by Pope Innocent III.'

'Our Reverend Lord is nowhere apparent, leaves us to our own recourse.'

'You use your authority unwisely, Grand Master.'

It earned him a kick, an application of brute force that sent him sprawling and semi-conscious away from the source of heat. Miracles were often inexplicable. Grand Master Du Plezier knelt beside him and murmured in his ear.

'I shall grasp your soul and tear the balls from it. I will break the Franciscan steel in your spine. You wish to learn of our intent, want to know how a simple beggar of no cares may attain above his station. From henceforth you are a galley slave. You will suffer and die to the beat of a drum and at an oar of our fighting fleet.'

And Brother Luke was pleased, for he would be sent offshore to the dungeons of Arwad and would use his time well. The Templars were involved in grand treachery in league with others unknown. He was in their midst.

*

January arrived as bleak and unforgiving as the month and year preceding. In the harbour of Arsur a trading-vessel sat low and heavy-laden in the water, a refugee from the Mediterranean winds migrating south out of Constantinople. Luck and high seas had kept it running hard and beyond the reach of pirates. Now, weather-beaten, battened down, it was ready to offload. Sacks were carried and barrels rolled, crew and wharfmen mingling and shouting in the patchwork patois of the Levant. Through them came passengers, a tall figure in black striding ashore and leading his followers behind. The Cathars had reached their appointed destination.

On the landing-stage, the Lord of Arsur stood to greet them. He had bided long for the rendezvous, had ordered his lookouts to scan the horizon these weeks past. The waiting was worth it. Disembarking was no ordinary visitor, but a *Parfait* and his band of Believers, a Perfect whose authority and command would seal the loyalty, the commitment, of an entire army of heretics. His presence was all. Of course, nothing lasted for ever, not even alliance, nor yet a promise. In time the Cathars would be dealt with, disposed of when their role was complete and Jerusalem taken. They would be handed as reward to the Templars, enslaved or butchered at will. Such were the nature and order of things. Thus were hierarchy and rule imposed. Baphomet was a cruel god.

'You come at auspicious moment, Perfect.'

The Cathar leader halted before him. 'We have braved much and travelled far. It is for the purpose of releasing light into the world, of seizing and levelling the religious sites our enemy the Pope and his demonic Church of Rome hold most dear.'

'To that end we prepare.'

'I welcome such report. We have sent many to safe exile here, thousands who escape persecution and grow strong for future return.'

'All receive our protection and care, are now trained in the proper arts of war and true conduct of killing.'

'For it, I am thankful, my lord.'

'While, for their presence, I too owe you recognition. Revenge is powerful motive, is it not?'

'Divine reckoning more so.' The Perfect gestured westward across the water. 'One day we Cathars shall land as mighty formation upon the shores of Europe, will sweep aside those who oppose us, will rip asunder the royal houses and bishop palaces of our foes.'

'Noble and worthy aim.'

'A dream and prospect that will be fulfilled. I shall lead my brethren to victory.'

You shall be long since dead, the Lord of Arsur mused. But he would encourage the man in his fervour and ambition, support him in the following weeks. There was reason for employing disparate groups with varying objectives, a time for cohesion and for later moment of revelation. Needs would be tended and self-interest flattered.

He gave a tight smile. 'You will be tired from your journey.'

'No, my lord. We are inspired at prospect of carnage, revived by the thought that each step we take brings us nearer to *Consolamentium*, to the point of our epiphany and salvation.'

'There is ample reward. I have gathered children in number for your sharpened blades, and will commit them to your keeping once the kingdom is mine.'

'You honour us, my lord.'

'Obedience and devotion are demanded in return.'

Their enthusiasm was touching. Conquest was ever founded on the blood of innocents, and this one would be marked with heavy and ritual spillage in the ancient valley of Gehenna itself. What better way to celebrate the passing of an era, to bless the introduction of the new. The Lord of Arsur beckoned the Perfect to follow. Much remained to be done. He would reserve the fate of the infant and purloined queen Yolanda for himself.

Other newcomers had found passage to Arsur. Captured and enslaved by the governor of Alexandria, they had been sent as tribute to the Sultan of Damascus. But intervention had occurred. Their caravan was attacked by the leper Knights of St Lazarus, the horde descending to liberate Moslem heads from bodies and plunder from the camel train. Prisoners did not find freedom. They merely passed to different ownership.

Carrying a flaming torch, the Lord of Arsur made his way down to inspect the human takings. It was happy accident they had fallen into his possession. He would use them wisely, cruelly, would add them to the sum total of the greater scheme. Bolts drew back, heavy oak doors swung wide. He was in.

They were subdued in their misery and chains, some sobbing futilely, others watching wordless as he walked among them with the flaring brand. He searched their faces, wishing to see the dumb desolation, wanting to feed on the piteousness and despair. Perchance they thought he was life and death. He would not be offering life.

'Your name?' He brought the flame closer and switched to German. 'What is your name?'

'It is Egon.'

The boy was a solid Rhinelander, had the large frame and inbred insolence of a village peasant. Scared naturally, but with a hint of resistance and anger. An intriguing prospect.

'And what is your trade, Egon?'

'A blacksmith, like my father.'

'Yet you are far from any forge.' The Lord of Arsur moved the torch before his face, and the eyes of the boy flickered. 'You are well received to our kingdom of Outremer, son of blacksmith.'

'Is this welcome?' Egon tugged at his leg-iron.

'Consider it necessity.'

'We are not beasts or thieves to be shackled. Like you we are Christians, pilgrims on holy mission to reach Jerusalem.'

'You have my oath you shall find it.'

'Word counts for naught when we are held in your dungeon.'

'Such spirit in the young ox.' The Lord of Arsur transferred his gaze to a younger boy. 'Who is this?'

'His name is Zepp, and he will not answer. Since his

brother died and we took ship from Genoa, his tongue has fled him.'

'I am certain it may be restored.'

As the light swept near, the ten-year old shrank back further in the straw. He was no longer the ever-cheerful child of the road, the ebullient optimist who had guided his blind twin each step of the way. What remained was shadow and the dead eyes of loss.

'Stay back from him!' The cry from Egon was fierce with distrust.

Around, there was the rustle of the young with-drawing to the imagined safety of deeper gloom, attempting to evade notice. They wanted no part in this, yearned for their mothers and fathers and a ship for home. Egon glared at his captor.

The Lord of Arsur affected surprise. 'A challenge?'

'Believe it so. You are master and lord, but I shall not let you harm him.'

'Your power to bargain is weak, son of black-smith.'

'A prisoner may fight.'

'To little effect. What if I should slit his throat, tease wide his belly with a knife?'

'You would be wise to do the same to me.'

'There are ways to punish misjudged threat, means to chasten animals which strain insolent at their leash.'

'I do not fear you.' Courage was in the countenance, lie was carried in the trembling. 'I do not fear you.'

'You should.'

Another voice broke in, the words soft and insinuating. Intrigued, the Lord of Arsur swung the torch, directed illumination towards a figure crouched low and angular in a recess. The boy was tall and spare, his head crowned by red stubble, his frame hunched in fawning supplication. Yet it was his face that merited interest. At once deferential and knowing, it exuded the confidence of survival, the craven submissiveness of one who understood authority and was choosing to serve it. All in a glance. The Lord of Arsur had found a willing worker.

Gunther, the woodsman's son, spoke again. 'Neither is of worth to you, my lord.'

'Are you of worth?'

'I will kill them both at your command, will obey you as they defy. Zepp has no speech. He is weak and broken. Egon is well trusted, will inspire mutiny and revolt among the rest.'

Egon shouted and tried to reach him. 'You dare say this?'

'See how he agitates, my lord?' Gunther leered mocking at the older boy. 'He is a brute who will cause trouble, a barbarian who will carry others with him.'

'You traitor.' The blacksmith's son quivered with rage and incomprehension.

'My lord, how he speaks to me is reflected on you. He is deserving of your harshest sanction.'

Egon stared. 'Why, Gunther?'

'Why must there be whys?'

The Lord of Arsur watched in calm fascination. There was stark beauty to suffering and injustice, an honesty and symmetry in seeing wrong prevail. Gunther was a fine discovery. As light drew the good, so darkness gathered deeper shades of black. It was the attraction of likes. The offspring of a woodsman had come over to his side. He would exploit it, would find employment for this busy and malignant young soul.

'You think too hard, Kurt.'

The youngster did not turn at the sound of Otto's voice. He was looking out across the rise and fall of hills towards the pale and distant bastion of Castel Blanc and the setting sun beyond. An enchanted place suffused in deepening gold. Here on the roof of the Warden's Tower, in the inner fort of Krak des Chevaliers, a child could abandon the cares of the world, might become absorbed in the mystery and splendour of the setting. But the pose of the boy suggested only worry.

'Do you remember how the old Hospitaller spoke, Otto?'

'He vowed he would not eat us.'

'More than that.' Kurt darted a glance of earnestness at his friend. 'He told us we inhabit an island placed upon a sea of troubles and buffeted by infidel storm. He claimed the Beast walks abroad, and soon will devour the world.'

'They are the ramblings of an ancient who resides too long in a cellar.'

'You saw him as I, heard his insight to our pasts and present. Out there is danger and darkness, Otto.'

'What I discern is a landscape of beauty, a sun that dips and casts its lengthening rays.'

'But we do not share the sight he possesses.'

'Be thankful for it, Kurt.' The noble boy approached and rested a brotherly arm across his shoulder. 'Whatever we face, we stand together.'

'I trust so, Otto. Yet many with whom I started have gone, many friendships have been broken by death. There was a girl . . .'

He paused, reminiscence and sorrow pulling him back into silence. They stood side by side, both sharing and isolated in their thoughts. Outside the walls were the opposing worlds of the Franks and the Mohammedans, the galloping hooves of horses, the flying arrows of skirmishers and raiding-parties. It was safer to hide, to stand remote on the roof of a fortress. Yet Otto already wore his *cuirie* armour, had once more donned sword and scabbard. It was coming to the moment of departure.

As though wary of emotion, Kurt resumed in low monotone. 'They are all of them vanished, and I will not see them again. Hans, Albert, Roswitha, little Lisa, Egon, Zepp and Achim. Every last one of the children in my village.'

'You are no child, Kurt. You stepped to manhood the day you took up staff and headed from Cologne.'

'So why do I ache? Why do I grieve? Why do I long for the peace of climbing trees and searching nests?'

'Because we each of us yearn for others to carry the load. Now we learn to bear our own.'

'Are you still intent to find your father?'

'As much as I ever was. Do you still wish to discover the True Cross?'

'It is why I am here.'

'Then our close and loyal band continues.'

The twelve-year-old nodded and stepped back. Brother Luke might be elsewhere, everyone he had ever known scattered, but he had walked through fire to reach this point and he would journey on and make the end. The shrivelled old Hospitaller with his strange symbols and coloured fire had been correct. Answer for ever lay within.

Otto walked him to the flight of steps, and the two of them descended.

From the harbour mouth beyond the walls of the Templar castle of Tortosa, a small boat again carried Brother Luke towards the fortress island of Arwad. This time he made the trip in chains.

✝

Chapter 15

Moonlight and instinct would guide their way. They had saddled up and ridden from Krak des Chevaliers in the silver dusk, had snaked down to the road running westward for Tortosa. A strange landscape of mist and half-light, of low ground obscured by night shadow and rising to escarpments glowing soft. With fortune kind, they would be greeted in the coastal stronghold by Brother Luke; a missed rendezvous, and they would travel south and unaccompanied by the friar to the Cistercian monastery in the hill folds above Tripoli. The plan was simple, a further staging-post in the onward trek to Acre.

Sergeant Hugh led. Behind, Kurt swayed to the gait of his commandeered steed, watched the figure of the bowman merge with that of the horse, listened to the thudding trot of twelve iron-shod hooves.

There seemed to be more, the muffled and irregular sound of others intruding. He cocked an ear. A vibration, a feeling, a trick of his mind or heartbeat. The noise came again, never quite rising to a clatter or falling below the vague suggestion of a presence. They were being followed.

'Otto.' He murmured a warning to the older boy riding at his side.

But the young noble had already heard. His sword scraped free of its scabbard; his mount gathered pace and the lead-rein was surrendered.

'You are now free-rider, Kurt. Do as I do, and abstain from sudden move or dash.'

'How are we to act?'

'With cool heads and steadiness. Run and we become their prey to chase.'

'They will have lances, arrows, swords.'

'And you have pluck and nerve, young brother.'

The twelve-year-old begged to differ at this moment, but his friend carried authority and conveyed confidence, wore leather breastplate and held a drawn blade. That blade had done much to save them in the past. He replicated the moves of the noble boy, staying with him as he quickened to catch the Englishman. In his ear, Isolda was whispering a prayer. The soft tremor in her voice, the tightening of her fingers on his sides were the main betrayers of her terror.

'It will be all right, Isolda. It will be all right.'

'Are they again slavers, Kurt? Do they come in vengeance to kill or capture us?'

'We will give them hard fight, whatever they intend.'

In muttered conversation, Otto and Sergeant Hugh were exchanging views, debating tactics. For ambushers, the trailing enemy were proving more timid than committed. Perhaps they were curious, or corralled the quartet towards an open trap. The bowman spoke sotto voce to his brood.

'Walls rise about us and our sole escape is ahead. On my command, you will continue steady for the beat of a minute before breaking into gallop. I will slip to the side, will drench them with a rain of arrows.'

'Ride with us, Sergeant Hugh.' The noble boy urged him in a low voice. 'You must.'

'Must? We have before had words about your knightly conceits.'

'Concern, not conceit, Sergeant Hugh.'

'Disobey me and I shall haunt you, Alzey.'

'We run together or will make our stand.'

'Sweet Jesu, you will yet dig my grave.' Exasperation saturated the words of the soldier. 'Very well, on my count you will ride as though hell itself were on your tails, will divide only when you find gorge or indentation to explore. One, two . . .'

'Sergeant Hugh!'

Kurt had picked them out, yelled with the fury of sudden discovery. They were a phalanx of silent horsemen, as still as the surrounding hills and just as impermeable. And they waited ahead while their brethren herded the Christians on.

'Put up your sword, Otto.'

'Submit without a charge, without so much as raising this weapon in our defence?'

'A good soldier is one who measures probability and event.' The Englishman reined to a halt. 'Our luck is out. Know and accept it, be composed in your response.'

'I will not take lightly to a swarm of quarrel-flights let loose in our direction.'

'Should they wish to finish us, they will do so in any event.'

'Meanwhile, Sergeant Hugh?'

The bowman gazed forward, exhaling in weary acknowledgement. 'It appears our plan is changed.'

He must have been a potentate of sorts, an aged and magnificent sheikh dressed in finery and courteous in a remote and regal fashion. Another sight to remember. Kurt observed the white beard and commanding eyes, the egg-sized emerald set in the pommel of his sheathed sword, the studied fawning of officers and servants. Clearly a leader of some influence and power, and currently their host. Sergeant Hugh must have recognized him. The Englishman was scowling, had the air of a man who knew he was in the presence of greatness, understood he was negotiating for his life. He had been pushed forward as the youngsters were held back, spoke with this ruler in the incomprehensible tongue of the Arab. It was not a meeting of minds or comrades. The boy could only watch and guess, huddle close as bystander to his sister and his friend.

Saphadin was imperious still. 'I come from Homs to hunt golden jackal and desert fox, to capture Hospitallers on foul sortie from their fortress. Instead, I chance upon a snake.'

'A benign snake, your majesty. One that wishes no ill.'

'One that nonetheless is worst of vermin, the most vexing and baneful kind of any heathen creature.'

'Such judgement is harsh, al-Adil.'

'You are in no place to contest it.'

And that was true enough. The Englishman did not struggle as a Mamluk guard bound his hands behind his back. He had fought or dodged the Saracen for the span of his adult life, hardly expected warm reception and convivial conversation. Saphadin was worthy of his respect. The sentiment went unreturned.

'It is twenty years since last we met, Hugh of York.'

'Time heals injury and calms the angry soul, al-Adil.'

'Or it permits wrongs to fester that go unpunished.' The Sultan radiated threat in his serenity. 'You escorted the emissaries of Cœur de Lion to our lines, were present when we tried to parley release of our captured garrison at Acre.'

'An unfortunate and ugly episode.'

'You were there too when your king sacked further strongholds and spared no lives, when he laid waste our lands and butchered our people.'

'War conjures much atrocity, al-Adil.'

'So it does.' The look was both distant and penetrating. 'I served my brother, the great Salah ad-Din. You served your English lord, Richard, King of England.'

'The part I played was of small effect.'

'Yet consequence is great. You were witness and accomplice, have the blood of True Believers on your hands. Now I am sultan and you are scavenging bones, a belly-crawler who feeds on the droppings and trinkets of honest men, who robs merchants and traders and profits from misdeed.'

'I help these children towards Palestine, your majesty.'

'For what gain?'

A curt nod from Saphadin, and the Englishman was forced to his knees. The decision was already made. Sergeant Hugh began to sweat, his eyes darting, his skin paling to a lighter shade of grey. Somehow, his past had caught up; some way, his gift for patter and dealing had fled. He crouched alone at his very own site of execution.

He peered upward at the ruler. 'There is peace accord between our nations, al-Adil.'

'Do you see peace?'

'Where there is obstruction and travail there is also hope.'

'In your case there is none, Hugh of York.'

The swordsman was brought, a tall figure in waistcoat and tighter-fitting clothes that would impede neither swing of the arms nor action of the blade. Translation was unnecessary. The steel instrument was keen and straight, its edges gleaming.

Isolda gasped. 'Otto, stop them! Sergeant Hugh, you must fight, must resist!'

'Hush now, little one.' The bowman stared ahead to an imagined point beyond the tented walls. 'I go to a place where every soldier ends.'

Wordlessly, the anointed slayer took position, adjusting his feet, correcting his grip on the leather-bound hilt. Calculations needed to be made. In the shadow of the impending strike, Sergeant Hugh was whispering urgently to the Sultan, driving a last bargain, striving for the release of his young charges to the freedom they deserved. They in turn watched, disbelieving in the horror of the situation.

The moment came. With a piercing scream of exultation, the executioner lunged, his sword arcing clean, his body tensing for imminent contact. Kurt flinched. He had heard the cry before, had listened and shuddered when four men gutted the hapless Hans on the track in northern Italy. The same shout, identical dread. He clenched shut his eyes and closed his mind. To his front, Sergeant Hugh was trembling, his gaze wide in dull expectation.

But he was not the target. His blade slashing wildly, the executioner rushed at Saphadin. He was frantic to achieve a kill, inspired by Allah and orders to ensure that the hated ruler of Islam would lead no more. It would be a blow landed for righteous followers of the Faith, a personal journey that would conclude in paradise. Religious fire was abruptly doused. Before he could reach the Sultan, the tip of a javelin had buried itself deep within his chest. Sound and momentum were cut and the man slumped dead. Heaven attained.

Emotionless, Saphadin scrutinized the outcome. 'As I suspected. He is *hashshash*.'

'Assassin?' Sergeant Hugh shook himself from his altered state. 'You stage performance to humour me, test me, al-Adil?'

'I create situation to flush out traitors from within.'

'It is no more than fooling with me.'

'Are not all of us trifled with, Hugh of York? Are not all of us stalked as prey by those who employ Assassins, by those who plot to bring our kingdoms to swift and bloody end?'

'I am no part of it; these young are no part of it.'

'Portentous times hold everyone in their mailed fist. You are fortunate I open debate with Outremer, an avenue for conciliation with the regent John of Brienne.'

'Your cavalry remain armed, your raiding-parties still raid.'

'As do those of your military Orders. Suffice for each adversary to take share of blame, for both to draw back and seek to confer.'

'I value your mercy, al-Adil.'

'It saves your neck. Be thankful to the Lord of Arsur, grateful he arranges meeting at start of your month of March between your regent king and myself.'

'We must hope it bears fruit.'

The Sultan directed his sight from the bowman kneeling close to the body resting closer. 'Should it fail, there will be tens of thousands of corpses strewn.'

Back on the road, Sergeant Hugh was in silent and reflective mood. It had been a challenging encounter, one that had improved from poor beginnings. Perhaps he would live to die on the battlefield after all. He rocked his head and checked reflexively at his throat.

Otto was first to speak. He echoed in jest the earlier advice of the longbowman. 'Like any good soldier, you measure probability and event, Sergeant Hugh?'

'I measure vulnerability of my neck.'

Kurt laughed, exultant again to have survived, to have outlived capture by a fearsome *razzia* group and worrying meeting with the lord of lords the Sultan of Damascus. There was much to tell Brother Luke. He was sure matters could only improve.

'Eat well, you dogs.'

Stale bread and rancid meat showered down upon the prisoners through the overhead grille. There was never enough. It was occupational humour for the Templars, a means of conditioning and control, of provoking a brawl between slaves that would sift the dominant from the frail. On the fortress isle of Arwad, the weak did not inherit the earth. They simply lost ground and sustenance and hope, and died.

Brother Luke made no move to join the grabbing fray. He sat in a corner, gauging the patterns, the actors, the haves and the dispossessed. Every struggle had its casualties.

Clutching his spoils, a bearded galley slave slumped beside the friar and began to devour his meagre ration. Then he stopped, broke off a piece of biscuit and held it out as offering.

The Franciscan shook his head in refusal. 'You won it in fair fight, my son.'

'What is fair in this stinking hole? Take it.'

'I cannot.'

'If you have no food, you will fade. If you fade, you will have no use. If you have no use, the Grand Master will bind rocks to your feet and drop you in the harbour.'

'God in His holy wisdom will provide.'

A bitter laugh came from the man. 'Thus far He provides us with shit to feed on, a rod for our backs, an oar to work.'

'He tests us as He tested His Son.'

'That He does, and worse beside. Now accept this paltry fare.'

Reluctantly, the friar complied. He did so as gesture of goodwill and participation, as a breaking of bread and shared communion. A bond was forged. Both prisoners chewed slowly, savouring the tasteless morsels and appreciating the moment.

'Bless you, my son.' Brother Luke gnawed at the crust. 'I thank you for such kindness.'

'Our jailers would strip us of humanity. To keep it is to win small victory.'

'You have a name, my son?'

'None that is important. Either you or I shall be dead before the rowing-season is done.'

'I am certain you are wrong.'

The stranger observed him close, masticating on a fragment of meat, contemplating with inner sight and experienced eye. Veterans were rarely duped.

'In here, we are reduced to equal share of misery.' The prisoner gestured to the scuffling throng. 'Christian, Jew, Saracen, we all brawl for air and space and scraps of food. Not you, father. You sit alone, untouched by troubles. You have the stillness of one who has seen it pass before.'

'My years grant me perception. I am a mendicant, a wandering friar.'

'There is more. Your eyes tell me so. They contain in them no fear, no surprise, no despair.'

'Faith bears me as it will carry you, my son.'

Discussion was interrupted. An informal delegation of inmates approached, their expressions hungry and intent menacing. Leadership rested on a short and swarthy man with the cropped ears of a criminal and the scars of a thousand clashes. A killer who saw challenge everywhere, perceived threat and disrespect even in submission. The Franciscan bit into the hard biscuit.

An order was given. 'Stand.'

Meekly, Brother Luke obliged. He was stronger than any of them, could snap them at will across his knee. But he would wait, keep violence in reserve and as last resort. Quickness to temper was the failing of many men. Jesus preached understanding and love; it seemed lost on this chief and his brutish crew.

'How may I help you, my son?'

The leader wrinkled his nose. 'We have a peace-maker among us.' His lieutenants guffawed without generosity.

'Is peace not the true path for each of us?'

'Not for those who wish to live.' The man squinted at the friar. 'They tell me you are a priest, a holy man. Prove it.'

'In what manner?'

'Forgiveness.'

The blow was hard and stinging, delivered as expression of authority and opening move. It generated a ripple of enthusiastic mirth among the audience. Blood was up and about to flow. Pleased with the effect, the master of ceremonies tried again. He would enforce his law, reduce an easy and obvious target to cringing ruin. Lest others forget. The new-found friend of the priest raised objection, but was kicked back into place.

'Give me the last of your bread, holy man.'

'It is not mine to grant you.'

'You plan to turn it to a thousand loaves? To feed us all?'

'I intend to sit and eat in quiet contemplation.'

'Bless me, father.' Another punch landed.

Sport would be excellent. The chief cocked his head, making assessment. He wore a look of confident superiority, was almost benevolent with the punishment he would mete. Time to raise his performance. He turned to his men, accepting their encouragement, gaining length and leverage for the return swing.

He read it wrong. As his fist travelled in, it was blocked and his wrist seized and crushed by a powerful hand. He opened his mouth to scream, but already fresh and instant pain cut into his nervous system. It made no sense. His nose was suddenly crushed, his knee shattered, his instep stamped down upon. And he dropped away, rolling among his followers in a tormented frenzy of concertinaed limbs and bubbling shrieks.

Brother Luke resumed his corner position and

retrieved his discarded rusk. The crowd had backed away, would soon return with pledges of loyalty and samples of food. He had won the admiration of the herd.

Beside him, his prison ally wiped away the streak of blood from a cut lip. 'A Christian friar who fails to turn the other cheek.'

'I aspire to godliness without ever reaching it.'

'Piety will not aid you here. The Templars prepare us for their galleys. They want slaves with steel in their backs and basalt in their hearts.'

'You believe they plan for something?'

'I know it.' The weather-worn features hardened in intensity. 'Their treasure-house fills, the pace quickens in their dealings, the regularity of their patrolling increases.'

'They have visitors?'

'Personages of importance, men of rank brought by cover of night or shielded from enquiring gaze. Not always hidden from me.'

'Describe what you see.'

'A pale lord with sombre air and mysterious aspect, one whom others fear and to whom all bow their head and knee.'

The Franciscan lapsed into silent thought. In days to follow he would bring pastoral and religious care to these pitiable creatures, would teach them of the healing power of Christ and the solidarity to be gained through brotherly kindness and state of grace. *A pale lord with sombre air and mysterious aspect*. There were many considerations on his mind.

His neighbour again spoke. 'I am a Dane, a Varangian guard who bore witness to the slaughter and bloodshed exacted by the Franks upon the great city of Constantinople. They tortured, killed, raped and stole.' The words were precise and undramatic. 'Worst among them was this noble, this same ashen-faced demon who comes to Arwad. He is Satan himself, father.'

In the background, the sometime and self-appointed leader of the prisoners crawled damaged to a more uncertain future.

Disappointment at their failure to find Brother Luke was tempered by gladness at reaching the monastery of Belmont. The old Franciscan had grown restless and headed south, the Templars said. He was ever the wanderer, always pushing on, seeking new landscape and the unenlightened to dwell among. Kurt and Isolda, Otto and Sergeant Hugh would surely catch up with him. And so they had travelled on from Tortosa and its forbidding defences, journeyed into the hills above Tripoli and alighted at this place.

Around them in the courtyard were the containing walls, a proclamation in stone of Christian belief raised high over the Mediterranean Sea. They were safe here, for it was home to the white monks, the Cistercians.

'We at last are where we should be.' Sergeant Hugh looked about with satisfaction from the saddle. 'Honest brothers and a meditative life.'

Otto grinned with scepticism. 'You are drawn to it, Sergeant Hugh?'

'Not at all. Yet I value their compassion. On instruction of Lady Matilda, I have left at least a dozen bedraggled children to their care.'

'Each earns you money.'

'My place in heaven is more important to me.' It was not said to convince.

Brother and sister too observed their surroundings. The twelve-year-old tried to share the ebullient contentment of the soldier, was pleased to have left the road. But unease plucked at his thoughts. It might have been the cloistered quietness, the manner in which glimpsed faces were averted, the lifeless melancholy that seemed to rest upon the whole. Or he simply missed the wise company of the friar. He shrugged to himself. Experience had taught him to accept with composure and without complaint and to ready himself for any event. Seated behind, Isolda was silent with her own concerns.

'Peace and Jesus be with you, friends.'

Greeting came from a stooped monk with the dry and learned tone of his years. Not unkindly, though hardly fulsome. Around his neck was a small wood cross, on his crown the tonsure of his creed and order. Nothing to denote his office save the authority of his bearing and the salutation of the Englishman.

'Good eve to you, abbot. I bring further number to swell your flock.'

'They replace those since departed.'

'Departed?' Sergeant Hugh swung himself down. 'Some dozen were with you when last I counted.'

The abbot pressed his palms together in practised sign of piety. 'Occasion overtakes us. Victuallers and merchants paid visit while on route for Tyre. The children went gaily with them.'

'It was not the desire of Lady Matilda.'

'We oblige her wishes as best we may. But we are a holy order with tasks and hours uncommon to the world beyond. Our monastery is no site or situation for the unversed young.'

'They are pilgrims, abbot.'

'And we are monks dedicated to the simple life and rigours of the Cistercian way.'

'Does this simple life not include charity? Is that charity not rewarded with silver from the treasure-chest of Lady Matilda?'

'We have discharged our duty, Hugh of York.'

Sharpness had entered the voice, an edge that signalled disapproval and faint warning. Sergeant Hugh was used to such response. He sniffed and beckoned his companions down from their steeds. With luck he would trace the cellarer and arrange food and drink, would shun participation in any act of religious worship.

The abbot appraised him. 'I remind you we are in a house of the Lord. You shall leave behind all weapons and armour in this stableyard, will enter our domain in humility and cleansed of warlike trappings.'

'I am more content with my bow and sword beside me.'

'Your contentment has no worth in the sight of God.'

'Hark to it.' The soldier grimaced at Otto. 'It seems we are to be shorn of our defence.'

The young noble was already unstrapping his scabbard. 'There are strong walls about us, a myriad holy brothers to man them and give warning of approach.'

'Habit dies hard.'

A thin frost of amusement settled on the countenance of the abbot. 'As does *soldatesque*, Hugh of York. Observe our strictures, discard your barrackroom licentiousness, or seek other refuge for the night.'

'I have no complaint, abbot.'

'That is to your benefit. Bring your cohorts and enter inside. You shall have your reward.'

As was custom, the refectory meal passed in contemplative and holy silence. Only the clatter of wood bowls and consumption of winter potage, the reading of a Gospel, intruded. If there was tension or awkwardness it was hidden well, disguised in the hand movements and signed language of the monks. Kurt sloughed off his returning doubts. A strange setting could often generate unreliable response. He was with Otto and Sergeant Hugh in the company of religious brothers who wished no harm.

Later they repaired to their own chamber in a distant part of the dark and lofty edifice. It was a large room, sparse-furnished with horsehair mats and a wooden crucifix fastened to the wall. Sufficient for their purpose. Yet it was redolent with empty abandonment, filled with the blank space of recent occupation by children who had gone before. Kurt would not admit to trepidation. Nor would his sister. She distracted herself, opening the shutters to peer over the edge of the sill into the night and plunging chasm below. Sergeant Hugh made himself comfortable. He was mildly drunk on honey mead, had deftly obtained a leather gourd of drink. It would while away the hours.

Liquor lent him insight. 'You are troubled, Kurt. Be at ease.'

'These monks barely greet us with much friendship, Sergeant Hugh.'

'Their zeal is saved for books and prayer. Unsmiling strictness is their way.'

'You do not feel their cold mood?'

'I do not.'

'You believe the other children left with merchants for the south?'

'I do.' The soldier quaffed from the flask and smacked his lips. 'Our holy brothers are generous when they try.'

'They do not like us.'

'Who could not like you, boy? Who would resent the presence of such agreeable guests?'

Otto had settled himself, lay back on bedding and rested his arms behind his head. 'What a quiet place this is, Sergeant Hugh.'

'Until three hours are past and next watch is called. Then you will hear the clatter of sandals on stairways, the rush from dormitory to chapel.'

'They will not call us to join them?'

'Should they do so, I am elsewhere.'

Isolda returned from the window and perched on a rolled bundle. 'We are placed so high up here, set on a cliff that would make an eagle faint.'

The soldier shook his bottle. 'The easier to protect.'

Or to prevent escape, thought Kurt. Conversation faded as the hour grew late and slumber closed in. Otto snuffed the lamps; Isolda said her prayers; Sergeant Hugh emptied the last reserved drops of his evening brew. In the morning they would continue south for the crusader ports of Nephim and Jebail and for Palestine beyond. Beirut was fifty miles distant, a long and arduous trek, a stepping-stone in their quest to reach the royal city of Acre. The dangers would keep.

A low sound of scraping, of objects being dragged, insinuated into the quietness. It stopped. Then it came again, closer, approaching. The shadow-form of Otto padded across the floor, brother and sister sitting upright to see, Sergeant Hugh continuing to snore. It was best to confront the unknown. Kurt manoeuvred into a crouch and waited, ready to support his friend. The latch rose, the door swung wide.

'Who comes?' Otto whispered his challenge.

'Please, brother. I am no threat.'

The youthful voice quivered with urgency. Possibly he was, as he claimed, no threat. But threat lay somewhere behind. Kurt bent lower, anticipating the inrush of armed men and of flaming torches, the ringing clamour of steel. Instead, there was the rattle of the stranger and his cargo, the tumbling explanation of his words.

'You are in danger. You must believe me.'

'We are in a monastery.'

'It offers no sanctuary. Rather, it is a cage in which to trap you, a prison from where the children will be taken, where you and the English bowman will be slain.'

'What is it you bring with you?'

'Your weapons and armour, the swords and bow kept safe by a lay brother in the stable. It is not intended you see them or daybreak again.'

His disclosure was interrupted by Otto wrenching him across the threshold. The door closed, the interview proceeding in hushed and breathless haste.

'Your identity?'

'A novice monk, a witness to events when they came and carried off the children.'

'And who are these men?'

'Not the merchants the abbot would have you deem. They were cold and ruthless souls, fully armed and rank with menace. They visit again this night.'

'You are certain?'

'I vow it on my life and on the Holy Book. You must flee and put distance from this place. The abbot himself is in league with these devils, is bound in strange communion.'

'Yet you aid us, forewarn us of such things.'

'That is my Christian duty, the oath I took when committing to God. I must act on my belief.' In the gloom, the young monk untied the bundle as Otto went to relight a lamp. 'While we attend our midnight nocturns the enemy will appear and strike his blow. Remain and you will die.'

'Then it is motive enough to steal away.'

As the light flamed, Kurt stared at the wan and fearful face of the visitor. The English soldier slept on. 'Otto, I think Sergeant Hugh is prepared to steal nowhere.'

'It seems we have scarce choice.'

That choice revealed itself in hurried retreat along a deserted passageway. Awoken, groggy, and requiring encouragement, Sergeant Hugh accompanied his charges on clumsy tiptoe. The unwelcome hour and rushed tale, the presence of a novice monk, had at first left him confused. But he had brightened at the discovery of his bow and quiver. Prospect of a fight could be relied upon to banish haze or residual annoyance. Another portal opened, the lantern lifted. The soldier muttered an oath.

'Of all the places we may be stowed, monk, you bring us to a wood-store.'

'Step within and you will find no ordinary chamber.'

'Oh?'

Sergeant Hugh directed his lamp, let its radiance spread across workbenches and stacked logs towards a wide and gaping archway. At the limit of the scattered beam, where the long and narrow space ended in a vertical drop, stone buttresses protruded. On them rested a large and sturdy platform.

'You jest, monk.'

'Neither I nor you have occasion for it.'

The soldier rubbed his eyes. 'This is your plan for our escape?'

'There is no other. You will be challenged should you leave with horses, intercepted should you take flight from any spied-on parts.'

'Better than seek flight from a mountain perch. I make a poor buzzard, monk.'

There was a hissed call from Kurt, who had ventured out on to the jutting stage. He favoured exploration over caution. And what he stumbled upon added tremulous animation to his voice, drew the others near. Before them was an apparatus, an amalgam of axles and wheels resembling the toppled undercarriage of a giant cart. Across it stretched a thick rope, attached to which was a basket gondola.

Sergeant Hugh had changed to scratching his head. 'I see no bells attached, monk.'

'Nor will any peal, brother. We employ it to bring up firewood from the forest ravine below, to save several hours' ride by mule.'

'Are we to act as firewood?'

'That is my intent and your salvation. Often the lay brothers travel this way, their weight in one basket balanced and descent slowed by burden in the other.'

'I would rather face the foe.'

Otto was already reaching for the basket. 'You would be wiser to face your fears, Sergeant Hugh.'

Debate was quickly ended and the procedure described. The novice did not lie. He was near-frantic with strain and haste, willing them to move on, to get away, to heed his counsel and descend to freedom. Gingerly, Kurt climbed into the swinging pannier and gestured Isolda to join him. The brake was raised, the basket swayed and jolted and began its slide one hundred feet to the valley floor beneath.

The whispered shout of the soldier followed. 'Whatever occurs above, keep onward and hold to your purpose.'

Wheels turned and the upturned faces were lost.

✝

Chapter 16

The young monk had departed and Sergeant Hugh was on his own. He had lowered Otto into the blackness, had given a cursory wave as the noble youth grasped the rope and swayed downward on his fragile transport. Three delivered. There was a certain peace in being the last, a particular madness to travelling by line and basket. Plainly the Cistercians possessed a faith he did not share. Yet their abbot was treacherous, and the hour of truth close. The Englishman placed his lantern beside the door, the better to observe and to mark his target. Perhaps by then his head would clear. He glanced again towards the window and its wide balcony, felt the chill air of the January night. The abbot deserved a gentle rebuke.

He had been right to predict the noise of feet on stairway. But it was not the patter of sandals carrying holy brothers to prayer. It was the percussive tramp of hobnailed soles bringing a party of hostile searchers to his lair. They were early. He thanked God that Otto and the children were safe beyond their reach. It would allow him to practise his craft, to create magic in the privacy and comfort of his own personal killing-range. He hummed a gentle tune, counting down while doors opened and angry cries eddied stronger through the emptiness. They were navigating in his direction. He ran his fingers along an arrowhead. The enemy were building to this point.

A boot struck the oaken exterior. '*Open or suffer full consequence.*' The single blow became a barrage.

Another voice. '*We will exact cruel punishment on all who defy.*'

'*Throw wide this door and put up your weapons.*'

'*You dogs will obey. We shall flay you, roast you, quarter you.*'

'*Surrender now or for ever have regret.*'

Frustration cascaded in a torrent of collision and threat. Sergeant Hugh missed neither beat nor note of his song. His adversaries would try to break their way through, were thronging at the entrance. Such rude awakening from his rest could scarcely go unchallenged. He fitted an arrow, drew deep, and let fly. Oak splintered and the door started to bleed. He discharged a second shaft of ash, the wood surface shuddering and extracting a repeated human howl. It would occupy them for a while.

Slinging his longbow, and without unseemly rush, Sergeant Hugh stepped out to the platform. He could only hope the contraption would hold, his companions remember to add mass to the opposing basket. Inside, axes were battering at the door. Outside, he was about to perform what he knew to be insane. Let matters commence and heavy objects fall where they might.

Offering up the slightest of entreaties, he sprang into position. He sank fast.

These were vexing times. The abbot knelt before a rough-hewn cross and tried to pray, attempted to sluice the worries from his mind. The Lord of Arsur would be angered by events, and that was not good. There had been casualties, upset, and after two nights the four fugitives remained at large. Matters were out of his hands, beyond the walls of Belmont Monastery. Yet he could still tremble at the thought of displeasing his patron and overlord. On troubled occasion he would find solace in God, would immerse himself in meditation and holy scripture. No longer. Everywhere was disquiet; every one of his monks was disheartened. They did not enjoy disturbance, were not gladdened to hold vigil for their young novice brother found dead from tragic and unexplained fall.

He stirred from his ruminations, muttered the words of a Latin psalm. It was an hour until the bell for early-morning lauds would toll. The world slept and he maintained the Faith, kept the secret of his duplicity to himself. His Saviour understood why he acted as he did. There was need for funds, for pilgrims, for crusade, for survival of this monastery and for the everlasting glorification of God. The Lord of Arsur rewarded loyalty well.

'How fare you, abbot?' Interruption was rude and unexpected.

The Cistercian started. 'Hugh of York.'

'The very same. Alive, though somewhat bruised by swift descent.'

'I believed you long departed from our care.'

'Your kindness brings me back.' Delivery was leisurely as it was ironic. 'Survival may often depend on the unforeseen act.'

'An act that is foolhardy will not prompt survival. You are a hunted man, Hugh of York.'

'And what does that make you, abbot?'

Sergeant Hugh approached the kneeling form, could see the sweat develop on the crown of the tonsure and the nape of the neck, the colour take flight from the skin. A scared man, a calculating monk who would be assessing his chances and constructing excuse. The face shifted in his direction.

'I am a simple brother of Christ, Hugh of York.'

'I a simpler soldier. It seems we are mismatched, abbot.'

'These troubled and desperate events are no fault of mine, nor of this abbey.'

'Yet you carry guilt of a criminal in your demeanour. I do not recall St Benedict promoting treachery as part of his monastic code.'

'Treachery?'

'Be upright and face me.'

Timidly, with the reluctance of a man condemned and eking out remaining seconds, the monk clambered from his knees. He turned towards the bowman. The Englishman held no sword, was not poised as vengeful executioner. There was room for manoeuvre, opportunity to negotiate. The abbot forced composure into his expression. He wanted to placate, to be reasonable, to play a churchman wronged. But, like his thoughts, his gaze roved for possibilities and exit.

'Misunderstanding arises, Hugh of York.'

'In my quarter there is no confusion.'

'Then we will surely find clear passage through such unfortunate occasion. Let us talk and make common cause.'

'Your cause differs from mine, your pacts hold the stench of disloyalty.'

'What I do is to the benefit of this abbey.'

'What you do is harm to your faith, is in breach of your sacred covenant and betrayal of those who turn to you for succour.'

The abbot sought to evade, to dodge the pressing company. 'I may explain.'

'You may not.' Sergeant Hugh moved close. 'I know nothing of church matters or affairs of state. But I recognize a worm or viper, a scorpion or grub.'

'Others will come. It is nearing time for prayers.'

'So begin now to speak them, abbot.'

'You will be captured, will be punished for your sins in this life and the hereafter.'

Sergeant Hugh sighed. 'Thus is the lot of any soldier.'

'Heed me, Hugh of York.' His face panic-mottled and voice beseeching, the abbot had backed against the wall. 'There are armed men loose, those who would do you ill.'

'I am content at present to deal with one. Did I not dispatch a pair with arrows in the saw-room? Did a third pursuer not plunge to hell in a basket when I severed the ballast as it left the ground?'

'May God have mercy on you, Hugh of York.'

'Your need is the greater.' The soldier reached and administered a percussive slap to the bald pate of the monk.

'Unhand me.'

'Or you will call out the guard, summon your garrison?'

'Your action is intolerable.'

'As yours is righteous, godly, true to your creed?' The Englishman shook his head in mild disapproval. 'Cleansing of your tainted soul will come only with repentance and confession.'

'Confession? To you?' A nerve twitched.

'Be satisfied I will escape, abbot. I shall be gone with my charges and shall have reached many miles hence before you are found. Whether they discover you as breathing prelate or well-mutilated corpse rests firm in your hands.'

Be satisfied. The abbot was far from satisfied. He was hyperventilating, his grey and marginal locks lank with perspiration. Vaguely he pondered the method employed by the maddening intruder to regain entry to his abbey. Hazily he chastised himself for his greed, for having accepted the three horses of these travelling companions as payment and prize. He was in no doubt that Sergeant Hugh would retake possession and that the soldier would carry through a threat.

His face creased in bitter surrender. 'You return for purpose of revenge, Hugh of York.'

'I come for information.'

'It is not mine to give.'

'You will realize it is mine to take.' Sergeant Hugh went eye to eye with the abbot. 'Distinct from young Otto of Alzey, I am not of noble bent. I have a brutish and unforgiving nature.'

'Please, I may not speak of the things you ask.'

The soldier did not pause. 'Who is behind this plot? Who sends armed killers to the monastery? Who seeks to snatch the children as he did the last?'

'Identity is unknown to me.'

'A name.' Fingers squeezed tight on the scalp of the quaking Cistercian.

'I cannot tell you.'

'You shall.'

Sergeant Hugh gave his most engaging grin and pulled a small knife from his belt. The abbot truly deserved his title of a white monk.

As the chapel bell rang the opening of the day, the monks filed to their chancel pews in the early-morning darkness. They chanted and sang, responded to the invitatory prayers, recommitted themselves to God in this holy moment of matins. The abbot led their sacred entreaties. Absorbed in worship, the candle-cast shadows about them, his brethren did not notice the pallor of his skin or the nervous tremor in his hands.

'Never.'

An old and grieving regent could be a stubborn one. The Lord of Arsur regarded his ruler through the mask of friendship and concern. This poor man had lost his infant child, was poised to lose his kingdom. It was the least a trusted courtier could do but attend, to advise and console as he might. It was the festival of Epiphany, when the three wise Magi had presented gifts to the baby Jesus and revealed Him to a waiting world. In a royal apartment of Acre, the Lord of Arsur made more poisoned offering to the earthly king of Outremer.

Again, John of Brienne thundered his rejection. 'I will not conceive of it, will not countenance such a rash and dangerous plan.'

'You agreed to parley with Saphadin, your majesty.'

'Where is agreement when he takes my child?'

'The more reason to reach settlement, to win back your daughter and the peace of your realm.'

'Reason?' The eyes of the regent were wild with anguished rage. 'All reason deserts me, is consumed by the passion of hate, by black thought of vengeance on the Saracen beast.'

'Be still and composed, sir. Your daughter, our queen, will be returned to you safe.'

'Why do they snatch her? Why do they strike such savage blow? Why do they drive an old man to the edge of madness?'

'To weaken you, sir.'

It seemed to succeed. The Lord of Arsur watched as the regent choked back a sob. He would like to have confided that little Yolanda was seized for the single purpose of sacrifice, and that it was not at all the hand of the infidel at work. But John of Brienne would not understand, would barely appreciate as his world dissolved that its replacement formed within. He would vanish along with so many manifestations of a former age.

'Is there no honour in these butchers, Arsur?' The voice was fragile with incomprehension.

'There is solely politics, sir.'

'They expect me to talk when they inflict such a grievous wound?'

'If you do not, the wound will be graver and the body will die.'

'And now you ask that I part with Lady Matilda from my court, that I offer up as hostage to the heathen my last light and solace.'

'Saphadin commands it.'

The Sultan of Damascus did nothing of the sort. It was merely further pressure on this ageing Frankish ruler, another nail to be driven home. John of Brienne would feel every impact. He was near-broken by events, his torment expressed in the jagged silence, in the deep furrows of his brow, in the balled fist brought tense to his mouth.

His stress-bruised eyes lifted. 'You are our constant and considerate friend. Yet you counsel me to go against my conscience.'

'Kingship demands more than conscience, sir.' The Lord of Arsur was gentle in his persuasion. 'We have chance to pluck true and lasting settlement from these boiling waters.'

'Though I scald my flesh to find it. Why does

Saphadin choose the port of Jabala in Syria for our meeting?'

For the reason that I require both you and the Sultan to be absent from Palestine when I make my move. 'He suggests it lies within easy sail of Acre, would stay the Christian fears of surprise attack. The emir of the town holds no grudge or hostility towards us.' *It nevertheless shall not save you.*

'Then why such hesitation in our convening? Is it not imperative we face each other before the slow-approaching month of March?'

'Waiting will not harm proceedings.' *On the contrary, it will allow me to place my forces well.*

'I want Yolanda back.'

It was said with the despairing vehemence of a father. The Lord of Arsur was certain daughter and parent would be reunited soon. All that was left was fine-tuning and concluding orders and the diplomatic swap of hostages. The talks would begin, the leaders die, the army march. A string of actions leading inexorably to the purest of outcomes.

'Sir, there is yet possibility for fair ending. It is why I sought out Saphadin, why I step forward as hostage with three other barons.'

'For all your sacrifice I am grateful.'

'The Sultan will consign his own son al-Mu'azzam to our keeping. Is it not good sign?'

'I am in no mood for signs.' The regent ground his fist into his palm. 'I lose my wife to an early grave, my sweet infant daughter to the hands of a vile thief. I cannot give up Matilda to unknown fate.'

'*Our fate is ready decided if I do not go, my lord.*'

Matilda curtsied low, had entered the chamber unnoticed, was solemn and correct in her composure. Yet her spirit glowed. So collectable a beauty, such effortless and untamed grace, thought the Lord of Arsur. Her eyes were as green as the most precious of emeralds, her hair raven, her skin soft and pure. Breeding-stock without compare. The regent desired her safe, did not wish for her involvement. But she was already enmeshed. She would be lured to a new destiny, taken if necessary by force.

She levelled her gaze at John of Brienne, her look one of resolve. 'My duty is to serve, sir. How could I turn away when Yolanda is imperilled? How may I live in indolence and comfort when there is effort to be made?'

'This is no matter for a noble maid, nor for one so young.'

'I am needed, sir.'

'You are required here.'

'To roam the palace halls, to play at my loom, to watch our lands wither from the vantage of the city ramparts?'

'Dwell where you are protected and not with the responsibilities of men.'

'Have I not assumed the mantle of my father and administered his estates?'

The aged crusader shrugged in tired perplexity. 'Should harm befall you, I am finished.'

'I merely share the burden that threatens us all.' She pressed her case as his resistance flagged. 'Your own

Maria, my dear and departed queen, would not sit idle by. She would spur action to restore her child and our battered nation.'

John of Brienne clamped his open hands across his face. 'Your truth cuts deeper than any knife.'

'Let me travel to the fort of Beit-Nuba, sir. Permit me to tarry there with the Lord of Arsur and the other noble captives.'

The Lord of Arsur nodded comfortingly in his support. 'On my honour and life, I will guard and reinstate her to your side.'

Pledges were so easy to break, declarations so simple to abandon. A distressed regent and an ardent girl were the most malleable of elements. The Lord of Arsur was solicitous in his attention. He had kidnapped the infant daughter of that regent, had long ago killed the father of that girl. They were none the wiser. A pity the late Sir William de Picton and Lord of Jebail were not present to offer guidance. But they were victims of their own credulous nature. It was ever the unlikely and the ordinary who became the greatest of tyrants. He would surpass them all.

Ill at ease, Matilda wandered beneath the barrel-vaulting of the processional corridor. She had agreed to be made hostage for the sake and future of the realm and for the duration of the peace talks. Yet conflict instead of calm attached to every thought. She did not wish to leave her regent lord at time of such dread magnitude, to abandon Acre and the walls of Christendom for the uncertain company of the Lord of Arsur and hospitality of the Saracen. But such petty and self-serving views were unworthy of her name. She tried to discard them, attempted to reason they were product of emotions frayed by recent happening. Still they remained. There were none in whom she could confide her previous and warning instincts concerning the wet-nurse of Yolanda. Now the infant queen was gone. Perhaps it was reparation, a divine form of atonement that she should spend time with the strange and hateful Lord of Arsur. God have mercy. She was bleakly certain that matters would soon worsen.

January was a treadmill. For many hours of every day, dressed in threadbare rags against the wind, Brother Luke trudged the slatted boards and slowly turned the wheel. The Templars had found labour for sore and bloody feet. Each step produced the echoed rattle of a chain, pulled wooden pails from the cistern deep below and tipped their contents into sluices. These channels took water to every part: to the troughs and baths, to the forge and the mills. The Franciscan walked at their centre. He was an assiduous worker, never complaining or slackening his pace, never once crying out at the casual application of the lash. Even when it was dark, and the only light came from the orange glow of the smithy fires, the ambient sound of hammers on steel, the elderly friar plodded on. The Franks were preparing, and he wished to see. Boats came and left, provisions were loaded, the occasional corpse of a slave was dumped without flourish at sea.

Such was life and death during that month on the tiny fortress isle of Arwad.

This morning he had a fellow prisoner beside him, a roped associate to share the load. It was the Dane, the former Varangian guard of Constantinople who had broken bread with him at the start of his incarceration.

'You think on everything or nothing, holy brother?'

'I dwell upon the happiness to be gained even in the simplest toil.'

'A noble example I find hard to follow.'

'Was it not a humble ass that carried Jesus to Jerusalem? We Franciscans seek no higher calling than to be similar beast of burden.'

'I can truly say you have found it.'

Brother Luke gave an enigmatic smile. 'Slavery is a soul confined and kept in irons. This wheel provides no real imprisonment.'

'You have been touched by the sun and on the road too long, holy brother.'

'Maybe so.' Another step and revolution completed. 'Yet I have more liberty than any here in the dungeons possess.'

'Greater resilience too, I note.'

They pushed on, pressed down, heaving against the weight of their rotating pathway. Brother Luke glanced to the side, mapped with the trained eye of an observer the route of the watercourse and location of critical labours. An innocent enough pursuit. Bored with the monotony of their own regime and in search of better pastime, the guards had sauntered away. Attention diverted was opportunity gained. It was in such moments a prisoner might pluck from the ground a pin or discarded shard of glass; it was in these seconds he could perform reconnaissance or conceal an item. The Franciscan was no apprentice.

The Dane panted through exertion. 'For myself, and for my sins, I believe the acts of my forebears are come to visit me.'

'How so, my son?'

'I am descended from kings, rulers who once raided your shores of Albion, who pillaged the holy isle of Lindisfarne, who enslaved thousands.'

'There is not a man alive whose lands have not seen occupation, whose ancestors have not been put to the sword or yoke.'

'It becomes our turn, holy brother.'

'You a soldier and I a friar. Both are callings of uncertain fortune.'

'Does a man of God expect to be caged?'

'On occasion it is what I have come to assume.' Brother Luke found amusement in the memory. 'I have ceased to predict the vagaries of life.'

'But Templars? Christian knights who inflict suffering and indignity on a Christian brother?'

'It is possible I provoke them.'

Silence again settled, their efforts directed to maintaining the flow of their task. Brother Luke had not stopped surveying the backdrop. His gaze took in every detail, alighted on an idling figure or moving cart, tracked the course of a passing patrol. He was counting, testing, arranging his future.

A murmured warning from the Dane. 'Put it from your head, holy brother. Escape will not happen.'

'As I have declared, I am loath to make prophecy.'

'You are one man on an island of many, an unarmed friar against the most martial of foes.'

'That they do not consider me their equal is at least a beginning.'

'It is as like to be your end.' The prisoner stared at him in wonderment and oblique admiration. 'Tell me it is delusion, a trick of an infirm mind.'

'An aged wanderer is permitted occasional flight of his senses.'

'I think you too wise and calculating for such flight. It makes it the more dangerous.'

'Nothing I do will imperil any captive on this isle.'

'You may yet inspire us.'

There was a sudden catch in the voice of the Dane, as though emotion had been stirred, a longing uncovered. Prisoners rarely had the chance to reach beyond the confines of their bars, to travel further than the radius of their shackles. Brother Luke seemed to stretch out beyond the realm of probability. The promise was tantalizing, the reality daunting.

'Is this wild jest, holy brother?'

'I merely study all routes and dwell on each prospect.'

'However the future, regard me as your comrade.'

'With willingness, my son.'

'*You, come with us* . . .

Interruption was swift and with its usual brutality. Guards had appeared, were dragging the Dane from his position and redirecting him in a flurry of kicks. It would be foolish to resist. Brother Luke did not pause, the Dane reflexively folded to deferential posture. There were sacks to be hefted and carried. With discordant shouts, the prisoner was driven on. He exchanged only a sliding glance with the tramping friar, blank and transient stares that signified nothing and communicated much. Sentinels could rarely decipher the language of their captives.

The incident was past, and Brother Luke continued to plan for his breakout.

His lambs had seen nothing like it. Kurt and Isolda crouched in the cathedral gloom of the cave, children awed and insignificant in the hollowed majesty of their surroundings. Below them the river Lycus rushed and cascaded through gaping caverns; around them the pendulous stalactites and jutting stalagmites emerged as a myriad coloured teeth. Any mortal would be impressed. A few miles from Beirut, and this was their latest hiding-place, a waystop on a journey that had taken them from mountain peaks to valley floors, which had seen them huddle in the ruins of Byzantine churches and lie low among the stone remnants of Greek temples. They had no wish to be captured.

'Otto and Sergeant Hugh are departed a long while, Kurt.'

'Patience, Isolda. They forage for food, scout ahead for any danger.'

'I once believed it was the infidel alone who wished us harm. Since the monastery, I am not so certain.'

'Hazard is everywhere. It is why Otto and Sergeant Hugh ride with senses sharp and blades drawn.'

'How blessed we are.' She turned to him, her face thin and delicate in the light of their single lamp. 'And how lucky I am my brother is constant at my side.'

He put his arm about her shoulder and rested back against the cold dampness of the rock. In truth, he yearned to be riding out with the young noble and the English soldier, to be performing brave deeds and charging down the foe. That was aspiration for a boy, the spirit of Cœur de Lion. After all, he acted as unspoken squire to Otto, was as loyal and accomplished as any born to better blood. What he needed was a sword, a fight, a proving-ground.

Beside him, Isolda sighed. 'Is this what the old Hospitaller at Krak des Chevaliers meant when saying we might be consumed in the darkness?'

'He spoke in tongues, not any I can explain.'

'We are far from the square where we gathered before the cathedral in Cologne.'

'Far from everything.'

'So much joy and hope was there, so many children.'

'We are what is left, Isolda.'

'I did not imagine it this way, did not think there was cost in what the preacher-boy Nikolas told us.'

'Perhaps we did not think at all.'

It had been an age since the image of the girl with

the flaxen girl had visited. She returned to him now, her smile as open and eyes as bright as they were when first she approached. He welcomed her back. There was no sadness in her face, no accusation or regret. She would never grow old, never need to run for her life or tremble in caves. He was grateful for that.

His sister was talking, her voice subdued against the heavier flow of the water. 'Not once have we learned of Brother Luke passing this way.'

'He travels to his own calendar, Isolda. While we move and live as mountain ibex, he walks the coast. He has doubtless already reached Acre.'

'I miss him, Kurt.'

'We will soon be reunited and sharing tales of our adventure.'

'You think he has escaped by basket from a clifftop? You think he has been dragged off by heathen traders into slavery?'

They shared the joke, entertained and amazed at the world opened to them. Nobles and Franciscans, Templars and Saracens, Cathars and longbowmen. None other in their village would have made such encounters. What lay ahead rested in the closed palm of God. He might give or take away, might reveal to them the True Cross. Kurt wondered if they would ever confront a genuine dragon or monster.

'Kurt, you hear it?' His sister clutched his arm.

'There is nothing but the river and its sounds.'

'A voice.' Her own was insistent. 'Listen.'

'It is no one.'

'Someone comes. He is calling to us.'

'Sergeant Hugh? Otto?' The twelve-year-old eased forward to concentrate. 'I still do not notice.'

The words crawled faint and indecipherable to him, a reverberation pushing through the background. His face wrinkled in the effort to interpret. Whoever called could be near or far, might never stumble upon them. He doused the lamp.

But illumination remained. It was growing from a single source, glancing from limestone, creeping subdued and ever closer. Behind it was that voice. Again it cried out, plaintive, seeking, probing ahead of the oncoming beam. Isolda shivered. And Kurt too began to quake, his mouth dry, his stomach tightening in involuntary spasm of alarm. He and his sister were being identified by name. *Kurt . . . Isolda . . . Kurt . . . Isolda . . .* He recognized the words. Worse, he knew their speaker. Hypnotized in disbelief, he awaited revelation. The intruder had leaped from past and sinister dream to present and living nightmare, might just as well have reached and seized him by the throat. He could scarcely breathe, hardly think. Gunther had joined them in the hillside chamber.

He was not the son of the woodsman as Kurt remembered. The sneering arrogance was gone, the bullying manner evaporated to leave a cringing supplicant who posed no threat. That alone was disconcerting. Bewildered, Kurt rose and tried to retreat. The older boy was on his knees, stuttering and imploring in his regret, his face strained and mucous-wet with tears and misery.

'Kurt, Isolda, I ask your forgiveness for what I have done. Please, I beg of you.' He wrung his hands, bowed his head weeping.

'Is this the boy who robbed, who showed no mercy, who was cruel to any weaker than himself?'

'I am changed, wish only to make amends and prove myself worthy.'

'You may offer explanation.' Kurt heard his own voice hard-edged with mistrust. 'How came you here? How could you find us? How might any know of our position?'

'Your companion, the soldier.'

'Sergeant Hugh?'

Gunther nodded and sniffed. 'I come from Beirut, where he now attends. I met him by chance, and by good grace have earned his esteem through my rescue of others.'

'His esteem?'

'This voyage has taught me much, Kurt. It has granted me peace, opened my eyes and ears to the beauty of God and the meaning of His Word.'

'I do not believe you.'

'Drive me from your sight if you wish, yet I come in friendship.'

'It does not happen. This is nothing more than magic trance.' Kurt squeezed his eyes tight-shut and opened them once more. 'You are the Devil.'

'I am Gunther, the son of the woodsman, the boy from your village.'

'Would that you had stayed there.' Kurt spat out the words with vehement rage.

'For all my sins, I will pay. But let me begin to heal wrongs, let me help you in your journey.'

'We have aid enough.'

'I have food, warm clothes, a guide to escort us these last few miles. Sergeant Hugh awaits you, trusts in your agreement.'

'He should himself return to us.'

'A soldier easily strays, an Englishman finds pleasure wherever he visits.'

'There is Otto.'

'Our guide searches for him now. Better to be in daylight than in a cave, Kurt. Emerge from the gloom and ride with me.'

'What of the danger?'

'I survive, do I not?' Gunther managed an appeasing smile, his face splitting into bony configuration of rotten teeth and drying tears. 'We each search for the True Cross. Is it not fellowship, a bond?'

Of a kind. Kurt wanted to take up a stone and dash out his brains, to kick the mortal remains of this trespasser into the deepest pit, but he would not act on the urge. There was a possibility Gunther spoke the truth, the smallest reality he approached in good faith. Miracle or curse, it was hard to gauge.

The red-headed boy read his doubt. 'Heed me, Kurt. We must depart before robbers or bandits discover you here.'

'Shall we depend on him, Isolda?' Kurt turned to his sister.

She was mute in horror at the scene, her expression mobile with confusion and conflicting conces

She could offer him no guidance. Gunther seemed transformed. Yet, however contrite and passive his new-found manner, he inhabited the same body, used his former voice. It was too much to grasp.

Isolda finally nodded. 'We should follow him, Kurt.'

✝
Chapter 17

Conditions were treacherous. With care they clambered over obstacles and slithered down steep faces, making for the distant entrance of the caverns. Once, Kurt slipped. But Gunther proffered his hand, hauled him to safety as though brother-in-arms, as if bad blood and unpleasant history had never existed between them. Division was ended. The younger boy was glad his grudging instinct had been proved correct. Gunther was merely a lad like himself, a youth brave enough to bury the past, generous enough to lend his aid. The son of the woodsman was eager too to talk. He told of how he had travelled from Genoa, how little blind Achim had died, how Egon and Zepp now awaited their old friends in the royal city of Acre. Such news was further reason to hasten their pace.

They emerged blinking to the outside, disorientated in the cool afternoon glare. Around them, cedar trees climbed the valley sides; below, the river disgorged strong and full in its seaward spate.

Kurt looked about him. 'How good to see the day. We thank you, Gunther.'

'What I do is for greater cause.'

'It was wrong of us to question you, to believe you wished us harm.'

'I cannot right the past, though I may try to change the present.'

'We stand here because of you.'

'That pleases me, Kurt.'

His glee was authentic and infectious. He embraced his companions, whooped and punched the air, joined them in their delight. They were on their way. Even Isolda, always careful, grieving for Achim, gave over to excitement. There would be food, proper shelter, a reacquainting with friends.

'Where now, Gunther? What action shall we take?'

The pale eyes of the boy shone with anticipation. 'You need not move, Kurt.'

'I do not understand.'

'You never did.' Gunther punched him hard in the belly, danced back as the youngster buckled retching to his knees. 'The Lord of Arsur will provide all answer.'

Strangers had appeared, were closing in from the trees with the drilled intensity of a planned outcome. Brother and sister were their focal point. Doubled over, still clutching his stomach, Kurt staggered to his feet. There was no mistaking what he saw, could be no misreading of the crime. A blind and choking fury seized him. He brushed aside the caring entreaties of Isolda, whirled floundering to meet the taunting challenge of his foe. Gunther stayed beyond the cramped radius of his reach.

There were other ways to resist and fight. Struggling to breathe, choosing his moment, Kurt levered himself upright. He raised his face to the surrounding slopes and began to call.

'Otto, it is the Lord of Arsur who does this. Hear us, Otto. The Lord of Arsur . . . The Lord of Arsur . . .'

A sack was pulled over his head, and his shouts abruptly ceased.

Otto heard and saw. It was fortunate he had detected the arrival of armed men at the entrance to the caves, had watched as they dispersed to cover and as the gaunt form of Gunther disappeared within. It could mean only a trap, for instinct and experience had taught him as much. So he lay on his belly and observed, did not move as Kurt and Isolda were led out, as the two children were cast once again into captivity. He could not reason why. His limbs were heavy with dread for them, his thoughts frenzied even as his body was still. There were no troops to call upon, no Sergeant Hugh with longbow close at hand. The soldier had his own itinerary in Beirut. To confront was wastefully to die. Yet he possessed information, intelligence of critical import and a name with which to conjure. *The Lord of Arsur.* That same identity had been prized from the abbot by the hard-drinking and bargain-driving Englishman. Correlation was made, conspiracy revealed.

He had to reach Sergeant Hugh, to deliver report and prepare for rescue. The children depended on him. For three hours he waited in the thicket of trees, holding position and nerve before venturing to recover his horse. Then, mounted, he picked his way along the forest-bordered track to the coast, was cantering south for the city of Beirut. The Arab steed moved well, its neck stretched, its hooves thudding rhythmic and free. No other breed of stallion could maintain such pace.

At the river edge, he paused. It would be the optimum place for an ambush. An arched stone bridge spanned the divide, and on each bank high cliffs rose above the wooded gorge. Armies in retreat or on campaign had passed this way, their fates varied, their journey marked with regiment names and legion numbers scored deep in the rock face. A graveyard of sorts; a lesson in history. Otto peered about. Beneath him, his mount whinnied fretfully and stamped. Perhaps it was impatience, or possibly it was warning.

The figures when they materialized were not as he expected. They were Franks, certainly, armed as knights and seated on chargers. But they were different. They had the quality of spectres, the menace of bandits, the cowled and hooded facelessness of men without identity. Otto counted thirteen of them.

'What is your purpose, youth?'

For a moment, he could not answer. The voice of his challenger came diseased and harsh, seemed to issue from a lifeless soul. Any would be unnerved. Controlling his horse, subduing his impulse to leave, the young noble faced the threat.

'I would travel onward for Beirut.'

'You shall not pass.'

'Says whose authority?'

'That of the sword and superior force.' The eyes of the stranger glared sickly at the Rhineland boy.

'It is not the law of the land.'

'There is no law beyond the convention of death.' The leader of the leper knights made no attempt to move. 'State your name, fair one.'

'Otto of Alzey.'

The briefest of pauses. 'A far way from home, a distant corner in which to lose your handsome face.'

'You test me?'

'I invite you to combat, welcome you to perish for our sport.'

'I tend to more noble pursuit.'

'To flee, Otto of Alzey? To foul your undergarments? To fall to your knees and pray for clemency?'

'None of these shall I do.'

In fair fight he stood a chance against this scarecrow-apparition, and would have worked his blade to advantage. But there would be nothing just or even in the coming bout. Behind the aggressor were a dozen more, baneful disciples who would avenge and dispatch. No going forward, no falling back. Yet duty, urgency and honour forced him on.

The hooded form climbed from his horse and accepted the one-and-a-half-hander sword proffered by an acolyte. Perfectly balanced, its spine and twin edges gleaming, the weapon could cleave in twain chain-mail or man. Despite the wayward and mercenary habits of the English bowman, Otto found himself wistful for his presence. He dismounted purposefully and drew his sword.

At either end of the bridge they stood, squaring off, their blades lowered. Otto studied his rival. The man appeared to be carrying a limp, to have a left arm that occasionally twitched. He would attempt to exploit it. On that plain before Rome, Brother Luke had once counselled him to fight not as princeling from a castle but as mean vagabond of the road. He would shortly know the effects of such tutelage. Opposite, his antagonist behaved with the measured ritual of an executioner.

'Commit yourself to God, youth.'

'He guides all that I do.'

'Soon will He pluck you from this earth.' The body swayed, mesmerizing, cobra-slow. 'Shout out your final prayers that we may hear.'

'It is you who should make peace with the Redeemer.'

'I find my peace in the screams of others, in the corpses which litter my path. Your life is at stake, youth.'

'Name and repute are of higher value.'

'Be on your guard.'

They closed in a ringing clash of steel, and the world narrowed. It had reduced to this, to a slender band of stone on which two men fought and where existence balanced. Otto lunged and leaped back, greeting the whirling blade in a flash and flicker of sparks. He heard his breath and the pulse of his blood, the grunts and hammer-strikes of close exertion. Brute force contained its own sounds

Moves were replicated, blows met and traded in

dancing and parallel flow. Otto deflected an attack and hacked for the head, driving back his adversary. Cross-guards locked. He peered into malice-framed eyes, struggled yelling against an immutable strength. There had to be a way. Speed, judgement and cunning, Brother Luke had advised. But the friar was not engaged in deathly effort with unearthly foe.

He lashed out with a foot, connected with a padded knee. It earned him slight reprieve. But the sword rebounded fiercer, battering hard, sweeping near. He was losing ground.

'Beg for mercy, youth.'

'I save my breath to curse you.'

'Submit and die.'

'I will not.'

Thrust and cut. The knight flicked the pommel with his hand, switched the angle of assault with velocity and skill. A trick garnered from the battlefield. Otto panted. He could not lower his defence, could ill afford error. Somewhere, a vision of his grave floated. He would do everything to avoid ending there, anything to prevent himself betraying his friends. Metal scraped on metal.

In violent riot, the blade severed space and glanced from his *cuirie*. He staggered back and fell, recovered to a crouch, and parried upward. Again the sword descended. He blocked, his gauntleted hand gripping and levering his tapered blade. Pressure increased. Quickly, he dropped to the side and released his hold. The enemy corrected, was too practised to overreach, to become entangled or unbalanced.

One on one, and he felt he faced an army. He was weakening.

'What ails you, youth? I have found fiercer adversary in miners of iron, in women of villages I have burnt.'

'Your taunts are nothing.'

'There are victims whose tongues I have nailed to doors, whose skins I have stripped free and stuffed with straw, whose bodies I have rent asunder between sprung trees.'

'For all misdeeds, you shall answer.'

'Yet not this day.' The sword arced, Otto sprawled, and the masked aggressor stood above him. 'Luck deserts you, Otto of Alzey.'

His weapon was also gone, sent clattering beyond his reach. It was too late for calculation or riposte. He wiped the sweat from his eyes, blinked passive as the razor edge hung still and lingering above. Seconds away from his butchering. An oddly emotionless affair, a respite before the inevitable. His old tutor Felix would have been disappointed in such an ignoble finish. A mortal pity he would never again see his father.

The steel tip grazed the surface of his leather breastplate. 'What privilege to tremble at the edge of oblivion, youth.'

'Act as you may, brigand.'

'Such defiance in your perdition.' The sword toyed as though itself making decision. 'Dignity and hope have no worth in the Holy Land.'

'I live or depart as I choose.'

'And you earn stay of slaughter.'

Threat and blade lifted with suddenness and no explanation. A signal to his men, and the knight of St Lazarus returned to his horse and climbed into the saddle. Farewells were unnecessary. In a press of spurs and spray of hooves, the band had dissolved from sight. Game was over.

For a while Otto lay on his back, happy to be alive.

As some were thrown into bondage, others took steps towards their freedom. On his prison island, Brother Luke walked his creaking wheel as he had these many days and weeks. It was a night like any other. The same cold wind, the same glow from the smithy furnaces, the same routines. Somewhere, Templar knights slumbered and patrols strolled their customary beat; somewhere, a guard dozed beside the treasure-house and slaves nestled in the dank foulness of their dungeons. He had them all mapped.

Diverted, the escorting soldier had not earlier witnessed him stoop and plunge his hands in the open container of olive oil. Nor had the man noticed as he worked free those hands to later slip their bindings. It had been a time-consuming process. But the hours, and now darkness, were on his side. Carefully, he removed the last tie and eased himself from the wheel. From hereon, recapture would mean certain death.

He had rounds to perform. There were no guards on the oil-store, and it was there that he first directed himself. Using touch alone, he applied his pilfered needle to the lock, pushing against the door as the simple barrel gave. He had defeated tougher obstacles before. Systematically, he opened window shutters, emptied amphorae, decanted contents into earthenware jars. Then he cut his ragged garment into long strips with his acquired and hidden shard of glass. The better to make fuse-string.

Progress was steady and unhindered, the friar circulating through the narrow alleyways with the quiet confidence of purpose and carrying a bulky sack. To be furtive was to excite interest and enquiry. Occasionally a hound barked or a cat slunk by on mission for rats, a goat bleated. With a sigh of relief, a sentry loosed his bladder against a wall and returned to his repose. Nothing to report. He had been unaware of the night-stalker lingering at the corner. Brother Luke passed by. A cache of armour and weapons provided useful source of cover. He made his selection, chose a javelin, a linen mantle, a helmet with nose-guard, and moved on. The flour-mill was next, beyond it the forge and the armoury. It was a circuit of a mere few hundred yards, a journey that seemed like an odyssey.

'As exciting as any tomb, brother.' A hand slapped his back.

He paused and half turned, his voice lapsing to the rough vernacular of the soldier, his body stiffening in expectation of a knife. The sour hint of fermented wheat clung to the breath of the man. It could offer advantage or drawback.

'To you I am Sergeant Brother.' His hissed response was domineering and unfriendly.

The soldier lurched confused. 'I mean no harm, Sergeant Brother.'

'Yet you create offence. You have task to do?'

'It is not my watch, Sergeant Brother.'

'So use these hours to sleep and not to drink. We each of us face battle ahead.'

'That itself gives reason to celebrate. Attack on Jerusalem deserves libation, Sergeant Brother.'

'It demands our preparation.'

'You are fine sergeant and stern master.'

'Likely to be harsher should my comment go unheeded. Spare your effort for the fray, or we shall all end in the tomb.'

Salutary advice deliberated in silence by the drunk. He appeared to be convinced. The commanding tone and nocturnal shadow, the expanded garrison of recent days, lent credibility to the lie and anonymity to the friar. Brother Luke had gained the upper hand.

He pushed against the swaying form. 'Begone now, before my patience ends.' It had the desired effect.

Just as well, for the Franciscan had been engaged in pouring oil through a hatch that led direct to the flour-store and the baking-ovens adjacent. At this hour, the residual dust would have been swept, the grates cleared. But the stones within would still be hot. A useful item to remember, and a place he intended to revisit.

The forge was his focus and objective. At all hours its frenetic industry never ceased, the hammering, the hellish glow, the wheeze of bellows, the clouds of steam infecting the air about. Bodies glistened and toiled. A process was in motion, fires stoked, bars and ingots of white-hot steel folded, beaten, plunged and tempered. Military campaign made demands of its suppliers. They were too busy to notice incident at the margins, too deafened to sense an aged prisoner appearing in a doorway.

Flame belched in sudden explosion. Men and order vanished, chaos entered, as ragged blasts tore and repeated through the building inferno. Clay jars arced and shattered, oil spilled to hasten and fuel. Within the furnace, shapes had become indistinct. Humans lumbered and tumbled, colliding in blind exodus, fighting for air and escape. Their small and efficient world had crumpled. Conflagration replaced it, and the fire was spreading fast.

'*Feu! Feu! Feu!*'

Shrieked warnings did not do justice to the incendiary scene. From their dormitories, knights and sergeants came running, adding to confusion, swelling the frenzy. They were well occupied. Through their midst, Brother Luke wandered. He had discarded his javelin, had acquired a steel pail of burning charcoal that he seemed to be removing from the billowing site. None asked questions. He was merely another pair of hands, a soldier abandoning his post and gathering in a street thronging with too many. The glowing cinders were deposited through the entrance to the cloth-house.

Further eruptions burst in untidy trail across the island, the walls and passages soaked in creeping light and desperate scenes. Arwad was ablaze, and the old Franciscan on the move. He had reached the treasure-vaults. On normal occasion they were well guarded, the gilded heart of a Templar Order whose burgeoning wealth was amassed in coffers here. But circumstance was changed and discipline spent. Waving and hollering, the friar rushed in, a convincing presence in a moment of uncertainty and crisis.

Fearful and in haste, a warder crashed against him. 'What happens, brother?'

'Arwad is consumed. We all must join to fight the storm.'

'Where should I head?'

'Wherever there is flame to douse.' The friar propelled the man for the doorway. 'Make haste, brother, and may God help us.'

He had lifted the keys from the leather belt of the man, knew the procedure well enough for entry to the sanctum. Close by, fireballs vented to the sky, secondary and tertiary detonations catching the oil-mill, overwhelming the kitchens. He would be quick in his choice. Ten minutes later he re-emerged, a hunched figure trundling a laden handcart, a friar turned soldier turned thief. The shoreline had become his destination.

At some point his absence from the wheel would be noticed. Yet he had already ranged beyond the deserted gates, ascended a defilade, and ventured with his barrow out on to a stub pontoon. Fire-fighting would detain his captors for a while. He busied himself in stowing his trophies aboard a little skiff, his labours lit by unnatural radiance cast and reflected on the dark surrounding water.

'Holy brother, they come for you. You have not much time.' His fellow prisoner the Dane had crawled unseen from his duties.

Brother Luke glanced at the dim shadow. 'You are present to bid farewell or sail with me?'

'Neither, holy brother. I am here to preserve your life and protect your flight.'

'Though you may forfeit chance for your own?'

It provoked a quiet laugh. 'I acquire a sword and will put it to use. Call it revenge or simple pleasure for a Varangian guard who once more has occasion to enter the fray.'

'Do not squander your blood on account of an old Franciscan.'

'There is no waste when it it is done in fraternal love.' Shouts echoed near, were accompanied by the martial tramp of feet. 'Make haste, holy brother, and pray for me. We shall meet again in paradise.'

A blade cut the hawser and the craft floated free. As he raised the sail and manned the tiller, Brother Luke glimpsed the foreshore in a momentary and fading pulse of light. Armed figures had converged, their swords rising and falling in act of murder. A crossbow bolt flew wide and slapped the sea, then another. They would not reach him now. He tasted the bitterness of ash and charred particles on the wind, heard a bell toll. Arwad was behind him, its searing heat replaced by coolness, its luminescence returned to night.

*

'Kurt! Isolda!'

There was no single or definitive expression on the face of Egon. Bewilderment and gladness, consternation and amazement competed for supremacy. He gasped their names again, kept staring. Then he was on his feet, tugging at his chains, stretching his arms wide to embrace and hold his friends. Beside him, resting on his haunches, Zepp stayed mute as brother and sister crowded round, as Isolda stroked his hair and kissed him.

'He will never answer.' The voice of the blacksmith's boy was cracked with feeling. 'Not since Achim died has he said a word.'

Isolda held the face of the youngster between her palms. 'Be restored, sweet Zepp. No matter our lot, we are with you now, shall always be beside you.'

'How came you here, Egon?' Kurt rested a hand on the shoulder of his comrade.

'Fate of the worst kind; fortune that delivered us to slavery in Egypt and by way of caravan to this dungeon.'

The twelve-year-old peered about him. 'So many children are present.'

'Yet not the traitor Gunther.'

'Give me a sword and I will run him through. He is the one who captured us, Egon.'

'I do not doubt it, for he serves his new master well.'

'The Lord of Arsur?'

Egon nodded, apprehension and disgust creasing his brow. The sturdy son of the blacksmith was afraid.

But the tension softened as he watched Isolda, his affection still there, his longing undimmed. Whatever their travails, however tortuous the journey, he could not disguise his pleasure in her company. It made the pain of revelation bleaker.

'See how we are shackled.' The blacksmith's boy rattled his bindings. 'We are kept for a reason, and that reason is to die.'

'You speak no sense, Egon.'

'Nor can I find it. Yet I know things, have been told by this black lord himself how events will unfold.'

'He gathers us to kill?'

'As sacrifice, Kurt. When time arrives, we are to be taken to Jerusalem and put to death as blessing for creation of a future kingdom.'

'No Christian would do this.'

'He is no Christian, no kind and proper lord. And what he plans fast approaches.'

'We may escape, have done so before.'

'Like this?' Egon was disbelieving.

'How often have we despaired, brother? How often have we then outpaced our hunters, found way through to freedom?'

'It was never from jail or fortress, Kurt.'

'Otto rides to aid us, Brother Luke too will collect support.'

'What are they against an army?'

'You have not met our companion Sergeant Hugh, once guard to the Lionheart Richard, longbowman without an equal.'

The older boy lowered his face, ashamed to show

his tears, unwilling to deal final blow to the hopeful-ness of his friend. To be held in irons was to see the human spirit reduced and robbed. Kurt would learn when it happened to him.

'Water . . .'

A child sobbed, and Isolda went to tend her. There were others beside, calling out to their mothers or to God, weeping while awake or in their wretched dreams. Brother and sister tried to comfort them. It was good to keep busy, to share clumsy and childish words with these poor and wasted creatures. How like they were to those who had arrived lame before the gates of Genoa, Kurt thought. They should have stayed there, should not have travelled to the ends of the earth in order to be slain. The innocent and pure were always the last to realize, the first to die. Now he was among them.

The adult voice was low and sonorous, and it was one he recognized. 'Did I not say we would meet again, child?'

Indeed he had done. The Perfect stood in the subter-ranean chamber, studied Kurt with the enquiring air of a herbalist who has discovered a rare specimen. And the subject of his interest glared back. He remembered well their last meeting, the shadow that had flitted over him in the hidden square of Nettuno, the way the figure in black had reached to tousle his hair and to menace. *We are chosen, elected to show the way and to harvest the corrupt flesh of man.* Like Gunther, the Cathars had returned to haunt him. Small wonder Egon believed he and his young fellow prisoners were damned.

He walked slowly towards the Cathar chief. 'What right have you here?'

'That of a keeper over his slave.'

'You have no power over us.'

'Words that have no meaning; thoughts which will soon vanish.'

'Brother Luke will take revenge.'

'Your friar?' The Perfect shook his head, could almost have been caring. 'He is captured, already most likely dead.'

'It is untrue.'

'Yet you are not certain.'

Confrontation was unequal, a boy set against a tall and solemn man who carried intent to harm. There was a calm hostility in the Cathar, a conviction that allowed him to dispense with obvious ill feeling. Killing children was merely a matter of faith. Kurt had his own duty, an obligation to protect each one of the young fettered in this place.

He balled his fists. 'You will not come near.'

'Your fiery temper and arguing spirit do not leave you, child.'

'I am no child.'

'To be sure, in the eyes of our true God you are progeny of evil.'

'Evil is to hold us here, to keep us locked away.'

'Open your eyes, child.' The Perfect frowned in commiseration. 'My *credentes* shall liberate and redeem your souls, act to banish wrong and benefit the world.'

Behind him, the Believers were gathered in

devotional silence, a posse of adherents the youngster had not encountered since Brother Luke punished them near the hanging-tree. Their presence was discouraging.

Kurt was not for surrender. 'Whatever you plan, you shall be brought before law.'

'The Lord of Arsur will rule Outremer, shall be our court of justice. And you shall be ash and dust.'

'Go from us! Let us alone!'

Fear prompted his attack, spurred him in wild fury to leap at the Perfect with arms and legs flailing. The onrush was checked. As he kicked and bit and was held firm, the Cathar leader leaned to address him.

'I vow I shall reserve my bluntest knife for you.'

Grim hours passed without surprise or incident, and the children sat or lay in simmering despair and silence, Isolda knelt beside Zepp and prayed; Kurt and Egon tried to sleep. The twelve-year-old was sure the gloating eyes of Gunther, son of the woodsman, were periodically upon them.

It had been a mistake to offer opinion to the regent, to make allegation without supporting proof. In the great hall of Acre, Otto and Sergeant Hugh shifted uncomfortably before the dais and throne. John of Brienne stared back. He viewed them as though they were village simpletons burst in upon a royal feast, dismissed them as though they uttered blasphemy. Above, heraldic banners hung in vivid profusion from the oak cross-beams. At ground level, matters were far less festive.

John of Brienne rose from his seat. 'Am I so weak, so infirm of mind, that I should take counsel from a stripling noble and a knavish bowman?'

'We are simple bearers of fact, sir.' Sergeant Hugh was prone to truculence when challenged.

'You are bringers of falsehood and cancerous rumour, Hugh of York.' The old crusader stamped his foot. 'Who gives you such devious tongue? Who permits you to mire the name of our noble Lord of Arsur with wrong accusation and vile calumny?'

'Circumstance, sir.'

'I shall give you circumstance to regret outrageous hearsay and untruth. You shall be lucky to escape whipping at the post.'

Otto cleared his throat. 'It is no way to treat your loyal servant, sir.'

'Hugh of York, loyal? He is as fickle and errant as wayside beggar or market harlot.'

'A beggar may have eyes, a harlot ears, sir.' The young noble respectfully met the thunderous look. 'At the monastery, the abbot revealed the dark hand of this lord in abduction of the child innocents. At the caves beyond Beirut, I witnessed his captains take my friends.'

'Would you have me alter policy on a whim? Would you have me abandon a true stalwart of our cause and kingdom?'

'I ask only that you judge the chance of foul plot.'

'There is no conspiracy, no treachery, no substance to these wicked and imprudent claims.' John of Brienne paced angrily on his royal platform. 'The Lord of Arsur finds us peace, establishes foundation for talk and accord with the Sultan of Damascus.'

Sergeant Hugh interrupted. 'Perhaps he creates foundation for himself.'

'Neither king nor noble need justify his course to a common soldier.'

'I merely venture an idea, sir.'

'You are not paid for it. In truth, you were rewarded by Lady Matilda to find and bring back stray waifs, child pilgrims you now lose. Do I see you return those sums of silver?'

'There was certain expense, sir.'

'And precious little sacrifice. Yet the Lord of Arsur of whom you speak ill has endangered his life for our gain, offers himself as hostage to Saphadin. Lady Matilda too, from whom you rob, goes as captive to Beit-Nuba. What advantage do you seek that is not for yourself?'

A ruler indignant could be hard to placate, harder to persuade. Otto observed him and the hushed courtiers about, sensed reason would not penetrate when his story seemed absurd. He himself could make no sense of it. These people had sound basis for their doubts, reason to question the character and standing of Sergeant Hugh. Yet he knew, without comprehending, that Outremer was imperilled, and that the Lord of Arsur was involved.

Lady Matilda smiled at him. In a single glance there could be so much. A warmth and understanding, a tender sorrow and teasing joy, a secret offer and shouted promise. He found himself staring, drawn enraptured to the green eyes, to the part-open mouth. Never before had he seen a girl so beautiful. Their sightlines touched and played and tangled, as sensuous as fingers, as enfolding as limbs. For a moment he resisted, wrestling the impulse. But the alchemy surged, elemental desire numbing his brain, clutching his groin, squeezing his gut. She possessed him.

The voice of the regent intruded. 'Let us put aside folly and abandon quarrel. You are my guest, young Otto of Alzey, and I welcome you as such.'

'You honour me, sir.'

'While you pay tribute with your presence.'

'I wish only to serve with valour and distinction and to restore my father to my sight.'

'Commendable aim.' The Frankish veteran nodded in approval. 'We need more as you, young Alzey.'

'All will rally to you, sir.'

'Our world crumbles, the shadow of war still looms. And Yolanda our queen, my infant daughter, is stolen. Yet we may dine.'

Otto pitied him his sadness and for all that he had lost. The old and dignified man was weighed heavy with his troubles. He should think of other things. Light-headed and slightly breathless, the young noble returned his attention to Lady Matilda. He wanted to hold her, to save her, to ensure that while he lived she would not fall prey to intrigue or the likes of the Lord of Arsur.

Leading a trio of roped donkeys burdened with Templar treasure, Brother Luke headed across the plain for the land of the Assassins. He no longer wore the brown habit of a Franciscan, but was garbed the stolen tunic taken from Arwad. Travellers and spies often had need of masquerade.

✝
Chapter 18

Matilda was in state of nervous perturbation. In all her life she had seen no boy like this. He was handsome beyond compare, had the charms of an angel and the physical form of a young and earthly god. It made her blush to think of him, to dwell on the uninhibited pursuits she might care to indulge with him. She repeated his name in whisper to herself. *Otto of Alzey*. Again it conjured the ache in her loins and belly, summoned his face to the forefront of her mind. The dancing blue eyes, the smile, the masculine-delicate features, the soft blond hair. She was shocked by her own response. It was both heady and disturbing to feel such things, strange and yet ordinary to imagine acting beyond her control. Emotion could be hard to untangle.

Then the pain deepened to more profound anguish and regret. Baby Yolanda was gone, the beloved regent a ragged shadow of his former kingship. For sure there was prospect of peace and promise of talks in Jabala. They might lead to settlement, could yet disintegrate into war. Matilda would play her dutiful part and accompany the hateful Lord of Arsur into temporary exile at Beit-Nuba. A small price for so sought-after an outcome. The chill noble made her flesh crawl as Otto of Alzey made it shiver-burn with craving. She was parting from her Rhinelander before speaking with him so much as a word. Need created a particular kind of grief.

She wandered to the balcony window of her chamber, looked out upon the rooftops of the city and the eastern line of its defence. How she wished her father were alive to guide her. Distant sounds wound and mingled in the dying February light. The cheer of archers at the target butts, the rattle of lances carried by a mounted troop of Hospitallers, the vibration of rigging from vessels in the harbour. And the smell of pitch coiled to her nostrils, the stench of a process that would end with the ignited substance tipped through channels on to an attacking Saracen force. Just in case.

A different sound, and closer to her. She peered over the stone parapet, tried to determine source and direction. The effort was wasted. With a grating clatter, the grapnel-hook caught and held, the attached rope tensed, and Otto swung himself over and into view. Landing at her feet, breathing heavily from exertion, he rose and straightened his tunic.

Suppressing a desire to fling her arms about him, she feigned annoyance. 'It is not custom to approach in this fashion.'

'How else may I reach you, Lady Matilda?'

'Nobility enter through doorways, pirates through windows.'

'I would not voyage from Alzey had I wished for simple journey.'

'The road scarce improves your manners, Otto of Alzey.'

'Though it sharpens my instinct.' He detected her smile, had not misinterpreted. 'I come to save you, Matilda.'

'Too late, for I fear I am lost.'

'Do you trust in me?'

'What answer may I give to a man I hardly know?'

'You have ever been part of me, as I have been part of you.'

'Such presumption and conceit.'

'No more than the truth.' He stepped toward her as she backed to the interior. 'Hark to my words, Matilda. You must not travel as hostage to Beit-Nuba.'

'We each of us fulfil our obligation.'

'Is yours to fall prey to the Lord of Arsur, to be victim of his malicious design?'

'You speak without reason.'

'Nor am I fluent in detail. Yet I believe this lord does wrong, recognize he snatched the children you strove so hard with Sergeant Hugh to rescue.'

'You pluck conjecture from the clouds.'

'And draw bad feeling from my bones. If the Lord of Arsur carries off the innocent young, can he not also abduct your infant queen Yolanda?'

'I cannot think he would do this, Otto.'

'Avoid thought, and instead feel.'

She was silent, recoiling from the message and yet drawn to its certainty. Otto had merely been the prompt. The Lord of Arsur had become chief counsellor and power in the land, hero of the hour and of Outremer, friend to the regent. He had also been present in the royal stables when Sir William de Picton and the Lord of Jebail were killed, had quickly dispatched their Asssassin murderers. A rock, a bulwark, a trusty. The man preached amity and proffered statesmanship, was all the while a traitor.

'What does he plan, Otto?' Her voice was whisper-small.

'Something or nothing, I have no insight.' He advanced to her and held her arms.

'He was ally of my father.'

'And is staunch companion to Outremer, to a regent who ails and who depends upon him, who grows isolated by the hour.'

'We would not convince my guardian of conspiracy, Otto.'

'More is the pity, much greater the danger.' He searched her eyes, attempted to fathom the depth of her feeling. 'Surely there is a way to avoid the grasp of this Lord of Arsur.'

'In a week I go with him as hostage.'

'Time is cruel, Matilda.'

'It may be used to comfort.'

Her kiss was the start. Lips parted and gently then fully connected, bodies engaged, fingers coursed over gently swaying forms. Frenzy took a while to build. It was a single stream of thoughtlessness that emptied the brain and swelled the groin, that emerged in broken gasps and beads of sweat and escalated from tender caress to the violent momentum of desire. They were losing themselves, finding each other, discarding their clothes in haphazard abandon. Naked, they staggered clumsy and laughing to the silk swathes of her divan. Boy tasted girl, touched and stroked, brushed his mouth across her neck and breasts, pulled her to him, lifted her. She responded, giving of herself and taking of him, her eyes widening, her throat opening to release and amplify a long and shuddering groan.

They rolled and bucked, she rising, he falling, their limbs stretching and entwining in chaotic flow. She clawed at his back, wimpered low, repeated she loved him in guttural whisper. He wanted to cry out in need and surrender, to claim victory and admit defeat, to share with her every part of himself and each future day of his life. This was the Holy Land. She tilted her pelvis and moaned, bit his shoulder in forgetful intensity. Above her, he rocked and worked his hips, let matters slide, felt her heat, clung in suspended state of animation. They were reaching together, coming through. The surge, the peak, the trough. Things went deep.

'A youth with smell of the rut and air of indiscretion.'

The hand on his shoulder was firm, the voice that of Sergeant Hugh. Otto had jumped the last few feet of his descent, had landed soft beside the fig tree and congratulated himself on departure well executed. He would be back, could barely stay away. Matilda was everything he had longed for and nothing he had ever known. From those sweet hours of charged frenetic passion and warm embrace, he had discovered wholeness, carried away the perfume of her body on his skin and her ease and comfort in his soul. Now the English bowman intruded to shatter his delight.

He glared at the dim presence. 'You spy on me, Sergeant Hugh?'

'I guard your back. A back, I wager, which is bruised and strained from its misadventure.'

'You will learn of misadventure from my blade.'

'As Lady Matilda discovers it from your sword thrust.' Sergeant Hugh enjoyed his own jibe.

'It is no concern for you.'

'No?' The soldier manhandled him roughly to the palace wall. 'A peacock without feathers or gizzard cannot strut, a bull without balls is not highly prized.'

'You have been drinking?'

'That would be my preference. But there is too much excitement loose, too great a danger to you beyond wet vestibule of a damsel or wrath of her royal guardian.'

'Here? Danger?'

'Waken to it, Alzey.' The longbowman communicated with a slap.

'Let me be.'

'So you may walk into trap and trouble?' Sergeant Hugh shook his head. 'Enemies pursued you in the Alps and stalk you close in Acre.'

'Your solution is to waylay me in the dark?'

'To escort you to rare meeting. Come with me.'

This was his environment, the royal city in which the English bowman had lived, drunk and brawled for twenty years since storming its ramparts with Richard Cœur de Lion. He moved with the confidence of ownership, and Otto followed, pacing fast as the soldier strode through the tangled confines. Moslem raids had forced many to seek refuge within the walls. They clustered in the streets and courtyards, huddled figures steeped in misery among their goats and poultry and random belongings of their departure. Waiting for better times.

Sergeant Hugh and Otto reached their destination. It was a basic structure built of stone and close by an inner revetment, little more than an open shed stabling rats and storing animal dung to dry for later use as fuel. Few would visit or inspect too close. The young noble remained silent, for asking questions would gain no frank disclosure. Besides, the soldier was busy, had lit an oil lamp and was heaving aside a pallet of droppings to raise the cover of a hidden entrance.

He beckoned Otto to join him and heaved himself down before taking the lantern. There was little choice but to obey. Gingerly, the youth lowered himself through, feeling with his fingertips the earth walls of a narrow passageway, smelling the musty dampness of ancient excavation. They went deeper, part crouching, semi-crawling, navigating a subterranean lair of recesses and crumbling shafts. Sergeant Hugh knew the way. The cramped labyrinth was his unofficial storeroom, repository for traded and stolen wares, treasure-house of gold, silver and jewels. Every soldier required a retirement fund. Otto was flattered, and mystified, to be shown it.

'The very foundation of our walls.' Sergeant Hugh slapped the keystone of a half-buried arch. 'Below us are wood props, the structures for which Saracen fire-troops will mine to set their flame and crack the earth, to bring our fortress tumbling down.'

'We are not yet at war.'

'Though we are all of us perilous close.' Anticipation made the eyes of the bowman gleam.

'You did not bring me here to confer on philosophy and stratagem, Sergeant Hugh.'

'Proof that a handsome head may also be a wise one, Alzey. Tell me again how seemed the leader of those who snared Kurt and Isolda.'

'I have described him on numerous occasions.'

'Once more.'

'He was of mean and knavish look, with the scar of a knife-blade apparent on his cheek even at a distance.'

'You would recognize him?'

'I could not forget him.'

Sergeant Hugh grinned a mischievous smile. 'That is to our benefit, for I arrange reunion.'

He did not lie. With a flourish and a wave of his lantern, he stepped back and revealed the presence of a prisoner bound and gagged. There was no mistake. The bulging and livid eyes, the angry wound scored on pitted skin, belonged to a lieutenant of the Lord of Arsur. And Otto had once seen him outside the caverns near Beirut, had witnessed him place a sack over the head of his young friend Kurt. Circumstance was reversed.

'I am poor judge, but it seems he is not yet grown fond of us, Alzey.'

'You bring him here?' The young noble was incredulous.

'He hunted you with a knife, tracked you as though he were your shadow.'

'I thank you for such meddling.'

'It was sound idea at the time but his master will be awonder at where he might have strayed.'

'How did you convince him to accompany you to this place?'

'With comradeship and a larger knife.' The soldier cuffed the straining face a playful blow. 'You hear him, perceive how he longs to sing?'

Strange and throaty sounds filtered through the bared lips and the rope-knot fixed between them. The man was not a happy captive. It did little to daunt Sergeant Hugh, who was proud to show off his trophy and pleased at chance to bait it.

'In exchange for his collaboration, I give him voice, welcome his merriment and mirth.' He leaned forward and, with deliberate roughness, loosened the muffle.

It produced instant result. Grunted invective became a torrent of bellowed abuse, the detained henchman struggling enraged and unleashing curses and threat. Music to the tone-deaf ears of the Englishman.

'Such hearty tune from my caged and precious songbird.'

'You will pay for this! You shall hang for this!'

'Come, my songbird. It is time for pleasantness and not idle menace.'

The prisoner spat his ire. 'You believe you may escape retribution, may take action against me without coming to harm?'

'Maybe you forget you are in Acre and nor Arsur, that your companions are there as mine are here.'

'It will not save you.'

'And who will liberate you?' Sergeant Hugh pulled a face of mock concern. 'One moment you swagger haughty and strong, servant to your lord. The next you are gone and none know where.'

'You will release me.'

'We merely begin, my songbird.'

'Do not fool with me, nor misjudge the penalty for your crime.'

The soldier cocked an eyebrow. 'What of your misdeeds and of the boy Kurt and girl Isolda you seized outside the caves?'

'Your anxious care touches me, Hugh of York.' The sarcasm was laden with hate.

'As violence will readily mark you. Tell me where they are.'

'There is nothing you may do for them.'

'Why does your Lord of Arsur gather up the young to his lair? Did he further plot and take the baby queen?'

'Matters exist beyond your comprehension and control, outside the bounds of your narrow realm.'

'Little exists outside yours. Confide in me, my songbird.'

A stubborn silence prevailed, the captive refusing to speak, the bowman declining to end his inquisition. Whatever it took, however bloody it became, he would break the man and gain information for his efforts. He drew a long and thin knife from a metal sheath and turned it in the lamplight.

'Your own blade, my songbird.' He held it before the eyes of the man. 'A Persian design.'

'You speak without insight, Hugh of York.'

'Yet I make connection, draw close to the truth. I have seen such weapons before, carried by Assassins.'

'What of it?'

'Is your Lord of Arsur in league with these zealots? Was he arranger of the murder of Sir William de Picton and the Lord of Jebail?'

'You will have your tongue cut out, soldier.'

'While you shall still be buried.' Sergeant Hugh dangled the blade, saw the face blanch and perspiration spring. 'You recoil, my songbird. Is it that the steel is treated with poison, that single scratch may kill?' He brought it close.

'Stay your hand.'

The bowman glanced at Otto. 'Intriguing that he consorts with Assassins, conspires with killers of the kind who pursued you to Rome. They lead to the Lord of Arsur.'

Otto spoke calmly to the prisoner. 'I live because of Sergeant Hugh, and in spite of your endeavour. You damn your master by your presence here.'

'My damnation is as nothing to your own.'

The captive was scowling, had regained the bravado

and arrogance of the wronged and righteous, of a lieutenant who was privy to the greater scheme and the role of every player. He would not be cowed. Others would replace him, would come to exact revenge.

He looked slowly at the bowman and the young noble. 'Confession from me will bring you no solution or relief, will go ignored before the throne. I took the children at the cave and have herded many to our charge. I was present at the deaths of Sir William and the effete Lord of Jebail, myself flung a prying stablehand from the high parapet of the Accursed Tower. Each of you will suffer similar and deadly fate.'

Sergeant Hugh viewed him with understated threat. 'What happens in Arsur, my songbird?'

'Destiny.'

It was a word spoken with conviction.

Along the harbour-front of Arsur, ships had moored and disgorged their cargo. They came from Cyprus and Tortosa, brought Templars and mercenary knights, carried the troops and supplies that would keep an army on the march and sustain a military thrust upon Jerusalem. Like a blanket of spring flowers bloomed too early, a tented encampment spread out on the plain around the town. Horses exercised, campfires burned, ox-carts were positioned and filled with catapult-shot and bundled arrows. A static location everywhere in motion.

Occasionally, scouting turcopoles and squadrons of mail-clad Franks galloped in from outlying patrol.

Their warlike cries and fluttering pennants added to the tension, built anticipation towards the moment when the trumpets would sound, the formations fall in, the whips crack and wagons roll. Preparations would not be disturbed. The regent king of Outremer was otherwise engaged, the Sultan of Damascus busy with cares of his own. Both men were readying for peace talks in Jabala; both men would be butchered when they met. It was far from Arsur, from the place where ambition was made solid and where a force five thousand-strong gathered and waited. Beyond it, masked by the ridgeline of hills, hidden in their wooded sweeps and gorges, the leper Knights of St Lazarus also stirred. All had motive and their orders.

Pace and planning did not abate. There were battle-scythes to sharpen, sword-skills to hone, pike-drills to practise and maintain. In the Cathar lines, the Perfects moved among their armed flock, laying on hands, leading prayers, promising salvation in just conflict against heretical Latins and heathen Saracens alike. Aloof from them, kept apart from those they would one day kill, the Templars accepted holy sacrament and knelt before the cross-guards of their swords. Between such factions, the hired warriors and professional thugs played dice and swapped stories of past skirmish and close escape, of towns razed and girls taken. Prospect of campaign and glory could forge unity in any tongue, win obedience to a single cause. Jerusalem lay exposed. No greater spur to action existed in all mankind. The Lord of Arsur was counting on it.

*

'A sad and piteous sight.'

'The one I see is more shameful, Gunther.'

But the son of the woodsman had no shame. At a safe distance from the shackled children, he gnawed contentedly on a boiled chicken leg and licked his fingers. Since Kurt had challenged the Perfect and been chained as punishment with his sister, it seemed fitting moment to approach. Gunther would not waste his chance.

'How does it feel to be prisoner, Kurt?'

'More comfortable than to be a traitor.'

'Traitor?' The redhead sniggered. 'It is not treachery I perform, but a duty, a calling, a service to my lord.'

'A means to line your stomach while we starve.'

'You chose the wrong cause, and I the right.'

'Where is right in keeping us here bound?' Kurt trembled in his indignation.

The older boy continued to suck the chicken-bone clean. 'You think you may appeal to my nature, win mercy for yourselves. There is no profit in it for me.'

'Reward is in heaven.'

'My prize is on earth, is to witness you suffer, to observe you carried off to die.'

'I do you no wrong, Gunther.'

'Yet I have hated you always, despised your well-liked and admired ways.'

'It is no reason to do us harm.'

'You are friend to the weak as I am ally of the strong.' The son of the woodsman threw down the bone and ground it beneath his boot. 'Struggle exists, and only one may triumph.'

'So you come to taunt us?'

'I am here to eat.'

'The hand that feeds, the lord who governs you, will wring your neck, Gunther.'

'First it will twist yours. And yours, loving and caring Isolda. And yours, silent little Zepp. And yours, large and hardy Egon. And yours, each and every last one of you.'

He delighted in the fear generated, in the tremor that coursed through the bowed and quaking group. They were his audience and his victims. The gathered young looked to him, stared at him, respected him. It could go to the head. He hesitated, a boy with a bullying manner and a wider stage, a figure of new-found authority who would abuse it well. There was no better privilege. Almost in afterthought, he rocked on his heels and directed a ball of phlegm straight into the face of Kurt.

'Learn who is your master.' With that, Gunther left.

The twelve-year-old mopped his face in silence, aware of the sympathy of his friends and relief of the rest. If as focus of loathing for the woodsman's son he protected them and drew punishment on himself, so be it. He would not break. Beside him, Isolda whispered her concern and Egon his impotent rage. Nothing more remained to be done.

With a sound they had grown to dread, and from which they instinctively shrank, the studded oak door again crashed wide. Only bad things and rank food arrived through that opening. Two guards appeared and came for Kurt. He put up a fight, resisted with the energy of several demons, kicked and struggled with all his might, added to the chorus of shouts with his own protesting yells. To no result. His feet barely touched the ground as they transported him away.

It had been a journey of winding passageways and endless stairs, of fluttering shadows and the tramp of hobnailed leather on echoing stone. Wherever he was, he was far from his companions and further from safety. But he could remain defiant. He blinked in the half-light, and could just make out the dark shape and pale face of a stranger in the centre of the room. The man did not smile, showed no emotion or surprise.

Kurt summoned the courage to stammer a challenge. 'What is it you want of us?'

'Your lives.'

'We are not important. We are pilgrims without money, children without value for any ransom.'

'Thus you shall not be missed.'

'My friends fall sick and hungry. They need food, air, the light of the sky upon them.'

'Such concerns will fade.' Tepid eyes studied the boy. 'I am the Lord of Arsur.'

'What you do is wicked and unjust.'

'And what you say is rash. Tell me of the friar and the youth with whom you travelled.'

'Otto is more noble than you will ever be. Brother Luke is guide and shield like no other.'

'An aged Franciscan more irksome than a gnat.'

'He causes you trouble?' Kurt brightened.

'His insolence will be short-lived as your smile.'

'They will free us. Otto, Sergeant Hugh, Brother Luke will bring force against you, will keep on until you are judged, are felled by staff or sword.'

'I regret they will not.'

Kurt saw that he spoke the truth, that none would hear the prayers of the imprisoned, not a soul would answer their plaintive cries. He noticed other things. On a far wall was the monstrous head of a deity rendered in gold, its horns curling upward, its forehead etched with the sun and moon and bisected with a burning torch. His confidence bled away.

The Lord of Arsur followed his gaze. 'It is why you are here, why I act as I do.'

'False idols will not bring you victory.'

'Victory is already mine.'

'You lie.'

'A child has poor understanding.'

'I comprehend enough. I know you to be evil, that the statue before me is of a demon and no God.'

'Your own God is dead.'

'Yours is metal effigy.'

'Truth and power reside in Baphomet.' The voice of the Lord of Arsur almost carried a frozen trace of feeling. 'For over twenty-five years I have served Him and prepared. Now I offer Him my life work, deliver unto Him the Christian world, the Holy City of Jerusalem.'

Kurt controlled his quaking, for there was no one to speak out but himself. If he was now to breathe his last, he would at least adopt the confident bearing of Otto or the relaxed assertiveness of Sergeant Hugh. He had seen sufficient death to recognize its closeness.

The Lord of Arsur viewed him distantly. 'Bow down and tremble before the Divine.'

'I am not Gunther to do as you bid.'

'Yet you are boy of flesh and blood, a mortal with finite time. Even your Christ is prisoner in my keeping.'

He gestured to objects arrayed to the side, their shape and nature obscured by the gloom. With measured movement, he lifted the shutter from an oil lamp and swept its light across the artefacts. Still Kurt was motionless. The youngster could make out the gleam of elaborate gilding, the dark pustulence of gemstones and splintered edge of ancient wood. Such items were plainly sacred relics, for he had seen similar on his travels.

'Are they precious things?'

'They are beyond value.' The Lord of Arsur swung the lantern. 'This, the Crown of Thorns that rested upon the head of Jesus. And this, the very tip of the lance that pierced his side.' His hand alighted on the golden sleeve of a larger piece.

'What is it?' Kurt barely heard his own voice, scarcely remembered to take in air.

'The object for which you and other pilgrims come, the most potent symbol and greatest relic of them all: the one True Cross.'

'You play diabolic trick.'

'There is no ploy or lie. It was rendered to me by Saladin at Hattin, a reward for my part in destruction of the Christian force. Once more it shall have its place, shall grant lustre and power to the throne of its owner.'

Reverentially, and because his legs were suddenly too weak to carry him, Kurt sank to his knees. He was unworthy, a sinner in the presence of the crucified Christ. No further explanation was required. He had found that for which so many had set out from Cologne, for which little Lisa and the girl with the flaxen hair had been buried at the roadside, Hans cut down by Assassins, blind Achim brought low by disease. All gone, all dying for the cause of a length of blackened timber.

The Lord of Arsur whispered as a ghost. 'Soon every man will prostrate himself and the world will tremble before me.'

Kurt already trembled. His eyes closed; his mind grasping for prayer and faith, he discovered only terror. An ice breath told him silently there was no hope and no escape, informed him it was the end.

Handover was under way. On a rock and mud field in Galilee, where the ragged borders of Outremer melded with the edge of the Saracen badlands, two sides met to exchange their hostages. There was pageant in the moment. Cavalry was drawn up, trumpeters called, the display and counter-show of rival groups lent tension and colour to the occasion. Much was at stake. From each camp, Frankish and Moslem, five personages of high birth and infinite value would be traded for the other. They were insurance and statement, indicator that talks to take place in the town of Jabala enjoyed hopeful prospect and were in good faith. John of Brienne, regent of Outremer, and Saphadin, Sultan of Damascus, were men of honour and of their word. Peace depended on it.

Otto too was there, by invitation and design. His days of furtive and tender rendezvous with Matilda, their hours of erotic affray, were over. He wanted to bid farewell, to take a final look before his love was cast to the Devil and the company of the Lord of Arsur. Nothing else could be done. Where his heart was recently light with passion, it was now heavy with the leaden weight of parting. His crime was one of inertia. He consigned her to the jaws of conspiracy and could not move, could not show his concern or grief, could not intervene. As passive onlooker, he was present to witness and record event.

That event unfolded before him with ritual and formality and an unhurried beat. It might as well have been an execution. Mounted heralds approached from either side and read proclamations; courtiers bowed and presented gifts. Patiently, the hostages waited. Among the Saracens was al-Mu'azzam, feared raider and son of Saphadin. In the Christian line were the lords of Caesarea, Sidon, Haifa and Arsur. Always the Lord of Arsur, unassumingly dominant, an inert presence who managed to control. Beside him on her Arab mount was Matilda, her head crowned with a circlet, her face covered by a silken veil.

The young noble craned to see, hoping she would turn her head, praying for a miracle. Instead, a different spectacle arose. The Lord of Arsur had wheeled his horse and came towards him at a walking pace. Then he paused, his eyes strangely knowing, his blankness communicating assured supremacy.

'Things pass, Otto of Alzey.'

Back in the royal city of Acre, John of Brienne wandered in contemplation through the silent halls of his palace. Occasionally he would linger, attempting to remember or trying to forget. Here his young wife, the late Queen Maria, had filled the chamber with her laughter and the heavy scent of flowers. There in the nursery their baby daughter Yolanda had smiled and kicked and cooed at his presence. Her crib was as empty as his soul, the room as cold as his future. He moved on.

About this time, the swap would be taking place, the parties of hostages riding voluntarily into mutual captivity. At least Lady Matilda remained with the Lord of Arsur, would return safe once dealings with Saphadin were through. He was thankful for the steady and guiding hand of his preferred baron. Yet the departure of Matilda was another grievous loss heaped on a mound of existing sorrow. He could merely pray and hope for peaceful resolution.

He reached his private chapel, its interior a welcoming cocoon dimly lit by burning tallow. There was little place else where a powerless king could seek comfort or refuge. The last sanctuary for an aged fool. He sighed and stepped inside.

'I have awaited you, John of Brienne.'

The regent stared towards the voice, discerned the rough habit of a friar and the creased and weathered countenance of an old man.

'You trespass in these chambers, holy brother.'

'As you intrude in my thoughts.' The Franciscan gestured to the regent to sit. 'I travel too far to be turned away.'

'I am short of comradeship and loath to spurn communion. I judge you no Assassin.'

'My vows and inclination would forbid it. I am Brother Luke of Assisi, a wandering friar, a preacher of redemption and of the love of Christ.'

'You have a freedom I do not.'

'We each of us strive for a better world, each make voyage to attain it.'

'Tomorrow I board vessel for Jabala.' John of Brienne eased himself heavily into an adjacent seat. 'Should I fail in my mission with Saphadin, there will be general war and eventual destruction of Outremer.'

'Is quest worthwhile if the trial is not hard?'

'On occasion it may be too onerous, the cost too dear.'

'Your infant daughter Yolanda?'

The regent nodded. It was reassuring to converse with a man of God, to find common cause with a battered ancient who had trod the earth these many years. They were both warriors of a kind. The stranger possessed kindness and insight, yet had the large hands and rugged frame of a fighter. Perhaps he was wasted as a humble penitent.

'Yolanda is gone, holy brother. So tiny a child may leave so great an absence.'

'She will be found.'

'You speak either in conjecture and cruel jest or with singular knowledge.'

'A man who trudges as far as I will see and hear what others do not.'

'Tell me what you learn, holy brother.'

'I discover ambition and plot, fathom the lengths to which the angels of Lucifer fly to gain conquest and dominion.'

'Who is this Lucifer?'

'Outremer is endangered, but not from Saracen source. Your reign suffers and kingdom fails, and insidious threat lies close.'

Impatient, John of Brienne leaned forward. 'How close?'

'The enemy has the face of a crusader.'

Brother Luke had won his interest.

Before the walls of the Holy City of Jerusalem a small band of Christians paused to give voice in thanks for the end of their journey. They were Lent pilgrims, some fifty of them, a further concession squeezed from Saphadin by the Lord of Arsur as gesture of goodwill and encouragement to new treaty. No harm done. Except that, at given moment, each of them had a specific role. While some would neutralize sentries and seize strategic points, others would seek out the Arab families tasked with guarding entry to the Church of the Holy Sepulchre. Sacred sites were about to fall to new ownership. As the chanting pilgrims passed through the gate, a woman among them comforted her baby and kissed and stroked its head. The infant queen Yoldanda was carried through to her preordained future.

✝
Chapter 19

Royal excursion demanded its pomp. From every building in Acre, banners hung; from every quarter, the city populace emerged to cheer and applaud. John of Brienne, the regent king, was departing for conference with Saphadin. Hope would sail with him, for soon it would be the campaigning months when ground hardened and armies marched and the Saracens would descend like a wolf on the fold. There had not been full battle for twenty years. The old ruler of Outremer had reason and need to prevent reoccurrence.

In ceremonial array, clad in mail hauberks and clutching their swords and shields, the royal guard and knights of the military Orders lined the palace steps. They added colour to the scene, provided a cordon of steel against which the deadly intent of a lurking Assassin might crumble. No chance would be taken. The killers could be anywhere, disguised as Genoese merchant or Pisan mercenary, as Levantine Jew or Arab herder. This fragile moment of optimism required protecting.

A serpent-horn blared, a kettledrum rolled, and the

regent appeared beneath the grand portico of his royal dwelling. On his head was the crown, at his side the sword of office, around him his squires and courtiers and the trappings of state. He seemed strangely diminished by them all. But the crowd shouted as one, calling out in respect and affection in swelling unison. They believed in him. He blinked, visibly moved, as though not believing in himself. It was possible his subjects expected too much, probable they pitied him the death of his young queen and disappearance of his infant daughter. A good deal had changed since he arrived in their land an impoverished knight, a reluctantly chosen suitor from Champagne. Those were the days before travail and woe, before Outremer was threatened with extinction. Before an old Franciscan friar had appeared in his private chapel.

He raised a hand and the clamour died. 'My subjects, good citizens of Acre and brothers of our most Christian kingdom of Outremer. I stand before you as we stand before destiny. With clear eye and firm heart, with expectation and resolve. God is at my right hand as He is at yours. We must pray and we must prevail. I sail for Jabala this day to meet with the ruler of the Saracen, the Sultan of Damascus. It is to win peace that I go, yet it is for war we must prepare. Ready yourselves and your defence. For when I return, it shall be either as maker of concord or as commander of hostilities. However it is decided, Christ is with us.'

With a concluding nod, he stepped from the stage and descended the stairs to tumultuous acclaim. The people loved their grizzled champion. Chanting and waving, they followed his route, pushing to trail his entourage as it wound through the narrow streets for the harbour. There, bedecked in flags, the royal galley lay. Aboard were the senior barons and lords who would accompany him to Jabala; below, on the rowing-deck, the Nubian and Maghrib slaves who would toil at their oars to transport them. Everything was in order and the beat-keepers ready. The journey would take days, a coastal progress that would pass the other ports of Outremer, that would pick up further nobles and additional ships to join the northbound fleet. Magnificence and spectacle were customary for such occasion. Offshore of their destination, the galleys of the Templars would heave into view. They appeared to guard John of Brienne, to add steel to his dealings. Their truer purpose was to prevent his escape.

Excitement climbed and whistles blew. Doubt could ever be abandoned when ropes were cast off, the rhythm was called, and oars dipped and swung. Saphadin might have the land, but the crusaders owned the sea. From the poop deck, the regent acknowledged the warm farewells, and the crowd roared in response. For a brief instant, he could forget and pretend, immerse himself in the frenzied outpouring. He carried with him the prayers and wishes of them all.

A final salute, a shouted order from the captain, and the steady bass-pulse began. Escorted by two smaller craft, the royal vessel nosed towards the sea. Eyes would observe and the lips of spies make report. Slowly, the sparse flotilla manoeuvred beyond the harbour mouth and swung on to new bearing. People watched, conversed in the low whispers they reserved for mourning and matters of importance. They had every right to be fearful. The ships grew faint and disappeared.

Many miles to the north, at the site of impending parley, a great tent was being erected in the main square of Jabala. An emissary of Saphadin stood aloof and kept careful watch. His lord and master had decreed there should be no error or breach of protocol, no possible interruption to the smooth course and outcome of events. More than dignity was at stake. There were peace terms to agree, the return of hostages to arrange, a lasting settlement between Mohammedans and infidel Christians to present for royal mark. After months of sporadic raiding and infliction of grievous harm, this single chance could not be squandered.

Cursing loudly, the official upbraided a clumsy labourer. The man had fumbled a bail of silk, was scrabbling to retrieve the fallen load. Around him, others toiled. From high walls and flat roofs, soldiers watched alert to any nuance. Security lapse was punishable by death, for weakness could be exploited, and such exploitation lead to swift and violent attack. Killers might be anywhere. In truth, they were. The same onlookers from their vantages would have been surprised to learn that several Assassins were already among the working throng. Revelation would wait until appointed hour. The levies heaving on ropes, the chosen servers of figs and dates, the minder of caged nightingales, the guardians of the entrance: all had been trained, indoctrinated, at the pinnacle-fortress of al-Kahf, and all answered to their leader the Old Man of the Mountains. Each had his instructions and his target. The Frankish inhabitants of Acre would never again see their regent; the Moslems of Damascus would linger until eternity to ever witness their sultan return. Not a single delegate, not one emir or lord, was intended to survive the coming encounter. A clumsily handled bundle of silk could provide useful diversion. Weapons were placed and infiltration complete.

Tucked into a castellation above the now-denuded harbour, Otto sat in dark and despairing mood. He had not participated in the leave-taking of the regent. There was too much sorrow to merit cheer, too little reason for him to hope. Those he loved were gone. *Things pass, Otto of Alzey.* So the Lord of Arsur had spoken, and so it would come to be. The confident optimism of the citizens below was ill-placed. Kurt and Isolda were held captive; John of Brienne had doubtless sailed into trap; Matilda was even now in mortal danger and in company with the Devil.

Ah, Matilda. The young noble slumped back and rested his head against the stone. It was too cruel she had entered his life and held him in thrall, too fateful and unkind he had lost his heart to a girl now lost to him. He whispered her name, summoned her image, looked for concealed answer. In her he had found sense and purpose, an end to searching. With her absence, there was only bleak and raw misery. Love could sap a boy.

'Have faith, young Otto.'

He started, almost fell, and jumped to greet his visitor. There, standing before him with easy calm and in warm solemnity, was Brother Luke. Eventful months of separation were reduced to a few feet. Otto crossed them in a bound and threw his arms around the old Franciscan. How he had missed the wisdom and titanic strength, the counsel and steadiness of his friend.

'You are returned to us, Brother Luke.'

'Did I not pledge it so?' The friar held Otto's shoulders and peered in his eyes. 'It appears your own journey has been as accidental and full of incident as my own.'

'Little you do is accident, Brother Luke.'

'Yet providence and conspiracy may overtake me, nonetheless. Tell me of what you find.'

'The children are taken.'

'That I have heard.'

'Do you hear also of foul plot, Brother Luke? Of how the regent sails to danger and not treaty? Of how Lady Matilda and her fellow nobles are delivered into Saracen hands?'

'I know even of the Lord of Arsur.'

'None listen or heed the warning I give.'

The friar offered a gentle smile. 'Is it not the fate of many prophets, Otto?'

'What should we do?'

'We may pray.'

'Surely we must act?' Alarm at the perceived indifference of Brother Luke flared on the face of the youth.

'Without God we are nothing but eating, spawning, dung and death. With Him we are invincible.'

'At present hour we are bested by the enemy.'

'I dare say on past occasion you have also thought it.' If there was rebuke, it was wrapped soft in the comforting tone. 'Force must be allied to insight, impulse to arms ever joined with faith.'

'I have tried to do what is right, Brother Luke.'

'And in such effort grow sturdy and set well.'

Otto could talk of encounter with Saphadin or escape by basket from the monastery of Belmont, the freeing of Kurt and Isolda from Saracen traders and their later abduction at caves near Beirut. He could tell of his combat with the brigand knight on the bridge across the river Lycus, regale the friar with stories of drama and daring. Or he could describe his aching love and bitter parting from Matilda. Secret or truth, somehow the ageing Franciscan would already be aware.

Brother Luke patted him on the chest. 'My brave and intrepid son, you shall make worthy knight some day.'

'Should the Lord of Arsur succeed in his ascendancy, the day will not arise.'

'He will be thwarted, Otto.'

'I am less sure of it.'

'Who advised you of the hostile approach by Assassin in Rome?'

'You did, Brother Luke.'

'Who used his wooden staff to break the heads of circling Cathars?'

'Again, it was you.'

'If you have learned from me, you will recognize I do not lightly promise.'

'Your word is more of hope than of firm and settled outcome.'

'This old and decaying friar from Assisi will not fail you.' The lined face carried a peacefulness of conviction that disarmed any doubt. 'I have been busy in my travel, ceaseless in my purpose. My legs have walked, and my ears and eyes perceived.'

'You remain one man.'

'With a host of angels at my shoulder and an army of light behind me. On matters different, where is Sergeant Hugh?'

Otto laughed at the jest. It was old times rediscovered: the conversations around the fire late into a starlit night, the supportive clap of a hand to his shoulder, the calm instruction in life and combat. Few things could lift his spirits like the company of Brother Luke. As for Sergeant Hugh, the English bowman was gone to ground and perchance gone for good. Reliability was not his strongest suit. The lure of brighter things and richer pickings, the chance to fill the coffers of his hidden treasury, might have taken him on further journey. Collapse and instability for ever favoured the mercenary instinct. Yet Otto had grown inured then fond of his coarse and brazen ways. A presence sadly missed.

'He is vanished, Brother Luke. Without warning, he slipped the bonds of Acre away into the night.'

'No harm is done by it. We shall recover my lambs without him.'

'You have a plan?'

'One that may yet challenge fate. Fetch your sword and *cuirie* armour, and find good horse. We embark upon crusade.'

Dutifully, and with eager spring of action in his step, Otto girded himself to obey.

Others were on mission of their own. As the royal galley headed for Jabala, a battered and less prepossessing sailing-ship made south towards Arsur. It might have been a trading-vessel, a carrier of food and men running late to resupply hidden endeavour. Instead, it ferried Sergeant Hugh. The Englishman had not waited for orders, would anyway have ignored them. On a whim, and fuelled by wild urge and prospect of a fight, he had commandeered a three-master, persuaded its crew, encouraged his drinking friends and sparring rivals to join him in pressing quest. They were a rowdy and motley crowd, easily convinced. Belligerent, tough, eager to believe in tales of gold, they followed the bowman on board. He understood them well, knew they would slit a throat or belly through inclination and not command. That could prove useful.

'There are thirty of us, brothers.' He clenched the longbow in his fist and lifted it above his head. 'We may encounter force of thousands.'

A shout came from the assembled. 'Does it not frighten you, Hugh of York?'

'It will make me rich.'

'Have you a scheme?'

'Depend on it, brother. It is to kill any who oppose us, to take what is not rightfully ours.'

Through the cheers another question. 'How may we outnumbered win in open contest?'

'Who considers it should be open? You are unruly dogs and pirates, the lowest of snakes and vermin. Yet I love you as my own, depend on you to light the wildfire of chaos, to fight foul and foulest.'

'You choose well in us, Hugh of York.'

'For I see you well.' He grinned at his companions. 'There is not one of you with whom I have not drunk or scrapped these twenty years. I thank you for it, respect you for it. Now I ask you to pay for it.'

More ovation and enthusiastic clamour. In Acre, they had grown bored of their inertia, fretful at the decline of Outremer. The chance to bloody the nose of the Lord of Arsur was a fine excuse for expedition, an opportunity to sharpen swords blunted by neglect and to squeeze into mildewed jerkins and rusted mail abandoned to posterity. Sergeant Hugh had touched a nerve, at this moment tapped resource. Midriffs might be fuller, joints ache, but these men could still put the fear of God into the soul of a foe or pitch a javelin hard between his shoulder-blades.

The Englishman hushed them with a shake of his bow. 'I recall how my king Cœur de Lion appeared as a strange and wondrous ibis through the feathered arrows placed in his side by wheeling and darting heathens.'

'We face no Saracen.'

'But you will fight like Lionheart himself.' He

rested his longbow at his side. 'I promise you treasure, pledge you the earth if you stand with me. The Lord of Arsur seizes children, imprisons Christian pilgrims for his ends. Will we allow it?'

'Never!'

'Shall we force him to submit, to beg for our pardon?'

'We shall!'

'Do we grant it?'

'No!'

Sergeant Hugh pointed the horned tip of the yew at his gathered brethren. 'A man has told me that in Arsur lies destiny. It is our destiny, and ours to take.'

Approaching sundown, the boat swung in mild and unthreatening turn for the low cliffs of Arsur. Run-in to the harbour was slow, came without incident or challenge. The waters appeared deserted, the fortifications overlooking them devoid of life, sentries or the predicted routine of a vigilant garrison. Too quiet to be acceptable. Sergeant Hugh stood in the prow. At any moment he expected the flicker of arrows, the erupting yell of a charge. But nothing emerged. If there was ambush pending, it was held back well; if there had been army present, it was since departed. The bow nudged against the stones of the abandoned wharf.

Fortune favoured the foolish. Signalling by hand to his men, the Englishman leaped ashore. Once committed, there was little point in attempted retreat. He had already noticed the watchman idling towards them, the unsuspecting manner of his bearing. The man did not anticipate trouble. Plainly, he had never encountered Sergeant Hugh.

The bowman greeted the guard with friendly aplomb. 'I have found graveyards more lively, my brother.'

'Alas, the campaign begins and our army has marched. You are too late for the fray.'

'I think not.'

He head-slammed the watchman flat and waved his men forward. They fanned out as he reached in his quiver and drew out the black shaft of a night terror.

At the fort of Beit-Nuba in the rugged hills that paraded towards Jerusalem, the Frankish hostages marked time and counted the days. When talks were done and peace achieved, when Saphadin returned to Damascus and John of Brienne to Acre, the five noble prisoners would be released. It was small sacrifice. Comfort prevailed, for the Saracen code was to show honour and generosity to high-born guests. No expense was spared, no extravagance denied. Yet guards patrolled and doors were barred. Whatever their rank, Lady Matilda and the lords of Haifa, Sidon, Caesarea and Arsur would not be making early escape.

In a large and vaulted chamber hung with tapestries of golden thread and swathed in the silken carpets and precious ornamentation of the East, the male prisoners sat and talked. They were powerful men of influence, ego and considerable fiefs. Not all were friends. But in this venture they had common cause and shared fate, could break bread and spend their sentence in cordiality and strained acceptance. The Lord of Arsur lingered at the periphery, as though waiting.

Tearing off and consuming a piece of honeyed pastry, the Lord of Sidon rested in his chair. 'What sorry pass is this? We eat, drink, dice and play chess. And still no word.'

'It will come.' The Lord of Caesarea studied the chequered board. 'Besides, my brother lord, what would you do in Sidon other than sit on your arse and eat sweet dainties?'

'There is always money to count, whores to pleasure.'

'Your beloved wife to avoid.'

The Lord of Sidon grimaced. 'That I were young again and had the power of foresight!'

'They say she was once a rare beauty.'

'It is certainly rare to transform to such an ogress.' A further morsel of pastry disappeared.

'Do as our brother Lord of Arsur.' The Lord of Caesarea moved an ivory *shtranj* piece and eliminated a carved Bedouin from the ranks of the Lord of Haifa. 'Is it two or three wives he has so carelessly lost?' The taunt went unanswered.

Standing and stretching, the Lord of Sidon gazed morosely through a window slit. He did not enjoy incarceration, had fared badly in previous encounter with the Saracen. Being held on their territory and terms was unhelpful to his mood.

'Time may wear down a man.'

The Lord of Arsur replied from the far side of the

room. 'Can it not also make a man reflect, a noble ponder his insignificance and vulnerability at great moment?'

'You philosophize too much, my brother noble.'

'Perhaps.' The Lord of Arsur seemed unconcerned. 'And perhaps you do not think at all.'

'What insult is this?'

'One that is the truth. One that shows you as dolt and dullard unworthy of respect.'

The face of the Lord of Sidon darkened choleric-red. He could not let offence pass, could not allow injury to pride and honour. In an instant, temperature and disposition had changed. The players paused at their chess, the affronted baron squared up. Opposite, his adversary was unmoved.

It was the veteran Lord of Haifa who broke the wavering silence. 'Withdraw your serpent words, my lord, or deal with their consequence.'

'Rather, I will tell you of things.' The Lord of Arsur folded his hands. 'I will advise you of the deaths of John of Brienne and Sultan Saphadin of Damascus. I will announce to you how their vassals and barons, emirs and senior knights fall to the blade in the tent at Jabala.'

The Lord of Haifa rose from his game. 'Satanic spell ensnares your mind.'

'On the contrary, my lord. It is you and your fellow nobles before me who are held ensnared, your brothers who lie slain in the square of Jabala, your lands and possessions that pass forfeit to me.'

There might have been violent riot once shock

had abated and rage set in. Interruption prevented it. Shouts and screams and the jarring percussion of swordplay poured through a door that slammed wide in sudden invasion. Dishevelled and bewilder-eyed, Matilda was pushed through. Her confusion was merited. Around her were unfamiliar guards, well armed, ferocious and already blooded. Their handiwork had been displayed in the corpses on her route.

The Lord of Arsur greeted their arrival with modest formality. 'I expected such occasion.'

'Explain this.' Matilda threw off the restraining hands of her captors.

'Explanation will come with the army that marches for Beit-Nuba, that will proceed unchecked upon Jerusalem.' He silenced the jabbering protest with a sweep of his hand. 'All will bow and pay tribute to me. The Saracen, the Christian, the Jew.'

'I will not.' Defiant, the grey-haired Lord of Caesarea shouted his response.

'A sad error of judgement and a life cut short, Aymar of Caesarea.'

The abrupt closeness of death could stall conversation. With a heavy downward stroke, the blade of a sword crashed through the skull of the seated noble. His head clove in a shower of bone and broken teeth, the divided sections of his face falling away until connected only by his beard. A grotesque and yawning gap. Matilda clutched her own face as though holding it together; the Lord of Haifa stared dumbly at the twitching remnants of his gaming-partner. Close by, the countenance of the Lord of Sidon had travelled through several hues to settle on a lighter shade of grey. The focus of their concentration slouched unrecognizable, his arm flung out and shuddering on the emptied chessboard. Checkmate.

An event of no consequence for the Lord of Arsur. 'Your game appears ended.'

'What of yours?' The words of Matilda were soft with horror.

'Mine is started. From cardinals in Rome to the commander of this fort, from the Assassins in the tent at Jabala to my agents in Jerusalem: all labour to my ends, everything keeps to plan.'

'You contrived war and then peace?'

'I set Mohammedan against Frank, attacked trade caravans and peaceful estates, brought fire and murder to the heart of each court. I pushed Saphadin and John of Brienne towards conflict and offered them chance of peace.'

'A chance they could not refuse.'

'Do drowning men ignore the overhanging branch? Decision that is their ruin.'

'With such act, you plant seed for your own.' Matilda glanced quickly at the scene of butchery and back to the Lord of Arsur.

'There will ever be casualty when object is greatness. I did not lightly strip power from John of Brienne, did not casually take his infant Yolanda or slay his companions Sir William de Picton and the Lord of Jebail.'

'You?'

'Purpose exists in every deed.

'Wickedness also.'

The Lord of Haifa stepped forward and was blocked by a sharp display of swords. 'I will show you purpose. You will not escape with this deception.'

'Have I not done so?' The tormentor stooped and rose holding a scattered and bloody chess-piece. 'What are you but an abandoned fragment of a toppled order, my scarred and battered Lord of Haifa?'

'I am soldier and noble.'

'You are nothing.'

'While you are traitor of the foulest kind.'

The Lord of Arsur observed him blankly. 'Recognize that I am your new king, that Lady Matilda will become my queen.'

Matilda stared. 'I would prefer to die.'

'Such wish may be granted once you provide my son and heir.'

'You believe this daydream and nightmare notion will go unchallenged?' The Lord of Haifa quivered in wrath and fear and impotent feeling. 'Saracens will unite against you; the princes of Europe will hunt you down.'

'The heathens will have no master, the Christian kings no reason to hate me. For I am conqueror, ruler of Jerusalem, saviour of all Palestine and the holy sites.'

'Pretender and knave.'

'Many are with me; the rest shall die.'

'Then I must die.'

The Lord of Haifa took it as a man, received the blade full and deep in the chest. He staggered back, his eyes rolling, his silk mantle blossoming wet-red to the impact, and fell. Two down. Blood created a particular outline and smell. Its effect on the remaining nobleman was marked. The Lord of Sidon was on his knees, pleading and weeping, pledging allegiance.

It was accepted with unblinking coldness. 'On your feet, servant. Fate speeds and I ride for Jerusalem.'

How things could change. In the quiet aftermath, when the Lord of Arsur had departed and the corpses were borne away, Matilda stood as the broken Lord of Sidon sobbed and rocked himself in huddled wretchedness. Around her, the spatter and detritus of recent event remained uncleared. It did not matter. She was somewhere else, in a protecting place, in the strong and loving arms of Otto.

'We will dwell in the House of the Lord for ever.'

Kurt fervently hoped so. He swayed to the jolting movement of the cart, felt the parallel rhythm of Isolda beside him. It was not quite how he had envisaged reaching the city of Jerusalem. Of course he preferred to live, but options were closed and death become his shadow. Above the loud and forceful prayers of Egon, he could hear the lowing of oxen, the rumble of wagons, the singing of hymns, the tramp of feet. They were not comforting sounds. An army was on the march, slow and inexorable in its progress, and the sacrificial offerings stood crowded and transported ever onward. 'Amen,' the children said. For all the good it would do them.

Strength and Bravery. He remembered well the exhortation of Brother Luke, could recall the days of companionship and delight, the weeks when struggle seemed worthwhile. That struggle had carried him through shipwreck and danger, had led him to threatening encounter of every kind, had ended here. Such a pity. He craned his neck and studied the grey and trudging forms, tried to count the sloped tips of pikes. Anything to while the time, to escape the confines of his open tumbril and the true nature of the journey. In other transports there were more children, some sick and some dying, all passing to oblivion. For the first day, he had thought an arrow of Sergeant Hugh would soar high and puncture the bad dream. During the second, he had believed Otto might appear and ride at full tilt to snatch them away. By the third day, numb acceptance had replaced all hope.

'What do they sing, Kurt?'

'They are Cathars, Isolda. Who knows what they mean?' He looked at his sister. 'I swear they are more content than we.'

'It would be no trial or contest.' She smiled uncertainly, and comforted the mute Zepp at her side.

'We keep our heads high and show no fear.'

'There is little terror left for me. What have we not together faced, Kurt?'

He leaned and kissed her cheek. 'Had we stayed in our village, we would never have seen the sights we have seen, never encountered Otto and Brother Luke.'

'Nor met Sergeant Hugh.'

He laughed. 'We travelled and witnessed no drag-ons or monsters, yet fell in with bodyguard to the Lionheart himself.'

'So many have fought for us, sought to aid our quest.'

'Now are are left to ourselves.'

A daunting prospect. Kurt again stared beyond the heaving edges of the cart. In this measured stampede, there was scant chance of escape. By day they were sur-rounded and watched; by night they were bound and still surrounded. The previous morn he had observed a boy drop from the rear of a trundling wagon and make suicidal dash for invented safety. Dodging and weaving, the youngster had leaped through openings and scrambled past feet, his legs pumping, his face strained, his dark mane of hair flying triumphant at the pace. Panic, fear, the elation of sudden freedom carried him fast. Yet the Cathars reached him, caught him, fell on him as a pack. Kurt shook off the memory. The boy must have been about his age.

Egon reached and patted his shoulder. 'Tell us of the True Cross.'

'It was a mystic and magic thing, like no other relic in its size and beauty or the precious gems with which it was set.'

A child called out. 'Were there rubies?'

'Rubies and emeralds and diamonds as large as any egg.'

'They say it will cure disease.'

The son of the blacksmith nodded. 'They further say it gives power to those who possess it.'

'We know it to be true.' Kurt gestured to the rolling scene. 'Where is there greater show of strength than this?'

'Will the Lord of Arsur let us live?' A little girl with pinched and tear-stained features asked the question most avoided.

'The True Cross may make him wise.' Kurt stroked her head. 'It may also render him merciful.'

'Should we forgive him his sins?'

'We at least must try.'

Egon begged to differ. 'I forgive him nothing, Kurt. I curse him for each day he held us in his dungeon, for every hour we are herded in this fashion.'

'Our quest was to reach Jerusalem, and now we shall.'

'And beyond it?' What of the valley to which we are taken, in which we meet our fate?'

Unexpectedly, the face that had darkened with grim anxiety lightened at discovery of a hidden joke. Egon, so steady and solid, began to laugh.

Kurt peered at him bemused. 'Share with us your mirth, brother.'

'I shall.' Doubled over, the older boy gasped for breath. 'You recall how we grumbled at unfairness of walking, complained at how the preacher-boy Nikolas enjoyed passage in leisure and cart? It seems now we have everything for which we prayed.'

They shared in his amusement, the moment sharpening and driving their hunger for relief. Circumstance could create its own frivolous and infectious madness. The children were lost to it, wept in their hilarity.

Levity ceased. Astride a black charger, threading through the onward mass of his Believers, the Perfect made his way towards them. He rode alongside and scrutinized his young captives with satisfied air. They met all requirements, would nourish the bare earth with their blood.

His gaze alighted longest on Kurt. 'Lift your eyes heavenward, child. It is where your liberated spirit is soon to dwell.'

In the van, the Templar arrowhead forged across the desert scrubland for the squat bulk of the Judaean hills. God was on their side. It was for Him they acted, for Him they crusaded, rode, sought the Holy City. With a single blow they would expunge the humiliation of Hattin twenty-five years before, would establish themselves again as rightful occupants and guardians of Temple Mount. There was symmetry and sweetness in what they did. Some would protest, might not understand. The fainthearts of Europe, the indolent rulers, the Pope whose permission had not been sought. But they would be convinced. Victory provided its own justification.

Grand Master Du Plezier slapped the reins of his mount and urged the beast on. There was no going back, no waiting a further quarter-century at the periphery of Palestine and on the margins of history. His warrior monks would again hold sway. True, the Cathars made strange bedfellows, the mercenaries were beneath contempt, the Lord of Arsur was an opaque presence he barely comprehended. Yet the new ruler would be strong. It was what the Christian world lacked, what would restore Outremer as bringer of civilization and scourge of the heathen. A proud and defining moment. Nothing would keep him from kneeling at Calvary where the Saviour was crucified, from prostrating himself across the Stone of Unction where the body of Christ was anointed, from kissing the marble of the Holy Sepulchre where the Lamb of God was once buried. Not even an aged Franciscan and his vexing antics on the island of Arwad could prevent the will and direction of fate.

What privilege to be a Templar, to wear the blood-red cross and march beneath the sacred black and white of their *Bauceant* banner. About him, the noise of hooves thudded with steel purposefulness through the linked rings of his mailed hood. The din of holy war and uncontested advance. Before them was Latrun, and beyond it the ascent to Jerusalem and greatness.

He raised a hand to shield his eyes, had seen what the scouts now scurried to report. The earth was alive. From nowhere and from everywhere, as though transformed from rock itself, an army shimmered into view. It spilled into a widening arc, its flanks racing and unfurling, its troops manoeu-vring in close and ordered array. There were the Mohammedan colours of green and black, the plumes of Turcomans, the pennants of Mamluks. And with them too was the unexpected: the white eight-pointed crosses of Hospitallers and black German symbols of the Teutons. The way was blocked. Leading the formation were two white-bearded generals, one a Saracen in magnificent silken robes of state, the other a doughty Frank armed and garbed for war. The Sultan of Damascus and the regent king of Outremer were arrived to give battle.

† Chapter 20

Surface tension, an invisible force that attracted and repelled, seemed to stall immediate action. The armies faced each other. Behind the forward line of *pavise* shields, crossbowmen crouched and cocked their weapons; to the rear of these, infantry stood with arms sloped and cavalry horses champed and fretted. Inertia would end with a single fire-arrow rising high, with a shouted command and downward sweep of a sword. Then the rush and slaughter could begin. But, for the present, only dread and uneasy near-silence prevailed.

Almost twelve thousand men whispered prayers or said nothing, listened to their own breath and heart-beat. Some stooped to take and put to their mouths a morsel of earth in final sacrament, lip service to be closer to God and to prepare for forthcoming return to dust. Each tip of a blade or spear was a nerve-end. Heavy steel helmets were lifted and donned. For their knightly wearers, the world was narrowed to the vision field of eye-slits, focus reduced to the separating distance and the need to kill. Two hundred yards. The death strip.

Under flag of truce, and accompanied each by an officer, Grand Master Du Plezier and John of Brienne trotted their mounts out to the centre of no man's land. They eyed each other with mutual antipathy and accusation.

'There is only damnation where you head, Du Plezier.'

'At least it will be with sword and lance in our hands and the name of Jesus on our lips.'

'Christian against Christian?' The regent gazed from the Templars opposite to his Hospitallers and Teutons waiting and massed. 'Is this why your Order was founded? Is this why you took sacred vow?'

'I pledged to fight the heathen.'

'Instead, you harm Outremer, endanger the very lives and faith you claim to serve.'

'Unlike you, I do not consort with Saracen army, John of Brienne.'

'Saracen army poised and ready. Saracen army that will devour our kingdom should we choose war over quest for peace.'

'Peace is illusory.'

'It is necessary.'

'Who else will take Jerusalem if not ourselves, John of Brienne?'

'Your vainglorious attempt is not in the name of God, but in the traitorous service of the Lord of Arsur.'

'He is strong as you are weak.'

'It is you who has weakened me, Philippe Du Plezier. It is you who shall pay.'

444

Impasse had physical form. The two commanders continued to sit in their saddles, Franks already engaged in battle of a kind. Too much had been committed for easy retreat. Positions had been taken, loyalties placed. Men would rather lose life than face.

The regent leant to scrutinize the features of the Grand Master. 'Did you imagine it would finish this way, Du Plezier?'

'Campaign is not done.'

'You cannot break through, though you may yet retire.'

'Retire?' The eyes of the holy warrior flickered resistance. 'When have you known a force of Templars to withdraw?'

'When Our Saviour would counsel it and reason dictate it.'

'I see no merit in frailty and cowardice.'

'Yet you discern purpose in leading your Order to oblivion, in being last and most thoughtless of Grand Masters.'

'I will write my own epitaph, John of Brienne.'

'Victors have that comfort. You will be no victor.'

For a brief instant, doubt clouded and faded on the features of the Templar knight. The regent saw. He had conducted enough negotiation, survived the vagaries and brinkmanship of sovereign rule, to understand when to commit and when to hold. He would break his opponent. If it killed him.

He jabbed an armoured finger at Du Plezier. 'Ponder beyond this barren field, dwell long upon your fate should you fail to die in battle.'

'I am in the hands of Christ.'

'You will be in the embrace of our torturers and executioners, shall face the ire of the Christian world. Neither the Pope nor kings of Europe will show mercy. You will be tied to the stake, have kindling placed about you, will smell and taste and feel your skin blacken and fall burning to the flame.'

A harsh laugh carried short in the throat. 'Who are you to think I fear?'

'If not in trepidation of superior force, then perhaps of the judgement of history.' John of Brienne waved an arm. 'See your brother Grand Masters who ride with me, the knights and holy crosses of their Orders beside them. Are they wrong?'

'They lack our zealous intent and purity of motive.'

'No greatness or immortality resides in failure, Du Plezier.'

'Nor in ceding ground.'

'We have learned in detail of your preparations at the fortress of Tortosa and the isle of Arwad, of how you intended your galleys to encircle and destroy me.'

'The aim was noble.'

'The result is ignominy and eternal shame. Your bones shall be dust and scattered with those of heretic Cathars, your memory cursed and spat upon.'

The collision of wills was a noiseless affair. The reckless error of his ways only slowly permeated the consciousness of the Grand Master. He had not meant things to happen in this fashion. Triumph was intended to be swift, the verdict kind. Instead, he had led his men and Order into morass.

He frowned. 'How may we atone, John of Brienne?'

'With humility and departure to your castles.'

'I will not abase myself before you.'

'That I do not seek.' The regent maintained his stone-faced glare. 'Be aware that none has shed sweat and blood for our values more than I or stood to arms when needed. Our deaths now are not required.'

'It is eternal battle in which we engage.'

'Live again to fight it.'

Deal was struck, yet not quite complete. It would be sealed with honour combat, the meeting of two warriors and the death of one. Agreement and reparation demanded ritual reddening. Better the token loss of a champion than the senseless slaughter of many. So the commanders returned to their lines and the gaping arena once more lay vacant.

A horse appeared and walked with deliberate and blinkered tread for the heart of the field. Its rider was a curious and unsettling sight, a bent figure in the worn mantle of a knight, a ghoul in sackcloth hood who clutched a shield and sword. There were mutterings among the soldiers, talk of Satan and of fallen angels. The apparition continued.

Completing his parade before the ranks, he turned towards regent and Sultan and removed the cover from his face. Collective horror spread in a single gasp. The army spasmed, shuffled as though seeking to put distance between itself and the diseased and ravaged presence revealed before it. The knight was a leper, a brother of St Lazarus. His raw disfigurement had erased all human semblance.

'Stare well, my friends.' The voice of the man was harsh with sickness. 'Is this not power, to make an army tremble at my approach?'

John of Brienne shouted to him. 'Begone from us, you demon.'

'Surely it is no way to treat a champion?'

'You are unclean, a stranger to our midst.'

'Even scavengers may bite, even outcasts offer challenge with sword. I am your reflection, John of Brienne and Saphadin *al-Adil*, product of this decayed land and image of the future.'

'You are an unworthy adversary for so precious a fight.'

'That is a judgement for any who would dare oppose me.' The grotesque threw down a gauntlet on the earth. 'I was once a noble, a pious and godly man. Yet fate consumed me, humankind despised me, Christ abandoned me. This day I return from the grave and raise my blade to all.'

He wheeled his steed, cantered to the midway mark, and dismounted. There he stood, a lone misshapen form hemmed in by weight of numbers and pressing expectation. Honour killing was demanded, and he would provide. The crowd stirred. A young man had stepped from the Hospitaller ranks and bent to recover the gauntlet, was crossing the ground with measured stride and presenting himself for contest.

The leader of the Knights of St Lazarus unhooked the shield from his horse and slapped the mount away. 'You are brave to face me twice, Otto of Alzey.'

'As you are unwise to offer second chance.'

'There is no such chance. On this occasion you will die.'

Otto flexed and turned his wrist, steadied his breathing, controlled his balance. The sword was ready in his hand. He did not plan a repeat of their last encounter, to again end prone and this monstrous fiend stand to decide life or death above him. That would be fatal. For present circumstance he wore an open helmet on his head, bore in his left hand a shield of the Order of St John. The Blessed Virgin would watch over him. Matilda would wait for him.

The leper studied his opponent. 'You believe yourself a knight because you come armed as one?'

'I aspire to knightly virtue.'

'What is virtue when men fight as baited dogs in a pit between two armies.'

'My cause is true.'

'And what is truth, Otto of Alzey? Control of Jerusalem? Dominion of one faith over another? Power in the Holy Land?'

'I did not barter my soul to the Lord of Arsur.'

'For you had no need.' Words grated through the lipless mouth. 'He alone offered the hand of amity, raised us up beyond the status of dung and scurrying beetles.'

'Violent misdeed has no defence.'

'And no redemption save butchery.' The knight stepped back and tapped his longsword on the stony ground. 'The beast will ever devour youth and beauty.'

Courtesies were done. With grand gesture and

sweeping suddenness, the leper brigand swung his blade for early kill. The strike went nowhere, skittering wide. Otto answered with bludgeoning thrust that too was parried. Duel had commenced in earnest. It would end when a corpse lay sprawled or a blood-trail led to a wounded man begging to be spared. There was no room for pause or pity in the conflict zone. Another hit deflected, a further adjustment made. In virtuoso sequence, blows were swapped and space traded, the rivals moving, feinting, darting close and fast. Minutes passed with visceral grunts and physical contortion, with cascading sweat, with metallic shock delivered and absorbed. Still no advantage.

The armies looked on. Before them, the pair of combatants circled and sparred. The young one was doing well, pushing in, holding his gain. But the deformed troll of a knight was no wet-nosed pupil. He beat away the onslaught with flurry of his own, the lightning snap and clash of his double-edged blade showing fightback and ferocity. It could go either way.

Smearing the perspiration from his eyes, Otto leaped back, drew the knight in, and dashed down with his sword. The leper stumbled. It was not enough to permit the terminal cut. The blade glanced from the battered shield, leaving Otto open, forcing him into hasty recoil. They were both tiring. Storm had abated to squall, to more occasional gusts of aggression. A period when attention drifted and mistakes were made. He thought of the bridge and their last meeting, watched the eyes, the direction of flow. The two of them were almost friends.

Breakthrough was unexpected. In a howl of pain, propelled by a jagged assault that tore rotten flesh from his face, the knight tumbled heavily on his side. Illness and injury conspired against him. He tried to drag himself up, but his leg was weak and would not carry him. He reached for his sword, but Otto stamped on his hand and kicked the weapon away. There was yet his dagger. He fumbled for it, found a larger blade in contact with his hand. His gauntlet leached blood and again he screamed.

Otto angled his sword for steep and backhanded stroke. 'Fortune turns, knight.'

'Is not that the stuff of life?' The leper was guttural-indistinct through the red swamp of his face. 'You are victor and inherit nothing.'

'I have everything for which I fight.'

'Honour and praise, the gratitude of all, the glance and bed of every fair maid in Outremer?'

'The love of one suffices.'

'And now you may present her with severed head of a Gorgon.' Uncompromising, the knight of St Lazarus gazed up at him. 'Take your prize, Otto of Alzey.'

'We have our reward. It is peace.'

The young noble stalked away. Blood had been drawn and his task achieved. Many would want to see his challenger dispatched. Chivalry and redress demanded it. Yet he had no wish to oblige, no appetite to exact revenge on one who had earlier shown him lenience. Kindness deserved reciprocity. He was saving retribution for the Lord of Arsur, reserving his energies for the ride to Beit-Nuba.

'Attend, Otto of Alzey.'

He called over his shoulder. 'I tarry no longer.'

'Would you place limit on time spent in company between father and son?'

'You do not know of what you speak.'

'I recognize myself once to have been Wilhelm of Alzey and you to be my progeny.'

Otto paused. There was no meaning in these lies, no earthly bond or symmetry between his beloved father and this murderous and foul spectre who twice had fought him. Reason proclaimed the man jested or was possessed. Experience dictated that mockery was part of the game, a weapon in the armoury. And yet . . .

He twisted to look, allowed his body to follow. The knight of St Lazarus was upright, standing unarmed, his expression hidden behind the lacerated and putrefying mask. His younger rival stared, hoping for confirmation, a sign, searching within and without for familiarity and feeling. Deadness triumphed.

'What is become of you, knight?'

'Sometimes the Devil may catch a man unawares and make him his slave.'

'You went willing to it.'

'Is it so?' A shrug of sorts. 'The steel hoop may close about the neck, the manacles around the feet, before one ever wakes.'

'We all have choice where we sleep.'

'There is no rest among the jackals, and I grow sick and weary.'

'As I am tired of excuse.'

'Pick more wisely than I whom to serve, my son.'

Obliteration pre-empted settlement or reply. Decision was out of their hands, the threat unseen until it was close and thundering down upon the leper. A mounted knight of St Lazarus was galloping in fast for the kill. There were scores to settle, a beaten and tainted commander to be put from his misery and beyond enemy grasp. Otto watched the glint of the raised war-hammer, its descent and shattering impact. The body dropped. His father was down. He did not run to the corpse, did not cry out. The field of battle was no place for regret or searing introspection. Such an ending was inescapable, a blessing, avoided the need for blame or acceptance, reduced the number of questions to ask. Final moments were merely a blur of hooves and the hollow strike of steel on skull. The way most warriors preferred to go. He would reserve his love and sorrow for others.

Disaffection needed outlet. The hired soldiers would not be paid; the Templars would never reach Jerusalem. It rankled. The Cathars too felt betrayed. Argument quickly escalated, altercation fragmenting into wider trading of blows. A knight was pulled from his horse and put struggling to the knife. He bled and kicked as well as any scapegoat. But it was insufficient to sate desire for vengeance, spawned a myriad further fights. Through the throng, the Grand Master of the Templars rode, his captains beside him, his sword raised high.

'My brethren, we are deceived and undone! Find

again our holy cause, commit yourselves to sacred war! The Cathars are our sworn enemy, the allies of Satan and opponents of our Church! Show no mercy in your zeal! Salve your conscience with their blood and restore the Order to its rightful place!'

They obeyed. The Templars were carving out position, battling for reinstatement and favour in a continued Outremer. No simple undertaking. Yet they could prove themselves through violence, had done so many times before. Saphadin and John of Brienne would observe and marvel at their prowess; the rival Hospitallers and Teutons would for ever show respect. They would massacre with gusto. So it began.

The Cathars did not go lightly or unprotesting to their deaths. Those who were armed hurled themselves at the advancing knights; those bare-handed threw themselves in the fray with equal vigour. A lance was wrenched from the grasp of a mounted Templar and turned against him until he hung pinned and wriggling like an insect. Atop a cart, a Cathar had lit a wildfire pot, was preparing to fling it at an encroaching mob of mercenaries. A crossbow-bolt through his head bowled him down, drove him among the rest of his incendiaries. Oil, pitch, resin and spirit ignited. Explosion followed. It erupted outward in instant pressure-shock, removing flesh from bone, air from lungs, life from a firestorm radius of fifty yards. Other wagons were consumed, building the chaos, carrying the flame. Another blast.

'Egon, we need weapons.' Kurt crouched low as a snub-nosed quarrel flew overhead, and squinted through a loose join in the sides of the cart. 'We cannot defend ourselves as we are.'

'As we are is sitting low and waiting safe.'

'Safety is nowhere here.'

The blacksmith's boy placed a restraining arm across his shoulder. 'No foolish daring, Kurt. We are better together, more able to meet the threat.'

'Unable to greet it with anything more than a cry.'

'Stay with us, Kurt.'

'Should we die, it will be as soldiers and not as children.'

Without second thought, he slithered over the cart's shallow walls. Quickly, he rolled beneath the axle, lying flat, scanning the eddying scenes of mayhem. Brute force could be mesmerizing. Horses reared, men screamed, bodies jarred and swayed in endless and ferocious scrimmage. It was reaching close. He reacted as a small figure fell into view and scrambled to his side.

'Zepp, this is no place for you.'

The youngster disagreed. He was already peering ahead for opportunity in the fire-framed tumult. He spotted it. With soundless energy, he darted into a cavity among the whirling action, disappearing momentarily, re-emerging with a scythe to crawl back to sanctuary. A second time, a third. Kurt joined him, waiting until a Templar was trampled and beheaded before stripping him of his dagger and sword. Hot work among the most hellish of landscapes. Beneath and around them, the ground shuddered and the temperature climbed.

A dead face landed inches from his own, its eyes confused, its mouth leering. He pushed it away. Zepp was passing another sword upward, adding to the armoury on board the swaying tumbril. The ox had staggered wounded and bellowing to its knees; its driver disappeared through a screen of exploding munitions. The cargo was going nowhere.

Kurt coughed and wiped his streaming eyes. The curling haze carried the stench of cindered flesh.

'We must climb back, Zepp.'

In turn they ascended, Zepp in front, Kurt behind, each wrenched upward by willing hands and propelled by shrill exhortation. As he tumbled to the floorpan and a billhook splintered wood where his neck had been, it occurred to Kurt he had turned thirteen years of age. Just a single thought joining others travelling random in his mind.

He clenched a short javelin in his hand and took up his station as the lookout. At least they had the means to inflict some punishment. The cart lurched on the heavy groundswell. Perhaps matters would be less troubling if he imagined he were on a ship at sea, believed the storm would soon pass. But there was no sign of lessening tempest.

Kill the young. He had not dreamed the words. Before him, the distant form of the Perfect was growing larger, nearing, pointing in his direction. The Cathar chief would yet have his consolation.

The moment for it arrived. With religious utterance on his lips, and the strain of destruction on his face, the Perfect leaped from his horse on to the cart.

Indecisiveness was not part of his creed. He bore a stabbing-sword, and intended to use it, would slay the children as he had always pledged. Even in these dying hours, when his Believers suffered and fell, he could gain for them everlasting reward. Their God would view them kindly for his act. He had not reckoned on Isolda.

She tore at him with the ferocity of a protective vixen, her rage boundless, her fingers clawing for his face and eyes. He tried to ward her off. But the attack was unrelenting, came from a girl who had endured enough and who was fighting for her life. It was poor contest. He lost first his sword and then his balance, his feet scraping for purchase, his arm flung out in vain. A puncture-wound toppled him; a blundering and panicked beast towing a burning wagon rapidly broke and buried his remains. The children readied themselves for the next onslaught.

'How easily man may descend to hell.'

Saphadin was a calm spectator. From his horse he surveyed the apocalyptic tableau, a bejewelled ruler undemonstrative before his troops and yet pleased with the result. As in the last moments on the plateau of the Horns of Hattin, a western army was being annihilated. Unlike at Hattin, the Franks were doing the work themselves. There was much to celebrate. His sultanate was secure, the threat neutralized, the kingdom of Outremer embroiled in its own debilitating and internecine conflict. Status quo had been restored. Allah was indeed Most Merciful.

Beside him, John of Brienne answered in Arabic. 'It is ever dismal to witness carnage of such kind.'

'Each thrust of a spear, every dart from a bow, is one less of the foe grasping for my throat.'

'We have both reached old age, al-Adil. That is miracle itself.'

'I know little of miracle and more of how we may be blinded by flattery and trappings of court and betrayed by those within.'

'This time, fate intervenes.'

'Not fate, but an aged holy man they call a Franciscan.'

The regent nodded. 'Without him, our bones would now be picked over by rats and scavenging birds in the streets of Jabala.'

It had been close-run thing. To alter their perception of the Lord of Arsur, to accept revelation of his duplicity, had taken leap of imagination and earthquake in reasoning. This was its consequence. The Holy Land was used to chaos and seismic shock, to the eruption of hostility and levelling of civilization. Strange alliance could also be forged. The two old men continued their arid contemplation of the scene.

John of Brienne glanced at his counterpart. 'I trust you shall disband your army, al-Adil.'

'I never broke my word to Cœur de Lion, will not do so to you.'

'Survival gives us new chance.'

'As war creates only piles of ash.'

'The lesson before us is stark, will for a while bring the Templars to heel. Zealots on both sides will be restrained in their ambition and cautious of adventure.'

'No more the use of Assassins, the thoughtless raid, the rapacious quest for land.'

'And no more the setting where infant daughter may be stolen from her father.' There was slight tremor in the voice of the regent. 'Christian and Mohammedan may labour together, al-Adil.'

'For the present.' Saphadin spurred his horse and wheeled to face his army.

Smoke drifted, and at the heart of the fires corpses glowed like magma.

Golgotha, the skull-rock. A place of suffering and absolution, of end and beginning; the site of crucifixion and the Church of the Holy Sepulchre. On Christian maps it was the centre of the known world. And here, where the transept bisected the choir, was its very core. Crusaders had fought to defend it, pilgrims endured to reach it. Many thousands had perished with its name on their lips. There was no location more sacred. It deserved something profound.

The Lord of Arsur stood before the high altar and marvelled at the majesty of the occasion. Deliverance was upon the earth. Against the wall was the empty throne of Jerusalem. He would fill it well, rule with an iron fist that had been lacking for millennia. Some moment; quite a prospect. He breathed in slow, let the pungent aromas of burning incense and juniper oil infiltrate his senses. An intoxicating experience. He was ushering in a new dawn, a fresh reality, a pristine rule. Jesus was no match for it. In this tranquil gloom, among the candle-tinted columns and dark recesses, throughout the ambulatories and hidden chapels, the pious had worshipped and called for the coming of the Lord. He was arrived.

It had been undemanding effort to relieve the Moslem wardens of their keys to the church, would prove no harder to introduce his forces to the city. His troops were even now marching for the gates of Jerusalem, would bring with them the catapults and mangonels, the paraphernalia of siege-defence, they found concealed at Beit-Nuba. Accompanying them would be his future wife Matilda. Later would be brought the gilt-bound relic of the True Cross. A womb and an icon. Everything dynastic reign required.

A small cry returned him to his purpose. Nestling in a rush basket placed upon the high altar was the infant queen Yolanda. How fitting she was present at historic point of sacrifice. The spilling of her blood would mark the end of her line and the beginning of his, bring to the world the supremacy of Baphomet. Other victims were journeying by cart and would be dealt with by the Cathars. His focus was on a single life and the one resulting death.

He moved to the altar, started the ritual incantation that would lead to the downward plunge of his knife. The baby smiled up at him. But he had no pity in his heart, no inclination to release her from her path. Destiny asked much of her. She frowned and began to whimper. He did not pause, for the schedule was imperative.

Interruption came with the suggestion of a presence behind and the quiet tread of bare feet on flagstone. He turned to see, straining to penetrate the shadowed dark towards the aedicule and holy tomb. Emerging from it was Brother Luke.

The friar did not approach too close, but loitered still and watchful at fifteen paces. 'Your army will not come; your followers in Jerusalem are all of them captured.'

'So speaks an ancient beggar and fool.'

'A beggar who travels the earth for this encounter. A fool who outfoxes your ploys and deception.'

'Brother Luke?'

'I answer to that name.'

'The Templars should have silenced you when they had chance in Tortosa.'

'Yet they did not. God is kind.'

'You will find my God is the greater.'

The eyes of the Franciscan narrowed. 'Cruelty and base horror are oft founded on such belief.'

'What do you believe, friar? That you will live? That I may be halted?' The Lord of Arsur waved his blade. 'Tell me, holy vagabond. Are you angel of vengeance or mere ragged pile of bones?'

'I do as my Father and Saviour commands me.'

'Thus to each of us a plan.'

'You would sully a place of veneration and worship with senseless murder of an innocent?'

'It has happened here before.' The joke was not delivered with humour or warmth.

'You are the darkness, Lord of Arsur.'

'And you the light?'

'*Firmitas et Fortitudo.*' Brother Luke delivered the words with the cool conviction of a mantra. '*Firmitas et Fortitudo.*'

'Neither Latin proverb nor your strength and bravery have consequence at this hour.'

'Though they are words present from my birth, the family motto I have borne on every step since England.'

'I hope they will comfort you in your death.'

'They shall haunt you at yours.'

Lowering his knife a fraction, the Lord of Arsur examined the obscured and distant features of the old man. The intruder certainly knew how to taunt and provoke, how to upset procedure and tax his patience. Worthy punishment would be later decided for his lies and insult, his rashness in confronting the rightful king of Palestine. That king could show temporary restraint in a trying situation.

'Who are you, Franciscan?'

'A man you betrayed and consigned to die.'

'It does not narrow the field.'

'The field in which I stood at dawn on fifth of July the year of Our Lord 1187 was winnowed enough to a single Templar.'

'Hattin?'

'A battle in which you delivered up our Christian army to Salah ad-Din, from which you rode as my brother knights were beheaded in turn on gathered stones.' Explanation instead of bitterness pervaded the voice. 'I was the knight who witnessed you with the True Cross, who raised voice against you.'

The Lord of Arsur whispered the words, pulled them from an earlier time. *'Judas. Betrayer of our cause . . . A curse be upon you.'*

'Well you remember it.'

'Bygone deed is owned but by the past.'

'I bring it to the present.' Brother Luke made no attempt to draw near. 'My vehemence earned me reprieve. The Saracens thought me brave, revoked my execution and sent me in chains and endless caravan to the furthest point on earth. I crossed deserts and climbed mountains, spent twenty years toiling in death and the deepest of mines to hew lapis from the ground.'

'We have each of us been industrious.'

'Not so industrious I was denied thinking each day of such moment as this, dreaming each night of escaping and trailing you to your lair.'

'You find me. Trailing is done.'

'I am not.'

Threat was implicit though not described. In some subtle way, the confrontation was rising, had become personal. The Lord of Arsur would play for time. Surely his guards would arrive, his hidden cohorts burst through to exact vindictive penalty on this tortured soul. Yet none came.

Outward composure had acquired a layer of perspiration. 'Let us call truce, holy friar.'

'Memory relates you use talk to murder those who oppose you, to gather rulers and nobles at a tent in Jabala and there see them slain.'

'Such insight and perseverance in one so old.'

'So much iniquity in one so human.' The friar seemed to study his subject for deeper revelation. 'Why did you send killers to Europe to end the life of Otto of Alzey?'

'For the reason that, should he be as good as his father is bad, Palestine would gain to my disadvantage.'

'That is all?'

'Not quite. The Assassins accepted invitation to serve me, and I in turn set them test of loyalty.'

'He was to die for mere trial?'

'Many depart this world for less.' The dagger edged towards the recumbent child.

'You shall commit no further harm.'

'I am menaced by former Templar?' The Lord of Arsur turned the steel to catch the light. 'Does not your sacred oath in the chapter ban violent act against brother Christian?'

'You are no Christian.'

'Yet you are Franciscan, a friar with binding duty against hurt to living soul.'

The aged wanderer did not answer. There were others less restrained than he. Perhaps a flicker of recognition sprang in the eye of the Lord of Arsur, an emerging realization of his mistake. It was quickly doused. With piercing yells, Assassins emerged from cavities behind the altar and fell upon the nobleman before he could respond. Brother Luke remained passive and aloof, an observer to justice enacted in a crimson spray and accompanied by garbled shrieks and revered handiwork. Assassins liked to be on the winning side; their allegiance had been bought with gold taken from the treasury of the Templars on the island of Arwad. Such irony was lost on what was left of the Lord of Arsur.

Twelve miles from Jerusalem, a troop of mounted Hospitallers clattered through the gateway to the courtyard of Beit-Nuba. At its head was Otto of Alzey. He had come for his beloved.

Survival was a desolate state. Kurt wandered alone through the deserted tanneries at the edge of Arsur. He had wanted the isolation, had sought out a place where he could forget everything and lose himself. Battle was fought and victory won, he and his sister returned to freedom. But liberation carried price and burden. His bones ached, his spirit was grey, his head drooped beneath the weight of fatigue and the heaviness of a thousand dead. He had seen too much. Maybe here he could find release, replace the smoke of war with the pungent fumes of the dyeing pits, exchange the colour of blood for the rainbow hues of more peaceful trade. The Lord of Arsur was gone, his plot revealed and territories seized. Yet the True Cross went undiscovered. It hardly seemed to matter.

Some horrors remained. As he strolled among the lead mixing-vessels, shuffled a stone from his path, among the drying-racks, he was confronted by odd and disquieting sight. He stared perplexed. Before him was craftsmanship: a row of severed heads dried and treated and laid out in display. So like the head of St

John the Baptist pulled from a sack on the cart in the cathedral square of Cologne. Nothing was sacred.

A further head had joined them at the end of the line. It was the most startling of all, for it was alive, red-haired, attached to a body. Gunther stood with the curving twenty-two-inch blade of a *faussar* in his hand.

The knife gleamed as wicked as the smile. 'Do I surprise you, Kurt?'

Enough to make him run. He covered the ground fast, dodging past piled hides and scrambling over heaps of broken and emptied murex molluscs and buccinum whelks. The shell fragments cut his feet and hands. He did not feel the pain, could not pause for gentle reflection. If he were cornered, Gunther would strike. Should he plead, the son of the woodsman would slit his throat. Creating distance was his principal aim.

'You fail to outrun me, Kurt.' The voice kept pace.

Alarmed, searching frantic for weapon or escape, the younger boy dashed haphazard amid the vivid palette of the dyes. Red, yellow, blue, pink, he traversed them all, each second bringing Gunther close, every false turn reminding that he was trapped. Wheezing in breathless fright, he stopped. No way out. Across the noxious pit of purple, his rival waggled the blade.

'See this colouring, Kurt? It is the pigment of empire and of the robes of kings.'

'Put up your sword.'

Gunther failed to comply. 'You would not suppose

so regal a thing would grow from so foul a stench or vile a process.'

'Stay from me, Gunther.'

'Why? Have you sharp weapon?' Amusement joined the freckles on the face.

'I do you no wrong.'

'Yet I still shall kill you.' The boy began to circle the periphery, reversing his course as Kurt stayed ahead. 'Come to me, brother.'

'The Lord of Arsur is no more, Gunther.'

'Your fate is set firm.' The son of the woodsman danced carefully about the rim.

Desperate, Kurt backed away. 'When we fought in Cologne, you told me it was the strongest who rule, the weak who submit.'

'Then submit.'

'Never.'

'I warned I would kill you, Kurt.'

'Your strength is gone, your allies and master with it.'

Gunther pressed in. 'You know of what I am capable.'

'It is the end, Gunther.'

'No, Kurt. It begins.' He slashed with his blade at the chest of the youngster. 'It was I who in the Alps slew the mountain-dweller. He screamed as you will scream.'

'You gain nothing.'

'I will take something with me.' Another lunge, a further circuit.

Kurt balanced, kept moving, noted the bloody prints left by his feet. 'We may talk, Gunther.'

'I prefer to put this *faussar* in your belly.'

Circular argument and repeated chase, and distance was shortening. Kurt tasted the dryness in his throat, felt the tightening of his chest. His time ended where he stood. He was staring at death or its earthly agent, holding back the inevitable for a few seconds more. The eyes of Gunther glimmered vengeful.

Then a screech he knew, the rushing flight of feathered ash as a she-devil split the space between them. Their ways parted. Gunther shied and fell, plunging headlong in the pit. And Kurt watched. His adversary sank and re-emerged, choking and vomiting, a macabre creation thrashing glutinous and drowning in the viscous soup. There was little to be done. The mouth gaped and closed, made strange noises and coloured foam.

Kurt reacted. He hurried to find a dyeing-pole, to extend not the hand of friendship but the branch of common compassion. He could never be like Gunther, would never turn his back.

The hand of Sergeant Hugh rested on his shoulder. 'He reaps his whirlwind, Kurt.'

'We must help him.'

'Leave him to God.' The soldier hugged his charge close. 'To be a man is to let others choose their destiny.'

Kurt hesitated, shivering on the brink, torn and conflicted by a hundred emotions and a single compelling sight. The pressure increased on his shoulder. Sergeant Hugh would not release his grip, would make decision for him. Eventually the youngster surrendered, breaking the curse, drawing away. He had been right to tell Gunther it was the end.

Sombrely, the two ambled from the place of execution. In one hand the soldier carried his longbow, with the other he ushered a thirteen-year-old boy silent in his thoughts. Behind them, a hand coloured imperial purple clutched feebly at air and sank beneath the surface.

✝

End

Preparations for departure were under way. Sergeant Hugh and his miscreant companions had secured Arsur, had made light work of killing its guards and lifting its contents. The odd yard of expensive silk fluttered discarded in the breeze; the occasional corpse bobbed inoffensive in the harbour. Only with the arrival of Otto had order been restored. He was to make inventory, impose martial law, report to the regent king John of Brienne now returned to the royal court in Acre. Saphadin still had an army. To once more reside safe within the coastal bastions of Outremer it was wise for the Franks to be vigilant.

The ship was loaded and the crew ready. It had been a profitable venture for its master to carry the English bowman from Acre, and would prove lucrative again to transport passengers back to Europe. Tired and elated, the children had hurried to embark. Bundles were stowed, berths taken, and the teeming young clung to rigging and leaned from the deck to fix their eyes on a land they had never called home.

For Kurt and Isolda, parting was less sweet. On the wharfside, they stood with Otto and Matilda, attempting to be brave, trying to stifle their tears. The young noble placed his beret on the head of his friend.

'It is token of when first we met, Kurt. Remember me well.'

'I could not forget.'

'We have had fine adventure. Peace is regained, the infant queen Yolanda restored. Few would have guessed at such exploit.'

'So many are dead.'

'Yet we are alive. There is chance for us to do good, to carry hope and faith in our hearts wherever we may end.'

Isolda spoke up. 'Why must you stay, Otto?'

'To atone for my father; to fulfil the duty that is asked of me.' He took the hand of Matilda beside him. 'And for the love I bear.'

'Shall we ever see you again?' The voice of Isolda came broken with sorrow.

'Are brother and sister ever apart? I will chance on you each day in my heart and mind and soul.'

'It is not the same.'

'Nothing is constant save my affection.' He drew the children to him, held them tight so they would not see him weep.

Kurt buried his face against the shoulder of the youth. They had been brothers-in-arms, companions in danger, friends since meeting on the path where Gunther had held a knife and Otto a sword. The young noble from Alzey had saved him so often. There were too few words and too little time to state everything he thought and felt. Perhaps he did not have to.

Otto murmured to him. 'I told you once we each of us have a path. Be steadfast in yours, young brother.'

'*Firmitas et Fortitudo.*'

'As a wise old man once spoke.' The young noble smiled and straightened, gestured to the ship. 'Now is the turn of Sergeant Hugh to travel with you. Let us hope he conjures lesser storm in Europe than the havoc he here creates.'

They laughed, their sadness interrupted. It was proper they should take leave with a song and not salt tears.

Matilda touched the face of Isolda and kissed her lightly on the cheek. 'Would that you will be my sister.'

'I would treasure it.'

'And I will remember and cherish your love and all your kindness to my betrothed.'

Whistles blew from the vessel and the moment was near. The four young held each other again and made their final pledges.

'There is another who would bid farewell.'

Otto pointed and the children turned, to the brown Franciscan robe, the bald pate, the aged face and upright bearing of Brother Luke. He held wide his arms, and Kurt and Isolda flew to him, their joy and grief unruly, their understanding total that this was reunion and last goodbye.

Dreams merged. Goat-faced gods and howling arrows, the red crosses of Templar knights and screams of burning Cathars: all entered his mind and fused with the creak of the ship and fluid slap of the waves. Each rattle of the rigging was the cart shaking its way to Jerusalem; every whisper of breeze was the groan of a child in the dungeons of Arsur. There was too the stained face of Gunther, rising from the dye, appearing from the sea. The past could haunt.

Kurt slept only fitfully on board. He would pace the deck or stare at the green trail of phosphorescence that led to the receding horizon and a land where he had left part of his heart and most of his childhood. He longed to return home, ached to see his mother and make his father proud, to be again the boy who climbed trees and stole the eggs of birds. But perhaps too much had changed. Over eight months and a lifetime divided him from a previous self standing restless in Cologne. The preacher-boy Nikolas was vanished; little Lisa, Hans and Achim were dead. Experience could kill young hope, would even kill the young themselves. He could almost smell the smoke of the woodfires, hear the bubbling call of the skylark, taste the first autumn blackberries. Life would be simpler within the confines of the hamlet. It would never be the same.

Mutterings and a low gleam of light stirred him from his dozing. He might have guessed it was not over, should have known that wherever Sergeant Hugh resided there was catalyst for trouble. The bowman had kept to himself these days past, had provoked comment and glance with his sly alertness and secretive manner. Not once did he leave the crowded enclave of his possessions or let his concentration slide. The crew talked and sharpened knives. Distrust was growing to mutiny.

Edging towards the stern, the youngster kept beyond the thrown light of lanterns, crouched at the periphery of what was turning to mob unrest. Before him was a tale easily read. At bay, perched on a plank, pointing his sword, was Sergeant Hugh, and around him an encroaching throng of armed objectors. The bowman was unstinting in his curses and colourful opinion. He appeared to be emptying bags of money overboard.

'Who bids me for this, you whores of Satan?' Another sack dropped from view. 'You wish to scrabble for gold or merely for your entrails?'

None volunteered for evisceration. The bowman prowled his makeshift stage, marginally drunk, always dangerous. His audience was rapt. With calculation and daring they could rush him, take him, damage him beyond recovery. But he posed no easy mark. He strutted and preened, presented his sword, paused casually to topple a chest of treasure over and into the brine.

A crewman advanced, was blocked by an extravagant sweep of the blade. Sergeant Hugh leered at him. 'For such audaciousness we lose a further bauble.' He selected a gem-set ornament and tossed it over his shoulder.

'We may parley, brother.'

'I would rather play.' A silver-gilt cross hurtled to the water.

Greed and urgency infected the voices. 'Stop, brother. You lose everything.'

'I gain my soul.'

'You cannot do this.'

'Regard.' They did so in horror as he heaved a larger item to the parapet. 'You think it has a price? Are you willing to pay it?'

'Stay your hand.'

He nudged the object into untidy dive. 'I thought not.'

'*We shall kill the children.*' The threat came from the captain.

'Shall you?' The bowman was unconcerned. He leaned and tapped a brace of clay amphorae lashed together at his feet. 'First perceive the vessels of wild-fire kept in my charge. Next observe the flint and pyrite lodged at their side. A single strike of my sword creates a spark that will produce inferno.'

'This is mad folly.'

'It is precaution. Eruption will come before I cut the tiller-rope. One death I deem unnecessary and there will be a hundred.'

In the background, Egon was quietly disarming a man of his crossbow. Other children moved to mark their targets, shadowing adults they did not trust. They had grown to be cautious. Sergeant Hugh was ready for finale.

He lifted an artefact to his side, threw off its sack-cloth cover to reveal a glinting and holy relic encased in priceless gems and sleeve of gold.

'The True Cross, my friends.'

And Kurt knew it to be true. He had gazed upon it as he viewed it now, had stared in wonder in the hidden chapel of the Lord of Arsur. There could be no doubt. Around him, some men crossed themselves or fell to their knees; others were too dumbstruck to respond. It was the effect the bowman wanted.

Suddenly sober, he rested a hand on the priceless lumber. 'It could bring me power and fame, wealth beyond compare. I care little for it.'

'There is nothing more precious.' The cry carried desperation.

'Nothing save friendship and duty, kindness and mercy, those things I have ignored for many a year.'

'Deliver it up.'

'To you?' Sergeant Hugh shook his head. 'Will it make you better man? Will it open your eyes and heart as it has failed to do with kings and popes? Will it earn you rightful place in heaven?'

'We shall send you there before us.'

'See, already it rots your spirit and curdles your mind. I have seen thousands die for it, witnessed the bloodlust in the eyes of Cœur de Lion as he sought it.'

Tension pulled nerves and vocal-chords taut. 'Step down, bastard knave.'

'I first have task to perform.'

The relic was already attached to a ballast stone, the stone pushed by a boot-clad foot. Almost as after-thought, the soldier sent the True Cross spinning.

Despair and fury followed on astonished disbe-lief. Men shouted in the agony of realization, ran to look, strained to catch glimpse of the lustrous cargo swallowed in the night and swell. They were to be disappointed. Above them, Sergeant Hugh swayed to the motion of the ship, enjoying the distraction, waiting for the consequence. Fait accompli.

'Accept what is done.' He smiled benignly at the commotion. 'Look within yourselves and not to any relic.'

'You malign and traitorous dog.'

'One who holds sword and offers Norse burial.' The tip of his blade twitched above the clay pots.

Rebellion subsided to sullen resignation as the master called off his crew. No mariner wished for fire on ship. They would have to swallow their pride, choke on their fear and disappointment. And pray. God would not forgive them their timidity and failure.

Remaining in the shaded light, the children assembled silent and accusatory. Sergeant Hugh clambered down and sat on a ledge to face them.

'Such mournful faces for those that are freed.'

'Freed?' Kurt blinked in consternation. 'You condemn us, Sergeant Hugh.'

'I release you from the burden that breaks the back of every Christian.'

'You discard the True Cross.'

'So I do. Yet I still stand, vent wind, may dance a jig or two.'

'Your deed is sacrilegious.'

'My words profane. But there is wisdom in them.' He placed his sword across his knee. 'Would you favour it if the True Cross fell in possession of thieves and rogues, once more dwelt with a Lord of Arsur?'

'You could take it to Rome.'

'Where dwell the greatest sinners.'

Isolda emerged from her tremulous silence. 'We will be judged, Sergeant Hugh. For a thousand miles or more we journeyed to pray before the Cross.'

'You need it no more, daughter. Without it you are grown strong, helper to the sick and dispossessed, mother and sister to all. And you, Kurt. You are my Lionheart, a boy who carries himself and others through every blight and hardship. You have learned so much. Become who you are.'

'What do you learn, Sergeant Hugh?'

The soldier paused. 'That young are worth saving.'

He winked at brother and sister and flipped each a golden coin. Gaining insight had not caused loss of shrewdness.

In the twilight stillness of the lamps, the ship eased back to its usual rhythms and the children slept or talked in exhausted clusters. Sergeant Hugh watched over them. Seated apart on a barrel of salted fish, Kurt stretched out and hummed a tune, observed as the silhouettes of Egon and Isolda met shyly and entwined in caring embrace.

A small hand took his, a voice he had not heard since Genoa spoke quiet in his ear. 'We go home, Kurt.'

Yes, they were home. He reached and tousled the

hair of Zepp, happy for his return, glad to be alive. Things would be all right.

*

Far off in Palestine, a Franciscan brother wandered on alone into the desert fastness. His pilgrimage was done.

✝

Historical Note

Nikolas the boy preacher was not seen again. The chronicles relate how angry and grieving Rhineland parents, in search of retribution, exacted their revenge by capturing and hanging his father.

In August 1225 the girl queen Yolanda was officially crowned in the cathedral of Tyre as Queen Isabella II of Jerusalem, Empress of Outremer. Later that year, in a strategic union, she was married to the brutal and dissolute King Frederick of Hohenstaufen. Consigned to his harem in Palermo, she was to die on 1 May 1228, six days after giving birth to a baby son. She was only sixteen years of age. Dismissing her father John of Brienne as regent, Frederick assumed her crown and kingdom. His chamberlain was a Templar; his tutor and mentor had once been Cardinal Cencio Savelli.

Pope Innocent III died in July 1216. His successor as pontiff was Cardinal Savelli, who adopted the title Pope Honorius III. It was he who unleashed the ill-fated Fifth Crusade in 1217.

Ousted as regent of Outremer, John of Brienne was even mooted as potential king of England. In 1228 he was to become regent emperor of the Latin Empire of Constantinople, and he retained this title until his death in 1237 aged eighty-nine.

Francis of Assisi set sail for Palestine in the autumn of 1212, but was shipwrecked soon after leaving the Slovenian coast. In August 1219 he again ventured east, and in Fariskur met Sultan al-Kamil of Egypt, son of Saphadin, to sue for peace between Islam and Christendom. His mission was to fail.

The Assassins' sect spread from Persia and its mountain base at Alamut and established a formidable forward presence in Syria throughout the twelfth and thirteenth centuries. Key strategic fortresses included al-Kahf, Khariba, Khawabi, Masyaf, Rusafa and Qula'ya. Some more notable political murders were those of Vizier Shihab al-Din (1177), Marquis Conrad of Montferrat, King of Jerusalem (1192), and Raymond, son of Bohemond IV of Antioch (1213). By 1265 the power of the Assassins was eventually broken through a combination of Mongol incursion and the growing dominance of Baybars, the Mamluk sultan of Egypt. They were to serve their new masters as trained killers for several generations to come. In 1272 the sultan employed his Assassins in an attempt on the life of Prince Edward (later to become King Edward I) of England.

*

It was in 1192, having taken Jerusalem, that Saladin assigned the guarding of access to the Church of the Holy Sepulchre to two Moslem families. The Joudeh were entrusted with the key, the Nusseibeh had custodianship of the main entrance. Their descendants retain the responsibility to this day.

When in 1291 Acre fell to the Mamluks and the Frankish crusaders were finally pushed from the Holy Land, it was the small offshore isle-fortress of Arwad that served as their last redoubt. Only in 1302 did the Moslems gain possession. The era of the Crusades was past.

In 1230, almost twenty years after the Children's Crusade, a priest arrived in Europe claiming to be one of its few survivors. His was a harrowing tale of hardship and suffering, of the young murdered or sold into slavery. Their holy quest had been in vain.

The True Cross was never found.

✝

Acknowledgement

Throughout the writing of this book, the current and real plight of so many thousands of children in myriad corners of the world was often in my mind. Exploitation abounds. Whether consigned to short and terrifying lives as Kalashnikov-fodder or held in prostitution, or condemned to exist as slave-labour or as refugees, children variously fall prey to adult greed, neglect, stupidity and evil. *Pilgrim* is as much about these young as it is about Kurt, Isolda and their companions. Lest we forget.

Read on for an excerpt from James Jackson's
new novel

REALM

The Armada is coming

✝

1587

Wednesday, 8 February

Martyrdom had its own rituals and rhythm. She had asked for more time, another day or two in which to pray and prepare and make her peace. But the stone-faced nobles of Elizabeth had sneered the more, had reminded her they were present merely to announce her execution for the following morn. That morn was come.

Only a few hours since delivery of their news, a few hours for her to write last letters and final testament, to speak and dwell upon the words of the Old Religion. As she had lain upon her bed in the quiet hours, her ladies had gathered round and read to her stories from the times of Christ. He had died for her. Now she was to die for Him. There was no greater privilege or comfort. She would show how a true heir to the English crown could meet her end, with dignified calm, with the strength and certitude of a Roman Catholic. No bastard offspring of the whore Anne Boleyn, no heretic usurper, would wrest the glory from her. Approaching six o'clock, drawing near to the appointed hour. The concluding act in the life and death of Mary Stuart, Queen of Scots.

Fotheringhaye Castle, a grim and forbidding place set bleak upon its motte. Her own personal Calvary. In the hearth, the weak fire did little to chase off the pre-dawn chill. It mattered little. She would not shiver or show fear. Her mind was on higher things and her fingers clasped around a gold crucifix on which the Lamb of God was fixed. What honour to shed her blood for the cause, to be a rallying beacon for the coming war. Those who had tormented her, those who had entrapped her, would one day lose their humour as they in turn were forced to mount the scaffold. She felt a visceral rush of excitement at such prospect. As God was her judge, it would happen.

'Your Majesty.'

She lifted her arms while her ladies-in-waiting busied themselves in respectful grief to fasten the jet acorn-buttons of her black satin gown. Much care had been taken in choosing her wardrobe for this moment. Set with pearls and trimmed in mourning-velvet, and with sleeves slashed in imperial purple, it would add presence and regality to the event. Your Majesty. She was indeed a queen, a queen wronged, a queen betrayed, a queen denied her rightful place upon the throne of England. Instead, her neck was to be rested on the block and her head struck from her body. By order of her own kinswoman and cousin Elizabeth. Yet vengeance was so close and these murderers so blind.

For a moment, she thought she could hear the hammering of carpenters at work in the great hall below.

The sounds were simply the imaginings of her mind, the residual echo of a night through which the artisans had laboured to create the stage for her passing. Each dull thud of a mallet or rasp of a saw, every nail-booted step of the guards outside, had made the outcome more solid and her destiny assured. Their efforts were as nothing to the great enterprise underway in Lisbon, to the provisioning and preparation of ships and the mustering of troops. King Philip II of Spain was embarking upon holy crusade against England. And she knew, had read of it in the secret communiqués smuggled to her by friends and loyalists. A pity she would not live to see the ancient faith restored or to witness the conquering Spanish enter London. A pity too those secret messages had been intercepted, those friends and loyalists compromised, caught and turned. Walsingham had brought her to this point.

That name, that dark eminence. Sir Francis Walsingham. The spymaster of Elizabeth had sent so many to the rack and scaffold, had placed so many agents, had revealed so many plots. She had been wrong to believe she could outwit him, foolish in thinking there was any sanctuary from his reach. Ever austere and always watchful, with the patience of a serpent, it was Walsingham who had uncovered her scheming and pursued her to the end. His henchmen would be secreted among the gathered audience, would soon report on her destruction. Perhaps he would raise a smile, a toast. She had other concerns. Besides, there was scant advantage in regret.

Her women fastened the girdle at her waist and

attached a rosary, placed a pomander chain and Agnus Dei about her neck. The finishing touches. She was forty-four years of age and in her nineteenth year of captivity in England.

She reached and lightly brushed the tear-patterned cheek of her favourite servant. 'No weeping, my sweet Jane. I beg it of you.'

'Forgive me, my lady.' The eyes and voice were hollowed in sadness. 'It is too much to bear to see you mistreated.'

'Mistreated? I am raised up, chosen by God to do His bidding.'

'We lose you, my lady.'

'Nothing is lost save the frailties of flesh and burden of existing. Be happy for me. I have prayed for this moment, for relief from my suffering. Now it is upon me.'

'May we not mourn for you, my lady?'

Mary smiled in gentle admonition. 'I forbid it. For I go resolved and willing as a penitent sinner to my fate.'

'You leave us behind, my lady.'

'To rejoice and to well remember and to keep the name of Mary Stuart, Queen of Scots, alive.'

'I could not forget, my lady.' The words of the lady-in-waiting constricted between sobs.

Drawing her women close, Mary comforted them, her words soothing, her arms embracing. For long years they had been her companions and confidantes. No secrets were left; nothing remained to be done.

In turn, she kissed them. 'For your service, I thank

you. For your friendship, I thank the Lord. Be strong. Our parting is but a temporary thing.'

Another servant wailed. 'You are our mistress and our very reason, my lady.'

'Even as dust I will continue to be so.' Mary stepped back. 'Now fetch the men so that I may say my farewell.'

They processed in, her surgeon, her apothecary, her steward, her porter, her groom, all stooping to press their lips to her proffered hand, each burdened with a private anguish. Then she took a few morsels of bread soaked in wine, the better to sustain her in the desolate drama ahead, and withdrew alone to her oratory. The Last Supper followed by Gethsemane. Her attendants waited.

Dawn brightened into day, the sharp February sunlight glancing between embroidered drapes and presaging a promised spring. New beginnings. Mary prayed on in silence and seclusion before a wooden cross. Doubtless her Protestant slayers would claim such clement weather reflected divine benediction on their efforts. They could suppose what they liked. Past eight o'clock.

'Open in the name of Queen Elizabeth! Attendance is called! Make haste!'

Interruption was rude, but expected, arrived with urgent shouts and a flurry of loud impacts on the oaken door to the bedchamber. The ceremonial escort was outside. Access was given, and a man officious and ill-tempered in his duties marched through. Maybe he thought the prisoner was flown, perchance he suspected the traitorous Catholics would pull one final trick. He would take no chances.

Kneeling and composed, Mary glanced up at him. 'Why, if it is not the sheriff of Northampton.'

'You are required, madam.'

'Solely by God my Saviour.'

'Your appointment is with the block. Let us away to it.'

'Is there such hurry?'

'There is engagement to keep and a delegation at the door.'

'Feign would I have them wait.' She raised herself to face him and scrutinized him further. The man was of a type she recognized, raw ambition wrapped in finery and a ruff. 'Each to our business, my lord sheriff.'

'We shall maintain it as such.'

'I will not protest.'

She turned and kissed the foot of the wooden cross before following him, pausing only while her ladies fitted her veil. It was a dressing of finest lawn edged in bone lace, attached with silver wire to her caul, and falling in delicate train down her back. She was ready. Tenderly, with the frozen emotion of departure, her ladies completed their task and curtsied low. The door opened and Mary Stuart made her exit.

Familiar and unsmiling faces greeted her. The dour countenance of her jailer Sir Amyas Paulet, the kindlier visage of the Fotheringhaye castellan Sir William Fitzwilliam; there too the regretful expression of the Earl of Shrewsbury and the choleric-hued eyes of the Earl of Kent.

The latter noble was spokesman. 'Events undo you, madam.'

'I remain unbowed and the Spirit of the Lord is with me.'

'Your composure does you credit. It will be needed, for you go to mount the scaffold unaided by your servants.'

'That is not the custom.'

'It is the order of my queen.'

'Am I not her cousin? Am I not anointed queen of Scotland?'

'To us you are mere traitor.'

'While to others I am but sacrifice and victim.' She peered in turn at the assembled. 'Is it not desirable the manner of my death should be observed and reported by those who know me? Is it not right that some dignity and rank be accorded me even as I face the axe?'

Quick looks were exchanged and agreement reached. Kent nodded. 'Very well, madam. Your steward and three manservants may join the foregathered in silence and obedience, two ladies may help disrobe you. That is all.'

'What of my priest?'

Anger emerged as a sneer. 'I am not so mutable and persuaded as a Duke of Norfolk, madam.'

Indeed, he was not. The old Duke had been a fool, had fallen prey to her coquettish and calculating ways, had served sentence in the Tower for his misjudgement. Kent was of a different humour.

He leant forward. 'Servants you may have, Popish

comforts you may not. Put aside your crucifix and carry instead your blasphemous faith in your heart.'

'Shame on you, sir.'

'No shame exists in what I do. It is my instruction.'

'Instruction will save none of you. England is for the fiery pit. Those Protestant lords who this day condemn me shall themselves be condemned. Those who believe themselves architects of my damnation will one day prove themselves draughtsmen of their own.'

'Be silent or be bound.'

'I will be bound by nothing but my religion.' She smiled benignly at the discomfort caused. 'My noble lords and sirs, today it is my reckoning. Tomorrow it is yours.'

'So let us dwell on the present.'

Mary kept her gaze steady and resisting. 'I lift my eyes to heaven. Now you shall see how Mary Stuart gladly meets her long expected end.'

Journey to the site of execution could begin.

Black canvas draped the scaffold. Set near the centre of the great hall, it was a simple structure some twelve feet square and raised two feet from the ground. Upon it, surrounded by quantities of scattered straw, and itself standing two-foot proud, was the focus of attention and grim totem of the piece, the block. And lying close on a fold of dark cloth was the axe. A stark scene for a portentous drama, one lit by the leaking sunlight, by the rows of tallow lamps hanging in their brackets, and by the warmer glow cast by a roaring blaze in the fireplace. Still the coldness clung.

An audience of three hundred had assembled. Behind a row of drawn-up soldiers, lords and notables were seated. To their rear, standing or settled on trestle-benches, were others. Local worthies and churchmen, the invited burghers and the curious, all had been brought together by prospect of historic and defining act. Expectation and low murmur filled the room, a festiveness that mingled oddly with drab unease. The weight of the moment could ever dampen the pleasure. It had passed the hour of nine.

A stirring, a craning of necks and swivelling of eyes, and whispers eddied through the crowd. It had started. Members of the retinue took their places and principal actors approached the stage. Here, the Dean of Peterborough, severe in his ecclesiastical gown; there, the executioner and his assistant, anonymous in their leather hoods and tight-fitting jerkins.

'The prisoner arrives.'

They rose in unison, not in respect for the condemned, but in deference to their queen who had signed the death warrant. Somewhere a drum beat a funereal tattoo. Then, preceded by the sheriff of Northampton, Mary Stuart, Queen of Scots, entered her arena. Shocked and collective silence fell upon the whole. She was not what they anticipated, not the alluring demon of their nightmares nor the devious papist siren who had served as talisman and rallying-point for rebellion against the Crown. Just a stooped figure, made stouter through imprisonment and moving slowly for the raised platform. Yet there was something undimmed in her manner, a majesty and serenity that transfixed. Beneath the veil, a half-smile played, and the famed auburn hair marked her steady passage through the crowd. Truly a royal presence.

With the aid of her two ladies, she climbed the three steps to the scaffold and halted to listen as the words of the commission for her execution were read.

Standing below her, the Dean of Peterborough began his address. 'It is not too late to renounce your sin, never too late to reject Catholic heresy and vile superstition and adopt the Protestant faith of this nation and our sovereign queen.'

'I am settled in my religion, Mr Dean. And I am here to shed my blood for it.'

'Then you will surely suffer the torments of hell.'

'On the contrary, I escape the torments of this world for the wonders of everlasting life.'

'Unburden yourself and become a child of Christ.'

'He shall receive me at this hour and at the moment of my death.'

'Be reconciled to our cause, my daughter.'

'Do not trouble yourself, for I rejoice in my own.'

The Protestant minister knelt at the base of the steps to pray in loud and sonorous tones. But Mary turned her back and prayed louder, her voice rising strong and her words in Latin echoing through the hall. Spectators shifted uneasily at the sound of the forbidden rites. They had not heard such utterance for many years. Undaunted on her podium, Mary stood her ground.

As the churchman finished, Mary knelt and clasped together her hands, changing to the English tongue for her plea of intercession.

'O, Lord, in Your mercy, wash free our cares, banish the afflictions of the English Catholic faith, have pity upon my son and allow Elizabeth my cousin to serve You in years to come. May the saints intercede for me, may the good citizens of this kingdom return to the path of righteousness, and may God avert His wrath from our beloved England.' She kissed her rosary, crossed herself, and spread wide her arms. 'As Christ suffered and died upon the Cross, so too must I stretch out my arms and be received into Your embrace. Forgive my sins, O God, and take me from this world of travail.'

She rose, the creak of her Spanish shoeleather loud against the muted backdrop. The pageant was inching towards finale. It was the turn of the axeman and his aide to beg forgiveness, a formal act lent trembling intensity on the stage. They lowered themselves before her.

'Will you pardon us for what we must do, my lady?'

'Willingly and with all my heart, for now it is you I hope who will end my troubles.' She murmured closer in the ear of the executioner. 'Should you perform with the skill and quickness of the carpenters on this scaffold, you shall have from me no complaint.'

There was convention to observe, the need to undress. Calmly, she seated herself on a padded stool and surveyed the throng as her ladies moved to her side. One removed her veil, the other the ornaments around her neck.

'I confess I have never before put off my clothing in such company.' Hands loosened her girdle; fingers that had so recently fastened the buttons began to unpick them.

'Majesty . . . ' Desolate anguish spilled from her servant.

'Reserve your sorrow for those without faith, dear Jane.' She returned to her feet, permitted her ladies to cluster round.

'May God go with you, my lady.'

'And always be with you.' Whispered conversation broke off as the Queen of Scots cast a warning look at the encroaching executioner. 'Touch me not, good man. You are no customary groom of mine.'

He ignored her and pulled free her gown. She had wanted dramatic effect, was counting on its impact. The audience gasped, its breath held in three hundred throats. In front of them, a slash of colour in the blackness, Mary was revealed in crimson satin bodice and velvet petticoat of brightest scarlet. The symbol of blood and of Catholic martyrdom. None could ignore its meaning or duck the visual shockwave.

Mary exchanged glances with her servant standing wretched with a silken scarf held in her hands. 'Ne crie point pour moi. Ne crie point.' The blind was tied about her eyes.

Mumbling their prayers, her weeping ladies were ushered away. On the bleak scaffold, the Earls of Kent and Shrewsbury had assumed their places on low stools and the execution team was ready and flexing. Beheading was performance art. For a few seconds, Mary was alone in thought at the threshold. This was her life, her reason, her consummate act. Let all see and let the heart of Walsingham quake. Fulfilment and ecstasy bathed her bound and upward-tilted face. She found the cushion at her feet and sank to it before the block.

'In te Domino confide, non confundat in aeturnum . . . ' In you Lord is my trust; let me never be confounded.

Carefully she reached out, her fingertips touching and tracing the contours of the wood. She was a pilgrim at the start of a journey, a supplicant at the altar. With her hands, she positioned her chin in the groove, laid herself out, and held wide her arms.

'In manus tuam Domine, confide, spiritum meum.' Into your hands, O Lord, I commend my spirit. Four times she called out. The assistant to the executioner placed a steadying hand on her body and the axe swung.

The blade bit deep, its contact thudding hollow and startling and ballooning into the shivering atmosphere. Yet it was no clean strike and steel had embedded in the back of the head. A messy undertaking. The mouth leeched an involuntary groan. Cursing to himself, the executioner prised metal from bone and arced the weapon again into the descent. Accurate and almost through. Bending to his labour, the axeman worked the edge and severed the remaining sinew. Butchery was done and the head fell away.

Sudden violence gave way to a dread and unsettled stillness. It was a pall beneath which people blinked stupefied or clenched tight their eyes, balled their fists, muttered oaths or prayers. Ten o'clock. On the dais, blood coursed and collected in rivulets.

'God save the Queen!' The executioner held aloft his detached and battered prize.

The Dean of Peterborough joined him in rousing cry. 'So perish all the enemies of the Queen!'

'Amen to it!' Parading near the slumped torso, the Earl of Kent gleefully entered the chorus. 'Such be the end of the enemies of our Queen and Gospels! May they all share this bloody fate!'

But few seemed to listen. They were concentrating on the ashen face of the deceased, on the lips that parted and closed and which seemed to curse them all. Surely, they had done wrong. With still less dignity, the head dropped from its wig and bounced hard on the boards, its aged features twisting, its hair cropped and grey, its mouth continuing in secret conversation. The axeman bent to retrieve it. Close by, the Earl of Shrewsbury wept.

There was more horror. In the aftermath, as spectators were herded dumb and troubled from the hall and the executioners worked to strip their carcass, a muffled whine sounded on the platform. From the deep folds of the petticoat in which it had been hiding a small Skye terrier, lapdog and treasured companion to the departed Mary, emerged cringing to the outside. It sniffed and whimpered, recognising the scent, disturbed at the strangeness, and crawled through the thickening slick to cower forlorn below the headless shoulders. The tiny canine would not be leaving its mistress.

Accompanied by a small retinue, the Earl of Shrewsbury rode hard and south along the Roman road for London. With luck, fair weather and the aid of fresh horses stabled on their route, they would cover the distance in good time and bring their news to the Queen. Behind them at Fotheringhaye the scaffold would be dismantled, the blood sluiced, the vital organs removed and burned and the corpse sealed in a lead casket. All signs, any relics or tokens of remembrance, were to be expunged. As though Mary had never lived.

Beyond sight of the riding party, far ahead, was another horseman. He too was making the journey of some eighty miles; he too had witnessed the grisly spectacle in the great hall. But his destination was different. He carried his report to the orchestrator of that day, the spy chief and principal secretary of state Sir Francis Walsingham.

Read more . . .

James Jackson

BLOOD ROCK

1565, Malta – and the greatest siege the world has ever known . . .

The legendary Hospitaller Knights of St John stand alone against the tide of Islam. The Ottoman Emperor Suleiman the Magnificent has sent the greatest armada that ever set sail to annihilate them. Time is running out. There is a traitor among them. Malta's doom is sealed.

But one man will never yield. Englishman Christian Hardy will stop at nothing to save the island. With a band of close companions – the Moor, genius inventor of demonic weapons, Hubert, would-be warrior priest, the orphan Luqa and Maria, the beautiful noblewoman who risks all to be with him – he must unmask the spy within, take a stand against an unbeatable enemy and change the course of history.

'This is history – and terrific history – on every page'
Frederick Forsyth

Order your copy now by calling Bookpoint on 01235 827716 or visit your local bookshop quoting ISBN 978-1-84854-098-9
www.johnmurray.co.uk